D1736244

BLOODLORE

Book 1 of the Cadis Trilogy

Krista Walsh

Best Wishes
Krista 10/15

Chapter One

Venn Connell's boots pounded against the dirt road as she ran, the *thud* of her soles a steady rhythm to focus herself on the man ahead. Shoving a Feldall soldier out of her way, she leaped onto the back of a fleeing bandit to send him crashing face-first into the dirt, trapped under her weight. Her heart pulsed with the thought of how many dead these outlaws had left behind and how much she would enjoy resetting the balance.

She reached around to grab his chin, squeezed his waist with her thighs to keep from being bucked off while he tried to fight his way free. Skin and sinew tugged the edge of her blade as she drew her knife across his throat. The body twitched and sagged, and Venn jumped to her feet to rush to the aid of a soldier pinned against a tree, a dagger inching towards his abdomen in his struggle to fight off his assailant.

"No, no," Venn crooned into the bandit's ear, sinking her own knife into the man's lower back. "Allow me."

Stunned by the pain, the man whirled around to face

her, catching her by the shoulders just as she forced a second knife up between his ribs into his heart.

She stared into the man's eyes and saw the wild terror and confusion as the life drained out of him. His grip went slack and he slumped against her before sliding to the ground.

"You good, soldier?" she asked.

He drooped against the tree and mopped his brow with his sleeve. Blood and sweat smeared his face, and he squinted as it dripped into his eyes. More droplets slid off his chin onto the green and gold hawk of Feldall embroidered on his chest, but from what Venn could make out, none of it was his. Between quick breaths, he nodded.

New recruit, she reminded herself. She turned away to give him a moment, and faced the other four soldiers in the road.

"That all of them, Rem?" she asked.

"Yes, sir," Remy Herrigan called back.

Venn cringed at the title. As proud as she was to have been knighted by the queen of Andvell for services rendered, it still felt odd to be reminded of it after having spent most of her twenty-three years thumbing her nose at authority.

She bent down to pull her blades from the man at her feet. "Good. Then let's call it a day and head back. Unless anyone wants to wait for more to show up?"

She waggled her eyebrows at the other troops and felt a twinge of disappointment when no one volunteered.

Wiping her knives on the grass before sheathing them,

she straightened her leather jerkin and smoothed the black hair out of her face with the back of her wrist. Sweat trickled down her neck as the sun moved west, its rays sneaking through the thick canopy of trees overhead. With a good pace, they'd make it back to Feldall's Keep by supper, and her stomach grumbled in appreciation.

As she headed towards her white stallion, Corsa, Remy fell into step beside her. Venn cast her a sidelong glance, taking in the mess of shoulder-length blonde hair, hazel eyes, sharp features, and the scar that ran from left eye to left ear — a souvenir from a Cordelayan knife fighter after her country had been demolished by a mad sorcerer. Venn knew people focused on the scar when they saw her, but she thought it gave Remy a touch of distinction. Proof that she had fought and won. A visible warning to anyone who faced her now. It was why she liked having the scout on her team.

Remy nudged her shoulder. "That was a good fight, wouldn't you say?"

Venn ran her fingers over Corsa's mane. "It was a fight."

"It would be great to know where they're coming from," Remy continued, not acknowledging Venn's lacklustre response, "but there's a certain satisfaction each time we take down one of their packs, isn't there?"

Venn forced a smile, appreciating but not matching the woman's enthusiasm. "It's good exercise, at least. Hundreds dead on the road thanks to those bastards, and we're only able to pick them off four or five at a time. I'd prefer running at the source and cutting the issue off at the head." She mounted up and settled in the saddle, patting Corsa's neck as the stallion pawed at the ground. "There hasn't been any news on that?"

Remy rested her hand on her sword hilt, shifting it out of the way as she mounted her own chestnut mare, Shalla. "None at all. It's like they're coming out of nowhere."

Venn frowned and glared down the road in the direction the bandits had come. "They can't be emerging from the mists."

"Are you sure?" Remy grinned, but the expression faltered at Venn's look of surprise. "I just mean it would solve a lot of mysteries. What did you think I meant?"

"It doesn't matter," said Venn, clicking Corsa into a walk. "As much as it would answer a few questions, the possibility of anything popping out of nowhere ended five years ago. Trust me."

She sensed Remy's confused stare, but didn't bother to explain. After five years, Venn didn't think she understood either. At least not enough to make of sense of it to anyone else. She pushed the thought away and stroked Corsa's neck to soothe the rising memories.

The ride home took a few hours, and as they passed forest and then field, Venn scanned the road for more bandits. For a land that had been devastated by magic and by dragon fire, she could never take this route without thinking of how quickly the territory had risen from its ashes. New cottages popped up along the way, creating small villages where before there had only been farmsteads. Gardens and crops flourished with the coming harvest, and people and land oozed a sense of prosperity.

They passed through the gates and headed right towards the barracks, reaching the stables as the sun touched on the horizon, the evening glow surrounding Feldall's Keep with a golden aura. Up on its hill, separated from the rest of the village, the rounded stone walls stood as a symbol of peace and stability. The closest place to home Venn had found in almost fifteen years.

She dismounted Corsa and allowed Paul, the stable-hand, to lead him away.

"Extra carrots tonight, all right?" she called after him. "He gave one of those bandits a good kick to the head and deserves the treat."

"Got it," Paul called back, giving Corsa a proud pat on the side.

"Will you eat with the soldiers tonight?" Remy asked, preparing to lead Shalla away.

Venn debated the alternatives, but a *whoop* from a scout as he bragged about their recent skirmish to some of the other troops made up her mind.

"You guys go celebrate. I'll run up to the Keep and fill in the family."

Remy tilted her head. "Everything all right? For a victor, even of a skirmish, you don't look too victorious."

"Just grumpy," she replied, and flashed a wink. "Only got off a few good punches."

Remy chuckled. "We'll hope for more action next time."

She raised a hand in farewell and headed off, leaving Venn to her grumpiness.

Not that she wanted to be in a bad mood. The soldiers

had done a good job today, clearing the road of the third bandit pack that month, and they had reason to be happy with their success. But she wasn't feeling it. She felt detached from the celebration around her, along with a certain discomfort in her detachment.

Turning her back on the laughs and stories, Venn plodded through the village, skirting people coming and going within the horseshoe of shops. To the right of the village were the homes of the household staff, and light from the lanterns cast a warm glow over the path as she walked between the cottages and the shops towards the Keep.

Sweat gathered under the layers of leather armour and cotton, and she felt more like water than flesh by the time she crossed the bridge and climbed the stone steps to the front door. Grunting against the weight of the door, she stepped into the cool foyer and stripped off the armour, knowing someone would be around in a minute to clean up after her. It was one of the perks of living in the Keep proper and having the Lady of the territory owe a few favours.

Down to her tunic and trousers, Venn heaved a sigh of relief and sagged against the wall, pressing the back of her neck against the cool stone as she closed her eyes.

It felt great to breathe. She still hadn't adjusted to the armour Arms-master Brian insisted she wear on scouting trips. The days when she was free to prowl in the shadows and leap on unsuspecting victims for their coin or food scraps were too ingrained in her habits and routine.

But those days were behind her. Now that she lacked for nothing, it was difficult to come up with reasons to prowl in shadows.

"Hey, you're back! That was quick."

Venn opened her eyes to see Magdalen Stanwell, House Feldall's blonde and bubbly enchantress, reach the top of the stairs that led down to her workshop, known around the Keep – either affectionately or with horror, depending on the smells and noises rising from the depths – as the Haunt. Her blue corset and white tunic were stained with some sort of black liquid, but years of experience had taught Venn not to ask. At least this time there wasn't any smoke trailing after her.

Anyone else's company might have grated on her nerves, but with Maggie, Venn didn't feel the pressure to force a smile. "Yep. Everything went according to plan. They're dead. Roads are clear. People free to come and go as they please. All in a day's work."

Maggie's smile widened at her apathetic tone, and Venn could see the understanding in her blue eyes. "Just a matter of routine at this point, isn't it?"

"That's just it," Venn replied, feeling the enchantress had hit the heart of the issue.

"Well, the people appreciate it, and therefore Jax appreciates it. If nothing else, you can pat yourself on the back for giving Lady Feldall some much needed breathing room."

Venn shoved away from the wall and headed towards the stairs. "I'd rather let Jax do the patting. I'm on my way to let her know."

"Oh!" Maggie exclaimed, and Venn turned back. "Did

you happen to see William while you were out and about? He was supposed to pick some herbs for me, but that was a few hours ago."

"Nope," Venn replied, popping the word. "Haven't seen your son all day."

"Oh. All right, then."

Venn heard the enchantress's false cheer, no doubt to cover her disappointment, and flashed an apologetic smile before heading up the stairs.

Subtle, Mags. Real subtle.

In spite of Maggie's best efforts, Venn hadn't fallen for Will in the years they'd known each other. Being only two years older than her, he'd become the closest thing to a friend she would admit to having other than Remy, but that's where it ended. No matter how much his mother— and he, she suspected—wished otherwise.

As if summoned by the mention of his name, she bumped into Will at the top of the stairs, too caught up in her musings to notice him until they collided.

He dropped the book he'd been reading, two others hitting the stone with dusty *thump*s, and grabbed her arm to keep her from falling down the stairs.

"Sorry," he said, releasing her to pick up his book. "The dangers of reading and walking."

Venn bent to grab the other two for him, but Will snatched them back, tucking them under the book he'd been so engrossed in. She quirked an eyebrow, wondering what it was about "Summonings and Banishings" he didn't want her to know about.

"Lucky you ran into me and not down the stairs," she said, allowing him his mysteries. "Reading anything good?"

He pushed his fingers over his short brown hair. "No dragons or anything, but it's an interesting perspective on the theories of—" He noticed her expression, cleared his throat, and answered again with a simple, "Yes."

Catching his chocolate brown eyes, she said, "Sounds fascinating, but you might want to pause the studying and head down to the Haunt. Your mother's looking for you."

Will's cheeks flushed, and he rested his knuckle against his upper lip. Venn struggled not to smile at his expense, knowing how self-conscious he was of being thought attached to Maggie's apron strings at twenty-five. She knew better, but liked to watch him squirm.

Because I'm a rat turd like that, she acknowledged to herself.

"Right. I guess I should bring the herbs to her. I wanted to grab this so I could start —" He held out the book and closed his mouth mid-sentence. "Anyway, sorry to have walked into you. I'll see you later, I'm sure."

He pressed his lips together in a tight smile and headed down the stairs.

Venn finally allowed herself the grin and shook her head, still smiling as she entered Jasmine's office.

Jasmine Reed, née Feldall, as she would always remain in Venn's mind, sat behind her large oak desk, cursing to herself as she tried to clear papers away from a puddle of spilled ink.

"Rough day?" Venn asked, righting the overturned

bottle and using an empty sheet to blot the mess.

Jasmine puffed a stray hair out of her face in response and tapped the pile of papers together to straighten them, setting them down in one corner of the desk before burying her face in her hands, her right elbow in the ink stain.

"You might want to move your arm," Venn suggested, dropping into one of the three chairs across from her. She leaned back and stretched her arms out along the armrests.

"Shit," said Jasmine, twisting her arm around to check the damage. She laughed an exhausted chuckle. "Not that it matters. I haven't bothered to get my clothes washed in five years. Found it easier to get the seamstresses to make new ones."

The cause of the woman's dark circles and stained wardrobe shrieked and ran down the corridor screaming, "Nononono!"

A second set of footsteps chased after her. "You get back here, young lady. Don't make me call for your mother."

"No!" the five year old stretched out the word as she turned around and started running the other way towards her room.

The girl's nurse, blonde hair wild and skirts twisted, poked her head into Jasmine's office. "I'm sorry if we disturbed you, my Lady. I'll make sure Naya stays in her room for the rest of the evening."

Jasmine waved a hand. "You're doing your best, Tanya. You can't help it if my daughter is part possessed demon. Do you need me to come help?"

Tanya leaned back to peer down the corridor. "I think I

managed to put the fear of you into her blood. She should settle down now."

She bobbed a curtsy and closed the door. As soon as she was gone, Jasmine's shoulders drooped, and she rested her chin in her palm.

Venn grinned. "It could be worse. She could be breathing fire as she runs around like a demon. At least you can rest easy that you birthed a normal child. Nothing strange or unusual about that one."

Her teasing words — only half in jest — made Jasmine's eyes crinkle with a proud smile.

"So, is there something I can help you with?" she asked, covering a yawn and slouching in her chair, "or did you just stop by to witness my scatterbrained exhaustion?"

Venn's smile grew, and she propped her boots up on the edge of the desk. "I'm glad I'm not you, Jax. I would have lost it years ago and killed everyone in the Keep. You're a better woman than I am. But no, I just wanted to give you an update on today."

Jasmine smoothed down the stray hairs escaping her long braid, straightened her papers again and sat up, the haggard mother gone and the leader of her people taking over. "What do you have to report? Did everything go well?"

"More than well." Venn crossed her hands over her stomach. "No losses on our side and only a few small injuries. I think it's the most successful mission we've had since these pissers started showing up. Only six this time, too."

"Any lead on where they came from?"

Venn slid her hands off her belly and back onto the armrests, picking at the peeling wood on the chair. After years of so many people doing the same, the furniture had begun to look aged and worn.

"Nothing," she said, pulling her attention away from the splinter poking the pad of her middle finger. She crossed her arms to help her stay focused and caught Jasmine smiling at her obvious restlessness. Trying to do a better job of hiding it, she dropped her feet to the floor. "Everything is exactly the same as all the other times. My opinion? They're a pain in the ass, but don't pose a bigger threat that the odd clearing out won't manage. These bandits aren't trained, and their armour looks like it's been pinched from wherever they could get it. Their weapons are usually half-rusted and they hardly know how to wield them. They're out for easy cash from the weakest people they can find on the road."

Jasmine tapped her thumb against the back of her hand. "We have reports saying most of them are refugees from Cordelay and the outlying areas."

Venn frowned, thinking of the damage Cordelay had suffered, the entire country devastated by a tidal wave summoned by a mad sorcerer. She was struck by the coincidence of two references in the same day to events that had occurred five years ago.

"The thought had occurred to me," she said. "But why now?"

Jasmine threw up a hand and sat up. "The dragon's

gone, the queensguard is finally starting to pull back its presence on the roads, so the way is clear for these refugees to cause all sorts of trouble. We might want to send some troops on a field mission to the ruined cities. If there are people living in the wreckage, maybe we can offer aid and cut down on the attacks."

Venn heard the subtle request in Jasmine's words for her to lead at least one of the missions, and sank lower in her chair.

"I'll start planning tomorrow."

Jasmine's lips twitched in amusement at her lack of enthusiasm. "I would have thought you'd appreciate the task. Better than sitting around the Keep all day waiting for them to come to us."

Venn tapped her toe against the floor. "You know me too well."

"So what's the issue?"

As much as she hated the thought of sharing anything so personal with anyone — or admitting that she had anything so personal to share — the frustration she'd felt building up over the last few weeks finally boiled over at the opportunity to vent.

"I'm *bored.*"

Jasmine's eyebrow rose. "Didn't kill enough people today?"

Venn frowned. "You make me sound so evil. I don't get off on killing people. It's a fun hobby, but that's not the point. They're just too easy to kill, you know? There's no challenge. Where are the undead wolves or those armoured cougar things? Where are the people who shoot fire from their fingertips?"

Jasmine chuckled, and Venn noticed the way her shoulders drew back and the lines around her eyes smoothed out, as if the reminder of what life had been like back then put today's troubles in perspective. What was an excitable five year old compared to a fire-breathing dragon and an armoured bear at the gate?

Maybe the dragon would be easier to tame... she thought before Jasmine spoke.

"As much as I can't bring myself to wish for a return of our troubles just to keep you entertained, I understand what you're saying. I'll get someone else to lead the scouts after the bandits. As for you, I might have another opportunity that would at least get you away from the Keep longer than a few nights."

She reached for one of the papers caught in the ink spill, the top corner of the page lost under the blackness, and held it out towards Venn, who recognised Jayden Feldall's messy scrawl.

"According to my brother's latest poor attempt at letter writing, their ambassador in Margolin, Jer Reddington, has gone missing. They'd send one of their own people in to look for him, but tensions with Margolin are running high. Jayden couldn't say much in his letter, but between the lines, they're worried. I know you don't find politics interesting or diplomacy worthwhile," she said this with a smile, "but there might be a place for you to help."

Venn pressed her lips together as she perused the letter,

considering. A missing diplomat in a sensitive political muddle—lots of potential for intrigue. And it had been a while since she'd mocked Jayden Feldall for anything. It would be nice to see the princess Ariana, too.

Still can't believe the bastard managed to snag a royal, Venn thought, the idea never ceasing to amuse her.

"All right," she said, tossing the letter onto the desk and slapping her palms against the armrests. "I like it. If there's a message or something you want me to bring your brother, leave it in the stables. I'll leave first thing in the morning." She stood up to move towards the door, and then paused, running her fingers over the back of the chair. "Thanks."

Jasmine nodded and pressed her lips together, seemingly caught in some internal debate. Finally, a slow smile spread over her face. "Repeat this to anyone and I'll have your hide, but some days I miss the old adventures, too."

***

Venn left Jasmine's office with a lighter step than when she'd entered it. She felt sorry for the poor guy who'd gone missing, but at least now she had a purpose. Something to plan and achieve. Maybe a few scuffles in the dust along the way.

Stripping down to her smallclothes, she pulled back the sheets and slid into bed, brain already busy plotting out routes for the morning as she leaned over to blow out the candle. The room fell into darkness except for the dim light of the fire at the end of the bed, sending shadows dancing over the covers.

Falling into a partial doze, Venn thought she saw one shadow rise up above the others.

Sleepy brain, she thought as she yawned and turned on her side.

A creak of the bed, and her sleepiness began to ebb. Slowly, so as not to disturb the blankets, Venn slid a hand under her pillow, reaching for the hilt of the blade she always kept close.

Before she could reach it, the shadow let out a yell and lunged.

Chapter Two

The shape's full weight landed on Venn's chest, forcing the air out of her lungs, and Venn wrapped her arms around the bundle to prevent further attack.

"I've got you now, you little monster. Nice try, but you still have much to learn."

Naya sagged on top of her in a dead weight, and Venn grinned at the small tricks the girl had picked up on her own.

She pushed the girl off her onto the next pillow, and Naya rolled onto her stomach, smiling up at her with the full power of her missing front tooth.

"I scared Momma last night."

Venn wrapped her arm around Naya's shoulder, tucking her in beside her.

"I have no doubt. You've come a long way."

"I'd be even better if Tanya would leave me alone. I want to sneak around in shadows like you, Aunt Venn. Maggie's kids don't get watched all the time. Why can't I run around like they do?"

Venn knew Jasmine wished Naya could have a childhood that didn't involve people watching her every second for symptoms of dragon fire, but what did she expect when the child's father delved into ancient dark magic he didn't understand to bind his mind with that of a dragon? Brady Reed had survived the encounter, but it had changed him, and the mystery remained about what effects the ritual would have on his daughter.

From what Venn could tell, other than a birthmark like a dragon tail wrapped around her arm — which she was convinced was an amusing coincidence — Naya behaved no differently than any other brat running around and screaming that she didn't want to go to bed. Thank goodness. Venn had had enough of other people's magical dabbling throwing her life into turmoil.

"Because you're too important. Can't have you being whisked off by sorcerers or falling down the stairs," she replied.

When Jasmine and Brady had first started referring to her as Aunt Venn, she had wanted nothing to do with it. No way was she interested in taking up knitting and babysitting the runt when her parents wanted alone time. Especially not when the question still lingered about whether Naya would start oozing smoke every time she threw a fit.

She'd been an okay infant — cried a bunch, made a lot of messes, looked kind of cute when sleeping. It was only when she'd reached her second birthday and started throwing things off tables and running away whenever she suspected it was time for her to do something that Venn started paying attention. That's when she made up her mind to adopt the child as her pet and teach her all the ways of being sneaky. That's when being an aunt became fun.

Not to mention, the kid was pretty cute.

"Shouldn't you be in bed?" she asked.

Naya raised a shoulder. "Tanya told me to sleep, but I don't want to. Sleep is boring."

"Ah, to be young again," said Venn. "Wait until the day when you recognise sleep as your best friend."

"You're not asleep."

Caught off guard, Venn nodded, as though giving serious consideration to Naya's observation. "You're right."

"Why aren't you sleeping?"

"I had to pack and get ready to go."

Naya bolted up and twisted to face her. "You're leaving?"

Venn grinned. "Just for a little while. I'm going to see your Uncle Jayden."

The child sat up on her knees. "Can I come?"

Venn reached out and tugged her back to the pillows. "Not this time, dragon girl. Your Momma would miss you too much."

"But I'll miss you." Naya hung her head and rested it on Venn's chest, wrapping her small arms around her waist.

Venn pressed her lips together and cleared her throat, uncomfortable at the warm feeling in her chest. This sort of happy-family emotion was still too new for her.

"Why are you leaving?"

For the shortest second, Venn thought about changing her mind and staying at the Keep, being happy to help Jasmine keep the roads safe. But even the thought made her skin crawl with restlessness.

"Because it's a big world out there, dragon girl. Someone has to go and see it."

The room fell into silence and Venn wondered if the girl had fallen asleep, but then Naya said, "Will you bring me back a present?"

Venn chuckled and kissed her auburn hair. "I'll see what I can do, kid. Now get some sleep. I know I need to."

Naya tilted her head up to bat her large green eyes. "Can I stay here with you?"

Venn considered it, imagining the rush of panic Tanya would feel in the morning when Naya's bed was empty.

"Sure," she said, pulling the covers over both of them and rolling onto her side to tuck Naya in next to her. "But keep those kicky legs on your side of the bed."

***

The next morning, Venn untangled herself from the blankets and tiny arms, and dressed in her usual travel garb of black leather and wool. The folks of Feldall might prefer their green and gold colour scheme, but she had always found it more effective to sneak around in darker shades.

She stuffed three black travel outfits into her pack, and pulled the leather strap over her head to rest on her shoulder, then went to the bed and leaned in to kiss Naya's forehead, smoothing down the wild hair.

"Catch you later, dragon girl."

The child didn't wake up and Venn sneaked out, closing the door behind her.

"Looking to run away without notice?" a voice behind her spoke up.

Venn jumped and turned to see Brady coming up the hallway hauling the usual collection of books in his arms, no doubt on his way to the library to start his day. Locks of ginger hair slipped over his ear and into his face, but with his hands full, he could do nothing but stare through it.

"I'm guessing Naya spent the night with you last night?" he asked, coming to a stop beside her. Balancing the books on his hip, he pushed the hair out of his face, clearing his grey eyes. "Tanya went to check on her this morning and found the bed empty. Came running to us in a panic."

Venn grinned. "I would have let her know if she'd asked."

Brady's ginger eyebrow rose, but the smile belied any disapproval. He shifted on his feet, rebalancing his books. "You're on your way?"

She nodded. "Figure I'll get an early start before the heat kicks in. And who knows, maybe I'll run into some early morning bandits along the way with the same idea. Get this trip off on the right foot."

Brady smiled. "That's one way to see it."

Venn felt uncomfortable under his searching gaze, and she shifted her own focus on the wall behind him. She wondered what he saw in her with that dragon brain of his.

"Is everything all right?" he asked.

"Sure," she replied without hesitation. "Why wouldn't it be?"

The counsellor chuckled, and Venn knew her answer hadn't come as a surprise.

"It just seems to me that someone so anxious to leave the comforts of home — leaving her friends and security — has to be searching for something. I thought I'd present the opportunity for you to talk it out before you left."

She laughed. "Insightful, Brady, and I appreciate it, but the fact is the only thing I'm searching for is a bit of adventure. Find this Reddington guy, bring him home, win some accolades. The usual."

He nodded, his grey eyes soft and warm. The counsellor may not have been very people smart, but he really was a rare decent human being.

"Then I'll wish you a safe trip," he said, "and hope you find whatever it is you need. Be sure to send a message when you arrive safely at Addergrove."

Venn saluted, ignoring the sudden emotion creeping up at his words. "Will do, Counsellor."

Brady started walking, but paused again when he reached her side and said close to her ear, "Be prepared for a travel companion when you head downstairs. Jax wrote to the captain to ask someone to ride with you, and I think Maggie's planning to send Will."

"Thanks for the heads up," she replied through tight lips.

Brady winked and disappeared around the corner. Venn

hesitated, debating a counter plan to get out on her own. The trip to Addergrove would take at least fifteen days and, with the wrong people, could turn messy. She'd have to turn them down, no matter how much Maggie used her big blue eyes.

If she had any small hope that Brady had been mistaken, they disappeared when she made it down to the stables and found Corsa already saddled, with a charcoal stallion waiting beside him.

"Hey, Hollis," she sighed, patting the mount's neck.

"Oh good," said Maggie, coming out of the stable cradling a leather satchel in her arms. "You're here. I figured you'd probably start early."

"Yep," said Venn, looking anywhere but at the enchantress, hoping she could think of a quick and good excuse to get out of there alone.

"I made sure the horses were loaded up with food and a few extra water skins, just in case. I know it's a long trip and everything points to a hot couple of days. Will's just getting the rest of his stuff together, but do you mind if he rides with you? Ariana wrote me to say her healer has discovered some unusual herbs around their estate and doesn't want to start using them until he knows their properties. I offered Feldall's services to do the research."

Venn cleared her throat. "I can't guarantee this will be an easy trip. It's long, and we don't know the condition of the roads. If the bandits are out in full force beyond Feldall, or—"

"Of course he can come," Remy's voice piped up behind

her.

Venn turned to glare at the scout who had come up silently, leading Shalla by the reins. "What are you doing here?"

"Going with you, of course."

Venn blinked. "You are?"

Remy pulled a piece of paper out of her pocket, and handed it to her. "The captain told me to show you this in case you put up a fight."

Venn glanced at the paper and recognised Jasmine's writing.

"Brady mentioned she'd sent something. You were the lucky winner?"

"No one else volunteered."

The two women shared a grin, acknowledging that Venn's reputation of riding into unnecessary danger without forethought, and being tough on soldiers who thought better of it, made her a less than desirable travel companion. She admired their intelligence, but thought little of their sense of adventure.

She still would have preferred to travel on her own, but if it had to be someone, Remy would have been her first choice.

Maggie threw the satchel over Hollis's saddle as if Remy's agreement had been the final say. "Excellent. It'll be one stress off my mind to know you three will watch out for each other. And before you roll your eyes at me, Will has more to offer than being bookish."

"We never thought otherwise," Remy said before Venn

could reply. "He'll probably be the one keeping us safe if he brings that fireball spell with him."

The enchantress's face turned red with suppressed laughter. "I'm not sure how wise that would be. He was working on improving it and, well, we ran into a bit of an issue with the ingredient ratios." She frowned. "I'm afraid I lost some tomes that will be very difficult to replace."

Movement in the corner of Venn's eye caught her attention, and she turned her head just in time to see Will trip over a pitchfork, catching it before it fell, but unable to right it because it had caught on his pant leg. By the time he got everything settled and reached his horse, his face had flushed a deeper shade of red than his mother's.

"I have the list of books that were burned," he said, staring hard into Hollis's saddle as he tightened the girth. "I'll see if I can replace them along the way."

Maggie's mouth fell open as she realised he'd heard her, and that maybe he wouldn't have wanted the story shared, and she struggled to compose herself. "That's not how I meant it, Will. It was an error on both our parts. You put the fire out before it could burn anything else, so it could have been worse."

Seeing that she wasn't making anything better, she laughed, her eyes sparkling with warmth. "Trust me to act like such a mother sometimes. Ah well, he'll get over it." She pulled Venn into a hug. "Travel safe and don't stay away too long, all right?"

Venn gave the enchantress a squeeze in return, having grown used to Maggie's displays of affection and liking her too much to brush her off.

"We'll do what we can. Make sure you keep this place in good shape," she said. "As much as I'm looking to shake things up, I like to think that home will be exactly the same when I get back."

Maggie grinned in such a way that made Venn ask, "What?"

"I've just never heard you refer to the Keep as home before."

Venn laughed, amused as always by Maggie's sentimentality. "And you might not again if I come home to find things have changed."

Maggie nodded and blew a kiss to her son as he mounted Hollis. "Let me know what you learn about those herbs."

Venn understood her unspoken request that he write home often, and saw Will's flash of relief that she'd refrained. The interaction made her smile as she pulled herself up onto Corsa.

Remy followed on Shalla and waved her farewells as Venn led them towards the gates.

"I hope you're all ready for ass blisters and sore thighs," she said.

"Ready and eager," Remy replied.

Will remained silent, and Venn twisted in her saddle to find him rifling through the satchel his mother had left him.

"Stanwell?"

He jerked up, letting the flap of the satchel fall. "Sorry?"

Venn grinned. "Drowning us out already, are you? Probably not a bad idea. I sing when I ride, and I'm a horrible singer."

Remy laughed, and Venn urged Corsa into a trot, then a canter, eager to get on their way.

***

By mid-afternoon, they had reached the forest crowding around the ruins of Treevale Fortress. Once an imposing structure with eight tall towers, only two remained standing, and nature had begun to reclaim it. The odour of the dragon Talfyr lingered in the air — the sour scent of rotting cattle carcasses he had hoarded up on one of his towers, and sulphur from his fire breath that had scorched the stone and destroyed much of the surrounding woods.

Since Talfyr's departure, these lands had been left untouched by all but the bravest and most curious scholars, but Venn couldn't shake the creeping sensation in her blood that made her feel like someone was watching her. Too many bad memories haunted these ruins, and most of them personal.

Not far now…

Within another hour they would cross the Andvell River, close to where she had discovered the corpse of her sister, Siobhan, second-in-command to the mad sorcerer Raul until she had betrayed him to save Venn.

Not that Venn had known at the time. Or that she had been in any real danger. She and Siobhan had lost touch over a decade ago, but it still hurt to know that she had lost the chance to reconnect with her down the road. They both would have had stories to share.

"Everything all right?" Will asked, his soft voice intruding on her dark thoughts.

She blinked and looked up at him, wiping the glower from her face. "Absolutely. Just impossible not to come this way without thinking of all the bullshit history we're passing through. Hard to believe how much of it has gone back to normal. Like it never happened." Forcing a dry chuckle, she added, "Considering how much the three of us lost because of what Raul did in this place, it's almost like we don't belong here. We're three scars nature can't cover up."

Remy rode up beside her and smiled, her scar crinkling. "Nah, we just give it character. Perfect is boring."

She spoke cheerfully, but the fingers of her left hand played with the twine bracelet wrapped around her right wrist, a familiar gesture that gave away her discomfort.

As the sun peeked through the trees, the gloominess of the scene melted away, and Venn turned her attention to the woods around them, picking up the call of summer birds, the rummaging of creatures in the shrubs and dead leaves. Soon the seasons would change and the trees would take on their autumn colours, but for now everything remained lush and fertile. Under the noxious odours of Treevale, she picked up the sweet scents of the earth and of the rushing river ahead. A recent rainfall gave the air a clean dampness, and Venn allowed her head to fall back to catch the slight breeze that made its way under the canopy of branches.

Maybe this is enough, she thought. A break from her

routine even without the action.

The thought trailed away as a twig snapped somewhere in the dense shadows of the forest, and she tensed, hand at her side, ready to grab a blade. The scurrying of smaller animals and birdsong faded, blanketing the woods in silence. She squinted into the depths of leaves to make out what had made the noise and saw nothing but green.

"Hey, Miss Jumpy," Remy said, drawing her attention. "What's up?"

"You didn't hear that?"

Remy and Will exchanged a glance.

"I hear nothing," said Will.

"That's what I mean. I've had the sense we've been followed since we entered these gods-be-damned woods. It disappeared for a while, and now it's back."

Remy twisted in her saddle. "I don't see anything. But then I don't have your training and uncanny ability to see things out the back of my head."

Venn grimaced. "I'm not joking around. There's something out there."

"There probably is," Remy agreed. "It's a forest."

Venn's thoughts raced with possibilities. Witches, bandits, fanatics, undead beasts — she had encountered all sorts of creatures in these woods, and wanted to be ready for whatever came.

After a moment, the normal forest noises resumed, and Venn forced herself to relax.

"Maybe I am just imagining things."

"It's better to be safe than surprised," Will said, drawing

Hollis closer to Corsa's side. "We'll keep a better eye out just in case."

They crossed the bridge over the river and left Treevale behind them, along with some of Venn's tension. She still felt like someone was watching her, but no matter how many times she turned around, she never saw anything except trees.

It took a few hours to accept that her imagination had taken over her reason, and she let her attention drift away from the forest and back to the road.

"What's that up ahead?" Remy asked, leaning forward in her saddle.

Venn rolled her eyes. "Ha-ha, I get it. I was overreacting. No need to make fun."

Remy didn't laugh it off. "I'm not making fun. Just to the side of the road. Looks like someone crouched behind a tree."

Venn's gaze followed the direction of her friend's attention and, as they moved forward, caught a glint of metal in the evening sunlight.

"Weapon," she said, reaching for her knife. "Maybe I wasn't so paranoid after all."

Remy shot her a glance and gripped her own sword hilt.

Venn dismounted and threw Corsa's reins to Will, who fumbled to catch them.

"I'll be back," she said, voice low so only the other two could hear. "Keep heading up the road and see if it draws him out."

"And where are you going?" Remy asked.

Venn smiled and batted her lashes, offering the image of innocence. "I'm going to see if he needs directions."

"Is that a good idea?" Will asked. He reached for the satchel at his side, and Venn heard the rattle of glass vials within. "We don't know if anyone else is waiting with him. If we can't get to you in time —"

"Don't worry about me," said Venn. "This is why I came out here. If fun's not coming to me, I'm going to go find it. Now get going before he sees you standing around."

Before either of them could say anything else to try to dissuade her, she pushed into the thick foliage. Within seconds, the road was blocked behind branches and leaves, and she picked her way carefully over the forest debris, watching for sticks that might snap under her weight.

A few steps in, she paused, thinking she'd heard something behind her, but her strained ears picked up nothing and she continued on.

Beyond the woods, she heard Remy's and Will's muffled voices carrying on an inconsequential discussion about the weather, letting her know that whoever was hiding hadn't come out yet. With a light tread, she crept forward, keeping her eyes peeled for movement in case someone else had the same sneaking ideas.

A flash of metal up ahead told her she approached her target, and she ducked down at the waist, moving along the back of the trees to come up behind him.

One solitary figure hunched behind the bushes, short sword in hand, clothes ratty and boots dusty from too many days on foot. Venn twisted her lips in disappointment.

Here, she had hoped for some sort of assassin waiting on the road for his hit, but it was just another bandit, and not even with the benefit of friends.

She darted forward and reached for the man, but at the last moment, he dodged out of her grip, swinging his sword towards her arm. She threw up her hand to avoid the attack, and jumped to the side as he lunged. Dancing around the tree faster than he could move, she came up behind him and shoved him back against the trunk, setting her blade against his gut. Although he stood a head taller than her, he remained glued to the tree, not testing her willingness to sink the knife between his ribs.

"Just out for an afternoon stroll?" she asked.

He raised his sword again, but she grabbed his wrist and slammed it against the tree until the blade tumbled to the ground.

"And here I was going to give you a chance to get out of here."

She braced herself to stab when Will shouted, "Stop!"

The man's baleful glare shifted from her to the riders on the road, and Venn rolled her eyes towards the sky, releasing a sharp exhale but not her grip on the bandit.

"Why?"

She heard Will dismount and approach, his untrained steps crunching over leaves and branches of the forest floor.

"You aren't even going to ask what he was doing?" he asked, reaching her side.

Venn glanced from the bandit to the scholar. "I gave him the opportunity to tell me. He tried to kill me instead.

I consider that the end of the conversation."

Will scratched the dark shadow of bristles on his cheek, brow furrowed as though considering her argument.

So much like Brady, this guy, thought Venn. Will had been the counsellor's apprentice from the time he was a child, and obviously the teacher's obsession with knowledge had rubbed off on the student.

On the other hand, his desire to *know* was keeping Venn from her desire to *act*, which she found infuriating.

"What's your name?" Will asked the bandit.

The man spat at his feet and said nothing.

Will didn't react. "I don't intend to let her harm you if you can explain your reason for being here. Are you in need of help?"

Venn held back from rolling her eyes. She sensed Remy coming closer, and glanced over her shoulder to see the scout holding the horses, watching the tableau with amusement.

Turning back to the bandit, she caught the man sneering at them, sniggering with bitterness. Behind his cracked, bleeding lips, his teeth were stained black, and his breath reflected the state of his oral health. His black skin was weathered, covered in wrinkles that appeared all the deeper for the build-up of road dust. He reached up to scratch his head with dirty, broken fingernails.

"Help?" he asked, his voice hoarse. "Are you really asking that? Sure, you can help. How about you give me all your money, and then come back to what remains of my country and give each person there all your money, as well.

That would help."

Venn caught the reference. "You're from Cordelay?"

She frowned, thinking his accent didn't sound Cordelayan, but the man's contemptuous expression deepened. "You're referring to something that doesn't exist anymore. You mean the wreckage that was once Cordelay. Nothing more now than a sewage heap with starving children and more rats than people."

Will's expression filled with sympathy, and Venn wished he wouldn't let it show so clearly. What had happened to the man's country was unfortunate, but not their fault.

"Why turn to banditry?" he asked. "Surely you had other recourse? Somewhere you could go?"

"Sure," the man said. "For the last four and a half years, we've been moving through Margolin. 'Doors wide open', they said. 'Make yourselves at home.' Bunch of us wanted to see if we could salvage what was left, but the masses fled. Til just two months ago, when they closed the gates. Threw us out. Put guards up along the border saying they'd use anyone who tried to get in for target practice. So piss on the lot of 'em. Now we make do on the roads. So if you're not going to help me, what's say you let me go so I can get back to work?"

Will left Venn's side to return to the horses, and she shifted on her feet to watch him, keeping the blade tight against the bandit's gut. She looked to Remy, but the scout shook her head, having no more idea of what their friend was up to than Venn.

He rooted through his pack and pulled out a bundle of

wrapped food that was meant for their trip, then came back and handed it to the man.

"Take this. At the very least it should last until you get to Feldall's Keep. Present yourself to Lady Jasmine Reed, tell her I sent you, and I'm sure she'll do something to help you and your people. If she knows the Cordelayans are starving, she won't let it continue."

The man spat again, this time the sputum hitting Venn's boots. She ground her teeth and pressed the knife a little deeper into his tunic, holding herself back for Will's sake.

"I wouldn't ask anything of that dragon-mating whore," he said.

Will blinked his surprise, and Venn's eyes narrowed, seeing red. This man was asking for her blade to sink right into his liver.

"What makes you say that?" Will asked.

"You think we don't know the story?" the bandit replied. "How the Feldall bastards sat by and let the sorcerer do what he wished with our country? They never answered for it. You want to help us? Go back in time and stop the madman from doing what he did. Maybe then we could look to Andvell and call you friends. Until then, we'll take what we need through blood and tears."

Venn tightened her grip on his shoulder, allowing her nails to dig into his ratty leather coat.

"I'll be sure to pass your regard along to Feldall," she said, and applied pressure, feeling the blade slide through his tunic and break skin. The man's breath hitched, eyes narrowing with hate.

"Wait," Will stopped her again.

Unsure why she listened to him, she paused, arm steady. "What now?"

"Killing him will do nothing but continue their belief that we're not allies," he said.

The man snorted, and Venn wanted to argue that nothing they did would smooth relations out with people like him, but Will continued, "We need to start repairing the damage. It's what Jasmine would want us to do."

Venn cursed under her breath, knowing he was right about Jasmine, and stepped back, yanking her knife out of the bandit's shirt, but not pointing it away from him.

"If we find you at this again," Will said to him, "I won't be so quick to stop her. Get out of here, and take the food I gave you. Maybe one day you'll see it as proof that your stories aren't entirely true."

Venn grabbed the man's jacket and hauled him away from the tree, pushing him down the road towards the river.

"Asshole," she muttered at his retreating form. She bent to pick up his sword. "Doubt he could have killed anyone anyway. Probably would have tripped over this thing before he could use it."

Remy stepped closer and took the blade from her, holding it up to inspect the workmanship. "Good quality, though. Better than most of what we find on these guys. Might be worth hanging on to."

She strapped it in with the rest of her bags on the saddle while Venn turned to Will. "If you're going to have a soft heart like that the whole trip, we might need to part ways.

Some people out here need killing. One death to stop many and what not. Do you have issue with that?"

"Not at all," Will replied. "I'm just a believer in getting answers first. Do you have issue with that?"

He raised an eyebrow in challenge, and Venn found herself smiling. "Nope. A bit of a delay has been known to increase the satisfaction."

She winked and enjoyed the way his skin flushed.

"Let's head out," she said. "Might as well try to find a good place to camp before it gets too dark. Besides, now that you've given away a third of our food, we'll have to go hunting."

She shot him a look before taking the reins back from Remy, who laughed at her as they mounted up. Shoulders sagging, Will followed.

As they urged the horses forward, Remy glanced up to check the sun's position. "How much farther do you think you want to go today?"

"We've still got a few more hours of light," Venn replied. "How about we cut through the woods while we can, see if we can't find a shortcut and maybe that bandit's camp. If he's been here for a while, it's probably safe to assume the area's free of most big scaries."

Remy shook her head. "You speak so oddly sometimes, you know that?"

Venn flashed her a wink. "Comes from living in a lot of odd places."

Behind them, Will chuckled, but said nothing to answer Remy's questioning stare.

Venn led the way into the woods, brushing branches out of her face as she rode forward.

A flash of colour caught the corner of her eye as a black-clad figure with a red hood raced through the trees alongside them, and the peace of the afternoon vanished. He darted towards them, scurrying in front of the horses. Corsa danced backwards, and Venn clung to the reins to keep her seat.

She was ready to dismount and chase after him, but by the time Corsa settled, he'd already vanished. "What the rotting pig carcass, guy?" she called after him.

"Maybe he really has to pee," Remy suggested, her voice heavy with sarcasm as she scanned the trees. "Looking for the perfect tree."

Venn grinned at the idea, but still didn't like the idea of someone other than them exploring these woods. Maybe that bandit hadn't been alone after all. She kept her eyes peeled, and they pressed on, deeper into the forest.

A few minutes later, she spotted the red hooded figure again, this time kicking aside leaves with his boot. He saw them coming and fled.

"If this guy's trying to go unnoticed, he's not doing a good job," she said. "Think we should give him a follow? I might sleep better."

Remy forced out a breath. "If he's okay to run away from us, I'm okay with letting him go. It looks like he's alone, so he won't be much of a threat against the three of us, and I'm hungry."

"It's starting to get dark. I doubt you'll be able to see

him much longer, anyway," Will added, siding with Remy.

Venn's blood raced with the desire to hunt, but she allowed her friends to talk her down.

Probably just another refugee looking for a safe place to camp, she told herself.

No sooner had she made up her mind to forget about it than she spotted him a third time, just a flash of red in the darkening woods. He seemed to be on his hands and knees beyond a screen of branches.

Ignoring the rational arguments of the others, she turned Corsa in his direction and passed through into a clearing. The hooded figure looked up, saw her, and ran.

Venn wanted to run after him, but something about the clearing made her hesitate, breath catching in her chest as she was struck by a startling sense of familiarity.

Impossible, she thought. *It's a forest. All forests look the same.*

But she couldn't shake the feeling, and as she looked down, she noticed her fingers trembling around Corsa's reins. Like a memory, she heard notes of haunting laughter on the air, and her skin prickled with goosebumps.

Impossible, she repeated to herself.

"All good?" Remy asked, riding up beside her.

"Fine," said Venn, but the word came out less than sure. Images drifted back to her of whirling lights, all blue, black, and white. An impossible jumping through worlds, as though she were in a dream. She remembered falling through the tunnel and regaining consciousness surrounded by the three witches known as the Sisters, the guardians of these woods.

But it doesn't mean it was here. It could have been anywhere. Big forest, Venn. Big fucking forest.

In spite of her denial, she knew in her gut this was where the Sisters had brought her after her inter-world journey.

So what had the hooded figure been looking for?

Without knowing why, but overwhelmed with a need to know, she dismounted and took off after Red Hood.

"Venn!" Will called after her, but she didn't stop.

Pushing branches out of the way, she ignored the scratches of twigs and the rips in her pant legs as they caught on nettles. She focused on the pounding of her heart and the pumping of her legs, searching the woods for any sign of her quarry, knowing he couldn't be far.

As she broke through another curtain of branches onto a riverbank, she saw him up ahead. He stood on the edge of the ravine, looking as though he were about to jump into the rapids.

Pushing forward with her last burst of energy, Venn ran at him and launched herself into his side, tackling him to the ground. He threw an elbow and caught her in the temple, shooting sparks of light across her vision. She lost her grip and slid off him, striking her head against a rock buried in the dirt.

He used the chance to free himself and rushed down the bank, stopping a safe distance away.

Venn shook her head to clear the stars, and propped herself up on her hands, watching him, wondering why he didn't keep running.

She saw his lips move, but could hear nothing over the roar of the rapids. In their struggle, the man's hood had fallen back, and she found herself looking at a man in his thirties, chin bristled with brown and grey hair, a cruel smile on his lips, a scar twisting the top left corner of his mouth. His eyes were cold and dead, and staring into them filled her with a sense of fear.

"What in the nine gods' names are you doing, Venn?" Remy demanded, panting, as she caught up with her, Will at her side.

They knelt beside her, Will brushing her hair back to inspect the cut on her forehead, both of them too absorbed in her to see anyone else. When they finally noticed Venn's attention glued to something down the bank, they looked up and saw Red Hood, who continued to speak those soundless syllables.

Venn remained frozen as the smile on his twisted lips widened and he opened his palm. Her gaze travelled down his arm to what he held: a large marble-sized glass sphere, filled with green, blue, and yellow swirls, looking like nothing more than a pretty paperweight. As she watched, the colours in the sphere darkened, morphing into a red and black dance.

Her thoughts, already off-balance by the memories in the clearing and the double blow to her head, stumbled and slipped.

Impossible, she said for the third time. *Oh shit.*

He gave her a wink, squeezed his palm around the sphere, and vanished.

Remy jumped to her feet and ran to where the man had stood. "What the frozen piss?"

She spun in a circle, searching, but Venn knew she wouldn't find him.

"Where did he go?" Will asked, eyes wide with awe.

"I have no clue," Venn replied, still staring at the spot of empty air where the man had been.

She tore her gaze away and found the others staring back at her with baffled expressions, as though she had grown a second head.

Only then did she realise she was smiling.

Her smile widened into a grin. "Things are finally getting interesting."

Chapter Three

"So let me get this straight," said Remy. "you've transported to other worlds?"

Venn counted it as the third time she'd posed the question. The scout sat with her elbows resting on her knees, twisting her bracelet around her wrist. The expression of bewilderment hadn't left her face since Venn had first done her best to explain the situation.

"You're going to have to tell me the whole story from the beginning again," she said, "because everything I was told about what happened in those days — and thought a horrible exaggeration — turns out to be not nearly as amazing as the truth."

Venn chuckled, "Like I said, it's not something you can believe unless you were there to live it. It's a spell called the Meratis incantation. Maggie discovered it, using it to send and summon people between—ow, shit."

She jerked away from Will as he put pressure on the gash on her forehead.

"Sorry," he said. "But hold still and it won't hurt so much."

His long fingers brushed her hair back and held her steady, tilting her head as he dabbed ointment on the cut. Venn flinched, but didn't pull away again.

"All right, I think I understand the spell part. So that glass sphere thing the guy was holding is the Merantis thing?" Remy pointed in the direction of the clearing where Red Hood had disappeared.

Venn held back a sigh and thought how well Jeff Powell, the reason the Meratis incantation had been cast in the first place, would have gotten along with her friend. Neither of them could follow a story through to the end. Which was especially ironic in Jeff's case, considering the man was a popular author in his own world.

"The sphere contains the spell," said Venn, fingers clenching the dirt as Will continued to poke and prod at her head. "I never figured out how it worked, but that's probably for the best. It likely would have stolen my soul considering who it came from."

Remy frowned. "Who did it come from?"

"It was a gift from the Sisters," Will replied.

Venn raised an eyebrow and winced as the cut pulled, rolling her eyes when Will *tsk*ed at her. She returned her attention to Remy. "You've heard of them, right?"

Dazed, the scout nodded. "Only as a legend. They're wicked forest spirits or something, right?"

Will smirked. "You might want to speak of them with reverence out here." He gestured to the river and the trees lining the clearing. "We're in their territory."

A gust of wind picked up, blowing their hair in all directions. Remy's eyes widened, and she whirled her head back and forth as if expecting the witches to pop up on the riverbank. Venn didn't want to break it to her how smart it was to be suspicious. The Sisters were known to do exactly that.

"But," she continued, "it turned out all the casting of the Meratis incantation to bring us across worlds created a tear in the veil. There was a fun month cleaning up that mess. After that, it was agreed: no more Meratis."

Remy blinked and stared out over the water. Venn didn't know if she was trying to piece her thoughts together or if they had overloaded her with too much information. Considering how wild the story sounded in the retelling, she thought either possibility likely.

"So what you're telling me," she said, drawing her gaze back to Venn and Will, "is that it's not a good thing that this guy has the Meratis sphere. What with tears in the veil and all."

"It's not a thought to make me sleep well at night," said Will. "Without knowing how he means to use it, the magic could potentially reopen the rift and put us in the same position we were in five years ago."

He seemed to have finished with the painful part of the healing, so Venn removed her fingers from the dirt, picking it out from under her nails. "I don't know if that's even what worries me most. If we forget his intentions for a second, how in sunfire did he know what the sphere does? Or, more importantly, where to find it? It's not like it's a large statue relic passed by hundreds of people a day. It's a small ball of glass that was buried under leaves in the middle of a random clearing in the middle of a random forest five years ago. Think he tripped over it on his way to the river and thought, 'Hey, I've been looking for one of these'?"

"He obviously had a way to track it down." Will sat back on his heels and started putting away his salves. "Do you think we should head back to the Keep and let Jasmine and Brady know?"

Venn prodded tenderly at the lump on her head, thinking what she could really go for was a hot bath and some ale. Since neither of those was forthcoming, she got to her feet and swatted the dust off her trousers and tunic.

"What would they do about it? He could be anywhere in the world, and not necessarily in this world. I say we ride on and keep an ear out for word of a guy in a red hood popping in and out of town. If we go back now, Jax'll just sent out scouts and tell us to wait until we hear from them. It could mean months of sitting around, and this ambassador's not going to find himself. Unless he does, which would be convenient."

Will pressed his lips together, and Venn interrupted any proposal of alternatives by adding, "Nothing stopping you from going back with the message if you want."

He rose to stand beside her, pulling his satchel over his head. "Nope. I'm willing to follow your lead on this. You know what we faced last time better than Remy or I."

Remy shook her head. "I still can't believe what you're

telling me. It's incredible."

Venn smiled. "Jeff liked to remind me that truth is usually stranger than fiction. It's best just to roll with it and keep an open mind." She tilted her head to stare at what was left of the sun, the trunks of the trees red as blood in the fading light. "Speaking of open mindedness, how do you guys feel about setting up camp here tonight? Sure we might run into the odd world-jumper, but at least we can go fishing in the morning."

When the others didn't make any argument, Venn set to work on a fire, unable to drop her smile as she heard her friend murmur, "Unbelievable. Absolutely incredible."

***

They started out first thing the next morning, and Remy kept the conversation going with endless questions about Venn's past.

"How have you never told me any of this before?" she asked. "We've known each other over two years and I've never heard half this stuff. You'd think that while you were bragging about facing dragons, you'd mention the world jumping thing. It's kind of impressive."

"You didn't even believe me about the dragons," Venn retorted. "Why do you think I've been so bored? Coming down from all that has been a nightmare."

"The nightmare wasn't facing off with the dragon? Did you really do that?"

Venn sensed Will staring at her, daring her to lie, and she rolled her eyes. "Fine. For the sake of history, I guess you could say I didn't *face off* with him. But I was there when most of it happened."

"Amazing."

Venn thought back to that night, trying to remember her own reaction. "I guess it was at the time. Looking back, so much incredible stuff went on in such a short space of time that it all seems pretty run of the mill now."

"Run of the mill?" Remy repeated. "You talk about it like finding a snake in the hay!"

"Sad but true," said Will. "Although we don't talk about snakes and hay. Especially not around Jayden. Bad memories."

Remy shook her head, staring from one to the other as though suspecting they were having her on. Venn could only smile. She was known to make up a good story on occasion, but having something fantastical and real to share was more fun.

"It's not like Feldall got all the adventure, though," Will pointed out. "What about your side of things? What that bandit said yesterday, was that your experience back home?"

The light in Remy's eyes faded, and she focused her gaze on Shalla's ears, reaching once more for her bracelet. "It wasn't much different from what he said. At least, none of what he said surprised me. I just lucked out and got myself a position in the militia before I had to turn to banditry."

Venn peeked at her from behind the black hair that had fallen over her eyes. Since the time she'd been introduced to Remy, she never pried into her history. People's stories never really interested her. For one thing, people lied. For another, when it came down to it, everyone faced the same sort of shit and either survived or they didn't, and either grew from it or they didn't.

But now that the subject had come up, Will's questions and Remy's reaction piqued her curiosity. She wanted to know what Cordelay had become after Raul summoned a tidal wave to wash out the coastal country or after he sent in his men and armoured pets to have their fun with what was left. No one came away from something like that without more scars inside than out.

Silence fell on the riders, and for a while no one made a move to break it, which surprised Venn since she knew Will would be just as plagued by questions as she was.

Finally, Remy broke it herself.

"I don't even know how to describe that day. I was sixteen, looking after my little brother and sister by the beach. We were far enough away from the main city that we could only just hear the screams as Raul sent in the first wave of soldiers and creatures to scare us all into hiding. I found a cave and rushed us inside. We saw nothing but the ocean, stretched out for miles. My little brother was eight, but he cried for our mother, and I could say nothing to make it better."

She shuddered and stopped, her throat bobbing as she swallowed. "You know what? I can't. It was horrible and terrifying, and I can understand that man's pain and anger. I can't say I felt much warmth towards Andvell at first, myself. Especially towards the people at the Keep once word came they were involved. They were supposed to stop him."

Venn couldn't find anything to say, and no other subjects jumped out at her. She looked to Will, who stayed focused on Remy.

"So how did you end up with us?" he asked. "The bandit mentioned many of the Cordelayans crossed into Margolin. Did you go there first?"

"Not right away," she said, and the tremor left her voice now that she'd returned to practicality and fact. "Enough of us managed to survive that we banded together to protect what was left. We had to salvage what we could. Or we felt that we did, anyway. But there's only so long I could stay there, reminded of everything we'd lost. I tried Margolin first, but…" Her frown deepened. "Even two years ago we didn't get the welcome we expected. The fact they've closed the borders surprises me, but not that they don't want to take in any more refugees."

"How do you mean?" Venn asked. "Talk to me like I'm stupid. I don't know anything about the politics of these places."

"Margolin and Cordelay have always been allied countries," Remy explained. "We had the fishing and ships for their armies, and they had better farming. The border between us was a sort of formality, just to keep track of the comings and goings. But when I tried to cross over, I had all my bags searched, and they insisted on taking the names of the city and the people I'd be staying with so they could find me if they needed to. It was nothing I'd ever experienced before."

It sounded strange to Venn, but she hadn't been to

Margolin in over ten years. A lot had changed since then.

Will, caught by the politics far more than Venn was, pressed her for details. "Once in, why did you leave?"

Remy shrugged. "Because nothing got better once I was there. Even the family friend who took me in noticed the way people stared at me. Everyone was suspicious of the number of strangers, and the local jail was full to bursting with people they'd picked up — seemingly at random. I thought it best I get out while I could, and the only other place I could reach was Andvell."

Venn knew the rest of the story. They'd come across the starving young woman on the road with nothing more than the clothes on her back and a few last bites of food. Even her weapons had been lost or traded in the journey. It had been so similar to Venn's own story that she suspected it was a big part of why she'd taken to the woman.

Will fell into thought, and when he came out, he turned his questions away from Remy's personal life and back onto more rational matters. "I think it's worth mentioning the bandit's news once we get to Addergrove. Jayden and Ariana probably already know about the border closing, but if it's connected with the other tensions they're facing with Margolin, it could be worth looking into."

Venn stuck out her tongue in distaste. "Think the ambassador's stuck at the border? That'd be a boring result. Red Hood guy, though. He's a mystery I want to get to the bottom of."

"Are you sure?" Will asked. He paused to lead Hollis around the centre of a large puddle in the road. "Last time we dealt with world jumping, we had a whole group of people trying to solve the problem and still almost lost the Keep. You're not afraid of getting in over your head?"

Venn smiled. "It's about time I learned how to swim."

***

The next four days passed quietly, troubled only by the occasional lingering sensation that they were being followed, which Remy finally picked up on, as well. No matter how often they backtracked or took unplanned detours through the woods, they couldn't shake their unseen tail. At night, Will took to casting wards around their camp to keep out unwanted visitors, but nothing ever set them off.

"Could it be the Sisters?" Remy asked as they broke their fast on the sixth day. "You said this was their territory."

Venn tapped the tip of her knife against her front teeth, bringing the image of the three scantily clad women to mind against the ongoing voyeurism. "It's not their style. Red Hood might be starting the same old problems for them, but if they really had concerns, they wouldn't sneak around. They'd probably pop up in all their nearly nude glory and threaten us until we agreed to help them. But it's possible they're keeping an eye on us."

With that thought looming over her, Venn's tension rose again, on high alert for the first traces of witches in the woods. Not that she was afraid the Sisters would harm them, but she hated the way they enjoyed taking people unawares.

Hardly surprising. It's probably the most entertainment they get out here in the middle of nowhere.

By the time they packed and headed out, Venn was ready for a change of pace. The novelty of travel had already worn off, and she stared down the road with nothing more than deep sighs, hoping for another sign of Red Hood, or maybe a bandit or two. No such luck. Even the sky persisted in being clear and cloudless, without the least hint of a storm to throw a wrench in their smooth journey.

Remy and Will didn't seem to mind. They chatted between themselves about their childhoods and education, comparing notes on subjects they shared an interest in. Venn listened with half an ear, understanding only a quarter of what they spoke about. Her upbringing hadn't included much traditional education. None, actually.

She'd never had reason to regret the lack of conventional knowledge, having put her time and effort into everything unconventional, but now she felt an uncomfortable sense of inferiority that she couldn't keep up with the conversation.

Probably boring anyway, she thought, shrugging it off.

Instead of trying to untangle their discussion on Cordelayan history, Venn turned her attention to the woods on either side of the road, letting Corsa fall back to ride behind the others so she could focus more on the trees.

The nagging sensation of being watched increased now that she had nothing else to distract her, and with her temper already out of sorts, the plague of not knowing the truth finally grew to be too much.

"I'm going into the forest," she announced.

The other two fell silent and turned to her in surprise.

"Why?" Will asked.

"Because I don't think I'm paranoid," she replied. With no other explanation, she dismounted Corsa, trusting him to stay put, and pushed her way through the trees.

Since the pursuit of Red Hood the other day, they had avoided going too far into the forest in case the man decided to make another appearance, and Venn was amazed by the difference in the woods on this side of the river. As though they had crossed seasons in the short time they'd travelled, these trees looked barer, the leaves paler in colour and the light brighter through the canopy overhead. She walked through rows of birch trees instead of armies of oaks, and the forest debris wasn't nearly as thick or untidy.

The Sisters don't own this place. It was the only thought that occurred to her as she plodded over the dead leaves. The atmosphere felt lighter, less oppressive, but lacked the unique richness the witches' magic had infused throughout their territory.

She never would have believed it, but she preferred the forests she'd grown used to, witch magic or not. Without the Sisters' protection, she felt vulnerable and out in the open.

On the other hand, she hoped it would help her spot their stalker that much faster.

"Come out, come out wherever you are," she sang in a soft voice.

A branch snapped behind her, and she whipped around, knives ready, forcing out a sharp breath of exasperation on seeing Will and Remy.

"What are you two doing?" she demanded in a hushed voice.

"You didn't think we'd let you go snooping around alone," Remy shot back at the same volume, short sword in hand.

Venn didn't want to hurt their feelings by saying she wanted to go alone to make sure no one heard them coming, so she raised a finger to her lips to shush them and jerked her head towards the path she'd been clearing.

A loud snort echoed through the trees to their left, and the trio halted.

"Did that sound like what I think it sounded like?" Remy whispered, taking a step closer to Will.

Venn's heart had jumped into her throat at the noise, and she pressed her lips together, wanting to agree and hoping they were both wrong. As one, the three turned towards the sound, and she could only feel pride that none of them screamed.

The sun streamed through the trees to enlighten the scene in front of them, an innocent warmth that had no idea what it exposed.

Venn's blood ran cold, the fingers around the leather grips in her hand shifting, sliding up and down the hilts to keep them from going numb.

Brown fur, thick and matted, caught the light with streaks of gold and red. Large eyes stared at them as the wet, pebbly nose twitched. The lips, black and leathery, pulled back over sharp teeth, and a low growl cut through the silence, sending flurries of fear down Venn's arms and making her clutch the blades that much tighter.

She would never deny that she was afraid.

Not afraid that they faced a bear who looked hungry.

Not afraid that it was the creature that had followed them for so many days, as her gut told her it was.

What scared her more than anything was the way it glared at them through red-hued eyes, and the way the sun glinted off what lay beneath the fur, off its teeth, and off the sharp claws stretching out from the massive paws. Metal. All metal.

They hadn't come across any regular old grizzly bear. They were being hunted by one of Raul's mutated armoured pets.

Chapter Four

Venn didn't know how long she stood statue-still, but in that stretch of time, they all might have been posing for a theatrical tableau. Not even the birds thought it wise to take flight.

The bear stood on all fours, its nose easily as high as her own. Based on the stories she'd heard — and right now she hoped Jayden had been lying through his bragging teeth — it wasn't yet full grown, but the knowledge did nothing to make her want to take it on. Not even her love of adventure carried such a death wish.

"Thoughts?" Will asked, his lips barely moving to keep from drawing the bear's attention.

Not possible. Dead. Supposed to be dead.

Venn kept her head still as her gaze twitched in the direction of the road, guessing how long it would take to reach the horses if they ran. Too long, if the bear pursued.

And of course he would give chase. As one of Raul's creatures, what else would he want but their blood?

The armoured bear attack on Feldall's Keep during Raul's reign had since become a favourite local horror story. More than the water that turned to blood, more than the attack of armoured eagles. Venn had missed it by a few months, but Jayden was living proof of the bear's ferocity. That monster had splintered the front gate and done irreparable damage to the training barracks. It had taken a full unit to take him down, and too many men had been lost.

"None at all," she replied to Will after her mind caught up with her body. She weighed the various scenarios in her head and turned up dead in all of them. "Unless you have some miracle spell, magic man? Any bear bait in that satchel?"

Remy glanced from her to Will, eyes wide with hope and fear. Will kept his gaze on the bear and lifted the flap of his sack to paw through the rattling glass vials.

"Are you actually looking for bear bait?" Venn asked, unable to keep the impatience out of her tone as he rummaged.

"The last time the Keep faced an armoured bear attack, the only way they could trap it was with Mother's binding spell. I could have sworn I packed some of it."

Venn thought of the blue smoke spell that had saved their lives more than once, and that it would have been poor planning had he forgotten it, but this time she clamped her mouth shut, her desire not to provoke the bear greater than her desire to berate Will for not thinking ahead. Why wouldn't he plan for running into a mutated bear that was supposed to be extinct?

"No binding spell," said Will. "I have all sorts of things in here, but nothing that would work at the moment."

Remy's tongue flicked out over dry lips and the hope in her eyes faded. Venn saw her terror and imagined how many painful memories were washing over her in that moment.

"Wonderful," she replied, doing her best to keep calm. "I don't think the 'lie still and play dead' trick would work on this guy, either. I'm not sure about you two, but I don't feel I have the right armour nor the right weapons to face it."

She wasn't ashamed to say she was more likely to break down in a panic than get close to it with a blade. The way the bear stared at her — nose twitching, drool oozing out around his metal teeth — Venn saw nothing but a silent threat. If they didn't find a way out of there soon, she doubted there would be much left of them to send home.

"What if we try backing away?" Will suggested.

"And pretend we never saw it?" she asked. "I thought you were supposed to be the smart one."

Venn regretted being snarky as soon as she heard it in her voice. Fear had made her cranky.

But Will didn't sound offended when he said, "It hasn't attacked us yet, so maybe it'll lose interest now that we've found it, and go home."

Venn and Remy exchanged a glance. Without having much faith in the plan, Venn saw no other options. She nodded her agreement, and they began the walk to the road, each taking careful steps, trying not to turn their backs on the beast, who continued to watch them through the trees.

Once they reached the dirt lane, Venn released her breath, her lungs aching from the pressure, and shakily boosted herself in the stirrup to swing her leg over Corsa's back. Her fingers trembled around his reins and she could find no words for a good long while, but after more than ten checks over her shoulder to confirm the road was clear, she demanded, "How is this a thing?"

She meant her contemptuous disbelief to be directed at the situation, but Will flushed when he couldn't find an answer.

Remy, like Venn, seemed to wish she could ride backwards to keep an eye on the road. "That creature was one of Raul's."

Venn watched her, concerned over her friend's pallor. Her own clammy hands had finally started to dry the farther they got from the beast. "You know something about them, Rem?"

"Seen enough of them to know it can't be good it's following us."

The more she spoke, the more her fear appeared to ease.

"I still don't understand how it's here," Venn murmured, looking to Will. "You heard Jax's story, right?"

"I remember," Will replied, his brow knitted in thought.

"What story?" Remy asked, and Venn knew it was less curiosity and more desperation that she wanted to hear it. Anything to keep her mind off that day in Cordelay.

"She found out Raul had cast a spell to keep his pets alive

and under his control," she explained. "He held the magic in a glass sphere, just like how the Sisters contained the Meratis incantation. When we smashed it, his pets were wiped out."

Remy tugged at her bracelet. "What about those undead wolves you fought?"

Venn frowned, picturing the decomposing wolf corpses chasing her across a field of snow. "Those wolves were raised from the dead. A poor man's version of the creatures we still have nightmares about. This bear is one of Raul's. Without a doubt."

"Unless someone else is playing with his designs," said Will, and the idea stabbed horror through Venn's gut. Another maniac with a desire to manipulate life? Gods, she hoped not.

"That thing followed us out of Treevale," she said. "No one could have found Raul's lab under all that rubble, and you and Brady collected his books yourselves. It has to be one of his. But how is it possible that it's not full grown when the monsters have been gone for five years? It doesn't make sense."

"Well—" Remy began, then fell silent.

Venn looked to her in silent inquiry, and she tried to dismiss it, but when Venn continued to stare she continued, "I don't know if it's true, but I heard rumours after the Cordelay attack. One of our soldiers worked for Raul before he came to us, and he had lots of stories to share."

Venn's eyebrows shot up in surprise, and a similar expression crossed Will's face, but Remy waved a hand to push the point aside.

"The guy was in irons at the time. I'm not saying we picked him up off the street and offered him a job, but he offered to share information in exchange for food and shelter — what little we had left of it. We agreed to help him where we could, and he started talking. At the time, we thought he was full of shit, spouting nightmare stories to make himself sound important. After what I've learned the last couple of days, maybe he was telling the truth."

"He knew something about the creatures?" Will asked.

Remy nodded, chewing her lip as she tried to remember. "He explained how Raul had created his pets, binding them to this spell to keep them under control — I guess that's the one Lady Feldall smashed. But Raul was paranoid of having his people or his creatures dependent on anything other than him, worried that if the spell was ever broken, or got into the wrong hands, he would lose power. Apparently, after he'd had enough practice making his bears and cats and whatever else he made, he started a new project."

An oily discomfort coated Venn's belly as she guessed what her friend was about to say.

"He tried to grow them. Organically."

Yep. Worst possible answer.

Venn thought of the bear they'd seen, its metal claws and teeth waiting to tear into some unsuspecting traveller's flesh. "So there could be more of these out there. Families of armoured bears."

It would take all of Feldall's forces to clear the woods around Treevale, but if there was the smallest possibility of warbear cubs wandering the ruins, it would have to be done.

"I really don't know," said Remy. "According to this soldier, Raul never successfully achieved his goal. The mothers kept dying, and he couldn't find a work-around. But that's just what we were told. I have no proof he was right."

Will grimaced. "Raul wasn't known for sharing secrets."

Venn looked over her shoulder yet again, still seeing nothing but not feeling much relief at the emptiness.

"If the bear is what's been following us, then why? Why would one of Raul's pets want to keep us in sight? Of all the theories I can come up with, none of them are good."

"I hate to be the one always throwing around suggestions you hate," said Will, "but we are still closer to the Keep than Addergrove. We could turn around."

Unlike after the run-in with Red Hood, Venn considered the option briefly before dismissing it, this time for reasons more practical than rash. "If you want to be the first one to pass by the beast again, be my guest, but I think getting as far away from it as possible would be the smarter choice. Although I wouldn't be opposed to picking up the pace."

Will made no further arguments, and Remy looked ready to start the race.

Venn clicked her tongue at Corsa and they eased into a gallop, but any hope she had that the bear would leave them, or that it hadn't been their invisible pursuer, disappeared when she caught sight of it twice more over the next few days.

As though it cared less about staying hidden now that they'd seen each other, every once in a while she heard it snuffling in the darkness while she tried to fall asleep, or caught the sounds of it hunting. More than once when they camped near the Redwater River she saw it splashing in the rapids, catching fish.

Other than its unnerving presence, the bear never caused the travellers any trouble, so the unspoken agreement remained to let it be. It plodded along at a distance, and every so often would disappear for long enough stretches to make them hope it'd gone home, but by the end of the day they'd see or hear it again.

Venn could never relax when she knew it was nearby, but it worried her more when it vanished.

"I don't understand what it's doing," she said.

The trio sat around a fire for their mid-day meal, and watched the bear shake itself off on the riverbank, water splashing into the trees, until the fish in its mouth stopped thrashing.

"Do you think it belongs to someone?" Venn wondered aloud.

Remy tore off a strip of her salted deer meat. "A pet got loose, you mean?"

Venn's mouth twisted, her mind racing with possibilities. "I mean like a spy. I wouldn't put it past anything Raul created to have some sort of homing device built into its brain. Maybe it's taking information back to someone when it disappears like that."

The scout's eyebrow quirked. "I'm going to assume

these ideas are related to your past experiences with world jumping, because most of what you just said makes no sense to me. You think someone can read its mind? Translate its growls?"

Will raised a shoulder, keeping his attention on the patterns he was doodling in the dirt with a stick. "It's not beyond the realm of probability. From what I've seen of Brady's sketches of the creatures, Raul designed them with all sorts of built-in defence systems. Metallic teeth and claws, poisoned whiskers, and metal spines in their fur. It wouldn't be such a leap to think he discovered a way to make them see for him as well. Keep tabs on his enemies."

"Exactly," said Venn, relieved he understood her concerns.

"But who would be controlling them now?" Remy asked. "No one is left that would know how to handle these creatures. And why would this mystery person send it after us? As far as anyone is concerned, we're just three people out on a random journey who happen not to like bandits. We're no one."

Venn rubbed her brow to smooth out the wrinkles, wincing as she accidentally rubbed against the cut near her hairline. "I'm pretty sure Red Hood knew I knew what the Meratis sphere was. Some random person off the road wouldn't have had a clue. It's possible we're not as anonymous as we think we are."

Remy dropped her attention to the fire, considering her point.

"No matter what, I don't trust him," Venn continued

after a while. "No wild animal would choose to stay this close to human beings for so long."

"It's a 'him' now?" Will asked with a smile.

Venn took another look at the bear now lying in the sun, his red-hued eyes never straying too far from their camp. "Sure. Looks like a him. Reminds me a teenage boy, anyway. All the staring and laziness."

Remy chuckled, and Will bobbed his head in concession. He added another flourish to his design, and Venn saw he had made a decent representation of their new not-so-furry companion. "We all agree he's no regular animal. But until he does something other than track us and eat, I don't think we'll find our answers."

Remy grimaced. "Here's hoping that 'something' doesn't mean slaughtering us in our sleep. If we could come up with any way to get rid of him, I'd be all for it, but for now I guess we're stuck with him."

Venn knew that if she was right, it would only be a matter of time before the person behind the armoured bear came after them. She hoped they'd be prepared when he did. If she was wrong, then the bear was just weird.

After they finished lunch, Will pulled his first aid supplies out of his satchel and moved towards Venn. She leaned away from him, pressing her hand against his chest to fend him off.

"What do you think you're doing?"

"Checking your head wound. I saw you earlier. It's still bothering you." He caught her gaze with all the force of his golden-hued brown eyes, leaving no room for argument.

Venn argued anyway. "No it's not. My head is fine. It doesn't hurt and I didn't even lose consciousness."

Will poked her forehead.

"Ow!"

"See? You're in pain. Stop fidgeting and let me take a look." He batted her hand away and leaned in, brushing her hair off her forehead with the back of his fingers. "I didn't push us going home after we had the run-in with the thief, or with the bear, but this is where I draw the line. If we don't clean it out, it might get infected, turn green and black, and your skin will slough off."

Venn frowned. "No it won't."

His eyebrow quirked. "Do you want to risk it? Besides, any sort of infection and you'll smell worse than you already do."

Remy burst into laughter as Venn muttered a few unflattering phrases under her breath. Will caught her eye and winked, the gesture taking any sting out of his comment.

"Fine. Do what you have to do," she grumbled, and tried to sit still while he soaked some sweet scented ointment on a cloth and dabbed at the cut. Once he finished and reached for the bandages, she pushed him away again. "We all have our limits and that one is mine. I'm not going to walk around looking like a mummy."

"Like his mother?" Remy asked, choking on her water.

"No," said Venn, amused by her expression, "but don't let Maggie hear you say that."

Will gave in to her argument and sat back on his heels

to pack up his supplies, while Remy rose to her feet to ready the horses.

As they worked, Venn stayed on the riverbank and kept an eye on the bear stretching out in the mud. Aside from the metal plates under his fur and the way he insisted on tracking them, he didn't act like anything she associated with Raul. His pets only ever had one purpose, and that was death. They were designed so they didn't need to make any effort to destroy everything around them — they just had to brush against it.

If Remy was right that this one was born instead of built, she wondered if it would make any difference in his behaviour.

Shaking her head as the bear rolled onto his feet and waddled into the woods, she brushed off her knees and joined the others in their walk to the road.

The wind picked up once they left the shelter of the trees, and Venn pushed her hair out of her eyes to take in the evening scene. The sun had reached the tops of the trees, dousing the birch bark in gold. Birds twittered around them, rising up into the sky like a black cloud to dance on the air currents before settling down. Ravens cried out their afternoon debates, and somewhere in the distance a wolf howled, raising the hair on Venn's skin as she closed her eyes and followed the call, waiting for the reply.

The sounds brought her back to the days before the Feldall twins had arrested her and brought her into her new life — the days when she had lived outside, only hiding from bad weather by sleeping in stables in exchange for useful information or fresh game.

As much as she liked having a roof over her head and food in her belly, she missed the freedom of the past. Then, she had to work for survival, honing her skills to track and hunt.

She lapsed into an old habit, listening to the chattering squirrels and joyful birdsong. There had been a time when it was second nature to know what these calls meant, but now she had to work to remember which cries were for hunger or direction. Or panic.

Venn's eyes flew open at the sudden rush of raven cries as they took wing, abandoning their roost. She scanned the road ahead, looking for what might have set them off.

Under the discontented caws and quorks, she heard a steady thrum of hoofbeats on the road rushing towards them.

"Remy, guard up," she said, shifting her grip on Corsa's reins to grab a knife with her free hand. "Will, either arm up or stay back. I think we've got company."

Remy leaned forward and squinted, then tightened her control over Shalla as the band of riders rounded the corner. "I'll never understand how you always know these things."

The approaching riders sped on black horses, dressed in scarlet from head to toe. They looked like soldiers, but the armour was nothing Venn had ever seen. Moving bloodstains on the dirt road, catching the sunlight in ways that seemed to absorb it instead of reflect it.

Something about them filled Venn's gut with unease, but she shoved the feeling away, guessing the armour had been designed to make their enemies feel that exact shade of dread. She had never been one to give in to expectation.

They charged without slowing, and she thought they might rush right past them, perhaps en route to some important show down. Seven riders weren't enough for a war, but maybe they were contestants in some lord's fancy tourney. Sure, it would be strange for them to be riding in full gear, but not if they wanted to make an impressive entrance.

Unable to come up with any other reason for these soldiers to be coming at them, she clung to the idea right up to the point when they unsheathed their weapons, the sharp edges glinting in the afternoon sun.

Venn bared her teeth and tied Corsa's reins around the pommel, steering him with her knees as she pulled a second knife. Remy released her sword, and Will nudged Hollis to the side of the road, holding a vial in each hand that Venn hoped did more than smell pretty.

"Hooded thieves and armoured bears, now these freaks? Why do I get the feeling we set out at an odd time?" Remy asked between clenched teeth, loud enough so only Venn could hear.

Venn laughed and readied herself for the fight, feeling the blood rush through her veins, speeding up her heart, sharpening her vision. People might think she was crazy for always throwing herself into danger, but nothing beat the buzz of battle.

"The best time you mean," she said. "Meet you on the other side of this, Rem. Either here or in the afterlife."

"I love your optimism," Remy replied, before she spurred Shalla forward.

Venn let out a *whoop* and bolted after her, two riders against seven.

One soldier broke off from the rest, leading the charge, and headed for them with his sword raised. Venn threw her first knife, cursing as it glinted off his helmet, but ready with the second blade, grabbing a third.

Remy clashed swords with him, and the soldier made a quick second swing towards her horse. Shalla danced away in time, but he pressed on, giving neither horse nor scout a break.

Venn didn't have time to watch them before two more soldiers reached her, both with raised swords that looked ready to cut her in three. Corsa turned at the last moment, and Venn felt the edge of one blade graze her arm, cutting through her tunic to slice the skin.

"Move!" Will yelled, and Venn ducked out of the way as a vial flew over her head, smashing on the road to turn the earth slick under the horses. One crashed to the ground, taking another with it, but the riders used their mounts to steady themselves and approached on foot.

Feeling hindered by Corsa's bulk, Venn slid off and smacked his rear — her order for him to do his own thing and stay alive. The white stallion reared up, his front hooves catching one of the approaching soldiers under the chin so he fell back onto the road, his neck at an awkward angle. His fall spooked another horse, which reared back, his heavy rider tumbling to the ground in a whirlwind of colour.

Venn saw the easy mark and pounced on the soldier before he could regain his feet. Steel plating covered him from the neck down, but a small gap showed beneath his helmet, and she plunged her knife into the weak spot. Blood spurted out of his neck when she yanked out her blade, seeping into the armour until it disappeared, leaving nothing to stain the road beneath him.

The sight baffled her, distracting her enough that she didn't notice one of the other unhorsed soldiers come up behind her until she caught sight of his shadow. Kicking her leg out behind her, she tripped him up and rolled out of the way so he fell face first onto his dead companion. Venn climbed onto his back and wrapped her hand around his helmet, tugging his head back to widen the gap between his armour.

Before she could drag the knife across his throat, a weight come down over her head. She rolled onto her back, raising her hand to block out the glare of the sun. Another soldier stood over her, the hilt of his sword still angled to hit her, as the first regained his footing.

Shit.

Her heart slammed against her ribs. She tried to tighten her hand around her knife, but realised she had lost the blade in her fall. Not bothering to try and find it, she snaked a hand to her hip for another one, freeing it just as both soldiers raised their swords.

Two of them? That's a bit much for one little girl.

Despite the buzz of fear in her veins, she grinned and flipped onto her feet, spinning out of the way as the heavy metal swung towards the empty ground.

"Must piss you off that all your weight slows you down," she said, dancing out of their reach. "My grandmother moves faster than you do."

Behind her, Remy still battled the same soldier, but she was tiring, her arm slowing while the soldier appeared to gain energy. Will and Hollis remained away from the fight, but the last two soldiers were caught in some sort of glue, unable to lift their boots from the ground. He launched another vial in their direction, this one releasing a vile smell that moved one of them to push his helmet up to retch onto the road. Venn noticed his pale skin, the dark bruises under his eyes, and took the opportunity to throw a knife his way. It lodged in his eye, and he slumped to the ground, blood pooling beneath his head.

She whipped around to face the other two soldiers, her energy flagging. She forced the fatigue away and replaced her thrown knife, searching for her best shot.

"Don't suppose you care to tell me why you want to kill me?" she asked, trying to give herself a few extra seconds to catch her breath.

The ploy didn't work, the faceless soldiers remaining silent, plodding forward with their heavy steel tread.

"Good thing I didn't get my hopes up," she muttered, and threw herself at one of them, taking him down with a clatter that made Venn think of pots and pans.

The image made her laugh, but the amusement faded quickly as she felt a shooting pain in her arm. Glancing down, she saw his sword had pierced her bicep.

"Guess you're not as slow as I thought," she said.

Not giving either soldier time to prepare his next strike, refusing to consider herself out of the game, she used the numbness of shock to get to her feet, the steel of the blade grinding against bone as it pulled from her body. Pain pumped adrenaline through her blood, and she knew it was only a matter of time before it gave out.

Might as well make the most of it.

She swung her good arm out behind her, striking the second soldier across the head. It hurt her more than it affected him, but he shifted on his feet to regain his balance and she used the chance to get out from between them.

The soldier on the ground stuck out a foot and tripped her, sending her flying into the dirt. She shook her head and tried to regain her footing, but behind her, a low, ear-rumbling growl made her freeze. A shadow appeared over her, and she only had time to drop onto her belly before the paw came down.

Chapter Five

She threw her arms over her head, expecting every second to feel a blow that never came.

"Venn!" Will called out, and she peered up from under her arms to find him on the side of the road. He'd come down from Hollis to crouch in the ditch and gestured frantically for her to come to him.

Head woozy with blood loss and too many tumbles, she hesitated, trying to find her breath and get her head back in the fight. She rolled onto her side to see the body of the soldier that had been standing over her, ready to swing his sword down on her prone form. Blood pumped out of his neck. His head lay a few feet away.

Another gut-clenching growl sounded behind her, and Venn wasted no more time before crawling forward on her elbows and knees, not getting far before her injured arm gave out and she collapsed, cheek scraping against the road. Will cursed and rushed to her side, sliding his arm under her chest to help her sit up. She shifted to rest against his knee, his hand on her shoulder to keep her steady, and they stared in wonder at the scene before them.

The bear tore through the remaining soldiers, his metal claws cutting through the armour of the rider who had finally turned his attention away from Remy. The scout lurched over Shalla's side, blood dripping down her arm towards the discarded sword on the road. Venn wanted to rush to her friend's aid, but Will gripped her shoulder to restrain her.

The red soldiers' horses fled from the new onslaught, but the riders were dead before their mounts could disappear around the bend in the road.

When the last glue-caught soldier crumpled under the weight of the bear's heavy paw, Venn scrambled to her feet with Will's help and limped over to Remy before she could slip from Shalla's back.

"I'm fine," she said, bracing against Venn to right herself. Her tunic was torn at the shoulder, and a bruise had started to form on her cheek where she had been struck, but Venn could see no other injuries. "One hard hit, but it left me reeling. Give me a minute to catch my breath." She accepted her sword when Will picked it up and handed it to her, and gave Venn a scan. "And take that minute to look to your own self. Gods-be-damned, Venn. It looks like he almost chopped your arm off."

At the mention of her wound, Venn wavered on her feet, feeling the first stings of real pain. She blinked to clear the haziness of her vision and twisted her head towards the blood-spattered bear, who sat next to the severed head, pawing it as a child would a ball.

He glanced up at her as though feeling her stare, and Venn felt trapped in his red-hued gaze until Will's other arm wrapped around her waist, catching her before she fell.

"All right, let's sit you down," he said, guiding her a few feet away from the bodies to ease her to the ground. "Stay put."

Venn didn't know where he thought she might run off to. The ground wobbled, and she dug her fingers into the dirt to make sure she didn't slump over. To keep herself focused and awake, she watched the bear, determined not to look at her arm.

She had no issue with blood — not even her own — but from the quick glimpse she'd gotten earlier, she knew the sword had gone right through and had no interest in seeing what else might be oozing out of her.

Not that watching the bear was much help, the way he played with the soldiers' innards like cake batter, spreading them around the road. After a few moments, Venn's brow furrowed with confusion.

"Am I really out of it—"

"I suspect you are," said Remy, coming forward and leading Shalla behind her.

"Let me finish," said Venn. "Tell me you don't see it either. Where is the blood going?"

Remy frowned. "Pooling pretty nicely under you by the look of it."

Venn glanced down to see the red drizzle from her upper arm bead on her elbow before dripping onto the darkening earth. She forced her gaze away and shook her head. "Not mine. Theirs."

Will returned with the satchel that had been far more help than Venn anticipated when Maggie first left it with them at the Keep, and she kept her attention away from him as he took out the stinging salve. The pain on her forehead had been bad enough; her shoulders tensed as she braced for what was coming.

Remy's face twisted with distaste as she shifted her feet towards the mess of corpses, but the disgust soon melted into amazement. "What on…"

"So it's not just me?"

Will, his hand half-raised to Venn's wound, halted, stunned to see the pools of blood roll back towards the bodies like a reverse tide, soaking into the armour, which darkened into a richer shade of red.

The bear tossed his head with a growl, the fur between his shoulders rising up in sharp spines. He batted the head to send it rolling into the ditch before rising to his feet and padding away from the corpses. As he pulled his lips into a snarl, blood from his maw dripped onto the road to join the tide.

"You know it's trouble when even the warbear has issue. That is messed up," said Venn. She hissed between her teeth. "And sweet merciful pancakes on a plate of turkey giblets, William — what is wrong with you, you sadist?"

She tried to wrench her arm away, but his grip tightened around her wrist and the sharp movement sent shooting pains up her neck into her head, which radiated down to all the other scrapes and bruises she'd accumulated.

"Try not to move," he said, the gentleness of his voice preparing Venn for how bad it would be.

Venn squeezed one eye shut and stared at Remy with the other. The scout gave a smile of encouragement, but that didn't help the pain when he applied the salve. The bear growled again as she yelped.

"Might want to be careful, Will," Remy warned, keeping her eye on the bear. "Looks like our friend has a bit of a crush on our fearless leader. Doesn't seem to like seeing her in pain."

Venn had to wonder what had pushed the bear to come out of hiding to save them against the red soldiers, but that was a problem for later. For now, all thought disappeared, and she could only press her lips together to keep from screaming as Will pressed the salve-coated cloth around the gaping hole in her arm. Blood oozed between her teeth where she clamped down on her tongue.

"He'll like it even less if we don't get her patched up and travel-ready. Hate to say it, ladies, but I think we're past the halfway point to Addergrove." He looked up to smile, although the expression lacked its usual mirth. "Since I know you'd consider turning around if you could." The smile faded and he increased pressure on the wound to work in the salve. "But we should get you to a healer as soon as possible. There's only so much my road kit can help you."

"It's less than ten days to Addergrove," said Venn, keeping her teeth clenched as Will bound her bicep under layers of bandages. She thought better about putting up a fight this time. Bleeding out on the road was not how she wanted to go. "We could probably chop a few days if we ride fast and avoid any more encounters with these blood soldiers. Help me up."

"Are you sure you're up to it?" he asked. "You might want to eat something first. Corsa's pretty tall. We'd hate to have you fall off."

He tied off the binding, and then grabbed another strip of it to wrap around Venn's neck, keeping her arm lifted against her chest.

"I'll feel better if we're moving," she said. "Not sure how I feel about setting up camp in the middle of the road. We don't know where those freaks came from, so there's nothing to say another dozen aren't right around the corner. I'd rather have the element of surprise by coming across them next time."

"Here's hoping we don't come across anyone," said Remy. "I'd prefer we skip any more excitement until you've got two good throwing arms."

Will kept his arm around Venn's waist as she got to her feet. She tightened her fingers around his forearm until the world stopped spinning, and Remy grabbed Corsa's reins as the horse passed by, holding him steady as Will helped Venn mount up.

Once she was in the saddle, and the responsibility of moving in a straight line fell on the stallion, Venn disappeared into her thoughts and allowed the others to lead the way.

Before the sight of the unexpected slaughter disappeared

behind them, Venn twisted around to take one last look at the dark red shapes on the road, stuffing as many details as she could into her addled brain to pass along to Jayden and Ariana. No way in sunfire the Andvellian princess wouldn't want to hear about these guys.

As she turned back around, she saw the bear disappear into the trees. It felt strange to her, considering what he was, but she was almost relieved to know he wouldn't stray too far.

***

Venn managed to keep her seat as the day progressed, but they had to stop more often than she liked as her arm bled through the bandages. Will did the best he could with the herbs they found along the road and the remedies in his pack, but as the bleeding continued, his concern and frustration slipped through the calm veneer.

"I know the basics, but I'm no healer," he said when they stopped for the sixth time. "The sling doesn't keep your arm high enough."

Venn suspected the man's ego was at stake, as though he was afraid to disappoint her with his lack of skill. She told herself the state of his ego had no effect on her, but figured it would be a friendly gesture to assure him he wasn't useless.

"I'm still breathing," she said. "Whatever you're doing is keeping me going."

He glanced up from his work and forced a smile, which vanished as his attention dropped back to her arm. "I just wish I knew how to get this bleeding to stop."

Venn's thoughts fluttered back to the last time a healer had given a patient something to stop bleeding. The result had been a lot of vomiting and a warning that similar projectile emissions might occur at the other end, as well.

"No hogglewort," she said. "For the love of the gods, I don't care if you have to leave my drained body here on the road, I will not take hogglewort."

Will smirked. "If I had access to hogglewort, I would cram it down your throat no matter how much you fought me. Unfortunately or fortunately, we're days away from anything that helpful. Remy, help me tie this tight."

The scout dropped her task of starting the evening fire, and came to kneel on Venn's other side. Between them, they tugged the ends of the bandage until Venn's fingers felt swollen, but Will checked to make sure the blood flow wasn't cut off before tying it.

Instead of sliding her arm back into the sling, he took her wrist and rested her forearm on the top of her head.

"Keep your arm up there as long as you can," he directed.

Venn twisted her mouth into a sharp grimace. "Will this accomplish anything other than give you something to laugh at?"

Will grinned, the first sign of sincere amusement he'd shown since the fight. "Above the heart. Keep it there. When you get too tired, make sure you put it back in the sling."

Venn groaned at the awkward position and tried to go

about eating her dinner one-handed until frustration won and she was forced to accept Remy's offer of help.

Once her belly was sated, she stretched out on a blanket, pointing her toes towards the flames to warm them.

Remy stayed busy taking stock of their supplies for the rest of the trip, and Will buried his nose in a journal, too wrapped up in his thoughts to engage with anything or anyone around him, so Venn stretched her arm above her head, and frowned up into the trees.

For most of the day, she had managed to direct her thoughts towards the goal of reaching Addergrove, putting the red-clad soldiers out of her mind, but now that night pressed in around her and she had nothing else to distract her, they weighed on her.

Had Venn and the others been the soldiers' target or had they come across them by chance and decided they didn't like the look of three young riders?

Weird looking soldiers raising swords at anyone they passed? We would have heard about freaks like that.

Then again, she would have thought they'd hear about a group of soldiers dressed in such flashy armour.

She compared them to the bandits she'd faced the last few months. Those men and women were unorganised, untrained. Many of them fled the moment they saw a sword, their own weapons and armour useless against quality supplies.

These red guys were different. They had known what they were doing, even better trained than Remy, which gave Venn pause. And what was with that armour, the way it soaked up the blood as though designed to clean up the mess of the fallen?

The missing ambassador, the bandit they'd set loose on the road, even Red Hood getting his hands on the Meratis sphere – none of them made Venn want to push the pace of their trip and get to Jayden and Ariana more than that group of red riders.

The bear's help added another element of curiosity to the already mind-boggling scene. She knew it was possible he didn't like the look of those guys any more than Venn did, but he hadn't revealed himself until she had been in immediate danger, and then he'd torn them down in a single breath.

More coincidences? He'd just come out of the woods at the best possible moment? Somehow Venn knew it was more than that. He had come out to protect her.

Why?

She groaned and pressed the hand of her good arm into her forehead, thinking she now knew what Brady and Will experienced all the time with so many questions buzzing around in her skull. That had never been a problem for her. She was always the person ready and willing to go with the flow, take what came at her, and preferably force a knife through it. This whole leader thing was more responsibility than she cared for.

I want the fight, not the decisions.

The faster they reached Addergrove and dumped these problems on Jayden, the happier she would be.

"What's got you troubled?" Will asked, looking up from

his book.

He leaned forward on his knees, fountain pen dangling between his fingers. Venn stared at the black ink bubbling from the tip before it dripped into the grass. He and Brady had fashioned the pen after the version Brady had taken from the other world, but she suspected it still had ways to go before they perfected the design.

"Everything," she replied. "And I don't like it."

"I thought you wanted adventure," he said.

She *hmph*ed, not thrilled at having her words thrown back at her. "We're going after a missing ambassador. I was prepared for a bit of stabbing, a bit of hunting. The world-jumping thief was interesting, and tracking him down might have been a fun way to spend a couple of months, but these red guys? Anyone else get the feeling they weren't on their way to a party when they came at us? And what about the bear? Is anyone else bothered by the bear?"

Will raised a shoulder. "I have to say I'm a little less bothered by the bear. Based on how he's behaved around us, I think it's safe to say he doesn't see us as a threat. Whatever his motivations are, so far it hasn't been to hunt us. In attacking us, the riders threatened his habits, his goal. I'm not saying I know all the facets of bear thinking, but if that's the case, we may be grateful he's chosen to follow us for the ride."

Venn grunted and scanned the trees to see if she could spot the beast among the shadows, but he was nowhere to be seen, having sauntered off to do whatever it was he did when he left them. She still didn't trust those disappearances, but was willing to accept them if he kept coming back in time to save their asses.

"I still wonder what it is about me that lets everyone know who I am," she said, adding, "And makes them want to kill me."

Remy smiled over the pile of food and blankets she had scattered on the ground in front of her to repack. "Probably because you keep laughing at them when they challenge you. I swear, Venn, I don't know anyone that smiles in a fight like you do."

Venn chuckled. "It scares people, so I tell myself jokes. You might not believe me, but I'm a very funny person."

Will laughed, but Venn could see the uncertainty lurking behind Remy's amusement. "Under any other circumstances, I'd say your arrogance was getting the better of you, Connell. But it's hard to shake off the belief that we've run into something bigger than some starving refugees."

"The soldiers can't have come out of nowhere," said Will. "Training like that, and in armour that rich, someone has to be funding them. I'm sure Ariana will have a few ideas once we reach her. For tonight, I've set up some extra wards around the camp. They'll only go off with magic, unfortunately, but by the look of that armour, it should stop our friends if more of them swing by for a visit."

Venn dropped her head to the side to peer into the forest, the flames from the fire throwing light into the shadows, creating shapes where there were none. She couldn't tear her eyes away from the possible monsters in the night.

"That's something, at least," she murmured.

She heard the crack of Will's jaw as he yawned, and turned back in time to see him pass a hand over his mouth. The gesture set off a similar reaction in Venn, and in an instant her eyelids drooped, the tension of the day catching up with her.

"Since we're not going to solve this tonight, we might as well get some sleep," Remy squeezed out around a yawn of her own. She set the packs aside and stood up to spread a blanket on the ground, then stretched out on top of it. "Will, if you want to be really helpful, why not pull some kind of enchanter trick and dream the explanations, kay?"

He chuckled. "I'll work on it. You two be ready with your blades."

Venn grinned, patting her pillow. "No worries there, my friend. I've got us covered."

Remy rolled her eyes. "And I'll be over here on this side of the fire. If you're the one that ends up with the dreams, Venn, I don't want to wake up on the wrong side of your nightmare."

She rolled onto her side away from the others as Venn laughed. Within a few seconds, her snores covered up the soothing monotony of forest noises.

Venn glanced at Will who hadn't yet readied himself for bed, determined to finish jotting down his notes.

"What are you writing?" she asked.

He rubbed his chin, leaving smears of ink behind, and glanced up at her with a smile. In the firelight, it looked like a smile hiding a million secrets. "Nothing anyone else would find valuable, I'm sure."

Venn yawned again and turned onto her side, facing the flames. She rested her injured arm on the ground, conscious of keeping it raised above her head. "Your way of saying mind my own business. I got it." She closed her eyes, sliding her hand under the blanket-pillow to clutch the hilt of the knife she'd hidden there. "You just keep writing, scholar boy. This trip has the makings of a pretty epic tale."

She heard the deep rumble of his laugh and listened for the quill to start scratching over the paper again, falling asleep to the sound of his words.

***

Sometime in the middle of the night, a howling wolf shook Venn out of her dreams, chills running down her spine. The wolf had featured in the dream, one of the undead monsters she'd had the pleasure of destroying five years ago. Only this time, the wolf had been winning, its black teeth clamped around her arm so she couldn't pull away or reach for her weapon.

Her body came out of sleep and her arm shot through with pain, making her gasp.

As her brain caught up with the rest of her, she remembered the injury, and realised she'd rolled over onto the wounded limb. Groaning, she pushed herself onto her other side. And froze.

In the silence of the night, beyond Remy's snores, she heard snuffling in the woods behind her, coming closer. She thought of Will's wards around their camp, but knew it wouldn't keep away any creatures who wanted to steal their dinner.

Another wolf howled, but it sounded farther away. Whatever was on the edge of the camp, it wasn't him.

The snuffling came closer, followed by a snort, and Venn felt the shock of cold metal press against her back, which warmed as the fur covering the plates settled against her.

Her heart raced, and her breathing quickened as she debated what to do. Catching him in his sleep would be the best chance she'd have of killing him. One less threat stalking them on their path, one less possible bear to clear from Treevale once they returned home. She squeezed the hilt of her knife, spots dancing in her eyes as the adrenaline rushed through her, but she couldn't seem to pull the blade from under her pillow. After the way he'd saved her, killing him seemed ungrateful. And if Will was right and the bear would stand guard over them — whatever his reasons, maybe keeping him alive was the greater benefit. For a while she lay still, so tense her arm began to ache, but the bear did nothing but release another deep sigh, and she forced herself to relax and release the knife hilt.

Just for tonight, bear, you have your truce.

She closed her eyes, warm against the thick fur, and after a few minutes sleep overwhelmed her and she fell back into her dreams.

Chapter Six

With the bear now travelling with them instead of remaining hidden in the trees, Venn suspected Remy would get her wish in seeing no more action until they reached Addergrove. The more she watched him, the more she appreciated how deadly he was. Along with the metal teeth and claws, she took the opportunity, from the safety of Corsa's back, to get a closer look at the sharp spines between his shoulder blades, which she'd only seen him reveal when he wanted to make a display. They didn't appear to ooze poison the way the spines on some of Raul's other creatures did, but she felt no need to test it.

For the first couple of days, Will and Remy had trouble keeping Hollis and Shalla calm. Both mounts were terrified whenever he came close, dancing away in a panic, eyes rolling, and lashing out with teeth and hooves. Fortunately for them, the bear didn't worry much for his safety, and when he proved he had more interest leaning against trees than attacking them, the horses relaxed into their natural rhythms.

Much to Venn's amusement, Corsa never seemed fazed by the bear's presence. Other than the odd glance in his direction, and the occasional tail-flick in his face, the stallion treated him as he would a nuisance, not a threat.

"My horse has seen way too much shit," she said, patting Corsa's neck with pride before swatting at a bug on her leg. The farther north they travelled, the worse the biters seemed to get. Her skin prickled with sweat, and she glanced up to see the sun peeking out from below the tree tops, wishing it would hurry up and set. "What are we thinking for time?"

Will pulled the map out of his pack and spread it out in front of him. "I checked at our last stop. Pretty sure it's only a few more hours. If we take one more break tonight, we'd get there early tomorrow morning."

The thought of making camp when they were so close to a roof over their heads and a full meal in their bellies didn't appeal to Venn. "Why stop? I say we press on and get there tonight. We'd be there before midnight if you're right."

"What about your arm?" asked Remy, face pinched with concern. "I know better than to ask how you're doing, but you look tired. And the last time Will checked, it wasn't looking so good."

Venn had glanced at the wound before Will wrapped it up, seeing how the skin around the gaping hole had turned red and warm.

"All the more reason to get me to their healer as soon as possible."

The hesitation never left their faces, so she gave one last push.

"I'm more than happy to ride on without you if you need a little extra shut-eye."

The suggestion broke through her friends' reserves, and Will's shoulders slumped. Venn saw how tired they both were, and if their asses were anywhere near as sore as hers, they just wanted to get off their damned horses and never ride again. But they would thank her when they were able to sleep in an actual bed that night, and eat something not heated over a campfire.

"Fine," said Remy. "But this is the last time I'm riding with you. Even my captain has more mercy on his troops."

"But does he take you to so many new places, Rem? Just imagine: a few more hours and we'll be sitting in the lap of luxury."

Venn had never seen the estate in person, but based on the letters Jasmine had read aloud from her brother, and the much longer, more detailed letters from Ariana, she expected something great and expensive. Like the Keep, but bigger.

Queen Ansella had given her daughter and son-in-law the house shortly after the wedding five years ago. Venn had thought it was a nice, pricey wedding present until Ariana explained it was a political move to have more royal presence in the north. Although, from what Venn gathered from later letters, the queen regretted sending them so far away after her grandsons were born.

At the thought of the twins, Venn sighed and braced

herself for what was to come. If Will or Remy expected a few days of peace and quiet while they recuperated from their journey, they were in for a surprise.

From what she remembered of them when they came to visit the year before, Kyle and Laren, Jayden and Ariana's four-year-old sons, were even wilder than Naya. Not having had the opportunity to mould these two into her own creatures, Venn wasn't sure how much she looked forward to spending her days with them.

Never too late to start training. If they keep popping out the kids, I'm going to have a whole squadron of minions in a few years.

The thought made her smile.

"I think we're passing into Addergrove territory now," Will announced as they approached a fork in the road. The forest had thinned out into open field, and all that remained was a row of trees on either side of the lane, standing sentinel. The first two clusters of trees twined together, creating a natural archway. The bear took an extra left to disappear across the field, towards the woods in the distance.

Venn sniffed, unimpressed with security. "I thought it would be a bit more like the palace gates."

"Except not so tall," Remy joked, referring to the giant-scale wall around the capital. "But I think it's pretty."

"Pretty saves no one," said Venn. "And from what I know of both Jayden and Ariana, neither of them had a say in creating such a useless welcome sign. It screams, 'Rich people, this way.' Stupid."

"Maybe they don't have the same issues up here as we do down south," Will suggested.

Two weeks ago, Venn would have commented on how boring that would be. After all she had seen on the road since then, she hoped Will was right. There deserved to be some places in the world untouched by the craziness of the rest of it.

"So now that we're here, maybe it's a good time to ask what I can expect," said Remy. "I've only met Lord Feldall once and the princess never. What's Princess Ariana like? It's difficult to get an impression from the way you two speak about her."

"First off," said Venn, "refer to her as 'Princess' and she'll send you out to sleep in the stables. She's a peach. Good with a sword, quick with her tongue, and willing to keep people in their places. She'll make a good queen one day. If she lives that long."

"Oh?" Remy's brow shot up with interest.

"She means Ana isn't so dissimilar to Venn," Will explained. "She doesn't like sitting around when there's something hands-on for her to do. It's got her into trouble more than once in recent memory."

Venn grinned. "It wasn't so funny when it happened, but you should have seen Jay's reaction when Ana insisted on leading her troops against a revolutionary tribe outside Kilbury. She was three months pregnant — although I don't know if they knew that at the time — but damned if she was going to let anyone else take her place at the front of the line. He insisted on riding with her, and with their constant inter-competition I don't think they needed the rest of the army to quell the horde."

"Neither of them has lived that story down," Will concluded. "From what we hear, Ansella nearly had a fit right in her audience room when the page came in to announce the news."

"Pretty sure her first counsellor stayed in bed for a week. I can just picture him." Venn flung the back of her hand to her forehead. "Cloth pressed to his face, smelling salts in hand, jowls wobbling with despair."

Remy's wonder lapsed into shock. "Should you really be talking about the queen's advisor that way? It seems… impolitic."

Venn hooted. "You've seen the guy, Rem. Try arguing the opposite. Besides, who's nearby to hear me?"

"Me, for one," a familiar woman's voice broke in, the owner of the voice laughing as she rode up behind them.

In the deepening dusk, they'd passed her by without seeing her, but now Venn looked over her shoulder to smile at Ariana as she guided her mount, Mara, up to Corsa's side. The princess looked as lovely as ever in her leather trousers and cream-hued tunic, her strawberry blonde hair pulled back into a ponytail tied with leather. Her fair features were still sharp, but Venn saw the fatigue under her eyes and a tightness around her smile that suggested all was not as well as the lighthearted greeting would suggest.

"What in the nine gods' names are you doing out here at this hour?" Venn asked. "We expected to surprise the whole family over tumblers of liquor. Or maybe even dinner." She waggled her eyebrows to drive the hint home.

Ariana's smile widened. "Just getting some air. You'll need the break, too, once you've been here for a few hours." She rolled her eyes up to the sky at the reference to her children, and then gave Venn's leg a nudge with her knee. "But you must have ridden like the wind to get here so soon. We didn't expect you for another couple of days. Is everything all right? Brady wrote to say you were coming to help us with our diplomatic mystery. It's serious, but you didn't need to run."

The three travellers exchanged glances. Remy looked to the princess and flushed, casting her gaze to the ground, picking at the dirt on her tunic. Venn guessed how uncomfortable she felt being presented to Ariana in her road-dirty, travel-weary state, caught throwing out slurs against the queen's adviser.

Will nodded at Venn to explain.

"As interested as we are in helping with your situation," Venn began, and raised the sling, "we ran into a few unexpected challenges that made it wiser to shorten the trip."

Ariana frowned at the sight of bloody bandages and gestured towards the road. "Come on, then, let's get you to Phil. He'll take a look at that for you."

"And what about dinner?"

The princess laughed. "I think we can fix something there for you, as well."

The ride to the house took longer than Venn expected, the road twisting left around the field and back towards the forest before curving right to follow alongside it. Moonlight guided their way, and Venn watched the pinpricks of stars fade and reappear, counting six falling from the sky.

"Your mother didn't go stingy on the land, did she?" Venn asked as they rounded another corner only to face more trees.

"She thought more land would keep us safe since walls wouldn't send the right image to our northern population. But it has proved more difficult to maintain security. We've had to increase the patrol, so the guards are on night and day watch. We either need to recruit more men or increase the shifts, because they're wearing out."

Will cast a glance her way. "Has something happened to make the increase necessary? It doesn't seem like you face much trouble up here."

Venn sniffed. "Seriously. This has been the quietest part of our trip."

Ariana pressed her lips together and flicked up her brow, sending a message of 'you'd think so'. "That was the case up until recently, but there's a change in the wind, and it's not blowing well for Andvell. I suspect we're going to see a lot of trouble in the months to come."

Venn's interest piqued. "It doesn't involve strange soldiers in red, does it?"

The princess shook her head. "Miners in black, covered in gold dust and metal filings. Might not sound like much of a threat, but it means more to our economy than anyone outside the north might think."

Remy rode closer to hear more of the conversation.

"Trouble with Orland?"

Venn shot her a look of surprise, not only that the scout had finally worked up the courage to speak in Ariana's presence, but also that she seemed to know more about the northern borders than Venn was aware of.

"You got it," Ariana said.

"Jax mentioned something about Margolin, but I didn't know Orland was involved." Venn worked to remember the details. "That's why she suggested I come to you, to help retrieve your ambassador to Margolin without increasing tensions with them."

The lines around Ariana's mouth tightened as she pursed her lips. "Tensions might soon become an understatement."

Remy's brow furrowed. "That makes no sense. Why would Orland want to pick a fight with us? We're their primary trade partner."

"And that's the question keeping our ambassador to Orland up at night ever since they forced him out a month ago. He's been staying here with us since then, trying to get a better idea of what's changed, but so far no one's replying to his letters."

"This all started a month ago?" Will asked.

Ariana pushed aside a broken branch as she passed underneath. "A few months ago. Taylor stuck through it, doing his best to smooth the way for communication and compromise, but apparently they have no interest in talking things out. I'm not sure what it means for the weeks to come. The root of the problem started about six months ago. I think Mother hoped our royal presence here might settle relations and smooth out any rising tensions. But it didn't. We also haven't raised tensions, so whatever problems they have, I don't think it's with the throne."

She flashed them a smile.

"If you guys want to hear more about our political upheavals, let's at least wait until you're clean, fed, rested, and treated. And then Jay and I can listen to the new problems you're bringing to our doorstep."

Venn forced a return smile, not looking forward to breaking it to the princess that the trouble they brought was a little more serious than unhappy miners. As Ariana said, though, that would be a conversation for later. For now, she was happy to enjoy the rest of the quiet ride.

As they rounded one more bend in the road, Venn got her first view of Addergrove. The estate matched almost exactly with what she had expected, but impressed her much more.

The pale colour of the stone gave the building a bright appearance that warmed and welcomed on sight. A large pond graced the centre of the front courtyard, which sat in the middle of the curved road. Stretches of flourishing gardens wrapped the front and side of the house, and Venn suspected the back would offer an even more stunning display.

She wasn't too into flowers, but she could appreciate that some people felt it worth their while to spend time structuring grass to be pretty if not useful.

"Nice," she said.

Ariana laughed at the lacklustre description. "Thanks. Wait until you see the inside. I promise it's not nearly as pretentious as it looks from here."

They rode up to the stable and dismounted, handing the horses off to two stable-hands. The men looked to be nothing more than simple country folk, but as she made to walk away, Venn caught sight of a sword hilt hidden behind a bale of hay.

Security wasn't quite as shabby as it appeared to be from their lack of gate.

"The rooms should all be ready for you," Ariana informed them as she led the way to the front doors, pulling off her riding gloves as they went.

Venn caught sight of four servants rushing towards the stables to grab the travellers' packs and satchels from the horses, a luxury it had taken her years to get used to, but that she'd missed the last two weeks.

I'm getting soft.

"I feel I should warn you that Kyle has learned how to create crossbows out of sticks and string. We've tried taking them away, but it only encouraged him to get more creative. He nearly put Laren's eye out yesterday." She sighed. "I've been trying to convince Phil to give me something to make them sleep. He refuses to do it."

"You can't find good healers today," Venn replied, shaking her head in mock sympathy.

Ariana rolled her shoulders. "I could use the sleep, myself. But at least here I can throw them outside to get into trouble in the garden if they want. I don't know if they would have had that much freedom in the capital. Mother's had to bring security down even heavier than we have in recent months."

"Trouble there, too?"

The princess looked over her shoulder and in the angle of light looked wearier than she'd appeared on the road. "Trouble everywhere."

The front door opened, and Venn grinned to see a familiar unbalanced form under the arches, his left hand tucked into the pocket of his jacket, with the right sleeve knotted at the shoulder to accommodate his missing arm. Crossing one foot over the other as he propped his shoulder against the doorjamb, Jayden greeted them with a roguish smile that took Venn back so many years. It hadn't been so long ago that she'd seen him, but it felt strange to arrive from her unusual trip to greet him instead of having him on the road with her. Kids, a wife, his own home — he'd turned into such a grown-up compared to the rash warrior he'd been when she first met him.

"Nice to see you, shrimp," he said, stretching his arm out to nudge her good shoulder.

"Hey, one-eye," she returned, punching him back.

Jayden's good green eye crinkled with his smile, the right one hidden under the black leather patch. The smile faded as his gaze dropped to her bandaged arm.

"What's this?" he asked, gesturing to the sling. "You're not trying to compete with me, are you? Even with one arm I can still kick your ass. You're not going to beat me by copying the style."

"You kidding?" she countered. "You're getting so old I could beat you without losing breath. But no, if it's possible, I'd like to keep my arm. This was just a run-in with some very odd soldiers in magical armour. Good times. Pretty sure they're evil. Can't wait to tell you about them."

"Hm," Jayden replied, pressing his lips into a straight line. "Jax wrote to say you were coming to help us because you're bored. That doesn't sound all that boring."

"Turns out we left Feldall at a good time."

The warrior's eye narrowed further and the lines around his mouth hardened as he looked over Venn's shoulder. He reached for the knife at his side.

"Get behind me," he said. "Ana, grab the others."

"Jay, what—" His wife's face twisted with confusion until she looked behind her. She released the dagger in her boot and stepped in front of Will and Remy. "You two get inside and make sure the kids don't come out."

If Venn were given three guesses as to what they saw, she knew she would only need one.

"Guys—" she tried, raising her good hand to catch their attention.

"Venn, move out of the way," Jayden ordered.

She saw the fear lurking behind his courage, and knew he wouldn't listen to anything she said. For the moment, her truce with the bear still stood, and she spun through the options of letting Jayden have his way, helping him and Ana take the beast down, or accepting that, by chance or contrivance, the bear had become part of her team.

What did I once hear about strange bedfellows?

Releasing a sigh, she turned to the bear, who had come up from the road, and marched towards him.

"Venn!" Ariana shouted and started to run after her. Jayden dropped his knife to grab his wife's arm, stopping her from getting too close.

"It's fine," Venn called over her shoulder. "Really."

The bear stopped a good distance away from the door and sat on its haunches as she reached him. Pausing, she stared into his red eyes, watched the way he cocked his head to stare back at her, and blew out a breath. No matter what risk he posed to them, she knew she couldn't stand by to see his blood spilled.

This is so stupid, she berated herself, but her gut had spoken and she'd made up her mind.

Slowly — having never attempted to touch him before, and hoping he wouldn't see it as a dinner offering — she rested her hand on his head.

"Don't choose now to go crazy and kill me, all right?" she said for his ears alone. He blinked his red eyes and stuck out his tongue to lick her wrist.

Releasing her breath, she turned back to the family in the doorway.

"See? He's not about to tear us all apart. I promise."

"What—" Ariana started, but couldn't find the words to keep going. Her brown eyes had widened until she looked like a caricature of herself, and she looked from Venn to each of the others, waiting for someone to explain.

Will raised his hands to fend off her silent questions. "We have no idea. He's been following us most of the trip and, if it hadn't been for him, the fight with the soldiers would have meant more than a sword through the arm for Venn and the black eye for Remy."

Venn smiled in an attempt to ease the tension. "I think I'll name him Frey. Figure Jeff might appreciate having something tough named after him."

She hoped to catch a glimmer of amusement in either Ariana or Jayden, knowing how much they had ragged on their other-worldly friend for not being the biggest and bravest of fighters, but the joke fell flat except for a smirk from Will, who rushed to hide it when he saw the horror and simmering anger still wrapped around the others.

"Tough crowd," she murmured under her breath.

Frey snorted and rose back on his feet. Jayden backed away as Ariana bent to pick his knife up off the ground.

"Get him off my land," said Jayden. "You guys are welcome here, but I don't want him anywhere near my children. Is that understood?"

Venn slid her hand over the rough spines in Frey's fur, giving him a pat on the shoulder as she walked away. "He's not much for listening, but he won't bother anyone. Definitely more a bodyguard sort of bear."

She walked through the door and patted Jayden's good arm. "And trust me, he's not even the craziest story we have to share."

Chapter Seven

Jayden relaxed once Venn convinced him Frey wasn't about to break down the front door. He took charge of showing Will and Remy to their rooms, while Ariana escorted Venn to the west wing where the healing ward stretched out on the main floor, overlooking the back gardens. Which, as Venn had guessed, were stunning even at night.

A tall man with light brown hair tied back above broad shoulders stood over a worktable along the back wall. The room smelled of herbs, and Venn's nose wrinkled as she caught a hint of something sour, like sulphur.

Ariana cleared her throat to catch the healer's attention, and Venn's mouth fell open when she recognised the face of the man who turned around.

"Phil?"

During the days of the rifts, Philian had been caught up in one of the vortices, summoned out of it by chance with the Meratis incantation. Venn hadn't seen him since the week he'd spent at Feldall's Keep recuperating, but this was the first she'd heard of him leaving his position as apprentice at Kariel's Keep to join Ariana.

The healer's face lit up, brown eyes twinkling. A smear of green crossed his left cheek, and he finished wiping his fingers off on a rag.

Venn looked to Ariana. "You poach him from Hamish?"

The princess laughed. "I would never do that. It would be rude." She rested her hand on Venn's shoulder. "The young lady is in need of some attendance. I'll leave her in your good hands and go see about having some food prepared for when you're done."

After the princess left, Phil gestured to a table covered in a white blanket. "Hop on up."

Venn eyed it warily — she hated going to the healers almost as much as the pain that took her to them — but did as she was told.

"What have you been up to that did such a good job almost taking your arm off?" he asked, untying the sling and unwrapping the bandages.

"Oh, you know, getting into fights with surprise soldiers on the road," she said, wincing as the last bandage pulled away from the wound, taking bits of skin and dried blood with it.

She watched Phil's expression as new blood rose to the surface and dripped down the side of her arm.

"Think I'll lose it?" she asked, half in jest.

He pressed his lips together and bobbed his head side-to-side in a "we'll see" gesture. "It would be the fastest way to get you out of this sling, but I think we can work around it so you keep your hand."

Venn relaxed at the teasing until he said, "First, we need to get this bleeding stopped."

Her stomach turned, and she tightened her grip on the blanket at her side. "No hogglewort."

The healer laughed and walked over to the wall of shelves stocked with jars and vials. He crouched down to grab something on the bottom shelf and came back with a jar full of light blue cream. "No hogglewort. I have something far friendlier in that regard, but it'll hurt like sunfire."

"Pain, I can handle. As long as I don't need to taste it."

"Then hold onto something."

Venn gripped the edge of the table with her good hand and squeezed her eyes shut, relieved Frey was nowhere nearby as she screamed through closed lips at the searing heat that jumped through her veins when Phil applied the salve. Sweat beaded on her brow and her stomach twisted in knots.

She almost wondered if it was worth skipping the hogglewort if she was going to throw up anyway.

But the pain eased, and she worked to slow her breath, her arm feeling better than it had in days.

"You okay?"

She saw his concern when he looked up at her, but didn't have the energy to put him at ease.

"Peachy."

"The worst is over. Just going to do the stitching and rewrap it. The salve also works to numb the pain. While that'll be great during the stitching, you won't feel it if you bump into anything, so make sure to watch where you're going."

She watched the top of his head as he worked, the hair that had escaped the leather strap falling over his eyes. To distract herself from the uncomfortable sensation of pulling skin, she said, "Maybe now that you've treated my arm, you can treat my curiosity. What brings you to Addergrove? Kariel piss you off one too many times?"

She'd dealt personally with Hamish Kariel. He was a bitter, miserable man, and she guessed the people in his household stayed more out of loyalty for who he used to be before he lost his daughter in Cordelay.

"Not at all," said Phil, eyes crinkling in a smile. "But Corban's been with Kariel a lot longer than I have, and has his own system worked out. He thought it best if I got my own footing, so he recommended me to Princess Ariana."

He rose up from the stitching, and started wrapping Venn's arm with new bandages. Her skin was tinged blue from the salve, blocking her from seeing the damage underneath.

"How is the old doc?" she asked, thinking of the Kariel healer with the sharp tongue and ridiculous sweet tooth.

"Getting old, but spry as ever. I'm pretty sure House Kariel will fall before he does." Phil tied off the bandage and tucked her arm back in the sling. "There you go. You're done for tonight. I'll want to see you every day while you're here to make sure it's healing well."

Venn puffed out a sigh and saluted. "You got it."

He crossed his arms. "And give a big hug to whoever got you to me. If it hadn't been so clean and well taken care of, I likely would have had to take the arm."

Warm relief rushed through her, her hands shaking at how close she'd been to living up to Jayden's joke of copying him. "I'll pass along your message."

Phil shooed her out of his ward, and Venn was directed by the servants towards the drawing room, where she found the others already relaxing on the chairs and sofa. A platter of food was spread out on the table in front of the fire, and Venn made a beeline towards it, stomach grumbling at the sight of cheese and fresh fruit.

She fell into a large chair and dove into the food, joining in on the light and frivolous subjects as they filled Remy in on old stories, and caught each other up on the last year.

The twins had already been put to bed so Venn was saved the trouble of facing them without a good night's sleep on a real mattress, but the food went a long way to pick up her waning spirits.

After they'd eaten, and the servants had taken away the trays and replaced the wine bottles, the conversation took a more serious turn. Venn, Remy, and Will took turns filling Ariana and Jayden in on their trip, and the lord and princess sat in rapt attention, horrified and amazed by what they heard.

Venn took a sip of rich red wine, enjoying the way it puckered her tastebuds before it went down, and sank back into the cushy chair by the fire, crossing her legs. Remy sat on one side of her, dwarfed by the large wingback, and Will on the other, his legs stretched out in front of him.

"Make anything of any of it?" she asked Jayden and Ariana.

Husband and wife exchanged a glance.

"Not the slightest," said Ariana. "The bandits we've heard about — we've had our own difficulties with them, even this far north — but it's good to know about the border with Cordelay. We only just received word from the capital that Margolin's closed it, but I'll be sure to let mother know the trouble it's causing."

Jayden rubbed his brow. "Of everything, I'm most concerned about the guy with the Meratis sphere. In the wrong hands, it could cause no end of chaos, and by the sound of it that man is definitely the wrong hands."

Venn picked at the bandage around her arm, wishing she could scratch at the healing wound beneath it.

"You didn't see those soldiers, Jay. I've never seen anything like them." She frowned. "Something about them terrified me."

"Do you get any sense of where they came from?" Ariana asked.

Remy glanced at the others and said, "It was a pretty empty stretch of road. Venn insisted on taking a lot of back roads to avoid the big cities, so it's impossible to know."

"Which is part of what worries me," Venn cut in. "We weren't on any main roads, and yet these people knew where to find us."

"And you're sure they were after you?" Ariana asked.

"Maybe not, but then why attack us?"

"What about the bear?" asked Jayden.

Venn bobbed her head. "Don't know what to make of that. But he won the day with those soldiers. Tore them down in a heartbeat."

He growled. "I'll bet."

Ariana reached out and ruffled his hair, pulling him away from his thoughts before he started to brood. He graced her with a warm smile and leaned his cheek into her palm.

Venn looked away from the intimate moment and drew her feet up under her. "So now that you're up to date and I can leave it all in your more-than-capable hands, why don't you fill us in on your situation? I'm not sure I'm up for a battle with some sort of blood clan, but if you have a bit more sneak-and-stab task, I'm all ears. How did you lose your ambassador?"

Jayden snorted and leaned back into the sofa, propping his boots up on the coffee table. Ariana kicked his legs down, and he shifted sideways to raise his feet onto her lap, nudging his boots off onto the floor.

"I don't know if stabbing would resolve the issues," Ariana said, as if breaking bad news, "but I appreciate the offer. As for the situation, this is the little we know: Ambrose Felpin, the Orlish ambassador in Andvell, left over a month ago. He claimed it was for health reasons and that he'd send a replacement, but he never did. The house was shut up and his people disappeared. Shortly afterwards, Courtney Taylor, our ambassador, was sent home without reason."

"You mentioned he's staying here with you," said Will.

Ariana nodded and rolled her eyes upwards. "He rarely leaves his room, but we figure he's still alive. We hear him pacing into the night, impatient to receive answers to his letters. He's written to my mother, but she hasn't learned anything more than we know. From what we've heard from our own people who live near the border, the Orlish have turned their backs on our markets. Our northern population make most of their money by trading with Orland, so for them it's been a huge blow. Their stock is overflowing and they can't afford to ship it south."

"And what do these Orlish people have to offer us?" Venn asked. "You mentioned gold dust?"

Jayden nodded. "They're rich in metals and gold, but the land isn't good for farming, which means they need to import most of their resources. We've had a treaty with them since King Ansel's time, made out of good faith as a thank you for harbouring people fleeing from the mad King Francis."

Venn tapped her glass against her teeth. "That's a good long time. What's changed?"

"That's what we don't know. They've moved all of their business to Margolin, but we haven't been able to figure out what Queen Rhoda is offering them."

Remy leaned forward, resting her empty glass on the table. "If the Orlish aren't talking, have you sent anyone into Margolin?"

Ariana frowned and rubbed the sole of Jayden's foot, a mindless gesture that coaxed a soft smile from Jayden, who reached up to brush a lock of fair hair off her cheek.

"That's where our missing ambassador comes in. Jer Reddington is one of the best contacts we have, never skipping a month in sending updated reports to the capital about his observations or concerns, but it's been two months now with nothing."

"And no one's been sent in to check?"

Ariana raised a shoulder. "We didn't want to escalate the issue by sending someone in officially. We sent word to other contacts in the Margolan capital, but the ones we've heard back from haven't learned anything, and the rest are just as silent."

Venn leaned forward to pour herself another glass from the pitcher on the table and gave the royal couple a smile. "Sounds like you two could use someone who knows what she's doing. The stabbing is a bonus, but I can just do the sneaking if it'll help. Don't forget that my survival hinged partly on acquiring useful information back in the day. It might be fun to flex some of those eavesdropping muscles again."

The princess's expression twitched with concern. "I wouldn't feel right sending you in alone."

Venn waved a hand. "I've spent more years alone than with people. It's fine." She sipped her wine and considered Ariana's doubting expression. As much as she would have preferred to go on alone, the trip hadn't been so unpleasant with her two companions. Remy could handle her own and might come in handy with her extra blade, and Will had proved himself more than useful.

If it means she'll let me go…

113

Taking another stab at persuasion, she added, "I'm sure if I asked nicely, these two would tag along for the trip."

Jayden and Ariana exchanged another glance, and then Jayden looked to Will and Remy, both of whom had turned to Venn with various expressions of surprise and amusement.

"What about you two? I don't want Venn to bully you into a situation you're not comfortable with. Will, I know your mother expects you to stay here and work with Phil for a while."

Will leaned on the armrest and rubbed his forehead until his eyebrow turned red, and then let his arm drop. "I'll go where I'm needed and where I might do some good. If you think there's information to find in Margolin, I'm willing to go along and ply my own skills."

"Remy?" Ariana asked.

The scout smiled and sipped her wine, clasping the cup between both hands. "I'm always up for some exploration. Besides, I want to find out more about their sudden discord with Cordelay. If they've closed one border and opened another, there has to be a reason for it. And if my people are going to suffer because of the change, I at least want to know why."

Jayden smirked at each of them, reminding Venn of a parent faced with a child insisting he was ready for his first sword. "Do any of you even speak Margolan?"

Venn waggled her hand in a "so-so" gesture. "It's been ten years, but I could get by."

Remy looked surprised, it not having occurred to her before Jayden mentioned it. "I know a word or two."

"I'm fluent," Will spoke up, and Venn rolled her eyes with a smile.

"Of course you are." She looked to Jayden. "See? We're your perfect team."

Ariana appeared ready to argue, but Jayden reached for her hand and gave it a squeeze. "It's worth a try. You would feel better, and your mother would feel better, knowing someone was looking into this. And she and I will feel even better knowing you're not going in yourself."

The princess smiled, and Venn felt the warmth from across the room. "No, I accept that this mission would be outside my skill set." She raised Jayden's hand to kiss the back of it, and held it to her lips before releasing a sigh, the smile gone and tension back around her eyes. Wife and mother had disappeared and the Princess of Andvell sat before them, worry-worn and out of options.

"I appreciate your offer, and I accept it."

"Make the arrangements," said Venn. "We'll set out as soon as I can use my arm."

Jayden sat up and tapped his finger against the table, catching Venn's blue eyes with his green.

"I've known you long enough to trust you, and to know you're able to recognise boundaries when you have to, but I need you to take this mission seriously, Venn. Tensions are high, and one wrong move could throw our countries into war."

Venn smiled and leaned back in the chair, swirling the wine in her glass. "Don't worry about me, Feldall. I'll be on my best fucking behaviour."

Chapter Eight

Venn slept most of her first day at Addergrove. She'd had a difficult time falling asleep — her injuries shooting pain through her each time she moved, and the mattress too soft after so long on the hard ground — but once her brain shut down, it didn't start up again until the sun was past its halfway point.

Between her arm, Remy's black eye, and Will's task of gaining information for Maggie, they spent a few days with the other half of her family, taking the time to recharge and explore the depths of the estate, including a few secret passages Jayden pointed out. Venn liked disappearing into the tunnels within the walls when the family became too much for her — especially the tunnel that led to the kitchen. By the second day, she had created a rapport with Mel, the cook, and talked him into sneaking her the odd snack between meals.

Every day, she spent a while in Phil's hands getting her arm doused with the stinging salve and rewrapped, which grew less painful as the days passed.

"Arm is healing well," he said on the fourth day.

Venn stared at the angry red gash and clicked her tongue. "You do good work, my friend. Amazing this happened only a week ago. The scar looks months old."

The healer's face broke out in a wide smile as he moved to his bench to grab more supplies. Locks of brown hair fell into his face, and he used his shoulder to brush it aside.

"How long do you think you'll stick around?" he asked.

Venn picked at a lint ball on the white sheet beneath her. "A few more days. We're all in riding form again, so now it's just a matter of hearing more about where we're going."

"That's too bad," he said, sending a smile over his shoulder. "I'll miss having you stop by my table." He returned to her side and poured a cooling lotion over the wound. The pain ebbed into a sweet numbness. "I think you can leave that unbound going forward. Just keep an eye on it, and come see me if it starts to get red. And then do your best not to get stabbed again."

Venn grinned. "No promises there. But thanks. You've done away with some of my loathing for healers." She hopped down from the table. "Send my regards to Corban if you're in touch. Tell him I expect to have cream tarts waiting for me if I stop by on my way home."

Phil chuckled. "I'll be sure to do that."

She winked and turned to head upstairs, but bumped into Will in the doorway, his gaze glued to his shoes.

"Ariana asked me to come get you," he said, raising his

head to give her a tight smile. "I think they've heard something from Margolin."

He shifted his attention over her shoulder to rest on Phil, and Venn felt oddly embarrassed as she glanced around to see the healer already busy with his herbs on the workbench. She turned back to Will.

"If they sent you to get me, it must be important," she said, nudging his shoulder to bring his focus to her. "You coming with?"

"Sure," he said, and cast one last look at Phil before falling into step beside her. "Your arm is looking better. Phil did good work."

Venn raised her arm to get a better look at the thin line stretching down half of her bicep. "It'll leave a pretty great scar, but, yeah, he worked a few miracles. I praised your work in getting me here alive, though. He agreed I would have been dead if you hadn't done so good a job."

She didn't know why she felt the need to add the soothing assurance, but something inside lifted when she saw Will's mood brighten.

They climbed the winding stairs up to Ariana's office, but found no one there except Kyle, who was on the floor playing with a toy soldier and horse.

"Hey, runt," Venn greeted, making sure to keep out of range of any projectile toys he might want to send her way. She'd already been the target of his tiny crossbows more than once since her arrival, and could only praise the kid's aim. "Where's your mum?"

Kyle shrugged, running the horse into his shoe and

throwing the soldier backwards across the room in the collision.

"What did he just run into?" she asked, crouching down beside him.

The child crawled on his hands and knees to grab the soldier and bring him back to his horse. "Raul's barrier spell. They can't get into the fortress to kill him."

Venn stepped into his vision and understood his leg was the barrier, which meant the pile of papers near the fireplace must be the tower that was about to go up in flames. She hoped none of the papers were important.

Will knelt beside her and pretended to drape something over the soldier's neck.

"I just gave him the same amulet my mother once created to help people pass through that barrier. It's made of souls to counter the force of the magic. He's free to go where he wants now."

Kyle hooted in joy and mounted the soldier back on his horse, riding him right into the stack of papers to send them tumbling into the fire.

Will leaned towards Venn, his warm breath tickling her ear. "Think we just ruined the country by burning those?"

Venn stared at the popping flames. "Not our problem. Kid would have found a way to get his soldier past the barrier with or without our help." Will smiled, and she turned back to Kyle. "So now that one crisis has been resolved, where's your mum?"

"With the bassador," he replied, wrinkling his nose in distaste. "He smells like bad oranges. I don't like him."

Venn grimaced and rose to her feet, Will standing at her side. "Thanks for the warning, I'll make sure to cover my nose. Have fun with your soldier. Make sure to watch for the dragon, though. He likes toppled towers."

Kyle grinned and pointed at the door where Laren had appeared, carrying a green-painted dragon in his hands.

"Oh no!" Laren cried out as he darted into the room. "Talfyr's on his way. Run!"

Will and Venn exchanged a glance, and she nodded, agreeing with his silent recommendation that they get out of the room before the dragon caused any more damage. They couldn't get in trouble for not stopping something they hadn't witnessed.

They headed down the corridor to the last door on the right, following the sweet scent Kyle described. An argument raged inside as an unfamiliar voice expressed his displeasure.

"Ridiculous and a poor decision, your Highness," the ambassador insisted as Will pushed open the door. His hands flew wildly, pushing through his grey hair to leave the neatly trimmed locks in disarray. "We can't allow untrained spies into the country to start trouble. Our hold on Margolin relations is tenuous as it is."

"Ambassador Taylor," Ariana cut him off, her tone firm and calm. She stood to one side of the desk in front of the window with her arms crossed and said nothing else until the man fell silent, his hands dropping to his sides. "Queen Ansella and I hold you in very high esteem as a representative of our country who has done his duty well for the last decade, but you are not first counsellor, nor have I asked for your opinion."

Cowed, the man bent his head and sank into the plush chair by the desk. Papers were strewn over the marble surface, with the afternoon sun glinting through the cup of red wine to cast a bloody glow over the vellum.

Will crept into the room, holding the door for Venn to come in behind him. Together they approached Remy, who leaned against the wall with her hands behind her back. Venn noticed how her friend had pulled her blonde hair into a tight bun, and guessed she'd aimed for a professional appearance to impress the ambassador. Venn didn't see much point. The man didn't look like anyone she wanted to impress. She settled against the wall beside her friend and crossed her arms.

Ariana closed her eyes and released a slow breath. She ran her hands over her hair, the wild strawberry blonde waves half out of their woven braids.

When she opened her brown eyes again, there remained no sign of the stress or irritation that had forced her sharp voice a moment ago.

"I realise you're as concerned about this situation as I am, Courtney, and know you have a unique perspective on the matter, but I did not make this decision lightly." Although she hadn't acknowledged Venn's arrival, it hadn't gone unnoticed. She turned to her with a formal incline of her head. "Sir Venn, I'm glad you're here."

Venn knew the situation was serious when the princess referred to her by title. Most people didn't — she rarely made the point to remind them she had one. Not that she cared much what this oaf with the ragged beard and loose-hanging clothes thought of her, but if it helped smooth things over for Ariana, they could throw 'sirs' around as much as they wished.

"Courtney — Sir Venn. She's the one who will lead the mission into Margolin."

The ambassador rose to his feet in a reluctant display, and bowed. After a sharp elbow jab from Will, Venn mimicked the greeting.

"Nice to meet you."

The statement came out as more of a question than she intended, and she cleared her throat.

"Have a seat." Ariana gestured to a polished wooden chair, and she threw herself sideways into it, draping one leg over the armrest and bobbing her other heel on the floor.

Remy shook her head in disapproval, and Ariana's eyes widened, but Venn ignored them both. Only Will smirked, as though understanding the purpose of her demonstration. Titles were one thing, but she wasn't about to flounce around like a pompous knight and give a false impression. Her casual arrogance was what made her perfect for the task.

"I hear you have issues sending me across the border?" she said to the ambassador.

Taylor dropped into his chair with a sniff of contempt, crossed his hands on the desk and stared down at her over his sharp nose. His bushy eyebrows, all salt and pepper, knit so close together they appeared joined. He stretched a hand out towards Venn without acknowledging her comment and said to Ariana, "This is exactly what I mean."

Venn smacked her lips and rolled her eyes up towards the ceiling.

Guy's missing the point.

Everyone's attention jumped to the door as Jayden entered the room and shoved the door closed to lean against it. Ariana's gaze flicked from Venn to Jayden to the ambassador. She appeared not to know what to say that would convince the man, so Venn dropped her foot to the floor and leaned forward.

"Listen," she said. "I might not be the buttoned-up class act you would prefer to send in there, but that's why I'm the right person to go. I'm a foul-mouthed, dirty traveller who knows how to hold her own. In the scheme of things, there are a lot more people like me out there than people like you. I'm better able to go unnoticed."

Jayden pushed away from the wall and moved over to the chair across from Venn. He took his wife's hand as he sat down and stretched out his legs.

"She's right," he said. "Venn might look like an unwanted drunken waif, but I've seen the woman work. She knows what she's doing."

"Does she realise how much is at stake?" Taylor demanded, still talking over Venn's head in a way that made her opinion of the man sink lower.

"Yeah, actually," she piped up before Ariana or Jayden could speak for her. "I've heard the story, and I know Andvell could slip into war if I open my mouth to the wrong people. But — and Jayden can speak from experience on this — I'm pretty damned good at keeping my mouth shut when I don't feel like talking."

Jayden shook his head with a smirk, and Venn winked. Their introduction was a fond shared memory. He had impressed her with his interrogation skills, but she had proved it was more unnerving to sit and smile than offer any reply.

Ambassador Taylor threw up his hands. "I'm obviously out-voted and see there's no purpose in arguing, but I wish you'd reconsider."

"And since I won't," said Ariana, letting go of Jayden's hand to grab the tall green chair by the fire. She gestured for Will and Remy to take the sofa and join the conversation, "perhaps you would be so good as to tell us any details that might narrow down what they should look for."

The man looked around the room, his gaze pausing on each face to find one person who would back him up. When no one stepped forward, he released a sigh and passed his hands over his eyes.

Venn grinned and slouched in her chair, once more propping one leg up on the arm rest.

"All right. Let's get to business."

***

Taylor had less information than Ariana had hoped, but more than enough to get Venn started. He knew the names of loyal people in Margolin's capital who they could go to for resources and places to stay. In other words, places Venn would avoid. No point ruining their chances of gaining the locals' trust by staying at inns known to be loyal to Andvell. Dead giveaway.

As soon as the ambassador shared everything he knew, Venn had thrown herself into preparations. A week's rest had been enough to heal her motivation as well as her saddle-sore muscles, and she wanted to get back on the road before either Will or Remy started thinking about the pleasures of home.

She spent the next two days chasing servants around the house, making sure they prepared enough supplies to last the journey to Margolin's capital, plus extras in case Will decided to play hero to more bandits.

The day before they were due to leave, Phil restocked Will's healing kit with various potions and salves, and offered his hopes that no one would need to use them.

Kyle and Laren wouldn't stop crying at the news that Aunt Venn was leaving, and Ariana had to send them to bed with extra sweets to make them let go of her legs. Venn didn't know why they were so heartbroken to see her leave, but just like Naya and Frey, the twins had never strayed far from her.

It's like cats, she thought. *Kids always know the person who doesn't like whiny, drippy creatures, and insist on attaching themselves to her.*

But when they disappeared from the room, hands caught in the grip of their nurse, Venn felt a slight pull at her heart that the next time she saw them, they might have forgotten how much they wanted to be around her.

Shortly after the sun set, Will and Remy retired to their rooms to get a last good night's sleep, but Venn couldn't bring herself to leave the comforts of the family so soon. She stood in the parlour window, staring out over the front pond until Jayden came to stand beside her.

"Everyone's on stand-by for tomorrow morning," he said. "Just give the word when you're ready and you'll be gone within the hour."

"Perfect," Venn replied, but she heard the force behind her cheer.

Jayden grinned, the scars on his cheek creasing, and nudged her shoulder. "Take a walk?"

Venn hesitated, not wanting to get cornered into any deep confessions, but agreed, grateful that Jayden had never been one for the heart-to-hearts, and relieved to have an excuse not to go to bed just yet.

He led her through the house and into the back gardens, the flowers lit up under the moonlight like so many fireflies.

She wrinkled her nose in confusion. "Why are the flowers glowing?"

Jayden bent down to clear the leaves away from one bright bloom, and Venn saw three white petals shining with blue-hued light in the darkness.

"I think this is one of the herbs Maggie sent Will here to check out. They're called tide blossoms or something like that. They hide under the leaves during the day and come out at night, reflecting any light so it looks like they're glowing." He picked one and handed it to Venn, who remained caught by the simple beauty of the petals.

Twisting the stem between her fingers, she said, "Never struck you as a flower man.

"I'm not," he said, guiding them down the path. "Neither is Ana, but it's nice to sit out here in the summer with the boys and hear her tell them stories about those flowers. They're happy to believe faeries are playing in the garden."

They stopped at a bench across from a lily-covered pond. The croak of frogs echoed around the song of crickets. A cool breeze brushed through Venn's hair, and she smelled incoming rain. Clouds had started to gather over the stars, and although the moon remained clear, she knew it wouldn't be for long.

A comfortable silence stretched between them until Jayden shifted towards her and said, "Be careful on the road, all right, runt?"

Venn chuckled. "You know me better than that. When am I ever careful?"

He furrowed his brow. "I'm serious. I know I vouched for you in there, and that I should be more worried for Margolin than for you, but we don't know what you're getting into. Take it slow and don't take chances. I'd hate to have to explain to the people who care about you that you were killed on a mission I sent you on."

Venn crossed her arms and stared into the water, watching the surface ripple as the wind picked up. It occurred to her that if she'd sent herself into danger six years ago, no one would have cared if she were hurt or killed. Now she had a whole slew of people threatening her to be safe.

She smiled. "I can't make any promises, but I'll do my best not to do anything stupid."

"That's all I ask."

They heard the first rumble of thunder in the distance. A streak of lightning shot down from the sky, and the tide blossoms brightened in response, the entire garden awash with light in that one instant.

"I see what you mean," said Venn. "That's pretty amazing."

Jayden chuckled, and tilted his head to catch the first drops of rain.

One drop fell on Venn's forehead, and then two, but that was all the warning they got before the storm came down in a torrent. Jayden bolted for the door, and she followed close behind him.

"At least your trip will start on a clean note," he joked once they reached the dry porch. He shook out his wet hair, and Venn grimaced as the droplets hit her face. "Get some sleep. I'll see you in a few hours."

He nudged her inside and, soaked and bedraggled, Venn shuffled up the stairs to her room. A fire blazed in the hearth, easing some of the chill brought on by the rain.

The thunder rumbled closer, ending with a crack above her head. She opened the window to lean out, catching the rain in her hair and the cool breeze on her face. The dampness cut through her bones, but for a few minutes she enjoyed the sensation, appreciating that tonight would be the last night for a while that she could enjoy a storm from a place of warmth and safety.

When the cold won over the pleasure, she pulled the glass pane shut and drew the heavy curtains, closing herself into the dark room with the crackle and pop of the fire. She undressed to her underwear and sleeveless shirt, and sank down on the carpet to dry her hair, exhausted but lacking the desire to crawl into bed.

Something's missing.

She wracked her brain trying to figure out what it was, getting up to rummage through her pack, messing up the sheets to remind her more of home, but nothing worked.

"You're just overtired," she said aloud, and crawled into bed. "Close your eyes and you'll fall right asleep."

She pulled the sheets up around her, tried to appreciate the feel of a soft mattress and pillow, sans roots or rocks or forest debris.

A few seconds later, she glared up at the ceiling, hands folded on her stomach.

"All right, Connell, stop dicking around." She got out of bed and stepped into her pants and boots. "You need to get some sleep tonight or tomorrow's going to be a horrible start to the trip."

Creeping out of her room, she snuck down the corridor to find the stairs and made her way to the front foyer. No other lights or noises came to her as she moved through the shadows, so she figured everyone else was already in bed and she could avoid getting into trouble.

Opening the front door, she peered into the murky courtyard, dark except for the odd flash of lightning as the storm moved closer.

"Psst!" she called, trying to project her voice outside without calling the attention of anyone within.

For a full minute, no sound echoed back to her except for the rolling thunder. About ready to give up and close the door, Venn paused and smiled when she heard the familiar snort and saw the glimmer of metal in the lightning. Frey emerged from the shadows behind the stable and paused at the front door.

For the week they'd been at Addergrove, he had remained hidden in the woods around the house. In Venn's wanderings of the grounds, she'd occasionally caught sight of the sun reflecting off his metal plates, but he'd never approached where others could spot him.

Too smart for his own good.

"C'mon in, you monster," she said, stepping aside.

Frey sniffed the air and took a cautious step onto the stone floor, his large frame barely making it through the doorway.

"Just keep quiet, all right? No one should be outside on a night like this."

She headed up the stairs, and sensed more than heard the bear follow her. Closing the door to her room behind them, she changed her wet clothes into dry ones and bundled herself under the blankets. Frey dropped down with a grunt in front of the fire, and Venn smiled to herself as her eyelids drooped.

Much better.

She eased into a sleep filled with tide blossoms, the glow

of their petals lighting her way down a dark path. With no idea where she was headed, she followed them without concern. Looking down, she could hardly make out her own torso and legs in the darkness, the black clothes blending in with the shadows, the light of the petals all she could see in the night.

Up ahead, the road curved, and she started to run, anxious to learn what she would find around the corner.

Before she could reach what she was running towards, instead of waking naturally to a bright morning wrapped in the warmth of her sheets, Venn was startled out of her dreams by a sharp scream and the clatter of breakfast dishes hitting the floor.

Chapter Nine

Venn lurched up in bed, knife in hand, which only served to draw another squeak out of the serving girl as she hurried out of the room.

Wiping a hand over her eyes to clear the sleep, Venn took stock of the room to see what had caused so much chaos. The sun had hardly come up and already people were screaming. Not a great start to the day.

She looked down to see Frey, his head twisted over his shoulder to look up at her, his red eyes deep and soulful.

"You scared her, bud," she said. "Try not to look so menacing."

The bear sniffed and rested his large head on his massive paw, making her smile.

Footsteps echoed down the corridor, and Venn groaned, bracing herself for more confusion.

Her feet had just touched the floor when Ariana rushed in, sword drawn, Jayden not far behind her.

"What is it?" she demanded. "What's wrong?"

"Nothing," said Venn, pulling the blanket around her shoulders as she climbed out of bed. "I think the woman panicked on seeing my house guest."

Jayden's gaze narrowed in on Frey and his concern morphed into fury. "I told you to keep him out of my house."

His voice came out no louder than a growl, teeth curled over his lip in a way that scrunched the scars running down the right side of his face.

"Jay…" Ariana said softly. She said nothing else, didn't reach out to stop him when his hand went for his sword, but the sound of her voice proved to be enough.

After a moment, he pressed his lips together, and though he still trembled with rage, he loosed his grip and clenched his fist at his side.

"A bear is not a house pet, anyway," he said. "Get him out of here, and I don't want to see him again before you leave."

He turned on his heel and marched out, leaving Ariana staring after him.

She blew out a sharp exhale, and Venn twisted her mouth in remorse. "Sorry about that. Think he'll be all right?"

Ariana nodded and tossed her sword onto Venn's bed, sagging down on the edge.

"He'll cool down eventually," she said, staring at Frey. "He's been on edge since you first introduced your… friend. Understandably, I guess. I think it's bringing up some pretty horrible memories."

"Shit, Ana, I'm sorry." Venn sat down next to the princess. "I knew he wouldn't be happy about it, but I've had time to hang out with this bear. I don't look at him and automatically think of Raul's fucked-up lab experiments anymore."

Ariana offered a tight-lipped smile and patted Venn's knee. "No matter what we think of him, I'm glad he was there for you. He does seem amazingly docile."

Frey twisted to stare up at Ariana, leathery nose twitching as he sniffed the air. When she shied away before he could reach her hand, he snorted and stretched back out on the floor.

"It's funny how you get used to things," said Venn. "For the first couple of weeks on the road, when I knew he was around but not if he planned to turn us into dinner or not, I didn't like him being so close. Now it feels strange not having him nearby at night." She reached out to pat his head, combing her fingers through his fur until they reached the cool metal plate underneath. "Still don't know the how or why of it, but as long as he's happy to guard us from the weird soldiers on the road, I'm all right to have him around."

"Like everything else, I'm sure everything will become clear. As much as my first instinct is to tell you to send him away, maybe the truth isn't as worrisome as I think it is. Maybe he just recognised a kindred spirit as you passed by." Ariana bumped Venn's shoulder. "Built to deal death, but with a big heart underneath."

Venn bumped her back. "Don't let word get round

about that. It won't do me any good if you tarnish my reputation of being a black-hearted bitch. But Jay should be okay after we leave, right? We'll head out in a couple of hours and he won't have to think about the warbear ever again."

The words were meant in jest, but when she glanced up at Ariana, she noticed an expression of sadness cross the princess's face.

"Everything all right, Ana?"

She forced a smile. "It's just a shame you have to leave so soon. We have a lovely home up here, with children we love to pieces even when we think about locking them in the secret tunnels until they wear themselves out, but it's lonely. I know Jay misses his family, and gods know I wouldn't mind seeing more of them. It's been nice having you here."

Venn's throat felt uncomfortably tight, and for a moment she said nothing, just dug her toes into Frey's back, creating patterns with his fur.

"Anyway," Ariana continued, getting to her feet and skirting around the bear. "I hope this doesn't turn out to be a stupid idea, us sending you into the middle of the problem."

Venn smiled up at her. "When am I not in the middle of the problem?"

The princess forced a sigh. "And that's what I'm afraid of."

***

With the serving girl pushing them into an early start, the horses were saddled and ready to go before the sun hit the top of the trees.

Remy and Will came down in time for breakfast, having been lucky enough to sleep through the morning's debacle.

"If you don't run into trouble," said Jayden, sliding a map across the table towards Venn, "the trip should only take you about six days by the main roads. I went over the route with Will last night to see where you might take a few shortcuts."

Venn glanced at it quickly before passing it to Will, who accepted the paper with a smile.

"I'll continue to play navigator, then," he said.

"Only way to make sure we end up facing the right way on the road," Venn replied.

Jayden shook his head. "How did you live on your own so long without knowing where you were going?"

"I got by just fine, thank you," Venn shot back. "I just prefer sticking to my own routes. With Will on our team, we'll get there in no time at all."

Will's face tinged pink as he laughed and tucked the map into the pack hanging over the back of his chair.

Ariana smiled at the banter, but her amusement faded as she returned to business. "We sent scouts out to survey the road to at least get you started, and by their reports everything looks clear. I just hope it continues all the way to the border."

Venn waved a chunk of bread in dismissal. "Don't even worry about us. Considering what we faced on the way here, the rest of the trip should be a breeze. I'm worried more about you guys. Think you'll be okay without us?"

The warrior growled, the dark look marred by the humour that had reappeared in his green eye. "I'll be okay without your beast hanging around, but I'd prefer if you sent word once you reached Margolin. Just to let us know you weren't immediately arrested for drunken debauchery."

Venn laughed. "I can't promise there won't be some of that, but we'll at least do our best not to get arrested."

Remy dabbed the butter from her lips with her napkin and set it down on the table beside her plate. "I'll look after her and do my best to keep her out of trouble. That's what friends are for."

"We won't let you be weighed down with that burden, Remy," said Ariana. "We know what Venn is like."

Breakfast over, they rose from the table and walked towards the front doors. Sunlight streamed over the tree tops and through the windows beside the door, flooding the foyer with warm light, pale and soft after the previous night's storm.

"Travel safely," Ariana said as she gave first Will and then Venn a hug.

Venn laughed to see Remy standing at attention, still not relaxed in the princess's company after the week of being a guest in her home. Ariana chuckled and threw her arms around the scout's shoulders. "It was lovely getting to know you, Remy. You're welcome here any time. The boys would like that, I'm sure."

Remy's wide hazel eyes stared at Venn over Ariana's

shoulder, begging her for help on how to react. Venn grinned and left her to figure it out, turning her attention to Jayden. Temporarily putting aside her avoidance of sentiment, she put her arms around his neck and squeezed him tight. With her mouth close to his ear, she said, "Sorry about this morning."

Jayden wrapped his arm around her waist and squeezed back. "Don't worry about it. But keep a close eye on him, all right? He might look at you with those sad and creepy red eyes, but that doesn't mean he won't snap your neck in your sleep. Don't trust him too far."

Venn murmured her promise and let go, waving goodbye to Ariana as she mounted up on Corsa and turned him towards the road.

"So what do you two say?" she asked Will and Remy as they rode up to flank her. "Do we follow the map or see where the adventure takes us?"

Will shook his head. "Not even a week from getting a sword through your arm and already wanting to dive into more trouble?"

Venn threw back her head and let out a maniacal laugh. "If you don't want trouble, you're riding with the wrong girl."

***

In spite of her suggestion that they stick to the back roads like they'd done most of the way to Addergrove, Will led them to the main routes. Within two days they passed through the township of Denbury, and Forburgh shortly after that.

"Too many places where people can see us and remember us," Venn complained as they left the town centre. Even without the bear by their side, Frey having wisely chosen to skirt the populated areas, she still noticed a lot of looks coming their way as they travelled. She brushed the white road dust from her black boots and huffed as she resettled in the saddle.

"On the other hand, with so many witnesses, maybe we won't be chased by terrifying soldiers in weird blood-absorbing armour," Remy pointed out. "I know you hate people, Venn, but I feel we're less likely to see those guys riding through town."

"Besides, we might as well get used to the crowds now," Will added. "Have you ever been to Margolin's capital? From the latest numbers I've seen, their population is nearly double that of Andvell's. It's going to be very loud and very busy."

Venn didn't bother to argue, seeing the validity of both their arguments, but she still kept her eyes peeled on the faces they passed, trying to commit to memory anyone that stood out as unusual or especially interested in them.

The one perk she saw of following the main roads was that they could spend most nights with a roof over their heads. Most of the inns they stayed at were shoddy, the rooms small and full of stale air, but even Venn had to admit it felt nicer to have a straw mattress under her back than the ground.

On the fourth night they reached the town of Treyhurst.

Most of the crowds had cleared for the evening, and the streets were lit only with lanterns from the odd late running shops and firelight from open cottage windows.

"We might want to restock before we head out tomorrow," said Will. "This is the last town we stop in before the border. I think Jayden said there was a good inn here, as well."

He hadn't finished speaking before the sign for the Bell and Candle Inn appeared ahead. Venn stared up at the two-storey building and thought of the coins rattling in her purse, relieved they didn't have much farther to go.

Will asked for two rooms, but when he showed Ariana's seal on her letter of travel, the innkeeper gave them a third for no extra charge.

"Should have tried to wrangle dinner out of him, too," said Venn as she hauled her bags up the stairs. She took the room in the middle of the floor, leaving Will and Remy to choose theirs on either side of her.

They enjoyed a rich dinner of meat and bread, plotted out their route once they managed to cross the border, and then Will disappeared to bury himself in his letters and notebooks. Venn followed Remy into her room, taking up camp on the floor beside the bed as Remy stretched out on the mattress, raising her feet on the pillows to ease the swelling of a hot day's ride in tight boots.

"I can't believe I let you talk me into going fifteen nights in camps," she said, moaning as she massaged the sole of one foot with the heel of the other. A pouch of tree nuts sat on her chest, and she flipped one into the air with her thumb to catch it in her mouth. "I'm never listening to your travel suggestions again."

Another nut flew upwards and Venn made a grab for it, tossing it into her mouth. She snatched the pouch around Remy's protestations and pathetic attempt to grab it back, and snagged a handful before dropping it back onto her chest.

"That's fine by me," Venn said around her food. "I've said it from the first — I'm not made for leading. Point me where to throw my knife, and we're good."

Remy stuck out her tongue in Venn's direction. "You know that's not true. I can think of a few people who would follow you into the demon's mouth itself."

She cast a blatant stare in the direction of Will's room.

Venn groaned over her hand as she poured more snacks into her mouth. "Oh please, not you, too. Do you know how much I get this from Maggie? Even Jayden started making comments before the end, and don't think I didn't notice the way Ariana was pushing us together. I don't need it from my best friend."

Remy pressed her hand against her heart. "Am I really your best friend? That's so sweet. Then listen to your best friend when I say you should kiss the poor guy before he falls for someone else."

Venn wrinkled her nose. "As my best friend, I would have thought your priority should be my happiness over his."

Remy giggled, and tossed up another nut, darting to the left to catch it. "Venn, I am thinking of your happiness. He could do much better."

Venn chucked a nut towards her friend's head, and Remy snapped it up, crunching it between her teeth with a smile.

"Some friend you are," Venn grumbled, getting to her feet.

"You know I love you."

Venn waved a finger in her direction as she left the room and went back to her own, pausing to listen at Will's door to check if he was still awake. At first she heard nothing, but then the familiar scratch of pen on parchment filtered through, along with some incoherent mumbles, and she smiled, happy to leave him to his work.

Back in her own room, she kicked off her boots and stood in front of the window, letting the breeze catch on the sweat under her arms and against her neck. The temperature had done nothing but rise since they left Addergrove, and her skin felt sticky with humidity.

Stripping down to her smallclothes, she pushed the heavier blankets to the end of the bed and draped herself with a single sheet.

But as much as she tried to turn off her brain and fall asleep, her thoughts continued to spin. Remy's words repeated in her mind, and the harder she tried to push them away, the louder they got. She'd known for years how Will felt about her. From the moment they'd met, he'd been fascinated. She remembered her first days in the Keep — how he couldn't keep his eyes off her, how mercilessly she had teased him because making him blush had been too easy. At first, Maggie had tried to stand between them, but at some point, as Venn became a part of the Feldall family, her thinking switched and she pushed them together.

But no matter what any of them said, Venn's stubbornness held, and she was determined it would continue to hold. Before she was fifteen years old, she'd been forced out of her community, moulded into a killer, and spilled more blood than she liked to admit. She didn't know if she could love, let alone if she deserved it. What she did know was that Will deserved better than her.

She shoved all thought of Will from her mind and focused instead on her plans for crossing into Margolin.

From what they'd picked up from the locals, tensions had risen even more in the week they'd spent at Addergrove. People were being turned away at the gate if they didn't have a good reference or a contact within the country. After crossing the border, the capital was another two-day ride. Easy enough to name one of Taylor's contacts there, but Venn hoped they wouldn't have to. Based on the little she knew of Taylor — and his obvious opinion of her — she didn't want his spies looking over her shoulder and getting in her way.

There's always Lewyn, a traitorous voice popped up in the back of her mind.

Venn grumbled and rolled onto her side, pushing the pillow over her head to block the voice out. But all it did was silence the other sounds in the room and make her thoughts louder.

Not saying you have to, the voice continued, *but if you*

run out of options…

There's not even a guarantee he's still in Margolin, Venn argued back.

You would have heard if he left and you know it.

Venn huffed, angry at herself for bringing up names better left in the past. Some people were meant to be forgotten.

She rolled onto her back again, and pressed a fist against her forehead, wishing the gesture would drive away all thought and help her fall asleep.

Before she could navigate her mind in any new direction, she heard soft noises outside in the corridor. Her skin prickled with wariness, ears strained towards the door.

Silence.

Then she heard it again: floorboards creaking outside her room.

Venn raised herself onto her elbows and stared at the door, her vision sharpening as her body went on high alert.

The creaking paused and she knew whoever was walking past had stopped.

She reached for the knife under her pillow and slid out of bed, wincing as her bare feet stepped on the edge of her boots, repressing the urge to swear. Moving across to the wardrobe on tiptoe, she grabbed a band of knives and strapped it to her calf, preferring to be over-prepared for nothing.

The floor outside the door groaned again and Venn's breath stopped in her chest, every part of her focused on mapping out what she would find if she left her room.

The innkeeper slept on the main floor behind the bar, so she knew it couldn't be him. Remy and Will were the only other occupants on this floor, one of the other rooms being a storage closet, and the other empty as far as she knew.

If one of the other two are playing tricks…

But she knew they wouldn't do that. She heard Remy's snores through the wall, and would have recognised Will's step.

Frey?

Venn moved to the window and peered out, seeing no dark shape anywhere below. Had he gotten in somehow and followed her up? But he would have made more noise on the squeaky floor, and wouldn't have tried so hard to hide his movements.

Taking a slow, silent breath, Venn stepped over to the side of the door and reached for the doorknob with her left hand, keeping the right raised, blade ready.

Her heart rattled against her ribs, and she forced her breathing to remain steady as she twisted the knob and pulled it towards her, easing the door open so only the barest hint of darkness from the corridor appeared.

As her eyes adjusted to the shadows beyond, she realised it wasn't darkness from the corridor, but something closer, something at the door blocking the way.

Her gaze travelled upwards, over the faint details of a leather vest, the studs and stitching worked into unusual designs, over the red pendant on a broad chest, and up to the thick chain around a thick neck, over the bristled chin of salt and pepper, which led up to a cruel, twisted smile.

A little farther up, she locked gazes with familiar cold, dead eyes peering out at her from under the edge of a red hood, and recognition cut through her just as dread forced its way down into her boots.

Chapter Ten

Red Hood gave her no time to speak, shoving the door inwards just as she threw herself against it to keep it closed. His weight carried more force than hers and she was pushed back into the room, the door swinging shut behind him.

Knife in hand, she lunged at him. He raised his arm and stepped out of the way, slamming the back of his hand into her cheek to send her crashing into the wall. She shoved off against the wood panels, but he caught her wrist, twisting her around to lock his arm around her throat, cutting off her breath.

"Goodbye," he whispered as he tightened his grip, his voice deep and gruff. Something in the simple word chilled her more than threats.

Letting her training take over to push away the panic, she reached up and grabbed the outside of his arm, pinching the muscle below his elbow until he flinched, then jerked her head back into his nose. He swore, and in his distraction she tore herself away and lurched forward. Before she could get far, he grabbed a handful of her hair, jerking her towards him. She wheeled around to swing her knife towards his face and he grabbed her forearm, shaking her hand until the blade clattered to the floor as his other hand clutched her throat.

The cold smile returned to his bleeding face, and he kicked out her ankles, slamming her down onto the floor to straddle her. Venn's head bounced against the floorboards so her teeth clapped together, and she tasted blood.

His steely eyes glared down at her, but he said nothing as he closed his hands around her neck. Except for Venn's grunts as she struggled to breathe, and the thud of her heels kicking against the floor, the room was eerily quiet.

Gripping his wrist with her one hand, his arm above the elbow with the other, she hooked her foot around his leg and arched her back. As they rolled, she grabbed a new blade at her calf and landed on his chest, pinning him beneath her with the knife at his throat.

"Tell me who are you and who you work for," she rasped around ragged breaths.

His lips curled into the smile that made Venn's insides feel as cold as his gaze. She pressed the blade deeper into his skin, slicing through the layers until a single bead of blood trickled down the side of his neck.

"Better luck next time, little girl," he growled.

Venn's brow furrowed. "Wha—"

Before she could finish the word, he vanished, leaving nothing beneath her but empty air. She toppled to the floor, her knife skittering away across the boards.

"What the actual gods-be-damned rectum of a sacrificial monkey totem?" she demanded of the room, but it offered no reply.

A shadow appeared in the doorway and Venn jumped, reaching for a third blade at her calf, and then breathed out in relief, bending over at the waist to slow her heart rate, panic catching up with her now that the Meratis jumper had disappeared.

Will started at her reaction and shifted his gaze anywhere but on her.

"I-I'm sorry," he stammered.

Venn glanced down to realise she stood in her underwear. Seeing no point in protecting her modesty, she did nothing to cover herself, just watched him peer into the room, scanning the shadows in the corners.

"I didn't mean to invade your privacy, I just wanted to make sure everything was okay. I thought I heard someone fall."

Venn wheezed a laugh, straightened up, and headed for the cup of wine on the night table, grateful her drink hadn't toppled in the struggle. "Heard the fall, but missed the fight?"

His mouth fell open, and he took a step closer, arm raised to reach for her. Just as his fingers brushed against her arm, he changed his mind and let his hand drop by his side. "A fight? With whom?"

He glanced over his shoulder to check the corner behind the door in case he'd missed someone, and then turned back to Venn, confused on finding the room empty.

"Neither of us is going crazy," she assured him, acknowledging that it might look like she'd been fighting herself in the darkness. "That red-hooded guy. The one who took the Meratis sphere. He showed up tonight and tried to kill me. I finally get the upper hand and the guy up and vanishes. So rude."

The marks on her neck — and no doubt a growing lump on her cheek based on the ache under her eye — must have shown in the moonlight, because Will changed his mind again and took Venn's arm to guide her closer to the window where he could see.

"Gods-be-damned," he whispered, running his fingers over what she guessed would be nasty bruises on her face in the morning. His fingertips felt smooth and cool against her flushed skin.

He lifted his gaze to meet hers and jerked his hand away. "I can take a look at that if you want. There might be something in Phil's care package that will ease any pain."

Venn held onto the softness of his stare, so refreshingly human after the cold deadness of her attacker.

"It doesn't hurt all that much, but thanks."

He sagged against the wall beside the window. "I'm sorry I didn't hear him sooner. That you had to face him on your own."

"And share my glory with someone else?" she asked, and smiled, wincing as her cheek shot pain up behind her eye. "Don't worry about it. I'm just upset he escaped before I could get any answers out of him."

Will offered a sympathetic smile. "Not to mention all

the new questions he raised. Like how he knew where we were staying. Where we were going. Maybe you were right about the main roads and busy cities."

Before he could apologise again, Venn gave him a light punch on the shoulder. "You're doing a great job leading us, so don't put yourself down. If he found us here, he would have found us anywhere. I'm starting to cave to Remy's way of thinking. If we're going to be hunted, we may as well sleep on comfortable beds."

Slowly, almost reluctantly, a smile appeared on Will's lips. "All right, I concede. But I'm still glad you're all right. Should we wake up Remy and let her know what happened? It might not be a bad idea to leave now, before he comes back."

He stopped talking and Remy's snores rumbled between them, making Venn chuckle. "I don't think we should interrupt her beauty sleep. Somehow I doubt the guy will reappear tonight. And if he does, I'll beat him again."

Will hesitated before nodding. "If you're sure."

"I am. Besides, you said we needed to restock before we leave," Venn added. "I say we both get some sleep so we can face tomorrow. If we're lucky, we'll get another crack at this guy before too long."

"If we're really lucky, we won't see or hear from him ever again. Hopefully he loses himself behind the veil."

She arched a brow. "Now where would be the fun in that?"

Will's smile grew and he pushed himself away from the wall to head towards the door. Before he left, he paused, hand resting on the door handle.

Venn remained by the window, waiting for him to speak, but a moment later he left, closing the door behind him.

***

Venn stood in the mouth of a cave so colossal she could see nothing of the ceiling except the dangling tree roots coming down from the land above her. A sharp breeze blew her short hair into her face. She pushed it back and shifted away from the wind to stare at the stream flowing along beside her, a steady current moving the water towards a river that rolled in harsh waves, the caps rising and crashing against the muddy bank.

At first it didn't strike her as strange that the water was a deep red. Only when it splashed against the walls of rock outside the cave, the droplets landing on the back of her hand, did she remember water should be clear, not dark and thick. The drops ran in rivulets through the creases of her skin before dripping off her fingertips into the earth, which looked dry and diseased instead of the fertile ground she expected to see.

On either side of the bleeding river ahead, endless rows of tall beautiful trees began to wither, falling in on each other.

Venn couldn't tear her gaze from the sight. Looking up, the tree roots shrivelled and curled in on themselves, and the rock trembled above her as the massive oaks fell. Beside her, the red stream grew wider, the ground beneath her feet drying out until it cracked.

Beyond, past the red river, the green fields faded with sickness: death as far as she could see.

"It starts with blood," said a voice on the air. A female voice that sounded familiar, although in the moment Venn couldn't place it. The stream rose again, and she shifted closer to the wall of the cave to escape its reach.

"Death strengthens death," a second voice spoke.

"Until the whole world bleeds," a third concluded.

Venn felt herself rise out of the cave and away from the blighted land, hovering above the tree tops and continuing to rise until entire cities stretched out below her, all ravaged by the same dark rot. The river of blood carried its way through each town, filling the lakes and coming down from the clouds. She saw no people in the wastelands. Nothing could survive such deep ruin.

The voices said nothing else, but Venn didn't need any more of a warning.

Trouble was brewing and the reach was greater than she'd realised.

A bloody wave rolled up from the river, carried on the wind and by the power of some unseen force. It swirled into branches, like arms that reached for her. She jumped out of the way to dodge the attack, hitting the ground on her injured arm.

***

The jarring pain forced her awake, and it took a few moments after she opened her eyes to realise she was no longer in bed, but on the floor. The cool floorboards pressed against her cheek, her healing arm trapped under her body.

Pressing her forehead against the floor to wake herself up, Venn slid up onto her hands and knees and used the edge of the bed to help her get to her feet. Her head ached and her mouth felt dry, as if she'd had too much to drink the night before.

Nothing like a good old-fashioned assassination attempt to make for a fun start the next day.

But that didn't seem right. The suddenness of awakening had left her mind empty and blurry.

Fragments of the dream came back to her. The river of blood and the blighted lands. As she ran through the scene, the words of warning slithered back into her mind, and the voices — so strange in her sleeping state — fell into place.

The Sisters had come out of hiding.

Shaking her head to clear the fog, Venn pulled on her travel-worn clothes and downed the dregs of wine in her glass before pouring another one. A few more sips cleared her head, and she stuffed the rest of her belongings into her pack.

Through the window, the sun had begun to peek over the horizon, washing the sky in light blue hues with hints of soft gold. As much as she preferred the richness of sunset, the promise of darkness to come, Venn had to give this sunrise a few points for being pretty.

Although she did wonder why in the nine gods' names she was up so early. They had no plans to leave until mid-morning, hoping to cross the border around noon.

Yet even as she considered crawling back into bed and sleeping another hour or two, there came a knock at the door. Her shoulders tensed, thinking of her unexpected visitor, but she made herself relax. Last night, he hadn't knocked.

"Come in," she called.

The door slid open and Remy, bleary-eyed and mussy-haired, poked her head into the room.

"You can't sleep either?" she asked.

Venn glanced at the disaster of her bed, the way the blankets had slid halfway off when she'd fallen to the floor. "Oh, I slept. Must have got a good twenty minutes in there somewhere."

Remy stepped inside and pushed the door shut behind her, shuffling over to the bed before sinking onto the edge, her hands dangling between her legs as she leaned forward on her knees. She yawned without covering her mouth, the scar on her face crunching into a red line before easing back into its usual white smoothness.

"I had weird dreams," she said.

Venn's hands paused over her packing, and she swiveled towards her friend, her hip propped on the table. "I don't suppose you saw a river of blood and rotting fields?"

Remy snorted. "No. What in sunfire were you drinking last night?" She fell backwards across the bed, stretching her arms out on either side. "I dreamed Frey got into Will's pack and ended up eating a whole bunch of those vials he's lugging around. We were smelling burnt bear farts across town. Woke up thinking maybe that wouldn't be the worst defence tactic if we could find a way to stay immune to the stench."

Surprised by the answer, Venn laughed with sincere amusement, thinking how perfectly villainous such an attack would be. But as her humour faded, and the bleakness of her own dream returned to her thoughts, she dropped into a chair and passed her hands over her face, elbows balanced on her knees.

More awake now, Remy sat back up, her eyes narrowed in concern. "You all right? And what in sunfire happened to your face?" Her gaze locked on Venn's cheek, and when Venn didn't answer, she said, "Whatever it was, I'm guessing bear farts didn't feature in your dreams, then. What do you think the river and blight meant? Stress about what we might find in Margolin?"

Venn rubbed her brow, trying to put her morning-murky thoughts in order to string a few good ideas together.

Another knock at the door and Will walked in. He looked just as tired as Remy, and Venn guessed none of them would be cheery companions for the day. Maybe it had been something in the food. She'd thought the mutton tasted funny.

Will sank on the bed next to Remy, scooting across the mattress to lean against the wall.

"You too?" she asked him. "Seems we all had a rough night."

He yawned, hiding it under the crook of his elbow, and then smacked his lips and jerked his head towards Venn. "Some more than most. Seems you and I got to sleep through the midnight knife dance."

Remy's eyes flew wide and she looked to Venn. "You were in a fight? I guess that explains the state of you this morning. Who was it? How did I not hear it?"

Venn grinned and let her hands fall onto her knees. "How can you hear anything over your snoring?"

Remy rolled her eyes, but continued to stare in expectation, refusing to be distracted. With a huff, Venn continued, "It was our friend, the red-hooded thief. He thought he'd come by for a visit, stick around for a murder. I nearly had him." Her smile faded. "He underestimated my skills, but I don't think he'll make that mistake again. I have a feeling the next time I see him, he won't be so easy to get rid of."

"How did he get away? Where did he go?"

With a shrug, Venn admitted she had no idea. "He used the Meratis sphere again." She knitted her brow. "I don't understand why I didn't go with him. The last time I used that thing, we were all close to it, so we all got caught up in the spell. This time it was just him." Goosebumps broke out over her arms as the truth seeped into her mind. "It's a scary thought, but I suspect that not only did he know what the sphere was and where to find it, he also has a better idea of how to use it than we do."

She didn't know what to make of that revelation, but it didn't sit well.

"I guess we'll find out," said Remy. "And likely in a way that won't make our day bimmelberries and cream."

"I think you're right about that. And as for my dream—

" Venn returned to their earlier subject.

"Dream?" Will interrupted. "I had dreams last night, too. Bugs." He shuddered, arms flailing as though he felt legs crawling up his neck. "They were everywhere."

"Hear any voices with that?" Venn asked, flexing her fingers around her knees.

"Nope."

"Thank the gods," she said, sagging into her chair. "Hopefully that means it was just a regular old night dream."

Remy watched her. "You don't think yours was a regular old night dream?"

Venn sank onto her elbows and stared at her fingernails, picking at the dirt accumulating under her thumb. "I do not. I think it was a message from the Sisters."

She relayed the dream in detail. The richness of the colours and the depth of her horror had all returned, allowing her to relive the vision when she closed her eyes, and the Sisters' voices echoed in her thoughts as she shared the words the women had spoken.

"Death strengthens death until the whole world bleeds," Will repeated. "Not the most reassuring words."

Remy looked from him to Venn. "I don't get it. Didn't you say these women usually show up in person? Why did they come to you in a dream? And why not tell us what's actually going on instead of giving you riddles and visions?"

Venn glanced at Will, and they shared a smile.

"Welcome to a world with the Sisters," he said.

"They don't understand communication the same way

the rest of the world does," Venn explained. "I'm not sure if it's a choice just to mess with people's heads, or if they're actually incapable of expressing themselves in a clear way. But it's up to us to interpret what they mean. And usually only after it happens."

Remy frowned. "That seems silly."

"It's ridiculous," Venn agreed. "As to why they came in a dream — I suspect we're too far out of their reach for them to make the trip in person. They're witches, but their spirits are tied to their territory. To the forest. Or at least that's how Brady and Maggie always explained it. With us being away from the woods, they're limited in how they can communicate."

Will's mouth twisted downwards as he stared into the empty grate. "Still, it doesn't bode well that they felt the need to contact us. It usually means something bad for Andvell."

Venn rubbed her thumb along the palm of her left hand, stretching her forefinger back and then running through each finger in turn. "If the blight I saw is an actual problem and not just some riddle in and of itself, I guess their worry makes sense. Their land is at risk again."

"And the river of blood?" Remy asked. "Do you think that's literal?"

Will rubbed his brow and drew his knees up towards his chest. "Jayden and Ariana did warn us the troubles with Margolin could lead to war. Maybe the Sisters were emphasising Jay's words about being careful how we act and what we say. That the repercussions could destroy both countries."

Venn considered Will's interpretation and saw the logic behind it, but something in her core told her the Sisters warned of more than just petty human problems. They could find ways to protect their forest from mundane violence. Her dream reeked of magic, and something far beyond their control.

But magic or war, Will's words still applied. They had to be careful.

"Anyone hungry for breakfast?" she asked.

In her mind, the leap from serious world-crumbling dreams to a hearty meal seemed straightforward, but the other two stared at her in surprise.

"What?" she asked. "Are we going to hide in this room talking about the potential problems we're riding into, or are we going to go ride into potential problems? If we're still planning to leave by mid-morning, I'd prefer we do it on a full stomach."

Will and Remy exchanged a glance, shrugged their agreement, and followed Venn out the door and down into the common room.

***

They hit the road a few hours earlier than planned, when the shops were opening and the roads were still quiet. On their way out of town, Will and Remy took over the shopping, restocking their packs with essentials for the rest of the trip, while Venn stayed with the horses. She paid extra attention to the faces that passed, always looking for the cruel smile of the hooded thief, and didn't relax in the saddle until they'd passed out of town and veered back onto the empty side roads.

Frey emerged from the woods to join them and stayed by Venn's side, head swaying back and forth to keep everything in view. Venn wondered if he knew about her late night visitor and wanted to make sure it didn't happen again under his watch.

"This is one of the shortcuts Jay suggested," said Will, urging Hollis towards a narrow path to the right. "It should get us to the Margolan border in a few hours, but we might want to take the time to plan our strategy once we reach it. Any hopes we had of passing through with a wave hello are out the window."

"Are we planning some devious cover story?" Remy asked with sarcastic enthusiasm. "Venn, you be the princess's lady-in-waiting, eloping with Jayden's valet, and I'll be another servant who wants to get out of the big city to achieve her dream of being a milkmaid."

Venn rolled her eyes. "That's the most ridiculous dream I've ever heard. Aim higher, Rem. At least dream of being the cheesemaker or something. And maybe hide the sword. It's a big giveaway that you're lying."

Will laughed. "While it's not a bad idea to come up with some sort of story, it doesn't need to be so complicated. Admitting we hail from Feldall's Keep would be the wrong way to go, but we can name a small town. Something far enough from the border that people probably haven't heard of it, but if they have we're not stuck. Either of you have any ideas?"

A name popped into Venn's mind, and as much as she hated the thought of suggesting it, she knew it made more sense to use a town they could pull details from to make the lie that much cleaner.

"Brindley," she said. "We come from Brindley."

Something in the way she said it must have warned the others off asking any questions, which Venn appreciated. She didn't want to get into her history, the dark past that had pushed her onto the road of murder and lies. She enjoyed the skills she had picked up, but didn't like to dwell on the reason she'd had to learn them in the first place.

"Brindley it is, then," said Will, casting her a quick glance. "What can you tell us about the place? Just in case people ask."

"Farming community in the middle of nowhere," she said to Corsa's twitching ears. "Not so far from Cordelay. Raul was going to destroy it next, but he was... distracted before he could complete the task. Halfway there he changed his mind and rushed to Feldall's Keep."

Sometimes Venn wished her friends had waited until he'd finished destroying the town before drawing him away. As it happened, the series of events had led to her sister's unnecessary death and sent Venn on a vengeance mission that turned out to be the wrong one. She had to be grateful for how it all worked out, but the cost had been high.

As if hearing her dark thoughts, Frey swung his head towards her and bumped his nose into her leg. Venn forced out a laugh and ran her fingers over his soft ears.

By late morning, they'd nailed down a solid and workable story of being three farmers with dreams of being merchants, on a scouting mission to gauge the markets in other countries. Venn hoped she'd never have to say one word on the subject of her supposed trade, not knowing the first thing about turning seeds into food, but it was agreed Will would be the primary spokesperson.

"Might as well put some of my education to good use," he joked.

As the sun reached its apex, sweat beaded on Venn's brow and drizzled down her face, catching in her eyelashes. No matter how many times she wiped her brow on her sleeve, she couldn't get cool. The trees around the road had petered out as they left the last village, until nothing remained along the road but tree stumps. Nothing to block the glare of the late summer sun.

Frey waddled beside them, head low. Venn imagined how hot he must be under the weight of his fur and the metal plates of his skull and back. She guessed if she reached out to touch him, her fingers would burn.

Raul had been a sick man to do that to a living creature.

Shalla kicked up a dust cloud from the road, and the sand blowing into Venn's eyes pulled her from her thoughts. Tears streamed down her cheeks as she tilted her head out of the breeze.

"What's going on here?" Remy murmured, so low that Venn hardly heard her. In a louder voice she said, "Think Margolin ran out of their own trees and are on a mass house-building spree, or have they gone overboard on security? It's like they don't want anyone sneaking up on them for leagues."

Venn looked from side to side and saw nothing but brown grass, as if it hadn't rained in months. But she knew they would have heard if Margolin was suffering a drought.

"They weren't just torn down," Will said. He eased Hollis to a stop and slid down from the saddle.

"Will, what are you doing?" Venn demanded, the hot day not leaving much room for patience. "At least while we're moving we can pretend there's a breeze."

But she, Frey, and Remy stopped to watch as he dug his toe into the ground, and grimaced as the grass didn't so much crinkle as squelch.

"It's rotten," he said, wiping the bottom of his boot in the dry dirt of the road. "The fields up ahead are barren. Nothing but packed earth, and diseased grass."

In the heat of the afternoon, a chill ran down Venn's spine. It reminded her too much of her dream.

Was this was the Sisters wanted me to see?

She glanced at the ground, at the choking dust of the road as it billowed up to catch in Corsa's fetlocks, turning his black hooves a sickly shade of grey.

Wandering towards the nearest tree trunk, Will bent down to get a closer look. Venn recognised his expression from all the time she had spent with Brady in his curious frames of mind.

"Please don't lick it," she said. Remy shot her a look, and Venn held up a hand to fend off her questions. "Don't ask, but it's a valid request."

Will refrained from tasting the stump, but he pressed against the bark, his finger leaving a mild indentation.

"Incredible…" he murmured.

"Disgusting," Venn corrected. "And not what we're here to look into, so maybe we should leave the experimentation alone and reach the border before nightfall."

She rolled her eyes and shifted in her saddle as Will reached into his satchel and pulled out the leather book and pen.

"You never know," he said, attention focused on the vellum, "this could turn out to be important. At the very least, it's probably related. How is Queen Rhoda supposed to feed her people when the land is rotting from the core? They can't farm land like this, and in blocking off Cordelay, that's more supplies gone. Orland has nothing to offer them in the way of food, and I doubt Ansella's about to step up to help Rhoda when it's her own fault for mucking about with the treaties. For all you know, this could be the key to the whole issue."

"Or," said Venn, "it's a sign they got too much rain and everything flooded. I don't keep that close a watch on Margolan weather patterns. What is it you find so fascinating?"

"How are you not fascinated?" Will asked, sounding sincerely surprised. "This sort of mass blight isn't from the weather, I guarantee you that. I've never seen anything like it."

He started walking out into the field, pausing every few steps to look around at the mess his footprints left behind.

"I don't believe this," Venn huffed, casting an incredulous glance at Remy, who just folded her hands on the pommel and smirked.

"I say we join him," she said, and when Venn's disbelief stretched to include her comment, her smile widened. "Maybe he's right and the source of everyone's problems is right here. We won't know until we check."

She dismounted, leaving Venn shaking her head at both of them.

"Unbelievable," she repeated to Frey, who snorted and looked away from her, apparently taking no sides in the argument.

Remy and Will walked farther out into the field as Venn remained with the horses.

"You should come out here," Remy called over her shoulder. "It feels like I'm walking through a bog. It's revolting!"

"Yeah, I'll get right on that," Venn replied, wrinkling her nose. "I guess neither of you feel like this is a waste of time?"

"Learning is never a waste of time, Venn," said Will. "It's an adventure. I thought you liked adventure."

She shielded the sun from her eyes and leaned forward. "I don't see you stabbing anything out there. You can keep your brand of adventure. But thanks."

Remy shrieked and teetered on one foot, catching Will's arm. He rushed to catch her, wrapping his other arm around her waist to pull her back.

Venn was already halfway towards them by the time

Remy steadied herself.

"You all right?" she asked. "What happened?"

Remy clutched her chest, slowing her breath. "I'm fine. That was close."

Will released her and shuffled over to the edge of a metre-wide hole. "This is unexpected."

Remy grabbed Venn's sleeve to restrain her as she moved up towards Will. Venn eased out of her grip, but squeezed Remy's hand as she leaned forward, staring down into the dark depths. Frey appeared on her other side, seeming just as interested in the strange chasm as her and Will.

"All right," she said, "I admit it. This is a little out of the ordinary."

Will glanced at her with a wink. "And you thought a trip into a field would be boring."

Thick brown antennae rose out of the darkness and tested the air, the narrowed tip of one brushing against Venn's knee. Thoughts racing with how big the hidden creature must be to have antennae so long, she jumped back with a yelp, Will not far behind her.

Swatting at her arms as though the antenna that touched her had sprouted into a million ants, Venn wriggled farther away. When she looked back towards the hole, all trace of the creature was gone. "What *was* that?"

Will started to inch back towards it, but Venn grabbed his arm. "You know what? No. I don't want to find out. Let's just go and pretend we imagined it. We all good with that?"

Remy's head bounced in a rapid nod as she edged away,

but Will hesitated, head swinging from the horses to the hole. Venn felt she had accommodated his curiosity long enough. Mould-sniffing and tree-poking she could handle, but bugs were an entirely different story. She shivered, still feeling whatever that thing had been — and anything that took up most of a metre-wide hole was bigger than anything she felt should exist — crawling over her skin.

Frey remained near the edge, giant paws batting at something within.

In a fight, Venn hoped to the nine gods that Frey could take down whatever it was, but she didn't want to have to be there to see it. Pushing a sharp whistle through her teeth to get his attention, she jerked her head towards the road, and he sauntered along behind them.

They reached the horses to find them skittish, Corsa dancing in the dust as Venn reached for him.

"Hush, boy, it's all right. Whatever it was, it's not coming after you."

She turned around to reassure herself as much as the stallion, and her fingers closed around the reins as the antennae once more appeared over the lip of the hole, waving in the air as though checking if it were safe to emerge.

Shuddering, she mounted and picked up Corsa's pace to get as far away from those long feelers as fast as she could.

Chapter Eleven

A gust of wind shuffled Venn's hair, and she slapped the back of her neck.

That's your hair, Connell. Not bugs, just hair.

An hour later and she still couldn't shake her disgust at the nightmare coming out of the ground. She usually boasted a strong stomach, but where bugs were concerned… She rubbed at her arms to clear the creeping sensation roving towards her elbow.

Wanting to maintain something of her reputation of being unshakeable and detached, she kept her attention on the road ahead, restraining herself from checking over her shoulder to make sure they weren't being followed by something with too many legs. Every now and again she reached out to pat Frey's head, relying on him to give her first warning if something hunted them. But when he sauntered off another hour later, disappearing across the diseased fields to blend in with the tree stumps, the tickles running down her legs and up her spine increased.

"How much longer?" she asked, partly to distract herself, and partly hoping she'd have an easier time putting her fears behind her once they were enclosed within the city's walls.

"It shouldn't be far," Will replied. He pulled the map out of his satchel and spread it over the saddle in front of him.

While he perused their direction, Remy said, "What about when we get there? Do we reach out to Taylor's men? I know you're not keen on the idea, and I can't say I am either, but it would be a place to start."

Venn snorted. "Only if you want to remove all hope of finding information elsewhere."

Remy tapped her fingers against the pommel of her saddle. "You don't think it fits with our story to contact our own people? Three Andvellian farmers arriving in an unknown territory. It's not so strange we would seek out those who speak our own language."

"How would we know they did? We're not supposed to know who they are. Besides, if tensions are as high as they seem to be from out here, Taylor's men might be hesitant to speak openly with us. Helping strangers? That's one way to draw unwanted attention."

Will shifted his gaze from the maps to Venn and then to Remy. "She has a point. Some of the names on Taylor's list are well established residents. They might not want to jeopardise their positions in a political minefield. Maybe it would be best to wait until we get settled."

Remy's shoulders slumped as she waded through their logic. "So do we go to an inn?" Her face wrinkled with uncertainty. "Can we trust anonymity to keep us unnoticed? It hasn't worked very well so far."

"Would you feel safer staying with someone that trussed-up sycophant recommended?" asked Venn. "You know without a doubt they would write to him before our head hit the pillow on our first night. No matter what we found or how we tried to find it, Taylor would know it all. I don't want someone watching over my shoulder. And who knows what Taylor would do with the information on his end. Not help us, I bet. Probably barge in and take all the credit for our hard work."

Remy laughed. "You're such a cynic. If I ever need some perspective on worst-case scenarios, I know who to go to."

"You want worst-case?" Venn asked. "Worst-case scenario, we all die. Everything else is realism. People will always stab you in the back if they think it'll work to their benefit."

Remy arched an eyebrow. "Always? Good to know what you think of me. And that I shouldn't count on you in a pinch."

She said the words jokingly, but although Venn smiled back, she couldn't feel the same levity. "Never count on anyone, Rem. Haven't I told you that often enough?"

"Okay, I got it. I think we're here," Will cut in. He stretched the map out towards Venn and Remy with his finger pointing to a spot along an inked line.

"This means nothing to me," said Venn.

Remy squinted to make out the details. "I don't think the road we're on is as squiggly as that one."

Will pulled the map back and twisted in his saddle to see around them. Hollis snorted and tossed his head, the patient steed bearing his absent-minded rider.

"I could give you a better idea if the trees were still here. We've lost a lot of landmarks. But the point is, we're close."

The final word still hung between them as the stone gates peeked up over a rise in the road ahead.

"I apologise, Will," said Remy. "Never again will I doubt the accuracy of your map-reading, squiggly lines or no."

Now that they'd arrived, Venn felt a weight drop in her belly. Their talk of Brindley that morning had already drawn her thoughts to the past, but crossing the border made her feel like she would be stepping into it. She hadn't expected to feel such a strong reaction to Margolin when she first agreed to the mission. It had been almost ten years since she'd been there, but the associations remained strong.

Big city, she assured herself.

Small world, a softer voice reminded her, and the words sounded ominous, echoing through her thoughts as the gates loomed closer.

"What do you think will happen to Frey while we're in Margolin?" Remy asked. "Think he'll go home if he can't follow us?"

A wave of panic washed over Venn at the thought of the bear not being close, her emotions already thrown off by the sight of those gates, but she swallowed it down with a smile.

"No doubt he'll come back when we least expect him," she said. "He'll probably teach himself how to climb over the damn wall."

Before she could give herself too much of a chance to dwell on what might await them, Corsa stumbled. He danced to the left to catch his balance, and Venn clung to the reins to keep her seat, heart jumping into her throat as she realised the stallion's quick action had saved them both from being impaled. A barricade of spikes had sprung from under the dust to greet them, the points angled outward to stare them in the face. Hollis and Shalla came to a sharp stop on either side of her, the three horses shifting backwards to give more space between their eyes and the sharp points.

"Courtesy's a bit lacking," said Venn, relieved to hear no tremor in her voice.

"I guess the rumours were true," Remy replied. "They really don't want any new faces wandering around."

Will leaned over Hollis's side to check the ground. "It's a metal plate of some kind. Corsa must have triggered it." He reached out to glide his finger over the edge of the final spike, jerking away as blood beaded to his fingertip. "Bit extreme. They're not messing around."

"Neither are we." Venn rose in the stirrups to get a better view of the gate and anyone guarding it. "We came here with business, and I don't intend to turn around now because of some pointed sticks. Someone has to be watching the road and I'm guessing we'll have an easier time dealing with human beings than metal spikes."

The barricade only stretched out as wide as the lane, she noticed, but debated the wisdom of riding around the side, figuring there would be more pressure plates hidden under the rotting ground.

"Here we go. Brace yourselves," Will commented, rubbing his hand over his mouth as a door on the left side of the gate opened and two soldiers marched out. "Looks like we're in for quite a welcome."

The two men — in regular steel plate instead of blood-hued, Venn noted with relief — approached, their hands on their sword hilts, and stopped on the other side of the barricade.

The visors on their helmets were raised, and Venn tested the waters by offering a sweet smile. Not surprisingly, the guards didn't return her cheerful greeting, but what did surprise Venn was their... dryness. That was the only word that came to mind. Their rich brown skin was parched and cracked, much like the packed earth of the land around them. One man didn't appear much older than Venn, the other maybe in his mid-fifties, but their haunted eyes suggested people who had seen too much, adding a decade to each man. She hadn't heard of Margolin getting caught up in much military trouble recently, but, by the look of these two, border patrol was no lazy-day tasking.

"State your business," Venn thought the older guard said. Her Margolan was rusty after years of disuse, and this man's accent ran thick.

Remy gaped, expression panicked, but Will squared his shoulders and replied, "We come on business. Farmers out of Brindley looking to trade with your country."

The guards hesitated, and the younger of the two tilted his head to look behind the trio. "You come to trade but bring no supplies with you?"

Will's fingers twitched against the reins, and Venn kicked herself for not thinking of that detail earlier. But they hadn't elected Will as spokesperson for his pretty eyes and smooth hair. With only a moment's pause, he said, "We didn't want to waste food if we found no interest in our goods. Our hope is to tour your country and do our research, but I didn't expect such a barrier to our arrival. This is a change from my last visit."

The first guard's expression clouded over, his dark eyes, pools of black ink, narrowing. "Much has changed in recent times. We're not as open and trusting to those who try to pass onto our lands without written invitation."

Remy nudged Venn with her elbow, shaking her head with a shrug of incomprehension, and, after Venn did her best to translate, asked, "Has something happened to provoke the change?"

The man cocked his head towards her and replied in accented Andvellian, "Just rumours, miss, but it is enough to put everyone on edge. You can see we are not in a great place to be discussing farming right now."

Will nodded his understanding. "How long ago did the blight start?"

Venn saw the younger guard's gaze shoot towards his partner in warning, but the older guard rolled his shoulders back and said, "It has been like this for the past three months. We had a solid month of heavy rainfall and it did not do much for the land. Choked and killed everything."

Will's brow creased and he started to speak, but stopped

and said instead, "That must put a heavy burden on your people. Maybe we came at a good time and can offer help. You're in need and we have produce."

The older guard jerked his head towards the gate. "You will have to take that up with the merchants in the capital, but I cannot let you in without an invitation. Is there anyone you know in the city to whom we can apply?"

Venn silently ran over the list Courtney Taylor had provided, sure that by now he would have written all of them to let them know she was coming. In spite of her earlier arguments, she knew it would be the easiest route, but, based on the spikes in the ground, even more dangerous than she'd originally thought. And not just for the contacts, but any of their associates, as well. As much as her first priority was her own safety, she didn't feel right dragging in people who couldn't fend for themselves.

The internal struggle she'd faced the night Red Hood had come to say hello returned to her mind, her past rising up from the dust just as those spikes had done.

And just as likely to stab me in the eye.

She saw Will reach into his pack, knew he was going to name one of Taylor's men, so before he could speak, and with a reluctance as sticky as syrup, she said, "Lewyn Kell. Write to him and say that Lynn Kenmore is here to see him. I'm sure he'll vouch for me." She sensed Remy's and Will's stares, and ignored them. Pressing her lips together she added, "Unfortunately, I don't know where he lives exactly. I know it's near the capital."

By the guards' expressions, his direction wouldn't be an

issue. The name had an immediate reaction as recognition flashed across both their faces, followed by a deeper scrutiny of the three before them.

Venn forced herself to remain stoic and silent under their attention, hiding her shock. If she'd known her old acquaintance had that much of a reputation, she wouldn't have been so quick to name him. At this point, he would be a man in his seventies. What sort of trouble could he be getting into? She wondered if she'd made a tactical error and given them away too soon.

But after a moment, without any further questions, the older guard nodded, and she felt the muscles in her neck relax.

"We know where to find your friend. We will send word to him and see what he says, but I would not get my hopes up. Lewyn Kell is not known to be overly social."

Venn's lips twitched. *Then he hasn't changed so much. But it would be nice to know what he's done to become so renowned.*

He's probably in jail, the snarky second voice spoke up. *You've just associated yourselves with a known Margolan criminal. Well done, Connell.*

"Until then," the guard continued, "you will wait here at the gate."

Corsa pawed at the ground, and Venn reached down to pat his neck, arching a brow at the guards. "Here at the spikes? Not a very comfortable campsite."

She thought she heard a soft sigh from Remy, and realised she should have let Will take over the talking again.

Diplomacy was not her strength.

"No," the younger man said with a smile that didn't reach his eyes. "Follow us, please."

He raised his arm to gesture at someone on the wall, and the spikes lowered into the dust, once more hidden from view. It came off as advanced construction, and Venn had to wonder where Margolin learned to craft them. It seemed they'd been doing more than playing with borders.

What is going on here that has them on such high alert? And how has Ansella not heard more about it?

"Thanks for your help," Remy said, her softer voice more cooperative than Venn's acidic tone. "It'd be great to have somewhere to clean up and wash off all this dust. It's hot as an inferno out here."

She ran her arm over her brow to clear the film of sweat that had built up as they chatted under the sun.

"I can't guarantee the accommodations will allow for much washing," said the older guard as he turned and started back towards the gate. "But you will be out of the sun."

Venn looked to Will and Remy, and Will shrugged, suggesting they go ahead. She frowned, not thinking much of the guard's mysterious words, but didn't see they had much of a choice. Releasing a slow breath, she urged Corsa forward.

Once they reached the gates, she waited for the large doors to open, hoping they'd be shown to an inn nearby, but the younger guard turned on his heel and grabbed Corsa's bridle. The horse snorted and jerked his head, but held steady.

"You'll dismount," the guard said.

Venn tightened her grip around the reins and straightened her shoulders, running through how long it would take to grab a knife at her calf and throw it into his eye. "Excuse me?"

Remy rested her hand on Venn's shoulder, holding her back. "What will you do with our horses?"

"They'll be taken care of until you're permitted entrance," he said. "But this is as far as you go."

Venn hesitated, running through the various scenarios. Some got her dead, others banned from the country. As much as she didn't like the thought of Corsa being too far out of reach, she'd comply if it increased their odds of getting them through the gates.

She dismounted onto the dry ground, her black boots immediately covered in a thick film of dust. Remy and Will did the same, and they allowed the younger guard to lead their mounts away while the older led the trio in the opposite direction, towards the door to the left of the gates.

"We're not going into the city?" Remy asked.

The guard shook his head. "As I said, you do not have permission to enter the country until we confirm who you are. Until then, you remain here."

"How long do you think we'll have to wait?" Will asked.

Venn was happy to let them ask the questions, her own teeth clenched as she tried to keep a clear head. Too many red flags were popping up as the guard pushed open the door, and she paused before stepping over the threshold.

"As long as it takes," he replied, standing aside to let them pass.

The urge to turn and run nearly overwhelmed her. Trained to avoid capture and disappear into the shadows, Venn had issue with voluntarily following someone into an enclosed space. She kept a close eye out for escape routes, but the rooms were small, the stone walls thick. All sound was muted except for the scraping of chairs ahead.

He led them into the guardroom, which looked quiet in the afternoon, most of the troops away on duty, she assumed. She wished he would leave them there, free to sit at one of the tables and wander outside if they wanted. But she knew better than to get her hopes up. They crossed the room towards another door, and he pulled it open to reveal a long corridor.

"I did tell you it might not be up to standard," he said. He spoke the words with amusement, but Venn didn't enjoy the joke. Torches along one side of the wall revealed a row of caged cells along the other. Walking to the first cell, he opened the door and stood aside. "If you will wait here."

He spoke as if inviting them to make themselves comfortable for an appointment. Never mind the dingy atmosphere or the locked door that would close on them with he left.

"I don't understand," said Venn, and held up her hands when Remy shot her a warning stare. "Not to start trouble or anything, but we've done nothing wrong. We only want access to the country."

The guard smiled, but it didn't warm his face.

"Which you will not get until we verify whether or not you pose a threat to Margolin."

Definitely something lacking in Margolin's welcoming committee.

In his cold smile, Venn didn't see a man who was used to being rude or sharp. It wasn't a cruel smile like Red Hood's but an expression of uncertainty and fear, and she suspected she, Remy, and Will weren't the cause — not directly. The realisation raised her curiosity about the guards' orders, and what they had been told to justify detaining every passer-by.

When they hesitated in following his instructions, the guard shifted on his feet, stretching his hand towards the door behind them. "If you do not wish to wait here, you are free to turn around and come back the way you came. It is up to you."

Venn still refused to move. Once locked in that cell, they would have no way of escape. If Lewyn didn't reply, would they be trapped?

Before she could think it through, Will stepped forward. She reached for his arm to pull him back, but he dropped onto the bench on the right-hand wall. "We'll wait."

Remy glanced at Venn, who released a breath, tucked her hands in her pockets and surveyed the scene, turning in a circle as she walked forward. "All right, I guess this isn't the shabbiest place I've ever set up camp." She sauntered into the cell and eased onto the bench on the back wall, locking her fingers behind her head and slouching down.

"We'll wait at your leisure. But I expect food."

The decision made, Remy edged into the small space after her, and the guard slammed the door shut, locking them inside.

Chapter Twelve

"Well, this isn't the start I expected," said Venn, after the soldier disappeared into the empty guardroom. The clang of the door had set her nerves rattling, and her mouth felt dry with unease.

To soothe herself, and so the others didn't notice her trembling, she pulled a knife from her waist and slid the blade under her thumbnail to pick away at the dirt. She was grateful the guards hadn't gone so far as to disarm them. Detained, but not arrested. A subtle but important difference. Hopefully it meant they weren't as stuck as the locked cell suggested.

From the silence of the other cells, she guessed they were the only people trying to get into Margolin that day. Either everyone else had learned it was a waste of time to try…

Or they're sitting dead in their cells, still hoping for their invitations.

Through the fog of her concern, she smiled at the image of skeletons, patiently waiting for approval.

"Anyone else feel the obstacles become more challenging the closer we get to our task?" Remy asked. "I doubt Ariana and Jayden would have agreed to send us here if they knew we'd be arrested."

She wrapped her fingers around the bars and peered first towards the empty corridor of the jail, and then towards the closed door leading to freedom. To Venn's surprise, the scout sounded calmer than she felt.

Forcing a laugh, she stretched her arms out in front of her, hands clasped so her knuckles popped. "I'm pretty sure Ariana and Jayden always assume I'll get arrested. I'm hardly the sweet and innocent child who gets off on following the rules." She brought her hands to her face to press her fingertips against her eyes and dropped her elbows onto her raised knees.

"I don't think they had any clue what we would find," said Will, crossing back and forth across the cell. "It strikes me that the only reason Ansella hasn't heard from Reddington is because Margolin doesn't want her to. They've probably been stopping his letters at the border, in and out."

"Sounds plausible," Remy said. "But they could hardly have afforded detaining everyone trying to cross into the country since the trouble started. This must be new."

Will paused in his pacing to turn to her and nodded. "And those spikes were designed by someone who knew what they were doing." He settled down on the bench to Venn's left. "I don't know if you noticed the metal, but it's the sort Orland exports. It could explain why Margolin's been fighting so hard to get them to change allegiances."

"Why not just hire them?" Remy asked, coming to sit down next to him. "The treaty with Andvell doesn't prevent them from doing business with other countries. Why cut ties with Ansella completely? Seems like a stupid way to go."

"If Rhoda's scared enough to have those barricades installed, I doubt she would allow much international cooperation," Will pointed out. "She might be afraid that anything Orland makes for her, they'll do the same for Andvell. No good having security measures your neighbours can match or even surpass."

"It's all too political for me," Venn said. "But I'd guess Will was right. Did you see those soldiers? They're scared shitless about something. Doesn't look like they've slept in months. For what? Sitting on a gate and watching empty roads? Without the trees blocking their view, they could see a single person strolling towards them hours before he became a threat. That's not something to lose sleep over. It's definitely more than a fear of being attacked."

"If they're not stealing his letters, our being locked up does give me some new ideas about our silent ambassador," said Will. "We're just outsiders wanting in. What do you think they're doing to outsiders already in? It's possible he's also been detained."

"If that's the case, our trip here will be a short one," said Remy as she slouched against the wall. She grabbed a few locks of blonde hair and started braiding the ends, only to undo the work and start again. "But why would they? Why not just oust him like the Orlish did to Taylor? They're more likely to bring enemies to their door by kidnapping the queen's representative than by sending him home." She frowned. "On the other hand, if he had an accident and died, I don't think they'd be in a rush to send word to Ansella, either."

The three fell into their own thoughts. Will stood up again to pace the short distance of the cell, his fingers tapping against his thigh, while Remy closed her eyes and pressed the back of her neck against the wall to stretch her spine. Venn watched them over the flick of her blade.

When Remy pulled herself back to the present, she asked, "Venn, who is Lewyn Kell? And Lynn Kenmore?"

After the silence, the question came as an unpleasant shock, but Venn had been braced for someone to ask. One didn't throw around random names, get that sort of reaction from the guards, and not raise some curiosity.

That didn't mean she wanted to explain. Telling the story meant digging up demons she preferred stayed buried, worried about what might be resurrected if she unearthed them.

Will leaned his shoulder against the wall, arms crossed, and he and Remy waited for her to reply.

Clearing her throat, she put the knife away, thinking it best to keep her weapons out of sight for a time. The only person who knew this part of her life was the man who'd pushed her through it, and she didn't know how her friends would feel once they knew.

She considered lying to them, but knew that would only get her so far. As soon as Lewyn showed up, he'd have no qualms about telling them everything, and she didn't trust what spin he might put on it.

"I can tell you if you really want to know," she said, "but it might change what you think about me. What you think you know about me."

Will smiled and crossed one foot over the other. "That's not likely. We've both known you long enough to see something of your darker side."

Remy nodded. "You're the one that smiles when she kills. It's not like that sort of thing goes unnoticed in the ranks."

Venn laughed, but felt no warmth in her amusement. "That's the thrill of the fight, a way to unsettle the enemy. Not so unusual. I'm not saying this to add drama to the story or anything. I just want to give you a head's up that it's not a cheery tale." She tilted her head back and looked around the cell. "Sort of fitting for the setting, though."

Will's eyes narrowed in concern. "Are we really sure we want to bring this Kell guy into it, then? You were opposed to Taylor's men because it might draw attention. This guy won't?"

Venn focused on rubbing her thumb over her palm. "I hope not, but I don't know. My only thinking when I gave his name was that we wouldn't need to worry about him running to the authorities, because he's not the type of guy who acknowledges authority exists. Your usual lone wolf. He might not help us, but he won't turn on us, either. At least, not to Rhoda."

Her fingers inched towards her blades again, and she

folded her hands, dropping them between her knees.

"Ten years ago, Lewyn Kell was my mentor. That's one way to put it, anyway. I doubt the word would come to your mind if I went in depth about his teaching methods. He's the man who trained me to kill."

She dropped the final word on them and waited for a reaction, but found none. Neither Will nor Remy moved, just watched her and waited for the rest of the story.

With a noise of disgust, having hoped they would be happy with the basics, Venn rolled her neck to work out the kinks and slumped against the wall. "I think you both know some of my history. Sister killed her abusive husband, was arrested, going to be killed, and I took her place to give her time to get away. By the time they realised I was the huddled lump in the cell, she was out of their reach and I became the brunt of their hate. Kill one tenant-lord…"

She threw in the line with a smile, which faded as the other two stared on with sympathy. Moving her gaze to the far wall to avoid their emotions, she continued, "Parents made my life miserable until the day they, and my entire community, chased me out of Brindley with sticks and stones. Ten years old and on my own. All right, boohoo, sad tale. I don't like to dwell on that part, because it's not what made me who I am. It's what came next. It's all thanks to Lewyn Kell."

Closing her eyes, she cast her memory back to the day she'd run out of Brindley with bruises on her arms, and holes in her shoes. How, for the first time in her life, she had felt in control. No one left to stomp on her or boss her around.

"For months after I left Brindley, I was on my own and liked it just fine. I could handle it. I traded the boots my parents had thrown after me for a knife, and that helped me hunt, make fires — all the things a kid in the wild needs to get by. In the summer, at least. As the seasons changed, it sank in quick that there's only so long you can survive without training, or good weapons, or proper clothing."

Drawing in a slow breath, she cast her gaze up towards the ceiling, feeling the dampness of her memories, the prickle on her skin as she imagined a cold wind cutting through her bones. "Winter hadn't arrived yet, but the chill in the air warned me it was coming soon enough. My toes started to freeze at night, and it was getting harder to find anything to eat. In the summer, I crafted lousy little shelters out of branches and leaves, but the wind had picked up and now they didn't last. And that year, winter made a striking first impression."

She shivered and opened her eyes, coming back to the dry warmth of the cell. Rubbing her arms to clear the goosebumps, she said, "I found an old bear cave and set up camp, fingers crossed it was empty. I built up a good fire, had nothing to eat because the forest had gone still with the threat of the storm, so I was starving. I couldn't see anything outside, the snow was falling so thick, and the wind was blowing all sorts of songs through the cracks in the stone. I never slept, positive that I would be snowed in and starve to death if I wasn't eaten by bears first."

She remembered how, the next morning, the storm

broke and the forest was whitewashed, the trees looking more like sketches than real objects. Ghosts of themselves. A smile came to her lips that she hadn't expected. It had been a long time since she'd stopped to admire the scenery. Shortly after that morning, her training had stripped beauty away from everything.

She caught the way her friends stared at her, horror mixed with sadness, and cleared her throat. "Anyway, after the snow stopped, hunting became more of a challenge. I was lucky if I had one meal a day. My clothes didn't fit anymore and it took too much effort to scrounge up something to eat when all I wanted to do was sit in that empty bear cave and stare at the walls. I don't think I would have lasted another week. Then one day, I caught sight of a stag and went after him. Hunger made me desperate, and even though I had no idea what I was doing, I was determined to take him down and sink my teeth into his flesh."

Remy cringed, which made Venn glad. She had no intention of sugar coating any of the story they'd asked to hear.

"He stood so close I could see his breath on the air. I was ready to go for it, knowing if I bagged him I would have food for a good long while without worry." She leaned in and lowered her voice to a whisper, amused to see Remy also lean closer, and Will sink down to the floor to catch her words. "I readied my knife, braced myself to run at him, when *thwack*!" She punched a fist into her palm, and the others jumped. "Arrow comes out of nowhere, beast falls, and there's this guy — all in black — coming up to take *my* kill!"

She laughed and settled against the wall. "You guys know me well enough to guess my reaction. I might have calmed down a little since I was ten, but not that much. I raced out and started screaming at him, waving my knife in his face, hoping to scare him away. I was sure I looked fierce." A bitter chuckle rumbled in her throat. "Of course, later he told me all he saw was a dirty, skinny girl with tear-streaked cheeks throwing a temper tantrum, but we all see things differently."

Pausing again, she waited for them to ask questions, or interrupt her, but the audience sat rapt, so she scratched a bug bite on her arm and went on. "I still believe his first instinct was to slit my throat and leave me for dead in those woods, but I guess he saw something that made him stop and think, because he set his weapons down and held up his hands for a truce. I didn't think much of him at first sight. Already an old man in his early sixties, his grey hair dirty and wiry against his dark skin, wearing a heavy wool coat full of holes, and fingerless gloves that showed off his thick-knuckled, purple hands. His eyes were a cold blue that maybe gave a trace of once being able to laugh, but I never saw that side of him."

She trailed off, lost in the memory. That moment had changed her life. If he'd killed her, if he'd walked away, she wouldn't have survived the winter, but she also would never have become the hard-hearted, bloodthirsty woman she was.

Giving herself a shake, she came back to the story. "He got me to calm down and told me his name was Lewyn Kell, that he was a hunter out of Margolin. He asked for my name. Which, of course, I made up. Which, of course, he knew. Now I can look back and roll my eyes at the poor attempt at creativity when I gave him Lynn Kenmore. After he got a good look at me, and, I guess, figured I wasn't about to start screaming again, or drop dead on the spot from starvation, he told me he could use me. That his job involved a lot of travelling, and he was looking for someone with a good eye to help him track. In exchange for my help, he would give me food, shelter, and training."

Venn shrugged. "Sounded like a sweet deal to me. What else was I doing with my life other than dying? So I took him up on it. I was ten years old and had no idea I'd just crossed the point of no return."

Remy's face filled with concern and she tugged at her twine bracelet. "Did he do what he said? Or was he... cruel."

Venn understood the actual question under her words and gave her friend a reassuring smile. "Nah, it was nothing like that. I don't think I'd ever call him a nice guy, but he kept his hands to himself." That was one of the few good things she could say about him. The smile faded and her memory moved to a quiet street on a dark winter night, standing ankle-deep in snow, a black shape at the side of a dark house. The moonless night added to the blackness, the light shrouded under thick layers of snow clouds. "Of course, it didn't take long to figure out that when he said 'hunter', he didn't mean game. What gave it away, you might ask? Oh, probably when he had me wait outside a house one night. He sneaked in the back door and from below the window, I heard a scuffle, a sharp cry, and then he was by my side again, sliding a bloody knife into the sheath at his waist."

Remy shook her head, and Will's expression darkened, but this time neither interrupted.

"He grabbed my arm and pulled me down the road, saying nothing as we left town and headed towards the woods. Once we arrived at camp — as a point of interest, the bear cave was empty, and, it turned out, the perfect winter hideaway — he jerked me towards him, and pressed the bloody knife to my throat. 'And that is how we hunt,' he said. 'You good with that or do we end this right here?' I think he expected me to be afraid, but he had already underestimated me. I was no weak little girl looking for someone to protect her. I was an angry, bitter little girl looking for a chance to get even and take care of myself."

She grinned and pulled her knees up to her chest, wrapping her arms around them. "I still remember the look on his face when I smiled at him, blinked my sweet blue eyes, and said 'I'm already learning.' He glanced down to find I'd pulled my own blade against his gut."

"That was a risky game," Will said, resting his arm on his bent knee. "He could have killed you right there."

"And what would that have mattered?" she asked. "Like I said, I was bitter and angry and had nothing else going for me. I saw the risks, and maybe part of me hoped he'd act on it, afraid of the person he could train me to be. But instead he grunted, and I don't think I've ever heard a sound express so much approval. That's when my training really started."

Venn ran her thumb over her wrist and the faint white scars that disappeared under her sleeve. In the right light, when she bothered to see them, similar scars were visible all over her body. A few of them were from recent years, but most of them from the time she'd spent with Lewyn. And the scars only gave away some of what he'd done to her. If bruises left permanent marks, her body would have been an art piece, awash in colour.

"He did nearly kill me a few times. Kell never believed training should be practice, but real life experience. As time went on, I got better. He would receive word that someone needed to be dealt with, and we would go deal with it. Usually I stood watch, but, depending on the situation, I'd go in while he went for a pint. I trained, and I got good. Really good. I could get up on a roof with no problem and enter through an upstairs window, in-stab-out before anyone knew I was there but the dead guy. Trouble was, Kell was getting old, and having a harder time carrying out his contracts. Eventually, he retired to his place in Margolin and set me up as his replacement."

Venn didn't know if either of them knew that part of her history, but the scout's mouth dropped a little, while Will's expression went blank and he pulled into himself. She felt a moment's concern that she'd just pushed her friends away.

It is what it is, she told herself. *I warned them.*

"You killed people for a living." Remy stated, more like she was confirming the facts than out of any form of judgement.

Venn tapped her thumb on the back of her hand, keeping her expression clear. "It was that or starve, so I made my choice. It's not like I was working for any big names or anything. Merchants passing through Andvell who needed a competitor out of the way, jealous spouses. Lots of nasty folks. People hired me who had grudges against rapists or robbers, but no other way to reach them. And some I did for fun because I didn't like them. The world is full of assholes, and I like to think I did my part in getting rid of a few hundred of them over the six years I was on my own."

"Hundreds…" Remy whispered.

Venn wanted to drop her gaze to the ground and avoid the horror she was afraid to see in her friend's eyes, but pride and stubbornness wouldn't allow it. She met Remy's gaze square on, facing her awe, which she couldn't interpret as shock or fear.

"You say that was ten years ago," said Will, his voice steady. A scholar out for information and nothing more. "You haven't been in touch with him since?"

Venn shifted her focus onto him, and something inside curled up to see his blankness. No reassurance or hate. His thoughts and feelings blocked off.

Pushing her worry away, knowing his opinion of her wouldn't change who she was or what she'd done, she shook her head, "And that worries me a bit. It's possible Kell won't acknowledge me. As far as the world is concerned, he's an old Margolin man, I'm a young Andvellian knight, and we've never met. He owes me no favours. In fact, the last thing he told me when he went off was to forget he existed. If anyone ever asked, I never heard of him. Coming to his country and throwing his name around is not exactly respecting his wish."

Remy's eyes flew wide. "He won't just leave us here."

Venn chuckled. "He's done far worse to me. Left me to get arrested more than once for crimes he committed. To be honest, he was always one of the assholes on the list of people I wanted to kill, but while I was with him, he was worth more to me alive than dead. And then he went away and I owed him enough for keeping me alive not to go after him." Her smile widened. "I wonder if he thinks I'm here to kill him now."

"Why would he think that?" Will asked, coming out of his reverie. "That life is behind you."

Venn raised an eyebrow. "He doesn't know that."

Will grimaced and went back to staring at his shoes. Remy followed Venn's gaze in his direction, and then looked to her and offered a soft smile, as though reading her concerns.

Schooling her expression to clear it of whatever Remy had seen, she got up and started pacing the cell between the bars and her bench. Choosing to lapse into silence now that she had shared her story and the others knew what they might expect — either if Lewyn came through for them or not — she returned to the bench and stretched out to stare up at the cracks in the ceiling.

"If he doesn't reply…" Remy began after a moment, then trailed off, looking from Venn to Will.

Will kept staring at his shoes, face knitted together with consideration, but replied, "We still have Taylor's men. If we don't hear back in another day, we'll give them another name. We're not without options."

Venn relaxed at the reminder that they wouldn't be trapped here indefinitely, and turned her thoughts to their situation.

She thought about the reactions of the guards on their arrival, and the spikes coming out of the road. To her, it all seemed excessive. Borders were supposed to have people crossing back and forth. No country could be self-sustaining. For Margolin to have shut themselves off to such a degree suggested a raging paranoia, and without having any idea why, she didn't know if it was justified or if the entire country had gone mad.

Without any hope that Lewyn would be of much help, if he offered any help at all, she tried to figure out what their next steps would be once they got into the city.

"Once we get to the capital, we should find an inn in the middle of town," Will said aloud.

"You reading my mind, Will?" she asked, not looking away from the ceiling.

"Not intentionally," he said, and she heard the smile around his words. "I just thought we should take this time to plan our next move."

Remy chuckled. "I was thinking the same, but came up with the opposite idea. If we already have that creepy guy coming after Venn, we shouldn't make it easy for him by staying in the obvious places. Like you said before, the capital's a busy area — it can't be that difficult to lose ourselves in it."

Venn debated both sides, happy to put her story behind them and move on to more practical matters. "If we try too hard to keep our heads down, we'll draw more attention. I say we stick with our story and take it one border at a time until we get to the capital. Hopefully once we're in the country, we won't run into this kind of problem everywhere we go."

"Where does your Kell friend live?" Will asked.

"On the outskirts of the capital, I think. At least, that's where he was ten years ago. It's possible he moved a dozen times since then. But if the guard knew his name that quickly, I'm going to guess Lewyn — who I would not call my friend — hasn't remained quite as retired as he was supposed to. Hopefully that won't come to bite us in the ass."

"We had to give it a shot," said Remy. "I think you made the right call. We might not know what this guy will do, but at least one of us knows who we're dealing with."

"And this is why you and I get along, Rem," said Venn, rolling her head to look at the scout. "You're just as untrusting as I am."

Will's gaze shifted between the women. "Taylor's the queen's ambassador and has been in her service for decades.

If we can't trust him, who can we trust?"

Venn sniffed a laugh and turned back towards the ceiling. "And that's why I'm glad you're with us, Will. Someone needs to be able to look at the world and not see monsters crawling out from under the beds."

"Says the woman who adopted a warbear as a pet?" Will posed. "Seems to me you have a strange concept of trust."

The words poked at Venn's heart like a fine blade, prodding old wounds so the blood rose to the surface. "I don't believe in trust at all. Like I said before, even the people you care about the most can turn on you if it works out best for them. It's an important lesson to learn."

"You don't really believe that," said Will.

Venn closed her eyes, watching the pattern of firelight on the inside of her eyelids.

"Don't I?"

Chapter Thirteen

The wait stretched out past the point of patience. They heard nothing the rest of that first day, and when the guard came to drop off their small, questionable dinner, which Venn debated the wisdom of eating, he had nothing more to offer than that no reply had been received.

"What'd they do?" she mumbled, kicking the bars. "Send the messenger out on a mule?"

They took turns sleeping as boredom won over conversation, the only change of scenery coming when one of them needed to relieve themselves, which meant a trade from a cell to a dark smelly room.

The next morning, another guard appeared with another tray of lousy food. Their tempers flared as their patience waned, made worse as first one and then two other prisoners arrived, only to be escorted out a few hours later, their contacts and invitations obviously easier to locate than Kell — or more willing to help.

"Think it's time we give them another name?" Will

asked.

Just as Venn debated between agreeing with him and finding a way to climb the bars, fling herself at the next guard to open the cell, and threaten to chop off an ear unless he released them, the guardroom door opened and the older guard who had greeted them at the gate called out, "Lynn Kenmore?"

Venn forced out a breath and pushed herself to her feet. Stepping up to the bars, she crossed her arms, and said, "Still me. Lucky you caught me. I was just about to go for a walk."

Remy kicked out her leg to nudge Venn's calf, but the guard only grunted, looking bored with her sarcasm. "It is a good thing, indeed. We would not have wanted you to miss your departure. Your friend arrived with your invitation."

Venn's mouth fell open and she leaned closer to the bars to stare at the guardroom door, wishing she could see through it to confirm he was telling the truth. It sounded too bizarre to be real.

The guard muttered in Margolan as he rifled through the keys on his metal ring to find the one for the cell, his words sounding more for himself than for Venn. "Doesn't look too happy to be here, but I'm not sure why he bothered to come at all. Written confirmation would have been enough." He peered up at her and, in Andvellian, said, "I am pretty sure I heard him utter a threat or two. You are sure he is a friend of yours?"

"Sure," she said. "We go way back. That's probably why

he's not too happy to see me."

She flashed a grin, but the guard didn't acknowledge it. He shoved the key in the lock and stood aside as the cell door swung open. Venn stepped lightly into the corridor, cautious, mistrustful of her freedom under the circumstances, but relishing the sensation of stepping on stones that hadn't become familiar with pacing over the last two days. She made sure to keep out of the guard's reach in case he got it in his head to come at her with a sword, claiming she was trying to escape. He didn't seem the type, but that wary look in his eye put her on edge.

"Thank you," Will said as he passed the guard, and Venn rolled her eyes, not seeing what he thought he was thanking the man for. Not killing them?

The guard led the way into the guardroom, which was busier that evening. By the grumble in her stomach and the clatter of dishware as a handful of soldiers crowded around a table at the back of the room, Venn guessed it was dinner time, and wished she could sneak something into her pockets on the way out.

They passed through the room and down the long corridors until light appeared ahead from outside. Venn blinked and turned her face away, letting her eyes adjust as they stepped out into the bright afternoon. After a few seconds of the sun beating on her head and the dust blowing in her eyes, she almost wished she could go back inside and travel to the capital via tunnel, but it felt wonderful to stretch out her arms and not come into contact with either Will or Remy.

Will let his head fall back on his shoulders to catch the wind, and Remy pushed her sleeves to her elbows to soak up the sun. They both looked pale for the two days spent inside, and Venn guessed she looked equally washed out.

She scanned the guards milling around the gate as they changed position, looking for a familiar face. Her guts twisted with unpleasant memories and emotions, not sure how she would react when she saw him. She felt thirteen years old again, preparing to face the only man whose opinion counted for something.

But once she found him, Lewyn Kell didn't look all that familiar. Gone was the robust hunter she had come across in the woods as a child, and in his place was a stooped, haggard fellow who relied on a heavy stick to keep his balance as he walked across the uneven ground.

"I'm fucking pissed to see you," he said in greeting, his Andvellian strong if faintly accented, and continued walking past them without stopping, headed towards the mounts the younger guard had taken from the stables.

Venn hadn't expected a friendly greeting, but she surprised herself by having to suppress a smile. No matter her feelings towards him ten years ago and whatever they'd evolved into now, no matter how much the man's appearance had changed, he was the only familiar spot in an increasingly unfamiliar world. A rat turd, but at least she could count on him to be a rat turd.

"Sir, you need to sign for them," the older guard said, hurrying after him, paper in hand.

"It look like I can sign anything in my condition?" the

old man snapped. Venn noticed one of his blue eyes had faded into a milky white with age, although the other looked as sharp as ever. "Make an 'x' on my behalf. You know where to find me if you need me."

The guard paused, about to argue, and then stepped back with a nod. "Yes, sir."

Puzzled, Venn followed her old mentor, wondering what in sunfire he had been up to over the years to have earned even such small commanding power over the Margolan authorities. It seemed strange to her that one of the better known — in the wrong circles — assassins of Andvell's and Margolin's history would have made such a big deal of himself in his own country.

But she knew better than to ask. In the years they'd spent together, she had learned to never initiate the conversation.

"Come on," he said. "Might as well start the long pissing trek home."

Remy leaned close to Venn's ear. "I can see where you developed your friendly speech habits."

Venn grinned and whispered back, "I learned from the pissing best."

The younger guard handed off their horses, who were tacked, ready to go, and looked glossier than they had since the first week they'd set out from the Keep. In fact, Corsa looked almost disappointed to be back on the road again.

"You're getting old and spoiled, boy," said Venn, patting his neck before pulling herself up onto his back.

Lewyn shuffled past them, his slow gait and the weight of his stick sending up more dust in his tracks, and hobbled up into the front of a cart pulled by two old nags that didn't look like they could outpace a turtle on a good day. Venn resigned herself to a slow journey, frustrated after two days of not moving at all.

But curiosity made her patient. Something had pushed Lewyn Kell to make the unnecessary two-day trip to the gate to collect someone he vowed never to see again, and she wanted to give him the time and space to decide if he wanted to explain it.

They travelled in silence for most of the day. Venn sensed both Remy and Will brimming with questions, but their guide quelled any desire to ask them. Other than exchanging the odd glance, and pointing out various scenes along their way, they seemed willing to be distracted by the wonders of the new country.

But for the first part of the day, there was nothing to see except more of the same. The blight stretched under the gate to consume Margolin's land, and all Venn could make out through the hazy heat were stretches of brown and black death.

Her dream stayed with her. Although the Sisters hadn't made any follow-up visit since that first vision, she no longer doubted the blight around that cave was the same as she saw in the waking world. She wasn't sure how the blood came into it, but she knew nothing coming out of this wasteland would surprise her.

As the day wore on and they passed through the first small towns, she saw life returning to the earth. It wasn't much, but the odd flash of green grass with bright seasonal flowers appeared in the yards of small cottages, and Venn saw Margolin hadn't changed as much as she feared from her visit ten years ago.

It wasn't until they entered the first city that the real cultural differences became clear. Venn had forgotten the extent of it, her memory smoothing out some of the more jarring contrasts and dulling the vividness of colours and scents, but now it all came back to her, along with how much she'd enjoyed herself.

Margolin was known for its exotic tastes and styles, and lived up to expectation. The country wasn't any farther south than Andvell, but the Margolan desert to the north and the ocean coast to the west brought warmer winds, and the milder temperatures allowed for more revealing clothing styles with lighter materials. Bare shoulders and midriffs were not unusual, and Venn snuck more than one glance in Will's direction to see how he enjoyed the view.

It didn't surprise her much, although she had to laugh, to find he focused most of his attention on the market and the architecture of the homes, so different than what they were used to in Andvell with the light shade of stone for the larger buildings, and different hues and textures of wood in the smaller cottages.

Venn allowed the voices of the people to wash over her without working too hard to translate the words, enjoying the novelty and seeming solitude in being apart from them.

These were not her people, and the idea felt liberating.

They passed out of the first town before nightfall, but Lewyn kept going at his slow pace without a single word of stopping for the night except to feed and water the horses. Venn dug through her sack to munch on snacks as they went, and she noticed Will and Remy do the same around the supper hour. Their last meal had been over a half-day ago, and her stomach was not willing to wait until they reached wherever Lewyn was taking them.

They rode until the moon dropped below the trees and the sky began to brighten, and only stopped when signs of another town appeared ahead, blocked by another gate. More guards appeared, but this time before any spikes could be triggered.

"Hold," one of them said.

Lewyn clicks his nags to a halt, the cart creaking as it slowed. Venn rode up along one side of the cart, while Will and Remy took the other, flanking him. They remained silent, but Venn saw Remy rest her hand on her leg close to her sword. She slid her fingers under the hem of her tunic, ready to grab her blades if needed.

"State your business," the guard said in heavier Margolin than the guards at the border.

"Going home," Lewyn barked, obviously more irritated than concerned at the delay. "Out of my way."

The guard's eyebrow rose, while the man at his side took in the riders accompanying the cart. "A little early for a pleasure ride, Kell. What's your purpose? And who are the people with you?"

"Guests," he said, and Venn rolled her eyes at his tone, as if he'd find more joy in saying they were auditors for the crown. "I signed for them at the border, so you can take it up with your brothers there if you have issue. Chances are I'll be sending them right back into Andvell tomorrow, but right now I want to get home and go to sleep. You have any reason to keep us?"

The guards exchanged a glance and the second man raised a shoulder. The first turned back to Lewyn. "Pass through. But mind yourself, Kell. It's risky for people to associate with foreigners. It's not a good time for strangers."

"It never is, boy," said Lewyn. "Pain in my ass more than anything else, no matter the situation."

He flicked the reins and urged the nags forward, the cart heaving as the weight rolled over the uneven road and through the gates into the capital. Venn allowed Lewyn to outpace her and fell in behind him, watching for any sudden movements from the guards until they were well out of sight.

Her first glimpse of the capital didn't give much of an impression — nothing to see except lanterns and torches, with the odd cry or shout coming from the inns and public houses. One man tumbled backwards out of a shabby pub, falling on his back with laughter before rolling onto his hands and knees, using a barrel to pull himself to his feet.

One of Lewyn's horses danced away from him and the cart lurched. Remy reached for her sword and Will for his satchel, but the scene didn't escalate past the old man growling at the drunk one.

Remy settled back in her saddle, but Venn checked the drunkard's face as they passed, still watching for the nameless Meratis jumper. She expected to see him everywhere, pretending to be drunk or not. She didn't know this man, but remained tense until they took a side road away from the centre of town and veered towards the countryside.

As the sun rose and the houses disappeared, replaced by fields that started to look dry and black again, Venn heard a familiar snort in the shadows and knew that Frey had managed to find his way around the gate. She caught Will's eye and knew he'd heard it, too. He offered a wink and squinted out over the field to try to find him.

Lewyn's head jerk towards the sound, but when the morning fell silent, he grumbled under his breath and returned his attention to the road. Venn released a quiet breath, relieved he hadn't gone in search of what had made the noise, like he would have done in the old days. No matter how skilled her mentor was, Frey would win, and she wanted answers.

Remy yawned and her head drooped forward, but she caught herself and reached for her water skin. Venn empathised, feeling the pressure on her spine from being too long in the saddle after two days with hardly any movement. She debated closing her eyes and letting Corsa do all the work, the horse not seeming fatigued at all, but she couldn't let her guard down.

To keep herself awake, and distract herself from the ache in her thighs, Venn's thoughts coasted towards the possible reasons for Lewyn's trip, which got her thinking about their last encounter. She heard his words as though he were saying them that moment.

"As far as anyone is concerned, Lewyn Kell the Assassin died in Andvell. The person who returns home is just an old man who's seen too much of the world, looking to pass the rest of his life in peace and quiet."

What could have happened to make the man who never broke an oath break a promise to himself?

And should we trust him not to screw us over?

The question popped into Venn's mind and refused to leave, making her worry that she had driven her friends into more danger than they needed.

Maybe we should have arrived separately, she thought. *Will could have contacted one of Taylor's people, Remy another, and that way no matter if one of us were wrong, the others would have found a good ally.*

Venn kicked herself for not having the idea sooner, wishing they would reach their destination soon and figure out what was going on. She played with the hilt of a knife at her hip, wanting to be ready if Lewyn should try anything against them now that they were away from prying eyes. Just because he was old and gave the appearance of being infirm, Venn knew him too well to think he wouldn't have a knife or two buried under the folds of his coat.

A cottage appeared in the distance, a shadow against a brightening backdrop as the sun took over the sky, and Venn's eyelids flagged with the changing light. The nags and cart followed the curving road towards the thatched-roofed building and finally picked up speed, glad to be home.

They stopped outside, and Lewyn climbed out, his stick

shaking under his weight as he stood by and watched the others dismount. As soon as Venn's feet touched the ground, he cleared his throat, summoning her over. Her legs wobbled from the days of riding, and she made sure they could hold her weight before letting go of Corsa and passing the reins to Will. She stepped towards Lewyn, arms crossed, waiting for the old man to say what he wanted to say.

"Now that you're here," he began.

Venn cocked her head, staying quiet.

Before she could blink, he slammed his stick down over the back of her neck, and the rising sun fell back into blackness.

Chapter Fourteen

Venn woke with a groan, the base of her skull throbbing. She didn't dare move until the room stopped spinning, knowing the dizziness would get worse once she opened her eyes.

Taking a deep breath, feeling the air seep into her lungs and soothe the rocking of her stomach, she eased first one eye open and then the other, finding Will by her side with a mug in his hands.

"You forgot everything I taught you," a rough voice scolded over her head. A voice that sounded no different from the one she had known back in the day. Just as brusque and strong, even with the slight wobbly quality of age.

She muttered something incoherent that everyone understood as a protest, and heard the *thud* of Lewyn's stick as it struck against the floorboard. The sound and resonating echo made her wince.

"No excuses. I left you in the prime of your career with

the best set of skills an assassin could ask for, and you've let them all go to waste. Not to mention the flab I see on your arms. You've been slacking."

"I found a place to live," she said, forcing the words out around a dry tongue. "Turns out it makes life a little easier."

"Makes you lazy. Easy to beat." He shuffled closer and stretched a mug down towards her. "Drink this."

She arched an eyebrow as she reached for the mug, trying to keep it steady from her prone position. "Trying to poison me too, Kell?"

"One lesson's enough for now," he said, shuffling away again.

"That doesn't sound like you." The drink smelled of spices and her mouth watered as the steam hit her nose.

He snorted, and chair legs scraped against the floor. "I'm getting old. I don't have the energy for more than one surprise attack in a quarter of the day. But drink that before I change my mind."

Will extended a hand and Venn took it, wrapping her fingers through his as he helped her sit up. Once she was steady, she let go of him and brushed her fingertips over the growing goose egg on the back of her head.

"He didn't go easy on you," Will said, confirming her assessment.

"Easy? Why would I go easy?" Lewyn demanded. "If I make it easy on her, would that make her enemies easy on her? Better she learn from someone who will teach. No mercy."

He brought another mug over for Remy, who sat

perched on the edge of an old bench along the wall. No comfortable furniture adorned the ex-assassin's small cottage. Almost no furniture at all, Venn noticed. Two chairs, the bench, and an iron-wrought bedstead set out in front of the fire.

Not the house of a man who holds sway over the guards at the gate.

The entire situation struck Venn as odd, but by the way Lewyn stared at her, and his disinterest in making a fool of her a second time, she figured she would learn her answers if she waited it out and didn't try to force his stubbornness.

The old man settled on a wooden chair, stick between his legs and his hands crossed on top of it. He locked gazes with her with his one good eye, and Venn felt him trying to bore into her soul and pull out her secrets.

"You've grown up," he said at last.

"Time does that to a person," she replied. "Doesn't look like it's been kind to you, either."

He sniffed, no hint of a smile moving his mouth, but neither did he appear offended by her comment. Just like he'd always been: a cold man through and through. Venn was relieved that some things hadn't changed. Even the pulsing in the back of her skull served as a good reminder that the past never really disappeared.

Remy and Will sat back and remained silent while the old acquaintances sized each other up, happy to sip their tea without drawing any attention to themselves.

Venn waited for Lewyn to move on to what he was going to say, but it took another few minutes of him staring.

Finally, he began. "I bet you're full of questions about why I bothered to come and get you. You know how I feel about satisfying curiosity, but the fact is you've come at an interesting time."

Venn's lips twitched upwards before she took another drink. "We ran into enough trouble on the journey here to tell us that much."

Lewyn frowned. "You've turned lippy since the last time I saw you. The Venn I trained knew when to keep her mouth shut and listen."

Remy sputtered on her tea and peered at Lewyn and Venn over the edge of her sleeve as she dabbed at her mouth. "Sorry."

Venn pressed her lips together, torn between falling back into the old habits and wanting to exert the independence she had worked so hard to claim. Her lessons won and she sat silently, enjoying the healing effects of the tea.

"You probably noticed the warm welcome you received before they locked you up inside the gate," Lewyn went on. "Those spikes are located at the entrance to every major city from here to the coast. They had someone from Orland come and build them three months ago. I can't tell you the number of idiots that were killed before they learned to feel for those pressure plates. Not even strangers from outside the country, but our own people."

A question tugged at Venn's tongue and she swallowed it with more tea.

Will shifted to sit next to her, like a child eager to hear a story, and Venn supposed in some ways that was true.

Lewyn would have details they needed — she just hoped Will didn't have it in his head that the answers would come so easily. Lewyn never gave anything away for free.

"I've spent the last ten years in this dusty hot city trying to keep my head down, so you can be sure I paid attention to what was going on. The changes started a few years ago when Rhoda heard of the devastation in Cordelay. I'd been here a few years by then, living in my forgotten circle of the countryside, and happy to stay alone until the end of my days. Unfortunately for me, and a few other people, it didn't work out quite that way. One night about half a year or so ago, a few monkey asses decided they wanted to sneak over the border by way of my land. This was before the spikes and the guard patrol at the border. I caught them, and they didn't survive long enough to reach the road into the city. Found out later they didn't have papers, didn't have a destination. Probably trying to smuggle something into the country. First thing next morning, the guards caught wind of the attack, and I was brought before Rhoda to give a report."

Venn repressed a smile at the irony of a man who had spent his life breaking the law and insulting the crown being forced to bow and scrape to explain himself.

The old man shook his head in disapproval. "Woman doesn't know what she's doing on that throne. Funny old bitty thanked me for my service and made me tell her my history. I made it all up, of course. No one needs to know that shit but me."

And me, thought Venn, but she kept her lips sealed,

suspecting that her knowledge of his past put her on his death list as much as he was on hers for his treatment of her. It was an awkward truce and she didn't want to be the one to upset the balance.

"Told her I used to be in her army and left the service because of my eye. As thanks, she tried to give me money. Almost laughed in her face as I turned it down. Here she is, giving me coin for doing what I've always done — what she would have locked me up the rest of my life for doing back in the day. What a joke. Besides, what's a man like me, at my age, going to do with money? Instead she tried to give me a position in her court. Some sort of military counsellor or some shit. Turned that down too. But she insisted on having me sit with her queensguard captain about Margolin's security gaps. Seems these people trying to cut over my land weren't the first border trouble they'd had, and they wanted someone with experience to help stamp it out."

Lewyn tapped his stick on the floor. "In that, I was more than happy to help if it got the queen off my back and trespassers out of my yard. I must have pointed out over a dozen security flaws, and the captain and I spent weeks coming up with strategies on how to fix them. Instead of listening to my suggestions, Rhoda threw my map away and that was the last I heard about it. She'd brought in a new first counsellor, I was told, and this man would take care of everything. Fine by me. I headed back here and waited to see what would come of it all."

Will began to speak, and then bit his tongue, but Lewyn

noticed and nodded at him. "Speak if you have something to say."

The younger man licked his lips. "I was just going to ask if you suspect a connection between this first counsellor and the changes that are being made."

"I blame nothing else. He's putting ideas into her head. I always suspected Rhoda of being weak-willed, but now she's proved it. She caves to everything he suggests. Turns out Captain Larimer is not an entirely horrible human being. He comes by now and again to update me on the situation and get my views on what should be done. I'm sure it won't surprise you to learn my only consistent advice has been to stab the man in the kidney the first chance he gets."

Friends with the captain of the queensguard. That explains his reception at the gate. Lucky us.

The idea of Lewyn getting buddy-buddy with any sort of authority figure — especially a law man — boggled Venn's mind. But then, she never imagined she would be knighted by the Andvellian queen and become aunt to the daughter and sons of one of Andvell's greatest families. Life worked out in funny ways, sometimes.

"Pay attention," Lewyn snapped at her, and Venn returned her focus to his story. "Since then, we've watched as she closed the border to Cordelay, preventing them from leaving what's left of their home, and she's proposing new treaties with Orland if they turn their backs on Andvell and ally with Margolin."

"Does she see it as an asset to the country?" Will asked.

"A tactical economic move?"

Lewyn sniffed. "You have a high regard for a small land-poor country, boy. They have nothing to offer us except their metals and their weapons, but it's enough for Rhoda. Never mind the foul blood it creates with Andvell. She seems determined to ruffle as much fur as she can these days."

"What about soldiers with red armour?" Venn asked, forgetting herself. "You mentioned the borders and the weapons, but what about another army? Something different than the men headed by your Captain Larimer?"

Her mentor glared at her and said nothing. After a while, he shook his head, and Venn realised his silence had been him considering her question, not berating her for asking it. That was new. "Not that I know of or that he's mentioned. Then again, I haven't seen nor heard anything from Larimer in the last month, so who knows what's going on in that palace."

"The paranoia goes that high up?" asked Remy.

"That's where it starts." Lewyn scratched the grey stubble on his chin. "Rhoda used to take a tour of the city every summer on Chiver's Day. That was two weeks ago. No one saw even a hem of her colourful gown. Other than the odd message going in and out of the palace, and the large retinues coming to visit and being sent away shortly after, you'd think she wasn't there at all. Nope, something's not sitting right about all this."

His blue eye caught Venn's again, but she couldn't look away from the white one, which she felt saw her more clearly.

"I don't know what brought you here now, Connell," he continued, "but as far as I can tell, what you've lost in reflexes, you've gained in timing. It wouldn't surprise me to learn that we're about to head into war."

***

That night, as Venn stretched out on a blanket on the floor in the corner, her thoughts raced with everything Lewyn had told them. Shortly after his prophecy, he'd ceased speaking and prepared a modest dinner of vegetables and broth with a small bit of meat. Venn had offered to go out and hunt something, but he'd waved her away.

"Meat's no good for my digestion anymore. Or my teeth."

He pulled back his lips to expose the yellowed enamel within. The cold grin reminded Venn of the bandit they'd met on the road, the one who had first informed them of the changes around the Margolin border, and she found herself wondering what had happened to him, and if Will's supplies had helped him get somewhere safe. With everything burning to ashes around them, it would be nice to know that one person was staying out of trouble.

Over the course of the evening, she watched Lewyn carefully, and the signs of his age filled her with a sadness she hadn't expected. It had been just short of a decade since they'd parted ways, and she knew she'd see a difference, but the loss of the man she had known into a shadow of his former self motivated her to fight that much harder to achieve everything she wanted before life forced her down the same path.

The window above her head was open to catch the faint breeze as it swirled past the cottage, and Venn lost herself in the chatter of crickets, and the hoots of an owl. The night called to her in a way it hadn't since she used to sleep under the stars, and she felt trapped within the cottage's four walls.

Desperate for air, she crawled out of her blankets, stepped cautiously over Will's sleeping form, and climbed through the window, thinking it would be quieter than trying to sneak through the creaking door. She landed on a bed of dry earth and padded out into the night, stretching her arms above her head to work the kinks out of her back and feel the wind flow over her skin, through the hair on her arms.

In this pose, she stilled, caught by a change in the air — a subtle shift that alerted her to someone else's presence. Keeping her movements slow, she dropped her arms to her hip, and as she danced to the left to avoid a strike, slipped a knife into her hand. She spun in a circle, blade raised, and caught Lewyn's strike as he brought his own knife down, her forearm blocking his.

He stepped aside and brought a second blade up in his other hand, aimed towards Venn's gut. She twisted sideways so it missed her, but her second weapon was already in hand to come up under his chin.

Grunting his approval, Lewyn raised his fingers in surrender. Venn had known him too long to believe the gesture, and remained poised, ready for another attack.

For the first time, she thought she caught a hint of a smile in the moonlight, but a cloud swam through the light and it disappeared.

"It seems you still remember one or two lessons, although I hope it's not just seeing me that's bringing your training back."

Venn smirked, taking the risk of putting her knives away. "I might have put on a bit of weight, Lewyn, but don't think I've spent the last six years sitting on my ass eating figs. We've been through some pretty crazy shit. So crazy even you couldn't have prepared me for it."

He inclined his head in a vague nod. "So I've heard, Sir Venn Connell."

Venn's fingers went slack at her sides as she stared at him.

"Close your mouth, girl, you look like a fish," he said, bringing up his stick to tap her chin. "You think we've lost touch all these years, but I haven't lost sight of you. It wouldn't have been in my best interests. If you stopped thinking about me, then perhaps a few new lessons are in order."

Venn dug her toe into the dirt. "I haven't been seeking you, Lewyn, but don't think for a second you ever left my mind. I watch for your face everywhere I go, and have ever since you left. The only reason I didn't come hunt you down was because I have a tiny bit of respect for you under all the loathing."

"Careful. That respect could be the weakness that kills you."

She flashed him a grin. "That respect would never stop me from killing you first if you gave me a reason to."

The old man sniffed. "That's my girl. You were always a pain in my ass, but at least the scrawny kid in the woods never disappointed me."

It was the closest the man would ever come to a compliment, Venn knew, so she took it to heart.

"Now, are you going to tell me what brings you to invade my country? I thought I was clear the last time we met that I never wanted to see you again."

"So let that be a sign that things are serious enough for me to break my promise," Venn replied. She pushed a hand through her hair and stared out over the expanse of empty land dotted with tree stumps. "It's not good, Lewyn. I don't know what's going on, or how much is connected, but it's big."

"It have anything to do with this guy?" he asked, nodding his head towards the shadows.

Venn followed his gaze, amazed that a man blind in one eye could make more out of the darkness than she could, but even though she saw nothing except a few undefined lumps, she guessed what he referred to.

She let out a whistle, and sure enough Frey emerged from the shadows.

"He's not the problem," she said, "but he is a very strange addition to it. We can't figure out why he's here, or why he refuses to leave my side."

"One of Raul's creatures?" Lewyn asked, eying the bear as Frey approached and stopped a few feet in front of them.

"That's what we think," said Venn, less surprised to hear Kell mention the mad sorcerer's twisted games so casually. She doubted anyone on this side of the world hadn't heard about Raul's methods. "But not one he made. Remy thinks Frey might have been one of the ones he bred instead of created."

The old man *hmph*ed, sounding impressed. "If that's the case, there must be more of them out there. This one's not even full grown. Definitely not five years old. I'd guess only a year or two."

Venn took a new look at the bear. "How can you tell?"

Lewyn cast her a sidelong glance. "Maybe I should have taught you some actual hunting in our time together. He's no spring cub by any means, but he hasn't grown into his paws."

"That doesn't explain why he's following me around as if I'm his mother."

"Maybe it does. I doubt any bear, armoured or not, would survive birthing a monster like this fella. Probably survived by mere chance. He likely senses something in you, kid. Something he can relate to. Probably your love of blood."

Venn snorted a laugh, but something in his comment weighed like a stone in her chest. She hoped other people saw her as more than just a bloodletter.

A sharp whack to her calf brought her attention back to Lewyn.

"I don't like that look on your face, Connell," he said. "Never forget who and what you are. I didn't train you to be soft, and you've seen enough in your short life to know the importance of the lessons I taught you. You want to live to be as old as I am, you'll follow them. You are shadow, and you are death. There is nothing else. Security, family — they're illusions of what we want. They don't last and we can't trust them not to be stripped from us."

Venn nodded, staring at Frey as he sniffed in the dirt.

"You're not going to disappoint me after all by turning your back on that rule, are you?"

"No, sir," she said. "Right now I have no choice but to keep it in mind. Too many people seem to be after me and want me dead. I need to stay focused."

"It's the only way to go. But," Lewyn added, stretching a hand out towards Frey. The bear paused in his sniffing and stared at the hand for a moment before coming closer and pressing his nose into Lewyn's palm. The old man slid his fingers over the bear's fur, over his head, knocking against the hard metal plate of the creature's skull, "it's not a bad idea to keep this one close. Trust him? Never. But he'll do more good for you than the enchanter in there and your friend. The scout seems quick and might be good with that sword, but stay away from the boy."

Venn snapped her head towards him. "From Will? Why?"

"Because he thinks he's in love with you," Lewyn replied, still eying the bear. "He's all wide-eyed and soppy, and he'll be no good to you with his attention diverted like that. I don't like magic, and don't trust everything it claims to do. Better a sword in the gut any day. He'll hold you back, weigh you down, and distract you if you're not careful."

"I'm not interested in Will," said Venn, her words firm. "He knows that. No matter how he feels about me, he won't get in the way of what I want."

"And what's that, kid? You rode away from the cushy life that made your arm soft — what is it you're after?"

Venn pressed her lips together, unable to put the desire into words.

The old man gave a hard chuckle. "You know the answer as well as I do." He turned around and hobbled back towards the house. "You crave the life. The feeling of a blade pressing into flesh, the smell of blood, and watching someone's life drain out of his eyes as you twist the knife. It's what you're good at. It's who you are. Might as well embrace it if you can't forget it."

He disappeared inside, and Venn stared after him, her boots frozen to the packed earth.

Frey snorted beside her, nosing her limp hand as it hung by her side. She reached up to pat his back, grateful for the solidness beneath her fingers. Lewyn's words had taken the ground out from under her.

Chapter Fifteen

The next morning, Venn rose before everyone else. Remy's snores were rivalled by Lewyn's, and it amazed her that she and Will had been able to sleep at all. She stepped outside and leaned against the side of the cottage, pressing her palms against the warm wood. The early sun was soft on her face, but it warned of another hot afternoon to come.

Staring out over the expanse of ruined field, she saw in the clearer light of day what the night had partially masked. Will was right: there was no way anyone living in Margolin could survive without finding some way to import food, because it would be impossible to grow it themselves.

A series of strange events.

In her experience, these strings of coincidences never led to anything good.

The door creaked behind her, and Venn turned to see Will step out, his arms stretched over his head until his back cracked, his mouth distorted with a yawn.

"Attractive," she said.

He rushed to cover his mouth, and when he finished yawning said, "Sorry. I didn't know you'd be right there. Sleep all right?"

"Hard not to when you have a lump the size of Frey's paw on your head." She reached up to run her fingers along the edges of the goose egg. "Better not have messed up my hair."

She winked at Will and he chuckled, leaning against the wall on the other side of the door. "Looks just as awful as it usually does."

"Good," she said. "I'd hate to think anyone believed I care about things like that."

"Strange welcoming practice he has."

Venn grimaced. "It was my own fault. Should have braced for it. Maybe he's right and I am getting soft. What about you? Get any sleep?"

He shrugged. "No dreams, so that's a nice change. Any more messages from the Sisters since we got here?"

"Nope," said Venn. She closed her eyes and tilted her face towards the sun. "Maybe they see we're already doing what we can. They usually only interfere when they think we're sitting around playing Triple Flip."

"It worries me they feel the need to interfere at all. After seeing this blight in person, I can only imagine how it could destroy Andvell if it reached deeper into the country. And by the blood you saw, I'll guess war won't be far behind."

Venn opened one eye to glance at Will's expression, the way his brown eyes had clouded over, his eyebrows knitted with the weight of his trouble. The sort of person to take the cares of the world on his own shoulders.

Closing her eye again, she nodded. "You're probably right. Rhoda can't be readying herself for war and be this paranoid without something having made her snap. Just as long as I'm the only one having the vision dreams around here and the bugs you saw stay out of it. War, I can handle." She shivered, ignoring Will's teasing smile and trying to push away the memory of those antennae coming out of the dead field. "We should write to Jayden and Ariana and let them know. No matter what we find today."

The door opened again and a bleary-eyed Remy poked her head outside. "What are you two doing out here?"

"Trying to catch a bit of extra sleep without you keeping us up," Venn replied.

Remy groaned and smacked her lips before disappearing, the door swinging shut. Will caught it and pushed it open, stepping in after her. Venn took one more breath to enjoy the silence before following him.

Lewyn appeared to still be asleep, the blankets high enough to expose nothing but the back of his short silver hair, just as Venn remembered it. Standing there, she imagined the twelve-year-old version of herself who had hated this man with all the passion of her childish soul. He had thrown her into sunfire, burning everything good about her to have only a black heart rise from the ashes. Until she'd learned to appreciate the value of what he'd given her, she'd spent many mornings standing over him this way, blade in hand, debating whether she should drive it into his spine.

"Do it now or forget about it, girl," he mumbled, the words echoing back through her past. The same thing he'd always said to her.

"Don't worry. Wasn't even thinking about it," she said, and the realisation surprised her. She used to think about killing him on a daily basis, but standing there now, she couldn't find a trace of the old desire. "But good to know you remember how I used to think. Maybe I can catch you off guard with some of the habits I've dropped since then."

He rolled to face her and slid his mangled feet on the floor — the little toe on his left foot black, and the middle toes on his right foot missing entirely from a frostbite incident so many years ago. "I doubt it. Seems to me you've picked up nothing but bad ones."

"We'll see, old man. Looks like we'll get a few chances to put it to the test in the days to come."

He grunted and shuffled towards his cupboards, the stick accompanying him with a steady pattern. *Shuffle, shuffle, thump, shuffle, shuffle, thump.*

"So what are we doing today?" Remy asked. She sat on the old bench, folding up the blankets and sleeping pallet to set them against the wall. "Hitting the beach? Seeing the sights?"

"To start," said Venn. "I thought we could rent a carriage and race through town to see what the merchants have to offer. Then break into the ambassador's house and find out why he's being rude to our beloved princess and not replying to her letters."

Will chuckled from his place on the floor as he helped

Remy tidy up. "So we'll go there first?"

"I want to know if he's actually gone or just barricaded himself inside." She grimaced. "These fusspots with the big titles and bigger egos often hide when they don't want to deal with the issues."

"And if he is gone?" Lewyn asked. He stuck a pot over the fire and the water began to boil as he readied the tea. The scent of the herbs was enough to get Venn's blood stirring for the day's task.

Not wanting to sound unprepared, she hesitated before saying, "We start asking around. He's an important person in the city. Someone will know something about where he went."

"There are Taylor's people," said Remy. "We made it into the country on our own steam, but they're an option if we need help."

"And there are Ambassador Reddington's servants," Will added. "They would have gone to market on a regular basis — how long has it been since anyone's seen them? Have *they* gone missing, or is it just him?"

Venn stretched a hand out towards her friends as though they had made her point. "You see? We have lots of options."

Lewyn snorted and picked up the pot to pour steaming water into four mugs. "If you want to waste your time, sure."

"Got anything better, old man?" she asked, reaching for one of the cups and blowing on the steam. The spices swam down her throat, tickling her tongue and warming her insides.

"You kids are overcomplicating things. You're talking to someone who knows the captain of the guard. If you find nothing at Reddington's place, talk to Larimer. He'll give you a better idea of what's going on than the spies of a sly, crafty son of a weevil's scrotum."

Venn smiled over the rim of the mug. "You've met Taylor, then?"

"I've met enough of them to know they're all alike. All smug, pompous rat turds who are out for themselves, fuck anyone else."

Remy approached the table to grab her own mug. "Isn't that what you think about everyone?"

"The whole world is out for themselves, but we're talking about aristocrats here. They're a special brand of smug, pompous rat turd."

He smirked, and Venn stared at him in amazement.

Kell? Cracking a joke?

"Hurry up and eat your fuel and then get out of here. You may be my houseguests, but that doesn't mean I want you screwing around with my routine." Lewyn stood up to shuffle back to his bed where he began stripping off his nightclothes.

Will and Remy looked away as he disrobed, but Venn had seen more than enough of him when treating his injuries to care. She stared at his back before he pulled a clean shirt over his knobby elbows. A few new scars marred the dark bony surface, the skin greyed and chalky.

He glanced at her over the collar of his shirt as he pulled

it over his head, catching her staring. Venn held his gaze and didn't back down until she caught a hint of a smile as he looked away.

***

They finished their light breakfast and headed out into the heart of the city. They'd taken Lewyn's nags and cart after he'd pointed out that they were supposed to be small town farmers. Even if the guard at the gate had failed to notice, the merchants were unlikely to miss the quality of their mounts.

The pace of the cart was slow, but Venn appreciated the opportunity to get a feel for the city. She had been to Margolin a number of times with Lewyn, but the capital only once, and in the middle of the night, so she didn't remember many details.

The air held traces of sweet spices and manure, and the roads were clogged with people milling about between houses and shops. Will hadn't exaggerated when he described the population difference between here and Andvell's capital, and it seemed to be more of a culture shock for him than for her or Remy. He stared in open-mouthed amazement at the world around them as he bounced along in the back of the cart.

"Pretty amazing, isn't it?" Venn asked, flicking the reins to steer the horses down a road to the right, moving away from the centre of town.

Remy twisted in her seat to face him. "I'm confused. You spoke with those guards at the border as if you've been speaking Margolan all your life, but you've never been here?"

Will remained silent, and Venn glanced backwards to see that a woman at a market table moulding a sculpture out of clay had caught his attention. The soft blue of her dress brought out the richness of her black skin, and Venn wasn't sure if he was watching her bare shoulders and stomach, or the way she worked the clay between her fingers.

"Brady made me practice," he replied without turning around. "I know the basics of all the countries that share a border with Andvell, as well as a few that follow the same language laws. He thought it would be smart when I left the Keep to find employment. This way, I can work as a scholar in any city."

Venn snorted a laugh and turned back to the road. "You, leave the Keep? I don't see that happening in a hundred years. You don't even walk out the gates unless it's to go to the Fountain."

The thought of the secret glen in the woods outside the Keep struck her with a sudden, brief yearning for home. Not for the routine of her life, she swore to herself, but for the greenery. As beautiful and exotic as the scenery was here, all the brown landscape and sand-coloured homes made for a bland view.

A jab to her side jerked her attention to Remy, who scrunched her eyebrows in a gesture of disapproval.

Venn widened her eyes and mouthed a subtle, "What?"

Remy rolled her eyes and turned away, leaving Venn to

guess what she'd done wrong.

The moment passed and they left the market, moving towards the outskirts of the capital where the houses were larger with more windows, fancier decorations, and a general appearance of smugness and opulence to match the people who lived in them.

Lewyn had told them they would know the ambassador's house when they passed it, and he'd been correct. Andvell's banner fluttered from a post over the door — the royal blue background with the silver winged horse in the centre. Similarly coloured curtains hung in every window except for the servants' quarters in the attic, which had simple white shutters to block out the light. Venn guided the cart through the wrought-iron gate, up the long entrance lane, and stopped in front of the house.

Peering down the road, her shoulders drooped. "I guess we couldn't leave the cart somewhere else and walk, but it seems silly to leave it out front for the world to recognise whose it is."

Will hopped into the dust and walked to the side of the house as Venn loped up to the front porch to knock on the dark blue door. A few moments later, he returned, jerking his head towards the back. "There's a stable over here where we can leave it. Not completely out of the way, but someone would have to come up this side road to see it."

"Better than nothing," said Remy, while Venn turned away from the door to check the side road, seeing nothing but dust.

"It'll do," she said.

Will reached the horses, sliding his fingers under the bridle, but paused before he led them away. "The stable's empty. I'm not sure what that means for what we'll find inside, but someone made sure to make it look like no one's home."

Remy stepped over to the other nag and the two of them led the horse and cart away while Venn knocked again, closing her eyes to take in the atmosphere of the house. She heard Remy's and Will's murmured voices as they moved towards the back of the house, and the banner flutter in the weak breeze. She felt sweat drip down her nose and forced her attention back towards the house. No sound coming from within — just a sense of emptiness.

To be safe, she knocked a third time and waited for the others to come around and join her on the porch.

"There's no one here," she said. "Any moral opposition to breaking in?"

Remy stood on her toes to peer through the window beside the door. "Looks pretty dark and abandoned to me. We came here to check it out, I say we do it."

She looked to Will, who shook his head. "No issues here."

"Good," said Venn. She pulled a blade out of the sheath at her hip and slid it between the door and the jamb. "Now you're officially co-conspirators if we get caught."

It didn't take much effort, which surprised her for a house so rich and boasting the height of modern conveniences. The door swung open silently, revealing dark hardwood floors, and a long curved staircase up ahead. An archway to the right hinted at a warm living room, over-stuffed with ostentatious furniture and decor that served status rather than comfort. To their left, another archway showed an office space, the wide desk covered in papers with a royal blue rug stretched out to cover most of the floorboards. Venn guessed the corridor straight ahead led to the kitchens.

No one rushed to yell at them or accuse them of trespassing, so she stepped inside. Will closed the door behind them, careful not to make any noise, but Venn suspected no one was around to hear them.

She wrinkled her nose. "Smell that?"

"I don't smell anything but dust," Remy said, and sneezed, catching it in the crook of her elbow.

"Will?"

"What is it? Something rotting?"

"Tangy," Venn agreed. "Watch where you step. I have a feeling we're going to walk in on an unpleasant surprise."

They split up to tour the first floor. Venn took the office, finding nothing that raised any alarm except for the fact that there was nothing to find. The fire had died down and nothing remained in the grate but ashes. A layer of dust covered every available surface, but otherwise it looked as though Reddington had walked out of the room with every intention of returning. A half-empty glass of wine sat on the desk next to a stack of angled papers, which suggested he'd been working when he left.

She stood over the edge and read what she could of the handwritten message he'd left behind. It looked like a letter, dated over a month ago. She moved over to sit in his chair and slid the paper closer.

Your Majesty,

As requested, I've kept an ear out for any developments of a threat to Andvell from within Margolin. Queen Rhoda continues to be civil and kind, with nothing to worry me. She assures me that she thinks highly of you and her relationship with Andvell, and I'm tempted to believe her.

She does, however, appear tired, and troubled about something, although she assured me it's been nothing but bad dreams due to the heavy rains we've been having.

The new first counsellor, a Guy Danos, is an interesting individual. He claims to come from Margolin, but from his accent, I would guess farther east. Perhaps his family hails from there. Rhoda appears especially fond of him. I'll keep you abreast of anything new.

One thing does worry me, and that is the continued blight to the country. It began a month ago, mostly in the outlying fields. Pastor's Field, which is not far from my own estate, has been worst hit. The grass is darkening into black, and the trees have begun to wither. At first I thought it was due to the weather, but now the rain has ebbed and the rot still spreads. I'm due to meet tomorrow with Thom Foley, a palace guard who's agreed to speak

with me about something he's learned. I'll send
another letter as soon as I return.

The letter ended there, unsigned, with no other information. But then, letters in the houses of people who had vanished never gave all the information one wanted. That would make things too gods-be-damned easy. But at least now they had another name to follow up on.

The fact the letter remained on the desk suggested Reddington hadn't been killed in the room, if he was dead.

Or he didn't mention the killer in the letter.

She pocketed the note and returned to the foyer to find the others. Will returned first from the living room, and Remy a moment later from the back of the house.

"Anything?" Venn asked.

"Lots of dust. No sign of a struggle or that Reddington has been injured," said Will.

"Same in the kitchen," Remy added. "Except that it's spotless and beautiful, and I wouldn't mind marrying an ambassador if it got me a house like this."

She tilted her head back to stare at the designs in the ceiling as Venn pulled the letter out of her pocket and handed it to Will.

"It doesn't say much, but something got him out of his chair before he had a chance to send it. Maybe we can pick it apart and make sense of it once we learn a little more."

Resting her hand on the carved newel post, she looked up the stairs. "What do you think? Ready to check out the rest of the house?"

The faint smell wafted down with a breeze from what must have been an open window, and Venn's nose wrinkled again. She hated that smell, being far too familiar with it.

Without waiting for the others to decide for her, she started up, taking slow steps to avoid the stairs creaking, although they felt solid under her boots.

She kept an eye on the upstairs corridor through the railings as she climbed, wanting to be prepared for anything they came across — ideally before it came across them. But no one and nothing broke the silence or emptiness as they reached the second level. She continued on into the master bedroom while Remy and Will again broke off to choose rooms of their own.

No papers littered any of the polished surfaces. The bedroom curtains fluttered with the open window, and Venn moved behind them, pulling them back with her forefinger to peer outside. She thought she saw a figure lingering behind the iron bars of the gate around the yard, but when she looked again the shape had disappeared.

It was enough to urge her to hurry, so she hastened her search of the bedroom and found Remy poking around the washing room.

"It's beautiful," she breathed. "I don't think I've ever seen anything like it, even at the palace. Ansella must pay her people really well, or it all comes cheap in Margolin. Either way, I might have to consider a career change."

Venn threw an arm around her friend's shoulders and guided her out of the room. "Considering this ambassador's vanished as completely as the Meratis jumper, perhaps you don't want to make your decision too soon."

They bumped into Will coming out of a guestroom. "Nothing there. I checked the other two as well. Empty. Doesn't look like anyone's used them in ages."

Venn frowned. "Nothing was touched in the master bedroom either. Even his clothes are still there. If he's gone, it's not by choice. But I think we already knew that." She took a deep breath and regretted it as the smell, stronger now, clung to the back of her throat with the metallic sharpness. "I guess we might as well go see the rest."

The stairs up to the servants' quarters were past the second guestroom, hidden behind a plain door. Venn braced herself as she opened it, making sure to take a breath before she did, but neither Remy nor Will was as prepared.

Will raised an arm to block his mouth and nose, while Remy let out a cough.

"I guess we found the source of the stench," she said, and nudged Venn towards the stairs. "After you."

Venn pressed her lips together and took the first step, these stairs not as well made or silent as the others in the house. Each step groaned, adding to the eeriness of knowing what she'd find.

Sure enough, as soon as she reached the landing, she saw the blood on the floor. Pools of it that had dried into brown, with more spray along the walls and across the bed sheets.

She'd also expected to find bodies, but there were none. Whoever had made the mess had at least done a partial clean-up. How considerate.

Going to the window, she threw open the shutters to get

some air, although the heat from the day did nothing to clear out the strength of the smell.

Will moved to the middle of the room, careful not to step in any of the blood. He spun in a slow circle, taking in the details while Remy and Venn remained on the edge of the scene. Venn poked through the night stand, finding nothing but a handkerchief and a small painted portrait of a family.

"If it weren't for the heat and close quarters, I'd say the smell should have been gone by now. The blood's not new." Will gestured to the large stain in front of him. "This person was likely stabbed. Probably with a sword. Likely a woman."

"I'd ask how you could possibly know that, but you're you, so of course you know," said Venn. She meant it teasingly, and was relieved to get a smile in return. Whatever she might have said earlier in the cart to bother him — which she assumed she'd done based on Remy's reaction — had obviously not hurt him too badly.

Lewyn's words from the night before came back to her, and she rubbed the back of her neck, wondering how people with actual feelings walked the difficult line between friendship and other. She didn't want to hurt Will, but she didn't want to lose him either.

And this is why I don't have feelings.

"The way the blood sprayed on the wall tells me some of it," Will started to explain, drawing Venn out of her thoughts, "and the pool tells me the rest. You can see the gap in the blood pool here, and it's small, so either a woman or a short man. Similar story over here, but she fell in the chair."

He pointed to the blue chair, upholstery faded and worn — probably a throwaway Reddington had replaced from downstairs. Blood stained the armrests and soaked into the seat, with the rest dripping down the sides.

"Why would someone take the bodies?" Remy asked, sinking down on the edge of the clean bed in the corner. "It isn't like anyone wouldn't know what happened here just because the corpses are missing."

Venn thought of the stories she'd heard of Raul, and the way he'd taken the bodies of his victims, transformed them into walking corpses to return them to Feldall.

"Because some people like to play mind-fuck games. It's probably something sick and twisted, and I would feel better if we got out of here."

Will shot her a look of surprise. "Blood making you squeamish all of a sudden?"

Venn rolled her eyes and moved towards the window to glance into the yard. "You kidding? I could bathe in the stuff if I had to and not care. But I don't like the guy I saw outside. Maybe it's best we head out and talk to Larimer. And if that Foley guy was willing to spill what he knew to Reddington, maybe he won't mind showing us the same courtesy."

She followed Will and Remy down the stairs, pausing at the top of the second flight to once more take in the silence of the house.

Two people were dead, another missing. Ariana wouldn't be happy.

They had come to Margolin to find answers, and as far

as that went, the mission was over, but Venn had no intention of letting it go without digging up more of an explanation than "Reddington's gone."

She hoped the explanations came before everything blew up in their faces.

Remy led the way outside, and Venn hesitated on the porch, scanning the yard in front of the house. Three wide trees stood to her right, the bark looking withered with the heat, and turning black at the base. Trees that hadn't been chopped down due to the blight, Venn guessed, but no life left in them.

Behind the farthest tree, something moved, and she caught a familiar glimpse of red. She broke into a run, ignoring Will's and Remy's cries as they shouted after her.

The Meratis jumper pushed away from the tree and darted down the road the way he'd come. Venn gave an extra push and closed the distance between them. When she was close enough, she launched herself at his waist and they fell onto the dusty road.

"Who are you?" she demanded, grappling for advantage. "What do you want?"

He did nothing but smile, wriggling on his belly towards a rock at the side of the road. Venn grabbed for his arm to pull him away, but he threw his elbow back, catching her in the throat.

She choked and lost her hold on him. Before she could catch her breath, the man reached the rock. He brought it down over her head so hard the world burst into stars before her eyes, and by the time they faded, he had vanished.

Chapter Sixteen

"Why does everyone go for the head?" Venn mumbled. She pressed a cloth against her hairline and watched Will rifle through his satchel.

"Because it's the only thing that makes you let go," Remy teased.

"I can't believe we lost him again." Venn couldn't bring herself to appreciate Remy's banter, too frustrated in her own failure. "Why was he here? How is he connected with Reddington?" She groaned and bent her head between her knees as the world swam again. "Any more questions and my brain's going to explode."

Will chuckled and pulled the cloth out of Venn's grip, tilting her head into the light to take another look at the damage. "I don't see any brains leaking out of this wound, although you will have an egg to complement the one Lewyn gave you. We might have to look at getting you a helmet. Maybe a warbear design?"

The image drew a smile from Venn, and she rolled her

shoulders to ease the bunched muscles in her neck. "If we come across a blacksmith in town, I'll see if we can work out a deal. Help me up."

Will grabbed her wrists and eased them both to their feet, Remy standing to catch Venn if required.

"I'll go get the cart," said Will, but he waited until Venn nodded before letting her go. She wavered, but managed to keep her balance.

He jogged to the back of the house while Remy and Venn stayed in the lane, Venn keeping her sights glued on the road in case the Meratis jumper returned.

"I wish I at least knew his name so my curses could be sent after someone other than Red Hood," she said.

Remy laughed and slid an arm around Venn's waist as she teetered. As much as Venn wanted to wave her away, she thought better of it.

"Too bad Frey wasn't here to crush the man's skull under his paw. Where do you think that bear is, anyway?" Remy shifted to watch the road in the opposite direction.

"Hanging out with Lewyn, I'm sure. Our friend seems to have taken a liking to him."

Remy nudged her shoulder. "Jealous?"

Venn realised there had been a hardness in her words and snorted a laugh. "Hardly. If Frey wants to stay here when we leave, he's welcome to. It's more —" She stopped, not sure she wanted to dig deeper into what she and Lewyn had spoken of the night before.

"More what?" her friend pushed.

Venn hesitated a moment longer and then tried for a

nonchalant shrug. "It's nothing really. Lewyn just suggested that the reason Frey chose to tag along with me is because he sensed my darkness and resonated with it, or some shit like that. I don't buy it."

Remy's attention moved from the road to Venn. "But you do, don't you? Or at least you're worried it's true."

Venn raised her shoulder again, keeping her gaze on the river of dust. "Maybe. No one wants to think something about her nature calls to an armoured bear that only exists to do the bidding of an evil mad sorcerer who destroyed her friend's country, almost destroyed lots of other countries and ruined everything he came into contact with."

Remy bobbed her head. "No, I suppose that's true. But at the same time, Frey's not doing any of those things, is he? He has darkness, but he doesn't act on it. Maybe, like you, he has a history and is looking to overcome it."

Startled, Venn looked to her, and Remy offered a soft smile, nudging her a second time. "None of us are who we were yesterday, Venn. We change all the time. It's what we choose to change into that counts. Maybe that's why you two mesh so well."

Venn grinned. "That sounds too sentimental for the likes of me. But thank you. I think I like your idea better."

"Did Kell say anything else you'd like me to talk away?"

Venn thought of what he'd said about Will and shook her head. "Nope. That was pretty much the end of the conversation."

Remy smirked, and Venn knew she didn't believe it. "All right. But if something comes up, I'm here." She paused

247

and then said, "He's not like I expected him to be, you know."

"Who?"

"Lewyn. From your story, I expected someone more threatening. Less of the making us food and tea and giving advice." She cleared her throat. "At the risk of you judging my taste in people, and still hating what he did to you, I kind of like him."

Venn cringed.

"He seems to want what's best for you. Even if he's got a messed up sense of what the best is."

"I will admit," said Venn, words stilted with reluctance, "he's not entirely the man I remember."

Remy gave her shoulder a squeeze. "Don't forget, you've grown up a lot, too. Maybe life has balanced things out in the end."

The cart creaked and rattled behind them, and Remy helped Venn climb into the back before jumping onto the front bench beside Will. As he guided the cart down the road, Venn thought she saw a dark shadow dart from nowhere and disappear into the house.

***

Venn's head throbbed with every jolt of the cart, and she heaved a sigh of relief when Will pulled to a stop in front of the palace gate. More guards stood in their way, but Venn wasn't worried. She had no interest in getting into the palace itself. This time she actually did want into the guardroom.

Remy raised her hand to a guard who pulled back his shoulders and lifted his visor to reveal a young man with deep brown eyes shadowed with dark circles, giving him a ghostly look. Was no one sleeping well in this country?

"Business?" he demanded in Margolan.

Chatty.

"We're here to talk to the captain of the guard," said Remy. On the ride over, they'd agreed she would take point as a soldier looking for a job in the Margolan army, hoping whoever they spoke with knew enough Andvellian to understand her. Venn would have volunteered, but knew she wouldn't come off as someone good at taking orders. "I believe his name is Larimer?"

The guard frowned. "Frederick Larimer is no longer captain of the queensguard."

His accented Andvellian was clear, and Venn was grateful to Queen Rhoda for training her men so well, but after what they'd just found in Reddington's house, Venn's stomach churned with the news. "Since when?"

The guard's gaze darted towards her, eyes narrowing in on the lump on her forehead. "Since he turned deserter and disappeared one night last week without a word. He's not in Queen Rhoda's good graces, and neither is anyone known to associate with him."

Venn thought of Lewyn. What might it mean to the old man that his drinking buddy had vanished and he might now be seen as an enemy of the crown?

I doubt he'd care. He's been known as worse.

"I don't know the man personally," Remy assured him,

drawing the soldier's attention back to her. "I'm a soldier from Cordelay, looking for work. I heard there might be room in the Margolan forces for extra border patrol."

The soldier crossed his arms, making Venn think about all the guards they'd seen since their arrival, each with the same stern expression and trace of fear behind his eyes. The false bravado they showed in the face of the many questions.

They have no idea what's going on, either, she realised. Mindless drones following orders without seeing the reason behind them, braced for something to trip them up and make them break the party line.

"At present we're not interested in anyone not Margolan-bred," he said. "There's too much tension between countries right now. Too many opportunities for spies."

Venn rested her arm on the side of the cart. "Do you know what started the tension? We've noticed the heightened security throughout the country, but everything seems to be business as usual. Precaution?"

"The queen's orders," the guard replied, his tone hard. "It's not our place to question what she deems best for our country."

And there's the party line.

"A contact in Cordelay told us to speak with Ambassador Reddington," she said, deciding to take the chance in mentioning him. "Do you know where we could find him?"

The guard's eyes narrowed again. "As a palace guard, it's not my duty to know the comings and goings of foreign diplomats. I have no idea where he might be."

Venn knew they wouldn't get any more information from him, so she turned to Remy. "I guess we'll have to stick with farming until something else comes up. We might as well get back to it."

Remy nodded, thanked the guard for his time, and gestured for Will to ride away.

Before they'd gone far, a soldier coming in from duty bumped into the horses.

"Watch where you're going," he snapped.

Will frowned. "Us?"

He said nothing more antagonising than the single word, but the soldier reached up, grabbed the front of Will's tunic, and pulled him close, glaring at him with startling green eyes.

Remy and Venn both hurried to the other side of the cart to help, but before they could touch the guard, he said in a hushed voice, "If you're looking for Larimer and the ambassador, start in Pastor's Field. Meet me at Reddington's the day after tomorrow. If you make it."

Venn caught the fear in his eyes as his gaze jumped to the men around him and wondered what it meant.

Louder, he said, "Show some respect and don't let it happen again."

He shoved Will back and stomped off, cursing to a fellow soldier about useless civilians as the trio in the cart stared after him in shock.

"What a guy," Remy said, settling back into her seat.

"I guess that's one way to get a point across," Venn

agreed.

None of them said anything more until they passed out of the market.

"What do you think about Larimer?" Will asked. Venn knew he was leaving the soldier's message as a subject best kept for the safety of Kell's cottage. "Think they're right and he deserted?"

Remy shook her head. "I doubt it. From what Lewyn told us last night, Larimer knew something wasn't right about this new first counsellor. If he was anywhere as loyal to his country as he sounds, he wouldn't turn tail and flee because of a change of power. He would want to keep a close eye on the changes." She twisted in her seat to face both Will and Venn. "Think he's dead? Maybe the same thing that happened to Ambassador Reddington happened to him?"

"We don't know what happened to Reddington," said Venn. "Maybe he's still alive. Why leave a bloody mess of the servants, but whisk him away and kill him somewhere else? If no one's seen or found Larimer, it's possible he's buried in the palace. Wouldn't surprise me if they threw him in the dungeons to rot for being too nosy. If he did leave, I doubt it was by choice." She paused, thought, and corrected herself. "Unless he had reason to run. To find someone who could help solve whatever's going on in the capital? Let's get back and talk to Lewyn. If he can't think of anywhere Larimer might have run to, maybe he knows where the guy lived outside the palace. Family members who might know something. And maybe he can tell us a little more about this Pastor's Field. It was in Reddington's letter, too. It's where he says the blight started."

Remy leaned in closer. "Do you think the guard was trying to give a warning about Lewyn not being in the queen's good graces?"

Venn felt a smooth smile twist her lips. "Gods help them if they try to mess with Lewyn. He hasn't lived to old age by not being savvy. I'm not worried."

***

They returned to Lewyn's cottage without incident, and found the old man whittling a block of wood out back. Frey stretched out under the sun, his snores almost as loud as Remy's.

"Never took you for the artsy type," Venn said, pulling a stump of old firewood between Lewyn and Frey to use as a perch. The bear twitched at the sound of her voice and wriggled closer.

Will leaned against the side of the house, while Remy overturned an empty water bucket to sit on.

"Need to do something to keep my fingers agile. Never know if my knife-throwing days aren't behind me for good." Lewyn didn't pause in his work as he glanced up at the three. "What'd you learn?"

Venn stretched her legs out in front of her, hands dangling between her thighs. "Nothing but a lot of bad luck."

Lewyn raised his knife to her eye. "Did I just hear you use the word luck?"

She didn't bat an eyelash. "I meant it in a metaphorical sense. Obviously luck has nothing to do with it. Just a lot of fucked-up coincidences that likely aren't coincidences. Your Captain Larimer has supposedly deserted the pack. He's missing."

Incredulity creased her mentor's wrinkled face, and his eyes, blue and white, bore into her. "That's impossible."

"But the truth. He's gone. And anyone who claims to have had an acquaintance with him is being warned to sever ties or face the consequences. At least, that's the message I got from the guy at the palace. He didn't actually come out and say it so clearly."

Lewyn went back to his whittling, sparing a quick glance her way before ignoring her.

Venn noticed how steady his hands were as he worked, how even his clouded eye had no trouble focusing in on the small details. She looked around and noticed his stick was nowhere to be seen. Trust an ex-assassin to play up his infirmities to appear more innocent and harmless.

"Larimer would never disappear like that," he said after a while. "He loved his queen and mistrusted this new first counsellor too much to walk away."

Remy cocked a brow Venn's way to acknowledge that she'd been right before she said, "That's what we assumed. It made us think he was either taken by force or ran while he could to find help. Can you think of anywhere he might have gone if he wanted reinforcements against his own people?"

"Bah," Lewyn said, waving the knife in the air. "He and

I talked history and strategy, not twiddle-twaddle like feelings or family. I have no idea who he had in the city other than his men. They were his life, the queen his first priority. If he went anywhere to get reinforcements, it would have been allies within his own household."

He rubbed his brow and stared into the face that had taken shape in the wood. It looked like a bear.

Behind him, Will said, "You also weren't wrong that it's worse than an increased border patrol."

"The queensguard is turning away help from anyone they don't personally know," Remy explained, nodding. "The paranoia is almost fanatical."

Lewyn blew dust off the face, picking stubborn splinters out of the eyes to give them more depth. "And it's going to get worse by the sounds of it. You kids did what you were sent to do. It might not be a bad idea to turn tail now while you can."

Venn ground her teeth and ran her fingers over Frey's back. "I'm not about to leave a mission half-finished. I was told to get information about Reddington's whereabouts. I've learned where he isn't. That doesn't help us figure out where he is."

"Stubborn as ever," Lewyn grumbled.

"What do you know about Pastor's Field?" she asked.

Lewyn's head whipped up, eyebrows high on his forehead. "Nothing. Why?"

Venn sniffed her disbelief. "You used to lie better than that. What is it?"

Her mentor rolled his eyes. "Really, it's nothing. Just a

name I haven't heard in a while. Bought up some old memories. Back in my contract days, there was a cottage in the field where I'd pick up my letters. The place has been deserted since I stopped doing the job. Why's it coming up now?"

Venn looked to Will, and the scholar came forward, sinking down into the dirt and scooping up a handful of dust to let it strain through his fingers. "A soldier came up to me as we were leaving the palace. He made a show of picking a fight, but then told us to check out the field if we want answers and said he'd meet us in two days at Reddington's house."

"After adding a friendly warning of, 'if we make it'," Venn interrupted.

"Reddington referred to both a soldier and the field in a letter we found," Will continued. "If this soldier is the Thom Foley mentioned in the letter, they were supposed to meet to talk about the situation."

"Why would he trust you to check it out?" Lewyn asked.

Venn's brow furrowed. "I've been asking myself that question since he left. He must have heard us asking the guard about Larimer and the ambassador. Remy mentioned she was a soldier, so maybe he thought we could help."

"More than his own men?"

"I don't know," said Venn. "Sounds like a spot of fun to me."

"You would think so," said Lewyn. "But as for what might be going on in Pastor's Field, I don't have a clue. Only way you'll find out is if you go. Why'd you come all the way back here first?"

He added the last question in a tone of deep contempt, and Venn scowled. "Since when did you train me to run into a situation before evaluating the possible danger? Guy comes up, threatens to hit Will, hisses a message we hardly understand, and we're supposed to ride right in?"

Lewyn watched her, and she saw approval slip into his unclouded eye. "So what are you going to do?"

"I'm going to go," she said, stunned into a quick response by his lack of argument. She thought of her conversation with Remy earlier about Lewyn's changing personality. So used to her memories of the gruff, hands-on mentor, she didn't know how to react to the man who treated her like an adult.

"Of course you are. When?"

The day was more than half over. By the time they reached the other side of town, it would be dark. She did not want to meet some unseen threat without being able to see it.

"First thing in the morning."

"Good. What will you do for the rest of your night? Sit on your thumbs and wait for the sun to come up?"

He picked up his carving again and shaved more off the side of the bear's belly.

"I think we should send a letter to Ariana," said Will. "They'll have been waiting to hear from us, and I'm sure they'll be interested in what we've found so far."

Lewyn arched an eyebrow. "Think it's smart to go spilling all your knowledge onto paper and sending it through the army's ranks, boy?"

"Only if I wanted to bring down all of Margolin's paranoid forces on your cottage," Will shot back. Venn expected him to be offended, but instead he smiled. "I happen to be trained in various forms of code. I'm sure they could break it if they tried, but I'll work to come up with something."

"Huh," said Lewyn, and looked to Venn. "This man's got his own world of secrets, hasn't he? None of you are what you appear to be." He switched his attention to Remy. "Except you. I don't know your story yet, but you seem the most open of the three."

Remy smiled, her hazel eyes twinkling and the scar on her face twisting. "I work very hard to appear that way."

Lewyn's eyes narrowed, trying to read her, and Venn smirked, although surprise swam under her amusement. Remy easier to read than Will? As far as Venn had always found, William Stanwell was an open book. She looked to him now, the way his dark eyes remained glued to Lewyn's face as though trying to do some reading of his own, and wondered how much more there was to her friend than she realised.

***

The snores of her mentor and friend once more pulled Venn out of her sleep, but this time she didn't mind so much. More blood had come to her in her dreams, and it was a relief to wake up finding none on the floor. The trip to Reddington's house had bothered her more than she realised, it seemed.

Not the blood. The mystery.

The distinction felt important for her to rationalise. Her time with Lewyn had made her more sensitive to the idea of losing her edge and growing soft. As much as she enjoyed being a part of the Feldall family, she didn't want them to define her. They could be taken from her at any moment, and she didn't want to feel the pain of their loss or of having to adjust to being on her own again. She was made to be on her own. It was the only way she could be sure of herself.

Giving her head a shake to push away the negative thoughts, cringing as both recent head injuries throbbed, she grabbed a clean tunic out of her pack and turned to face the wall, tugging off the dirty one. Topless, she strapped one band of sheaths around her waist, another two around her forearms, and the fourth around her hips, counting to make sure all fourteen blades were in place. Once she was comfortable, she pulled a clean undershirt and tunic over her head.

When she turned around, she found Will staring at her. She arched an eyebrow, expecting him to turn pink at having been caught, but his chocolate eyes bore into hers without losing any of their intensity. Emotions twisted in her belly that she didn't recognise. Embarrassment? Regret that she didn't feel what he hoped she'd feel? She hated that she was the one who had to drop her gaze first. Stuffing the dusty tunic in with the rest of her laundry, making a note to wash her clothes sooner rather than later before she ran out of clean options, she sat on her heels and scanned the room, unable to settle her attention on anything, still sensing Will's gaze on her.

"How's your arm?" he asked. "You don't seem to have trouble moving it anymore."

Relaxing a little now that he seemed ready to let the episode pass, she raised her arm and lowered it again, extending it at the elbow. "It's perfect. Between you and Phil it's like it never happened."

He rose up on his knees, the white shirt he wore under his tunic clinging to his stomach with the stifling humidity that had already clogged the air. "Mind if I take a look?"

Venn shook her head, and he inched forward on his knees, pulling her sleeve up over her bicep, the backs of his fingers drawing along her skin so goosebumps rose on her arm.

"Cold in this heat?" he teased.

She forced a chuckle, but couldn't come up with a quick response. After sensing his eyes roaming her before, it felt odd to have him so close. She wanted to push him away and run out into the empty field before those unfamiliar feelings returned, but the moment passed, and his attention was on the scar, raising her arm to see where the blade had gone in and come out.

"This looks really clean. The scar will fade with the rest of them." He released her and retreated to his own blanket, head tilted. "How did you get the one on your back?"

Venn instinctively reached for the mark that marred her lower side. The one that should have killed her and hadn't.

"I gave it to her," Lewyn said, pulling himself up in his

bed so his feet touched the floor.

Venn didn't know when the second set of snores had stopped. Remy's still droned on, making the sheets tremble with every inhale.

Her mentor kicked the blankets off him and rose to his feet, reaching for the stick Venn now suspected he didn't need. At Will's open-mouthed stare, he replied to the unasked question. "She was sleeping with her back to the room, in spite of what I told her. Remember the words, girl?"

"One eye open," Venn repeated the lesson as if it were yesterday. "Never trust an empty room."

"And what did you do?" he asked, tapping the stick against her knee.

She bit back a flinch and said, "I was an idiot and thought you had my back in camp."

"That's right," he said, and left her side to grab the pot to put over the fire.

Shuffle, shuffle, thump.

"And what did I say after I slid the knife into your back?"

Venn glared at him as the memory of that morning came back to her. "You said next time you'd slide the blade in two inches higher and get my kidney."

"And did it ever happen again?"

"It did not."

Lewyn nodded to Will, whose shock had faded into grimness. "And you see? She's still here today. If you don't believe it, you don't learn. The world is always going to look for your weaknesses. The chance to take you unawares.

Always allow yourself to be underestimated, and then you have the advantage."

"Lectures this early in the morning, Lewyn?" Venn asked, her temper flaring as he tried to instill the same lessons in others.

Will had no need to know this stuff. So far their journey had proved more dangerous than she'd expected, and she worried he'd be in over his head, but she'd promised Maggie she'd have his back. Now, with Lewyn trying to manipulate the man into believing the worst in others, she swore again that she'd get him home safely. When their mission was over, he would return to his library to study with Brady. With his books, he wouldn't need to worry about being stabbed in the back by someone he thought he could trust.

She hoped not, anyway.

"There's always room for lectures, girl. Especially when you're about to ride into the unknown."

Remy started up with a gasp and wiped her mouth with the back of her hand. "Was I snoring again?"

Venn grinned, glad for the distraction. "Don't worry about it. You were the perfect symphony for the morning's routine."

Remy groaned and rolled her eyes towards the fire. "That tea almost ready, Lewyn?"

He grunted and got the mugs ready as she hauled herself to her feet and went over to help.

Will's gaze had fallen back on Venn, but this time she didn't stare back, getting up instead to join Remy at the table.

"Did you get that letter written last night, Will?" the scout asked, pouring steaming water into the mugs.

Will sat on the bench, grabbed a piece of paper from his pack, and smoothed it out on his knee.

"'Dear Mam,'" he started. "'The weather is hot here in Margolin. The mission we set out on, to see if there was an interest in bringing our produce to a new market, hit a bit of a snag. With the weather as rough as it is, without any sign of rain, I don't see how we could arrange the transaction. I might stay for a while to see if any new deals can be worked out, but might have to come home empty-handed. Give my love to dad. Cris.' What do you think?"

"Reads like a child wrote it," said Lewyn. "But it doesn't send off too many red flags. Does your princess know the story you're running with?"

"No," Will said, "But they'll understand the basic idea. The important thing is that it sticks with our story for being here. If anyone finds the letter and it comes back to us, we can stick with the same lie."

"You might not be as dull-witted as you look," Lewyn said. "But you still need to get your head out of your pants and start focusing on the world around you. Keep your eyes to yourself and we'll get along fine."

Remy sat up in her chair, head twisting from Will to Venn, giving her a questioning look. Venn pressed her lips together, trying to keep herself from laughing, while Will's cheeks turned pink, obviously more bothered by Lewyn catching him than being caught by her.

"Now," Lewyn continued, ready to move on after

making his point. "Leave the letter with me and I'll make sure it's sent. You three heading out?"

"First thing after breakfast," Venn replied.

"Ready for anything?"

She patted the various knives hidden under her clothes, Remy reached for her sword, and Will grabbed the satchel of healing salves. Venn got a glimpse of rope peeking out the side of the satchel and silently thanked him for being so practical.

"Then I wish you all the best," said Lewyn. "Try not to get dead."

Chapter Seventeen

Will tried to convince them to use the nags and cart again, but Venn insisted they bring their own mounts for the mission

"For one thing, we have no idea what we'll find in this field and I really don't want to risk owing Lewyn anything. We've lived our lives pretty happily not being in the other's debt. For another thing, if something does happens, it'll be a lot faster to bolt out of there on horses that are used to our shit instead of controlling the cart."

"The same could have been said yesterday," Will pointed out. "You insisted on taking the cart. Nothing has changed. If anything, we're more at risk of being noticed. If anyone knows we're staying with Lewyn, and if Lewyn is under the crown's suspicion for his association with Larimer, we're being careless in drawing attention to ourselves."

Remy stepped between them to saddle Shalla. "While you two debate it, I'm going to get ready to head out. You may join me if you choose."

Seeing he was outvoted, Will threw up his hands without further argument and draped the satchel over his head, moving towards Hollis.

"Any idea where we're going?" he asked.

Venn smiled at him as she eased the bit between Corsa's teeth. "You're map guy — tell us where to go."

He grumbled under his breath, then flashed her a wink before pulling the map out of his bag. "From Reddington's letter, we know Pastor's Field is somewhere near his home, so we'll start on the same road as yesterday. I'll try to find the rest of the route as we go."

They followed his direction, and while they rode, Venn watched the soldiers they passed, looking for the man who had given them the message, but without success.

As they passed the road leading to Reddington's house, she scanned the ground for traces of new marks on the lane, but the blowing dust had covered up all signs of their visit, so she had no idea if anyone had shown up after Red Hood.

I better watch out I don't become as paranoid as everyone else in this country.

Will took point, having found their place on the map, and they followed him past the last house on the road — a large white estate with burgundy drapes, tall columns, and rocking chairs on the porch — and into the middle of nowhere.

Remy craned her neck to gawk, and Venn smiled. "Not happy in an officer's barracks anymore, Rem? Have to search for something bigger. Need a room to yourself like a spoiled little child."

Remy laughed, but Venn saw sadness creep into her eyes as she reached for her bracelet, and turned the subject onto safer ground.

"I wonder what you'd have to do to get a house like that," she continued, wanting to pull her friend out of her dark thoughts. "I'll guess sexual favours for the queen."

"Venn!" Remy gasped. "You can't say things like that about a monarch."

"What?" Venn laughed. "Why couldn't it be true? She obviously liked them enough to give them a big house."

Will glanced over his shoulder to get another look at the estate and chuckled. "As it happens, Queen Rhoda's been widowed for ten years. Anything is possible."

"I like my idea," Venn said. "Either that or it's some cranky old aunt and Rhoda doesn't want her living in the palace, getting in her way."

The jokes continued until the house fell out of sight, and the blighted landscape sprawled out in front of them. Once the colours had leached from the land, and nothing lay before them but the sun-bleached brown of the earth and the odd black patch of rotten grass, they found nothing more to laugh at.

But the blight wasn't the only part of the field that left them speechless.

"What in the nine gods' names happened here?" Venn asked, sliding from Corsa's back and leaving him to stand in the dust. With nowhere for him to forage or water himself, she hoped he wouldn't get bored and wander away.

If he did, she thought it likely the ground would swallow him up.

The field was scattered with holes. At least two dozen of them before she lost count, spaced sporadically across the plane, and all about a metre wide. Like the one Remy had nearly fallen into on their ride to Margolin.

"Some strange new irrigation system?" Remy offered, sounding as baffled as Venn felt.

Venn kicked at the dust and a cloud of it billowed up, settling over her black trousers in a fine layer.

"Would have been nice if that Foley guy had more time to tell us why we're here," Remy continued. She walked to the nearest hole and leaned over it. "Think they're poorly dug graves of all the people that have been killed? He could have sent us to where the murdered servants were buried."

They heard a snort and turned around to see Frey waddle up towards them. His large head swung back and forth as he took in the scene, and Venn imagined him registering his own amazement at the empty and collapsing land.

Will joined Remy and stared into the hole. "It might have been their attempt to stop the blight when it first started. Everywhere else we've seen, they're cutting the trees down to prevent them falling and causing damage, I suspect. If this is where the problem started, they must have tried to stop it by pulling them all up. Right from the roots."

He slid his boot along the ground and kicked a pile of dirt down the hole. They froze and listened to it skitter down the edges before going silent. Not too deep, but deep enough that Venn would much rather stay on the surface. She shivered in spite of the heat and again remembered what they'd seen at the last hole they'd encountered.

"You stick with me, all right, buddy?" she said, resting her hand on Frey's head. "One sign of whatever that was and you kill it. I don't care if it's some weird guy wearing a costume headband. Just make it gone."

Frey extended his long smooth tongue and caught a small centipede that had caught on Venn's trouser leg. She shuddered to see it and when another crawled up towards her boot, she stamped down on it.

"I really hate bugs," she said. Looking up, she noticed Will and Remy had walked farther out into the field, pausing from time to time to stare down the holes.

"Seeing anything?" she called.

"Nothing," Will shouted back. He shielded his eyes from the sun, beating his shirt against his chest to create any sort of breeze in the heat of the early afternoon, and turned in a circle. "There's nothing to see. Nothing to find."

"Has to be something," Venn said to herself, keeping near Frey's side as they moved out towards the others. "No one pretends to threaten someone in the street to give a secret message if it doesn't have some importance." Her shoulders slumped as she absorbed the size of the field, and she rubbed a hand over the back of her neck, feeling the heat from her burning skin. "Maybe we should have brought a shovel."

"To what?" Remy asked. "Add to the holes?"

Venn grinned. "Maybe that's what these are. Someone

else's attempts to find whatever that guy sent us here to find. They could have been one metre away from the entire mystery. Or we misunderstood him. My Margolan's not as strong as it used to be. Could be he didn't tell us to check the field — maybe he meant someone's name."

Remy's expression turned to horror at the idea, and she looked to Will, who noticed and shook his head. "She's giving you a hard time. A sorry attempt to lighten the mood."

Venn stuck her tongue out at him and sauntered away.

"He told us to come here," Will assured Remy. "Just wish he'd been able to tell us why. What about that cottage Lewyn mentioned?"

Venn squinted against the sun, seeing nothing but sand and glare, but when a few stray clouds passed overhead, she thought she made out some extra humps under the dust. "The cottage is gone, but the foundation might still be over there. May as well check it out."

Keeping Frey close and watching her footing, she moved towards the frame of what once might have been a small shack. She slid her boots over the dust, clearing away the top layer and finding nothing but what looked like an old spoon.

"Unless this is a cursed spoon from Dungaron," she said, holding it up like the sword, "I don't think this is why we're here."

Will passed a hand over his face, smearing dirt across his cheeks, and turned back out towards the field. "Then I guess we walk."

Remy and Venn released a groan, and each took a direction from where they stood. They walked out slowly, kicking away dirt piles and checking under rocks. Frey stayed by Venn as she'd requested, but so far she saw no sign of the giant antennae of the other day, just various sizes of the same brown centipedes, scurrying over the ground as if in a rush to get somewhere.

"These things grow big here," she said, kicking at one that stretched the size of her palm. It turned her stomach until Frey's tongue rolled out again and he caught it up, crunching down with his sharp teeth. Venn patted his shoulder. "You know, Frey, I was glad you were with us when those red soldiers attacked, but I don't think I've ever been more grateful that you tracked us than I am right at this moment. Keep eating, buddy."

The bear took her words to heart and waddled off, following the centipedes as they scrambled over the uneven earth.

When the holes stopped appearing and she'd gone as far as she thought useful, she turned around and started back.

"There's nothing here," she called to the approaching forms of Will and Remy. "Whatever reason he sent us here, we're either not going to find it, or someone else has already been and taken it. How much time do you want to waste kicking around in the dirt?"

She nudged over a rock with her toe and tipped her water flask into her mouth, grimacing at the warm, dusty flavour.

Will did another scan of the land and slouched, looking

as defeated as Venn felt. "You're probably right. Could be whatever he sent us here for is staring us right in the face, but I'm done. Rem?"

She shrugged. "It would be one thing if there was somewhere to hide something, but other than under that rock over there — and don't worry, I checked — there's nothing. It's hot, I'm cranky, and at this point I want to go home and give myself a bath. Maybe we can dash back to Reddington's house and use his washing room before heading home. I wouldn't mind giving that copper tub some real good use."

"I'm not sure I'll second you on the tub, but the rest sounds good. Not to mention, there are too many gods-be-damned bugs around here." Venn stamped her boot on a collection of smaller centipedes that had crawled out from under the rock she'd tipped over.

As she brought her boot down, the earth trembled beneath her feet. She stretched out her hands to catch her balance and Will grabbed her arm, wobbling to stay upright. Remy stepped backwards, but they shared a look of horror as they heard a thunderous crack, like the world breaking in half. A fissure grew from the hole beside them, and before Venn or Will could jump out of the way, the earth opened and swallowed them into the darkness.

Chapter Eighteen

Hard earth and small rocks tore into Venn's back as she and Will skidded down into the depths. She scrambled to catch onto something, trying to twist onto her stomach to claw her fingers into the dirt, but the rolling dust kept her moving. The echoes of the mini rockslide rumbled in her ears, blocking out all other sound.

They started to slow, and the slide ended, followed by a short drop over a sharp edge. Venn landed with a grunt, her right ankle collapsing under her weight.

Will caught her before she fell, his arm tight around her waist. In the light streaming down from above, she saw blood dripping down his face from a cut on his forehead, with bloody scrapes all down his cheek.

"You guys okay?" Remy shouted down to them, her face a shadow with the light behind her. "What in sunfire happened?"

"You all right?" Will asked, keeping hold of Venn.

She nodded, working to catch her breath. Easing out of

his grip, she rested her thighs against the edge, and leaned along the slope to look up. "We're fine, Rem. Now how in the most blessed treenut do we get out of here?"

Will cupped his hands and bent down. "Let me give you a boost."

Venn stepped on his palms with her good leg and he hoisted her onto the slope. Digging her torn and jagged nails into the dirt, wincing as small rocks jammed under the broken skin, she made it a metre before the ground gave and she slid back down. Will caught her before she tumbled over the edge again.

"No good," she said, twisting her arm to blow the dust off her skinned elbow. "We won't be able to climb out."

A chittering noise echoed in the blackness behind her, and she reached for Will's arm.

"Did you hear that?"

Will nodded and pulled her closer, as if to guard her. Venn wanted to push him away and run, but her legs shook and he became the only thing keeping her on her feet. She scanned the darkness and saw they hadn't landed in a hole so much as a meeting of tunnels, with four branches leading off from where they stood. It reeked of sulphur and moist earth. Beneath her feet, the dry earth had softened with dampness.

Something brushed against her leg and she lurched back, pushing Will away from the sound of something skittering towards them from one of the tunnels.

They weren't alone in this hole, and whatever else was there, Venn didn't think it sounded like anything she wanted to see.

Ahead of them, the sun reflected off something shiny.

Not shiny. Glossy. Like oil.

It moved farther out of the tunnel towards them, and Venn saw various shades of brown in all sorts of distorted shapes. As her eyes adjusted, her hand flew to her mouth and she tried not to gag.

The oil-like orbs were the faceted eyes of an insect. A giant, larger-than-her centipede.

She couldn't get an idea of how long it was with part of its body still hidden in the tunnel, but it took up the width of the space, and more if she included the endless rows of long hooked legs bent in against its body, braced upwards along the walls. She stopped counting at ten pairs, her attention caught on the sharp oozing pincers coming up beneath its lower mandible. Black eyes stared at them, the long brown antennae reaching out towards them.

"Sweet piss boiled up to throw on a fire of fuck," she hissed.

"I don't know what that means," Will whispered, standing as still as she was, "but I guess my bug dream was a message from the Sisters after all."

"If I ever get my hands on those witches…" Venn began, but couldn't finish. Her stomach twisted and her body tensed with a panic she had trouble forcing down. She didn't do well with bugs.

Worse, she heard more in the darkness. Even with this one paused in the tunnel, she felt them crawling over her.

"What's happening down there?"

"I think we found what that soldier warned us about," Venn replied over her shoulder, trying to keep her voice at a volume that didn't startle their host. "Be ready to run if you have to."

"Why, what—"

"Shit," Venn interrupted her.

Another set of antennae appeared over the first as a second centipede crawled on top of the other one, moving towards them. A third appeared in the next tunnel.

Venn's thoughts buzzed with terror, jumping up over the edge to try once more to crawl out of the hole, but she slid down as an antenna reached up to grab her leg. She kicked out, catching it in the head, and it moved to Will.

More of them came through the tunnels, squeezing in, legs a jumble as they pressed towards their visitors.

"Stay back," Will said, stretching an arm out.

"I don't think they'll listen to you," Venn replied through clenched teeth.

"Not them — you."

He reached into his pack and launched a vial at the oscillating monsters. It smashed, the smell of oil mixing with the sulphur and mould.

"*Insa!*"

A wave of flame burst into the room, catching the insects as the oil spattered and spread. Will pressed backwards into a rounded corner between the wall and slope, turning his face away from the force of the heat. Smoke oozed upwards, and Venn blocked her mouth and nose with the crook of her elbow, pressing herself against the wall as one centipede skittered up out of the hole to escape the flames. She shuddered as a leg brushed against hers, the small spines tearing her flesh. Being so close to it, she counted another dozen or more pairs of legs, its length at least as tall as her, if not as Will.

She heard Remy scream above, heard Frey growl, and the sounds of a brief fight.

Down with them, three centipedes shrivelled and curled in the middle of the room, while four more skittered back down the tunnels, wreathed in flame and carrying the oil with them. They heard more cracks and pops as the fire caught down other tunnels, and more rushing feet as the centipedes tried to get away from the threat.

Their own space remained quiet except for the crackling corpses, and Venn felt tears on her cheeks. She struck them away, wincing as the salt sank into the scrapes on her cheeks, and rested her forehead on the back of her hand to try to clear the spots from her eyes.

Will looked over his shoulder and smiled, reaching up to brush a lock of hair out of her face. "You all right? They didn't sting you?"

She shook her head and swallowed her disgust. "You?"

He ran his hand over his stomach, lifting his shirt to expose a red mark. "It didn't break the skin. I should be all right."

"What the *fuck* was that?" Remy shouted down. Venn heard her own hysteria matched in her friend, and released a breath.

"I guess we know the reason for all those holes," Will

breathed, tilting his head back to look at the row of holes leading down the right-hand tunnel. "Ventilation."

"Great to know that I'm standing here surrounded by them," said Remy.

"At least you're not in the middle of them," said Venn. "Throw down the gods-be-damned rope and get us out of here."

"What rope?" Remy asked.

Will rested his hand on her shoulder, and Venn's gaze dropped to his satchel, the rope visible under the flap.

"Oh gods," she said. Her chest felt tight, like she shouldn't get breath. "I need to get out of here."

For a third time she tried to scramble up the slope, desperation bringing her almost within reach of Remy's grip before she lost her footing and fell, fighting the whole way down for purchase.

"I can't be here. Find me a way out, Remy."

Remy disappeared to follow the order, but returned a moment later.

"The other holes all look steeper than this one," she said.

Will frowned. "It makes sense. Otherwise these things would be crawling all over the field. It was the landslide that made this one so level."

Venn clutched the front of her shirt, waving it against her chest to try to get any air. Her skin buzzed, and more tears stung her eyes, though she refused to let them fall.

Will left Venn's side to grab a length of thick tree root from the ground, and she had to restrain herself from pulling him back, feeling vulnerable and open with the empty space. He stuck the root into the oil and flame, and held it out in front of him.

"I guess we'll have to walk through," he said.

Venn clutched at the wall. "Are you in*sane*?"

He grinned. "I don't think I've ever seen you afraid before. Could this be the moment where I find out Venn Connell's deepest darkest fear?"

She sniffed, tried to clear her expression into stoicism, and failed. "I just hate bugs, all right? I hate them when they're small, I hate them when they crawl over me, and I especially hate big fucking giant bugs that want to devour me."

"That's all reasonable," Will said with a nod. He grabbed her hand and gave it a squeeze, tried to pull her forward.

She shook her head and remained dead weight on the slope. "I can't."

"Give me some of your knives," he said.

Venn clutched the bands around her waist tighter against her. "Why?"

"So that we can protect each other down here," he said. "Unless you want to do all the work?"

"Hang on," Remy called down. "I have something that might help with that."

She vanished again, and Venn stared into the dark tunnels, crossing her fingers that nothing emerged from the blackness.

"Try to think rationally," Will said, his voice soft and soothing. "If we have to walk through here anyway to get out, we can tear down as many of these fuckers as we can. Better than knowing they're here while we go home and coming across them by surprise later, right? Especially now that they can get out."

Before Venn could retort — or cry — at the idea, Remy returned above them.

"I still have the sword from the bandit we ran into. It's a decent blade and might offer more reach than the knives." She sent it sliding down the slope and Will grabbed it, looping it through his belt.

"Thanks, Rem. What can you tell from the one up there? Anything we should aim for?"

Remy groaned and left the hole a third time, but they heard her mumbling to herself. Frey's head appeared in the hole and he let out a soft growl. He set his paw down in the dirt as though to join them underground, but the loose earth slipped beneath him, unable to hold his weight, and he pulled back.

Remy returned. "I hate you for making me look. It looks like their bodies are segmented. Hard plates, but squishy between them. The underside is soft. Eyes, maybe. The last segment is right under their heads, so nothing but squish between that and the skull. And watch for the pincers. Even dead they're oozing something."

Venn's panic rose at the description as more noises echoed down the left tunnel.

Will grabbed her hand again. "Come on, Venn. Where's your sense of adventure?"

She shuddered, unsure how he could be so unruffled,

but stepped over the edge onto the tunnel floor, keeping hold of Will's hand.

He tilted his head back towards Remy. "We're going to head down this tunnel to our right. Try following the holes to stay with us. We might end up driving more of those things up your way."

Remy rolled her eyes. "That's great, guys. Really appreciate it. Just stay safe down there, all right?"

Her face disappeared, and Will waved the makeshift torch in front of them.

As they walked, he turned to Venn. "Did you hurt yourself in that fall? You're limping."

"I turned my ankle. It'll walk off."

"Are you sure or are you saying that because you don't want me to take a look?"

Venn pulled her hand out of his and crossed her arms. "I'm sure. It's twisted, not broken."

Will held up his hands. "All right. We'll go with what you say. But don't come whining to me tomorrow when it inflates to the size of that centipede's eye."

Venn jerked again as she felt something crawl up her arm. "Not funny." She ground her teeth when she heard him chuckle. "What about that oil and fire stuff? How many more of those do you have in that trick satchel of yours?"

Will handed her the torch and peered inside. "Four more vials of oil." He let the flap drop and reclaimed the torch. "But the spells take a lot out of me. I could probably manage it once more. After that you'd have to carry me out of here."

"If I cared to," she said, and hated the shake in her voice. "But all right, one more big burst of flame. Hopefully we don't need it."

More skittering approached from behind them, and Venn reached for the knives at her hip, shoving her fear under her battle lust. The hilts filled her palms as the centipede came around the corner, and she launched herself over his head, not giving those pincers a chance to get near her. She landed on its back, its legs giving out under her weight before gaining purchase on the damp earth, and sank one knife between the segmented plates. It twisted backwards to reach her and she leaned away, trying not to see more of its ugly face than she had to. The pincers snapped and she snapped back, aiming the second knife at the soft spot under its head. An antenna wriggled towards her, brushing over her cheek, and she released a string of curses under her breath as she pulled the first knife out of its back and stuck it in beside the other one, slicing through with both blades so its head fell forward, partially detached from its body. Jumping down, she cut through the rest and watched it tremble and collapse.

"That was…" Will began.

"Tell me later," Venn interrupted as another came around the corner. She hurled a knife towards its face, saw the blade lodge between its eyes, but it kept moving forward. "Fuck, I hate bugs."

Using the dead insect at her feet as a launching pad, she hurled herself at the other one. The pincers stretched towards her, oozing their venom, but she dodged it and skidded underneath him, blade up to cut through the soft underbelly. His insides spilled onto the ground, and she rolled out of the way, shaking her hand free of the sticky mess that covered her.

Ahead, Will had the sword out to face a third. The bug's antennae had looped around, locking him in. He swung the blade with quick precision, aiming for the eyes. When the centipede stretched out the pincer, Will slashed down and cut it off. Before the monster could retreat, he wheeled the blade up under its head, the crack and squelch loud in the silence of the tunnel as the tip of the sword pierced through the top of the skull. It dropped to the ground, the venom from the broken pincer seeping into the earth with a noxious scent.

Venn coughed and twisted her head the way they came, hoping to catch a whiff of fresh air from the hole they'd fallen down, but the corpses of the bugs she'd faced blocked the breeze.

"Ready to keep moving?" he asked.

She wanted to say no. Backing down from a fight never came easily to her, but damned if she had any interest in voluntarily facing more of those creatures. But forward as the only way out.

After retrieving the knives she'd left behind in the centipede corpses, she begrudgingly followed Will, trying not to trip over the legs, of which there were too many to acknowledge without that oily sensation of panic crawling through her veins.

To distract herself from what might lie in the darkness, she asked, "Where and when did you learn to wield a blade like that?"

Will glanced over his shoulder, twisting his wrist to slip the sword back through his belt. "Brian's been training me for a few years now. After everything that happened with Raul, the dragons, the mutated animals, Brady insisted."

Venn's eyes widened. "Years? And you never told me."

Will grinned. "What was it Lewyn said earlier? Always let people underestimate you. Guess I already live by that philosophy."

"A man of many mysteries," Venn murmured.

The smile remained on Will's face, but the warmth leached out of his eyes. "You have no idea."

He turned away and Venn let the subject drop. The idea of Will having deep dark secrets made her want to laugh even more than the idea that he was difficult for Lewyn to read. She had known him more than five years, had fought alongside him. He was the good boy who did his lessons and obeyed his mother and spent all of his time in the library. She would have believed there was nothing mysterious about him.

But it seemed even he kept secrets.

She stared at his back as he led the way through the tunnels, always choosing the right-hand fork when they reached one.

"Have a plan in mind or are we going to wander through the maze until we starve to death?"

Will waved the torch ahead of them to light the way

down another tunnel. "We know where to find something to eat if we get peckish."

Venn narrowed her eyes. "That's not funny."

They lapsed into silence, and she strained her ears to catch any more skittering. Nothing echoed around her and she breathed easier, hoping the ones they'd crossed had been the worst of it. They'd dealt with the threat, and now they could go home and she could drink herself into oblivion to wash out the image of those human-sized creatures.

Light beamed down at random intervals as they passed under the holes in the ceiling, and once in a while they heard Remy chatting to herself — or maybe to Frey — above, but the holes became rare. The air grew more stifled, warm, and damp, and Venn sensed they had gone down a slight incline, moving deeper underground.

"I think this is the opposite of finding our way out," Venn whispered, and winced as her voice fell dull between them, louder than she'd expected.

Will slowed down to walk closer to her, and they edged forward, unable to see more than half a metre ahead. To keep herself from stepping on his feet or losing him, Venn grabbed hold of the back of his shirt.

Once in a while, her boot crunched through something on the ground, and she swallowed hard, trying not to think of what it might be.

The air around them changed, the odour thicker and more putrid. Venn thought the tunnels were narrowing, but when she stretched out her free hand to follow the wall to her right, it gave way to nothing. Ahead of her, Will stumbled, wavering forward, and Venn hauled him back, holding onto him until he found his balance.

She moved up to stand beside him, and her breath caught in her chest. The torchlight didn't reveal much, but it was enough to twist her gut into knots.

The centipedes they'd faced earlier had only been the smallest hint of what hid in these tunnels. In the height of the afternoon, they were sleeping, but even asleep, the giant insects writhed before her. She counted fifteen sets of pincers in the pit below, and more legs than her mind could process. She knew there were more that she couldn't see, and was grateful she couldn't get a good idea about the size of the room.

In the edge of the light, she saw a human skull half-buried in the dirt.

Still clutching Will's shirt, she pulled him backwards.

"I think this would be a good time to use your last oomph," she hissed into his ear.

He waggled his head in a rapid nod, handed the torch to Venn, and reached into his satchel, his movements slow and deliberate. Without making any noise, he slid out one vial of oil and poured it in a line on the ground between them and the pit, and then took three steps backwards, pushing Venn with him.

"Get ready to run," he said, taking back the torch.

She half-turned and set her toes into the ground, ready to push off into a sprint as soon as he said the word, hoping he would keep up with her. She didn't know if she could bring herself to go back for him if he couldn't. Her thoughts scurried into the dark corners of her mind, and it took every ounce of strength not to scream and melt into a gibbering panic. No matter what she'd been through in the past, never before had she felt such a sense of helplessness.

Her weakness felt more pronounced in the face of Will's smooth confidence. She knew he was afraid, and that he knew as well as she did the next few minutes could be their last if they couldn't get out of reach of those centipedes, but she wouldn't know it to look at him.

His hands not even shaking, he took another two vials out of the bag and flung them both at the same time into opposite sides of the room. The length of time it took to hear the smash of glass raised Venn's heart rate once again as she imagined how many pairs of legs were hidden from sight.

As soon as the vials broke, the activity rose in the pit. The centipedes close enough to catch the light of the torch stirred, crawling over each other with their long extended legs. A dozen pincers turned towards them, the mass rising up to leave the pit and come after them.

"You ready?" Will asked. "This is going to be hot."

"Gods yes," said Venn.

Will turned to the horde and raised his hand. "*Insa!*"

Before Venn started to run, light filled the room as the oil caught and the fire blazed, and in that moment, she saw the nightmare that would haunt the rest of her life. Not dozens, but at least a hundred of the monstrous creatures lay out in front of her, the brown bodies writhing as they lifted themselves out of the twisted heap. Bones, some animal, others distinctly human, lay discarded around the edges of the pit or buried under the heavy bodies of the insects. The sound of their legs striking the rocks, of the pincers snapping in their silent communication rattled her brain.

They had to get out or would end up being the next centipede meal.

The fire licked up the walls and curled back in on itself, catching on their legs, and snapping at their antennae. The vial Will had emptied at his feet created a thick wall of black smoke and fire, and the centipedes in front of the horde were caught up in their rush to reach their dinner.

Venn's feet stayed frozen to the ground in her horror, but Will shoved her forward as the bugs and the fire began to chase them.

The insects were quick — too quick for the fire to consume them all at once — and Venn hadn't reached the first turn before the mass reached the tunnel, carrying the fire with them. As one centipede died, the others rushed over it, undeterred by the obstacle, but caught by the flame it left behind. They tracked the oil on their feet, spreading the damage as they skittered through the tunnels.

Venn pushed herself harder, her heart beating against her ribs, and her lungs straining for air not filled with fumes. Her ankle screamed under her weight, but she used the pain to fuel her speed. Glancing once over her shoulder to make sure Will was still behind her, she saw the tunnel behind him clogged with fiery monsters, the light reflected in the hundred facets of their bug eyes.

She turned back to the front and released a sharp scream as another centipede came out from the opposite tunnel. Skidding to a halt, foot slipping out from under her, she took a sharp left and left the new bug to join the masses. The way ahead looked clear, and she gave a final burst of energy, racing down a tunnel lit only by the fire behind her, which slowly faded as more bugs died out. But more legs scratched against the dirt, and her own legs began to tire. Light from one of the holes appeared ahead, and she crossed her fingers that it would be the one to free them from the stampede.

"It'll be a miracle if we make it," she called over her shoulder.

"What kind of attitude is that?" Will shouted back, and her chest flooded relief that he didn't sound far behind her.

She looked back to check and saw him stop and turn around. Skidding to a halt, she raced towards him and grabbed his arm. "What are you doing?"

His chest heaved with his exertion, and, around breaths, he grimaced and pulled out the final vial. "Hoping for the best."

The sound of the centipedes drew closer, and Venn spun around to face the other tunnel, watching for more of them to come up the opposite way, every now and then checking to see what Will was doing.

"You going to wait until they crawl over us?"

"That might be the best time to catch them," he said. "But let's see if we can time it better than that."

She heard them round the corner, heard the vial smash,

and felt the wave of heat as Will threw the torch into the oil. The next wave of bugs got caught in the flame, and this close, Venn could hear the whistle and cracks as heat expanded their segmented bodies. Will grabbed her arm and they backed away, but this time no more centipedes raced after them. The earth, already drier now that they'd risen from the depths of the nest, hardened and crumbled.

Lumps of dirt fell into Venn's hair, and she looked up to see the hole widen. She only had time to cry out before the roof caved in.

Chapter Nineteen

Tightening her grip on Will's arm, she tugged him out of the way, but he tripped and knocked them both over. She landed on her back with his solid frame covering hers as the heavy earth collapsed behind them, filling the air with dust and blocking them from the centipedes.

And hopefully crushing the pissers.

When the dust settled, Venn blinked the dirt from her eyes and did a quick scan of herself to make sure nothing was broken. Satisfied with her own state, she looked to Will, who had frozen with his elbows braced on either side of her, his head twisted to face the dirt pile. She pressed against his chest to get his attention and pushed him off. He rolled away, while she scrambled to her feet to sag against the wall, tilting her head towards the light above.

"Next time someone pulls us aside to give us secret directions," she said between pants, "we don't listen to them. All right?"

Will forced a laugh and pushed his hands through his

hair, the dark brown waves almost blond with the dust. "But then we wouldn't have found all these new friends to play with."

"And learn what?" Venn shoved herself away from the wall and stretched her arms out towards the tunnels. "Other than the fact that these disgusting, unnatural insects are breeding under this field, what do we know now that we didn't know before? I, for one, would have preferred the guy to pull us aside and say, 'By the way, Pastor's Field is riddled with toxic bugs' instead of sending us here in person."

Will moved to stand in front of her, his hands resting on her shoulders as he trapped her gaze with his. She stared into the brown depths and wondered how he could stand to be so cool after everything they'd seen.

"Breathe, Venn. They're not crawling over you and they're not going to get you, all right?"

At first she didn't understand why he spoke to her as though she were panicking, then she realised her breathing had quickened with her desire to run, and focused on calming down. He nodded and let her go, looking around them.

"It can't have just been the insects," he said. "They're interesting enough, but that can't be why he sent us here. How do you feel about continuing on?"

Venn rubbed her arms to clear the goosebumps, and followed him down the tunnel, dragging her feet. "If that wasn't the only nest in this place, I'm never speaking to you again."

"Somehow this is connected to Larimer and

Reddington," Will thought aloud as Venn trailed after him.

"Think someone fed them to the 'pedes?" she suggested, thinking of the bones in the pit.

Will stuck out his tongue in distaste. "That wouldn't be the way I want to go, but it's not beyond the realm of possibility. I guess then the question would be why."

"Easy clean up and the advantage for a twisted mind to have a few laughs?"

The next turn led to another incline, this one more gradual. With a soft cheer of relief, she raced up, stopping halfway to crane her head towards the hole. "This is odd. There's a grate."

Will leaned forward on his knee to see. "Huh."

The hole was wider than the others they had come across, but an iron grate rested across the opening, a lock dangling between the bars.

"So these centipedes weren't as much of a surprise to someone," said Venn. "They were actually being kept. Like pets." She shivered. "I question that someone's sanity."

Will stepped down and whirled in a circle, scanning the ground around him. "Now we return to the why." He stopping before reaching his original position, and his face lit up as he let out another, "Huh."

Venn cocked her head. "What now?"

He waved her over, and she released a sigh as she slid down, her twisted ankle throbbing with her weight. Following the direction of his pointing finger, she noticed two large wooden barrels near the slope, previously hidden in the shadows.

Hesitant, dreading the idea of more baby bugs squirming around inside, she punched off the lid, darting her face out of the way.

"Nothing's going to bite you," Will assured her, leaning in. He tilted the barrel towards the light, and Venn grimaced to see it full of something grey and slimy.

"It reeks. What in the nine gods' names is it?"

"If I had to guess — and to put you at ease, I'm not about to touch it or taste it — I'd say it's centipede venom."

Venn gagged. "Why?"

He scratched the back of his neck, brow furrowed in thought. "Something you said earlier gave me an idea, but it disappeared before I could grab it. What were you saying about the soldier who sent us here? Something about how you'd prefer it if…"

Venn waited for him to keep going, but he lapsed into silence and looked to her to fill in the rest. She chewed on her lip, trying to remember. "I think it was if he'd told us that Pastor's Field is full of toxic bugs. That what you mean?"

Will snapped his fingers. "Yes, it is. And now it fits even better. Centipede venom is toxic. In most people it'll make them ill, and in other cases can cause severe allergic reactions, like bee stings."

"All right…" said Venn, not picking up on her friend's train of thought. "Have you heard of an epidemic of mysterious allergic reactions that I missed?"

"No, but that's just when it's injected into the blood in its pure form. If it were diluted, let's say in water, and ingested, it would lead to nausea and, I'm sure, hallucinations. Maybe some paranoid delusions."

His direction now dawned on Venn. "You think someone's poisoning the queen? Breeding these things so he can collect their venom and dose her?"

Will grinned, the professor proud of the student.

Her expression clouded again. "Why do they have to be so big? I've never heard of 'pedes growing to be the size of, well, me. Is he planning to release them later on?"

Will frowned, eyes shifting as he thought it through. Venn saw when the epiphany struck, and he raised his gaze back to hers. "Quantity. Whoever's behind this must be dosing more people than just the queen. There's no way they'd manage to milk enough of the venom from the regular-sized insects."

Venn shuddered. "Why couldn't they have chosen snakes? I could have handled a pit full of snakes."

Will grinned. "Twenty-metre long snakes?"

"Just stop it," she groaned. "This conversation isn't getting any better." She stretched her arm across his chest to push him back. "We've already dealt with one issue while we're down here. If this is part of the problem, we might as well deal with it, too."

Bracing her foot against the first barrel, she kicked it over, knocking both to the ground. The venom sank into the earth until nothing remained but a slimy puddle on the surface.

Exhaling a sharp breath of satisfaction, she crossed her arms. "*Now* can we go?"

Will grinned. "Yes, if we can find a way out of here. There might be more barrels scattered throughout the nest, but good luck to whoever's collecting it. The debris should keep them busy."

"Venn?" Remy's voice sounded from above. "Will? Are you guys alive? What in the nine gods' names is going on down there?"

Her face appeared above the blocked tunnel.

"Trust me, Rem, it's better if you never find out. Save yourself the nightmares." Venn climbed up to the grate and shoved against the bars. "Think you can get that lock open?"

Remy knelt down and pulled the lock up to get a better look. "Not without a key."

Will leaned back to look down the tunnel, "I think there's another hole not too far that way." He pulled the rope from his satchel and handed it to Venn, who passed it up through the bars to Remy. "If you throw the rope down, we can climb up. Unless you're too shaken?"

He directed the last question at Venn, and she scoffed at the suggestion. "I'd learn to fly if it got me out of here a second sooner."

She scurried back down the slope and led the way through the tunnel, groaning when she heard the unmistakeable sound of another insect rushing their way.

"What do you say?" she asked, turning to Will as she pulled another knife from her waist. "One more for old times' sake?"

He grinned and grabbed the sword from his belt.

A single centipede skittered into view, and Venn threw

herself at it as the rope fell down behind her. She lodged the knife into its eye, but the pincer shot out, catching her shirt. She lurched away before it could reach her skin and heard the cotton tear. It came at her again, raising its front legs as though prepared to crush her. Backed against the wall, Venn had nowhere to move and braced her knives in front of her. With the insect focused on Venn, Will punched his blade underneath its head, below the pincers. Its insides seeped out onto Venn's boots before it collapsed, oozing more sulphurous smells into the earth.

Venn wiped her blade on the dirt of the wall, and blew a stray lock of dusty hair from her eyes. With a last shudder at the sight of the dead insect, she grabbed the rope and started up, Will close behind her.

***

When they arrived at Lewyn's cottage, he wouldn't let them inside until Remy had thrown bucket after bucket of freezing water over them to rid them of the dust and centipede goo.

In the heat of the afternoon, after the tightness of the air in the tunnels and the sensation of bugs still crawling under her clothes, Venn didn't complain. But the water trickling over her skin made her jump after every shower, and she stripped down as far as modesty would allow, not covering herself until she was sure she was bug free.

"So you think you accomplished something important today?" Lewyn asked.

"No," said Venn, shaking out her hair so water droplets

sprayed in every direction. Frey snorted and tossed his head, making her laugh, but her smile disappeared as she caught her mentor scowling at her, and she rolled her eyes. "I think we achieved something. We won't know what difference it makes in the scheme of things until we solve the twenty million other mysteries staring us in the face. We answered a few questions, and wound up with ten more. But that's the process of these things, right? What would be the fun of finding it all out right away?"

"And we're not at a dead end," Will pointed out. "We still have to meet with the soldier Foley tomorrow afternoon. He wouldn't want to meet us again if he didn't have more information to share."

"That's a naive point of view, boy," said Lewyn. "For all you know, he could work for whoever was breeding those things, hoping you'd go in and not come up. When he learns his plan failed, he might sink a knife into your gut."

Will nodded. "That could very well be true, and I'm sure we'll be on our guard in case it is, but it won't stop me from hoping he can shuffle these puzzle pieces into some sort of picture."

Lewyn sniffed. "Hope's a dangerous thing to have, as Connell here will tell you, I'm sure. At least you'll have her with you to manage the situation if those hopes crash and burn."

Venn clenched her teeth, thinking how Will's magic had saved her in those tunnels, and how she likely wouldn't have made it without him. Her fear from the morning blossomed into hot rage at Lewyn's insinuation that Will couldn't handle himself, or that she would be better off without him and Remy. She glared into his blue eye. "You're right. I will be. We'll stick together through this."

"Don't make promises you can't keep. Especially not ones it'll ruin you to break. But go on," he jerked his head towards the door. "Go inside and get yourselves something to eat before the stew gets cold. And thank the bear for tonight's dinner. Turns out he's useful for more than taking down a stray 'pede."

Venn glanced at the deer carcass hanging out back to dry, and looked to Frey. "How come you never went hunting for us?"

"Obviously you're not training him right," Lewyn answered for him. He reached out with his stick and nudged Venn inside.

***

Exhaustion guided Venn to her pallet earlier than the others, but sleep never claimed her. Every time she closed her eyes, she heard the Sisters' words of warning echo in her thoughts.

Death strengthens death until the whole world bleeds…

It made no more sense to her now than it did when she first heard them say it. The blight was only the start. Next would come the blood if she couldn't solve the rest of the mystery soon enough.

She thought of Ariana and Jayden, and the way they had been so quick to defend sending her to Margolin when Taylor put up a fuss. Venn hated the thought of letting them down and making things worse when she'd just wanted to help. Have fun and get into a few fights, sure, but achieve something in the process.

After the fight with the centipedes, the sight of that nest of hundreds of insects, all being bred for some larger purpose, it made her wonder if she'd be enough. If she'd be *good* enough to accomplish what she'd set out to do. Last time it had been Jayden and Jasmine, with Brady's brains and Maggie's magic, who had saved the day. She'd just gone in to help clean up the mess. Now more of the responsibility weighed on her shoulders, and she didn't know if she was up for it.

Bringing her fist down on her forehead, she blinked up at the ceiling, accepting that sleep wasn't likely to happen any time soon. She let her head fall to the side to stare out the window at the sliver of the waxing moon. A few dark clouds cut over the stars, blacking out the night, and in that moment there was nothing she wanted more than to go outside and watch the rain come in.

She crawled out of the blankets and headed for the door, careful not to trip over Remy, who was sprawled out beside her.

Opening the door slowly so it wouldn't squeak, she stepped outside and was startled to find Will standing in the yard, hands in his pockets, face tilted up towards the sky. She didn't want to scare him, so she cleared her throat, and he looked over his shoulder.

"I thought you went to bed hours ago," she said, coming to stand by him. "Guess I'm not the only one having trouble sleeping tonight."

"Not surprising," he replied. "After what we saw today, it makes sense our thoughts are running around like—"

Venn held up a hand. "Don't say bugs."

Will grinned and allowed his sentence to fade away. The smile disappeared and he rubbed the back of his neck. "If we're right that someone's using the venom to drive the queen mad, Andvell could be in more danger than we realised. There's no rationalising with someone that can't think rationally."

She nodded. "But if they're preparing for war, where are the signs of it? Other than the border control, where are the soldiers? Something still doesn't sit right with me."

"Hopefully the soldier can help tomorrow."

Lacking Will's natural optimism, Venn wasn't so sure. Closing her eyes, she felt the midnight breeze brush through her hair, the scents in the air sweet and light compared to the heaviness of that afternoon. She wished she could stay there forever. Everything felt so much easier standing in the shadows of the field instead of trying to act on all the questions she faced.

In the distance, they heard the first rumble of thunder. The silence between her and Will felt comfortable, and although she was loath to break it, Venn felt she couldn't go much longer without getting the uncomfortable out of the way.

"Thanks for today," she said, dropping her head to stare down at her boots. "For saving me and getting me out of the bug pit and all."

"That's what friends are for, right? Pushing each other to face their deepest fears and then helping to get through it."

Venn snorted and raised her head. "In theory, sure. In reality, it was all kinds of horrible and awful, and I'm tempted never to forgive you for it."

"That would be a shame," he replied, and the tone of his voice sounded far more serious than the reaction she'd intended her teasing words to have.

Her heart sped up, and she almost wished she was back in those tunnels as the tension in the quiet night heightened. She rushed to come up with something to say that would change the subject, or at least put them back on the playful footing she preferred remain between them. Her talk the other night with Lewyn spun through her thoughts, wrapping her heart in cold practicality. All this from one soft sentence.

To her embarrassment, the best she could come up with was, "Anyway, thanks."

She started back to the cottage, disappointed that her reprieve had been cut short by such awkwardness.

"You know I'm in love with you."

The words fell like dead weight in the air, and Venn's hand stayed frozen on the door handle, torn between facing the moment head-on and going inside and pretending he hadn't spoken.

You faced giant centipedes today, Connell. How can you not deal with this?

But the centipedes definitely felt like the smaller issue

now.

Bracing herself with a short breath, she dropped her hand to her side and turned to face him, fingers curled to rub against her palm.

"You don't know me, Will," she said, amazed that her voice sounded so steady when her mouth felt so dry. "You love what you think you know."

She expected to see the hope die in his eyes, or a look of disappointment. But he didn't seem surprised by her reply, his lips twitching in a smile. "I know you better than you think I do."

She swallowed hard, wishing she had any sort of skill with words to explain things to him in a way that made sense to either of them.

"I know what you think you see," she insisted. "You think I act hard to cover up a gooey, big-hearted core. But it's an act. I work to appear vulnerable. I bat my eyelashes when it works to my advantage, but the truth is I'm just as hard on the inside as I am on the outside."

He raised her gaze to hold hers. "I don't believe you."

So simple, and so matter-of-fact. To hear him say it, she almost felt convinced she'd been lying. That she would rather be the woman he thought she was than the woman she knew herself to be. But even if she gave in to him and tried for a week, for a month, her nature would always come out. It was best he accept it now and save himself the pain.

"Believe it," she said, keeping it short to make sure no tremor had worked its way in. She clenched her fists at her sides to channel the truth of her next words. "I am shadow and death, and I can't love you back."

That's not true, a small voice said, but she pushed it down before it could get any louder.

Around them, the wind picked up, and the sliver of moon disappeared under the building clouds, as though to give weight to what she said. He continued to stare at her, his gaze now blocked by the darkness.

Without being able to see his emotions, she found it harder to speak.

"When this is over," she continued, "go back to the Keep, and your library. Settle down with some sweet brilliant woman who will hug your mother and carry your brood of adorable, intelligent children. Forget you ever had feelings for me."

She thought she saw him about to speak, and rushed to add, "I'm not trying to be coy when I say you don't deserve me. You'll be better off in the long run. I'm sorry, Will, but you're too good a man to be with someone as wicked as me."

She started to turn away again, wanting an end to the conversation, wishing she hadn't had to hurt her friend in order to protect him.

"Venn."

Reluctantly, she stopped, but didn't face him, not sure she could see that blank expression without feeling something more than guilt.

"I'm not as carefree and innocent as you think I am, so maybe neither of us know the other as well as we think. We all have secrets and demons we want to keep hidden, but yours don't scare me."

Venn turned. "They should."

"They couldn't." Will stepped closer so she had to tilt her head to face him. "If you're not interested, I can respect that. I'll move on and never bring it up. But if I get a hint that you feel one ounce for me how I feel for you, I'll fight for you til the bitter end. I refuse to hide in my books when what I want is right here."

Venn's mouth fell open, her heart skipping a beat, and all words vanished.

But Will didn't seem to need anything more from her. He walked towards the door, reaching his hand out to brush his fingers against hers as he passed, and then he was gone and she remained on her own in the field, staring after him in shock. She might have stayed there for hours and still not had any idea how to process what he'd said, but the first drops of rain landed on her face, bringing her back into herself.

I did the right thing, she said. *We'll both be better off.*

But that small voice asked who she was trying to convince.

Lightning flashed a steady pattern across the sky, and thunder rolled over the field, wrapping her in sound and vibrating under her feet. Stretching out her arms to catch the rain, Venn greeted the storm.

Chapter Twenty

"Something happened last night you're not telling me about."

Remy flapped out the damp tunic and slung it over the line, shooting Venn a sideways stare, which Venn did her best to ignore.

When she recognised she wasn't going to get an answer, Remy snatched the next shirt in the pile and threw that over the line beside the tunic.

"Fine, don't tell me. But keep in mind I'm not just asking as a friend and because I'm concerned about you. I'm also your partner on what's turning out to be a dangerous mission. I need to know if something's going to affect what we're doing."

When Remy had suggested they take the time to wash out their clothes that morning, Venn had thought the woman just wanted clean clothes. Now she realised the task was a way to get her on her own and bombard her with awkward questions.

Venn ground her teeth and squared her shoulders. "It's not. It was an issue, I dealt with it. Nothing should carry over today."

Remy arched a brow. "If that's true, why have you been ignoring Will all morning? And why is he staring as if waiting for you to tear off your shirt and dance the latest *carna*?"

Venn grinned at the image. "If that ever happens, Rem, you're allowed to be worried. And maybe to lock me up somewhere that I'm not a danger to myself or others. Until then," she rested her hand on her friend's shoulder, "relax. Everything is fine."

She flapped out her own black tunic, frowning at the tears and the mud that hadn't come out with the scrubbing.

"Damn bugs ruined my best shirt," she grumbled, and tossed it onto the line next to the rest, not about to throw away a good tunic for the sake of a few rips and stains, no matter how Ariana might stare and shake her head when Venn got back.

Will rose from his place next to the door and sauntered over to them. "You almost ready to head out?"

He stayed close to Remy, but directed the question to Venn, who threw her final items haphazardly over the line and tossed the basket beside the washing tub. "Done."

Remy rolled her eyes. "And this is why you always look like you just rolled out of bed. No one would ever mistake you for an aristocrat."

"Nor would I want them to. I have a reputation to keep."

"For being a slob?"

Venn smiled. "For being a shadow. No one's supposed to see me anyway."

She followed the others into the cottage and waited by the door as Will grabbed his satchel and Remy her sword, her own knives already in place under her clothing. With no idea what to expect from the soldier Foley, she was glad to see they all wanted to be prepared.

"We'll get to Reddington's house by mid-day," said Will. "Hopefully Foley makes the trip worthwhile."

"I had a thought," said Venn, pulling out one of her knives and squinting into the edge to make sure it was up to standard. "Maybe you should take the market today. I feel like time is running against us, and the faster we gather information the better. Now that we've uncovered one secret, it could be time to go to Taylor's men and see what they know."

Will tapped his finger against the table. "I see. And how will you communicate with this soldier? Your Margolan isn't as fluent as mine."

"I'll get by."

He crossed his arms and shifted his stance, staring at her with such intensity that Venn had no choice but to lift her gaze from her knife to meet it.

"Why don't I go with you, and Remy talks to Taylor's men? We know they speak Andvellian, and that way there's no confusion over whatever this soldier has to say."

Remy's head moved back and forth between the debate, and Lewyn slouched in his chair, arms crossed and watching them as though critiquing their arguments. Venn wished both would disappear.

"You're the one who trusts Taylor enough to ask for help, so it only makes sense for you to go," she said. "If either Remy or I approach them, they might not be as cooperative. I can't guarantee I'd be polite."

Remy held up a finger. "I don't mind—"

Venn interrupted her, keeping her voice hard. "I want you with me. You're in the Feldall militia, so that might give us an angle when we go to a Margolan soldier. We don't know who he is or what he wants, and I want our bases covered."

When no one spoke up with more counter arguments, she jerked her head in a nod. "That's settled then. We might as well not waste any more time."

Lewyn grunted his approval. "Finally some words of sense out of you. Although I don't know if splitting your resources is the right way to go."

"If I want your opinion, I'll ask for it," she said, sliding her knife into the sheath at her hip. "I don't know what's going on, but I'm not going to wait for it to happen. After yesterday, I'm ready to up the pace."

"Rushing leads to mistakes."

"And hesitating leads to missed chances," she shot back, repeating the other half of his old lesson. "Keep your eyes open, watch for opportunities, and then leap. Don't hold back. You see? I haven't forgotten anything."

Lewyn's blue eye softened, and Venn thought she saw something she'd never seen in him before. Guilt? Regret?

Then it vanished and he nodded. "If you think this is the way to go, do it. It's not my game."

"Not this time," she agreed and looked to the others. "Let's head out."

She heard the sharpness in her voice and didn't like it, but the thought of spending more time with Will after last night tied her stomach up in knots. The way he acted as if nothing had happened was maddening. She knew he meant it when he said he would respect her wishes, but she didn't know that meant pretending everything was normal.

Without looking to see if Remy followed, she walked out of the cottage and strode towards the stable, not slowing until she reached Corsa. The stallion reached his head over the stall door and snorted against her cheek, nudging her shoulder. He stamped his feet, and Venn knew he wasn't looking forward to going out again.

The day before, after Remy helped Venn and Will climb out of the tunnels, four remaining centipedes had crawled out after them. Between the three of them and Frey, it had been an easy task to take the bugs down — with Remy nearly getting stabbed in the gut with one of the toxic pincers — but the real challenge had been calming the horses afterwards.

"I promise today will be easier, buddy," she said, running her hands over his milky white neck. "Just a simple ride into town."

She hoped she wasn't lying.

Remy guided Shalla out of her stall, and as the two tacked their mounts, Venn kept one eye on the stable doors, hoping to be gone before Will came out to prep Hollis.

But what's taking him so long? What's Lewyn saying to him in there?

The thought made her pause and look towards the cottage, tempted to go and check, but Corsa stamped his hoof and drew her attention to her task.

"Now will you tell me what in the nine gods' names is going on?" Remy asked, brushing Shalla before throwing on the saddle blanket. "What's wrong with you this morning? I know you hate planning, but you usually show some rationality. Kicking Will off the team at this point is a stupid idea."

Venn ground her teeth, hating that Remy was right, even if it wouldn't change her mind. "I already told you it's nothing."

She guided Corsa out in the yard to mount up and Remy snorted, following her. "It's obviously not nothing. Not only does your plan make no sense, you hurt Will's feelings and didn't even care."

Venn felt her stoic expression slip into a scowl as irritation rose up in her belly, swirling through her thoughts like black sludge. She urged Corsa forward, reaching out to twist her fingers through his mane for support.

Glancing over her shoulder to make sure no one was there to hear her, she said, "We had a talk last night, that's all. I told him he needs to grow up and understand I'm not interested in him. I know what he wants, Rem, but he's not going to find it with me."

"That's some short-sighted bullshit right there, but you

already know my thoughts on the subject." Remy's gaze scanned her over. "So this is the new Venn? Letting personal problems affect the task at hand?"

"It's not just what happened last night," Venn argued, refusing to be put down. "Yesterday was rough. We don't know what we're facing today, so I thought I'd give him a break. I'm sure he'll be safer with Taylor's men."

"For a woman as clever as you, you can come up with the stupidest excuses, you know that?" Venn bristled, but Remy shot her a smile and a wink. "I love you anyway. But don't think you can push me away now that I've told you."

Venn reached out to give her a smack on the arm, and Remy laughed, pushing Shalla into a canter.

***

The ambassador's house looked no different than it had the other day, still with the same hovering sense of abandonment. They led the horses into the back where they'd stored the cart on their previous trip and left them with feed and water.

A third horse was already stabled, a skinny piebald that looked like it might fall over soon if he didn't get something to eat.

"Think we should throw some extra feed his way?" Venn asked.

Remy had already moved to do it, hanging an extra bag outside the stall.

"It's probably the blight," she said. "I imagine there's a lot of hunger going around these days, in human and beast.

But still, if he's a soldier in the queensguard and his horse is in this condition, what does that tell us? Not even the queen is faring well."

Venn sniffed. "About time the rich suffer as much as the poor. Maybe they can get a good idea what it's like on a regular basis." She rolled her shoulders back. "But that's not why we're here. I guess we might as well see what's waiting for us."

They went around to the front porch, and climbed up the steps to find the door ajar. Venn leaned against the side of the house and reached out a hand to swing it in, keeping an eye on the foyer. Remy rested a hand on her sword hilt and stayed on the other side of the door.

The foyer appeared to be empty, and Venn heard no noise inside. Remy shot her a look and Venn saw the same concern that coursed through her. Had someone beat them there and killed the soldier before he could tell them what they needed to know? Were they about to find more blood sprayed on the walls?

Venn took the lead and slipped inside, keeping her back to the wall as she craned her neck forward to check the living room. Empty. Remy moved beside her and did the same with the office, shaking her head to indicate that no one was there either.

Ahead, the floorboards creaked, and a tall lanky figure appeared silhouetted from the rear of the house, coming in from the kitchen.

"No need to sneak around," he said in thickly accented Andvellian. "No one else is here."

He stepped into the foyer and, in the black skin and vibrant green eyes, Venn recognised the soldier who had sent them to Pastor's Field. She didn't relax her stance, but relief flooded through her that it wasn't the man she'd dreaded it would be: the Meratis-jumper with the cruel smile.

Dropping her hand away from her hip, she pulled the letter she'd found on Ambassador Reddington's desk and held it up between them. "Are you Thom Foley? The soldier who was supposed to meet with the ambassador?"

The soldier's gaze jumped between the two women and the door, and his hands twitched towards his sword when the house creaked. He gave them a small smile. "I should be glad the letter got into your hands and no one else's. That man must have been thick to write it out. No skill in being covert, that one."

Remy eyed the soldier warily, resting her hand on her sword hilt. "I guess he didn't see a reason to be. I gather the situation in Margolin has worsened in the recent months. Would he have needed to be more careful prior to that?"

"The position he was in, one can never be too careful," said Thom. He crossed his arms and cocked his head. "So you know who I am. Do I get the privilege of knowing who I'm speaking with?"

"If you don't know who we are, why did you ask us for help the other day?" Venn asked. They had so many questions for him, she figured she would start right away.

His tongue darted over his lips and again he looked to the door. "I had to take a chance. You can't understand the danger we're all in."

Venn and Remy exchanged a glance, and the scout gave her a nod. Venn hesitated a moment longer, but decided that if the soldier could take the chance to trust a bunch of strangers, she could take the chance of giving her name.

"Venn Connell. And this is Remy Herrigan."

"Under different circumstances, I'm sure it would be a pleasure to know you both," he said, and with their names, his shoulders seemed to relax. He nodded his head towards the kitchen. "Close the door and follow me. I don't want to sit where too many eyes can see us."

Remy took the first step after him, and Venn slid the door shut. They followed Thom past the curved staircase into the large room at the rear of the house. A long table sat in the middle of the kitchen with two large shoulder-high hearths along the far wall, each with its own massive black pot. The other walls were lined with worktables, and the most modern cooking devices.

"For a man who lived alone and doesn't seem to have kept company, he sure liked a large cooking space. Did he ever come in here himself?" Venn asked.

Thom looked to the worktables. "Not likely. I only dealt with him a handful of times, but he didn't strike me as the type to roll up his sleeves and work up a sweat. Nice enough for all that — a good diplomat — but more at home among his papers than his workers."

He grabbed a bottle of Margolan Amber — a bottle of nift pricier than Venn had ever seen in person — from a cabinet on the far wall and sloshed three tumblers full before setting them on the table.

"So what happened to him?" Venn asked. She sat down and took a glass, but didn't drink from it. "I'm sure you know his servants are dead. Where is he?"

Thom's gaze dropped, and Venn saw a flash of sadness behind the green and gold flecks. "Shame about that. Rhasha was a friend of mine going way back. It's because of her I agreed to talk to Ambassador Reddington to begin with." He took a large swig of his drink, skin flushing with the heat of the alcohol. "As for Reddington himself, I don't know. He's one among many that have disappeared in the last two months, but I've no idea where they end up."

"Then why are we here?" Venn eyed her drink, glanced at Remy, and took a small sip. The nift was strong and smooth, and she tasted nothing but the alcohol.

Doubt any poison would last in this stuff. It'd all burn away.

Even still, she pushed the glass aside to give it a few minutes, hoping Remy would run for help if she keeled over with a blue face. The scout had so far abstained from taking anything.

"You said you had to take a chance on us, that we're in danger. Considering we were just three people in a cart, some might think you bestow your trust a bit too easily."

Thom passed a hand over his face. "I heard you ask after my captain and the ambassador. I heard this one say she was a soldier." He gestured to Remy and leaned forward to rest his elbows on the table. "I saw you pass in the morning heading towards Reddington's house, so guessed you already knew he wasn't home. To ask after two men that disappeared — it raised my hopes that maybe you'd be willing to help. Did you go to the field?"

"We did," Venn replied, spinning the glass between her fingers. "Would have been nice to get more of a warning before we did."

Thom frowned. "I know. I'm sorry. My men were getting too close and I didn't want them to hear." His gaze shifted from Remy back to Venn, brow creased. "Is your friend all right?"

"Our third is safe and sound, thanks," she replied, her voice sharp, unwilling to let him off the hook too quickly for sending them into that demon pit. "How did you know about the 'pedes?"

Thom's forehead smoothed and creased again, the lines around his eyes hardening and his hands trembling as he reached once more for his glass. "Mistake. I never saw them myself, but Rhasha came to tell me not too long before she died. That's when everything started to make sense."

"Someone's using them to poison the queen," said Venn.

The glass froze at his chapped lips, and he flicked out his tongue to wet them. After a moment, he finished taking a sip and the glass rattled as he set it down. "You picked up more than I thought you would. Did you see them for yourselves?"

"We killed them."

His surprise grew to awe. Venn tilted her head and smiled.

"Killed?" he said, pushing his hand over his short hair. "Unbelievable. I swear I thought I was sending you in to find them, not fight them. I knew you weren't from around here, so all I wanted was for you to see them for yourselves. Didn't think you would believe me, otherwise. I thought if you knew what we faced, maybe you could bring my request for help to someone who can step in. But you're more capable than I realised."

Remy frowned. "I'm guessing no one's believed you before this?"

Thom scoffed. "Who is there to tell? There's been no one."

"What's going on here? Tell us what you know." She kept her voice softer than Venn would have.

Thom swallowed hard, eyes wide as panic crept up in their depths. Venn tensed in response and scanned the windows behind them, looking for anyone peering in.

"The dead insects could really fuck things up for a lot of people," he said, "and not in a good way. I don't know what the bastards behind the poisoning will do if they find their plan has been ruined."

Venn reached for her glass and took another sip, wishing the alcohol would push the nightmare of those insects out of her mind. "They'll probably react the way most crazy poisoners react. They'll try to find another way to get what they want. So we should probably stop them before they change methods, don't you think?"

Thom stared from her to Remy, again running his tongue over his dry lips. "It's not just the queen they're using that stuff on. It's the soldiers, too."

"Why?"

"Control?" he suggested. "It's easier to get people to believe scary shit is about to happen when all they can see is scary shit. It's making everyone paranoid, afraid of anyone they don't know, and even mistrustful of people they do know. I've seen childhood friends at each other's throats because they've started believing one is trying to kill the other. It's rampant in the ranks, no matter at what level. And the queen is just as bad. Not that I have any direct access to her, but I used to be assigned to the gardens, and watched her wandering the paths with her ladies and pets. To hear tell now, she doesn't even leave her rooms. The only people allowed access are First Counsellor Danos and the new captain of the guard, some man called Brannagh. Never heard of him before, never seen him before, and yet he's the one giving orders. Half the time we don't know where to find him. Surrounded by madmen, how can I know who to trust?"

His face twisted with disgust, and Venn understood his frustration. Having a commander you could rely on, someone you've worked with to know he was up to the task, was important when your job was life or death.

Remy reached for her glass and twisted it between her fingers. "How about you start from the beginning. How did you first notice people were being poisoned?"

Thom picked at a shard of wood poking up from the edge of the table. "I didn't know right away. It started gradually, the men whispering about something they'd seen late at night. It changed depending on the day. One would claim he saw a fish man peer into the room, skin all scales with jaws full of razor-sharp teeth. Another saw a shadow sneak into the queen's room and swears he heard her scream, but by the time he reached the door, it was locked and he couldn't get in. It took three men to calm him down and assure him Queen Rhoda was unharmed. She appreciated his valour, but after that he was sent to guard the kitchens. The queen herself began to look haggard, and the easy smiles the men were used to vanished. Then the nightmares became more common, and the delusions more powerful."

He pressed his fingers into his eyes and dropped his hand on the table. "I got worried that maybe it was a sort of fever. My wife died a few years back of something that looked like this. But it took her in a few days while this one lingers. I noticed it was getting worse. Up until that point, I hadn't experienced any symptoms and didn't want that to change, so I went to the healer. He's an old man who's been with Queen Rhoda since she was an infant. I shared my concerns, and he admitted he was just as worried. He had never seen anything like it, but so far no one was coming to him complaining of other ailments. It was all in their heads. He told me to come back to him if I saw anything else."

"And?" asked Venn, too caught up by the mystery to be patient.

"I paid more attention. I noticed the delusions and hallucinations got worse in the evening, after the sun went down. At first I thought it was connected to the darkness, but the seasons changed, the sun going down later, and the symptoms started at the same time they always did. That's when I realised it."

He paused to take another sip of his drink, and Remy and Venn both leaned forward.

"Realised what?" asked Remy.

"It's in the dinner wine. Whatever they're being dosed with, that's how they're drinking it. It might be slipped into the queen's wine as well."

Venn sagged back into her seat. "Then why weren't you affected?"

Thom offered a weak smile, his teeth bright against his black skin. He picked up his glass and swirled the contents. "I don't drink wine."

"Did you warn them?" Remy asked.

His smile faded. "At first, I tried. I told my men not to drink, that their nightmares were caused by the wine, but they didn't believe me. They started looking at me with suspicion. I let the matter drop in case word got back to the person dosing the wine."

"No one noticed you weren't drinking?" Remy kept her gaze locked on his. "Someone's going through a lot of effort to make sure the guard believes something is out to get the queen or the country or whatever, but no one's noticed you haven't been had the same reaction as the others?"

His face pinched as the fear returned, and he reached for the bottle to top himself up. "I learned to fake it. See, during the day it's almost easy to believe everything is fine. The troops are wary and they're exhausted, but someone coming off the street to talk to them might not realise anything is wrong. It's only when the poison first hits their system that everything starts to go crazy. The nightmares are the worst." He took a drink. "They started off bad, tossing and turning, waking up in a shock. But now they're enough to keep me up at night. I hear the men screaming, and in the morning they go on about what they saw. Horrible things that would strike fear into a person's heart no matter how strong a soldier he was. I started screaming when they screamed, waking up in a sweat when they did. It wasn't hard. All that fear in the bunk lingers in the air, affecting everyone, poison or no poison. I don't know how strong the dose is anymore or if the person behind this is letting the horror feed off itself now."

Remy's face paled, and Venn's stomach clenched. She dropped her boot onto the floor and leaned forward, waiting for him to continue.

"It's reached a point where I have trouble keeping up, and I'm worried for my safety. The visions they're having, I'd have to reach into the darkest centres of my mind to make up something half as disturbing." He buried his face in his hands, and then slid them down, peeking his green eyes out over his fingers. "That's why I had to take a chance on you. My men are too far gone, and the people are terrified. Rumours are spreading about a war, and if my queen's people can't believe she'll protect them, the hysteria will boil over. Please. I'm begging you for help."

Remy looked ready to reach out and pat him on the shoulder to reassure him, but Venn remained still.

"With the centipede nest cleared out and the barrels of venom lost, we might have bought you some time. Do you have any idea where to look next? Can we get into the palace somehow to talk to Rhoda?"

Thom shook his head, clasped hands dropping onto the table. "She's not seeing anyone. I'm not high enough in the ranks to get you an audience even if she wasn't barricaded in her room."

"What about Larimer? Any idea where he went, or are you also of the opinion that he deserted?"

"Not him," the soldier stated. "I've never met nor worked with a man more loyal than the captain. I don't know what might have happened to him, but I'd guess he and Ambassador Reddington suffered the same fate, whatever that might be."

"Help us out here, Foley," Venn pushed. "There's only so far we can take this if we don't know what to look for."

Before he could answer, the front door opened and slammed shut. Venn grabbed her knife at the same time Remy and Thom freed their swords. She edged towards the doorway and peered out into the foyer. A shape sagged down to the floor, hand clasping his stomach. A familiar mess of brown hair fell over his face and a shock of fear shot though Venn's heart.

"Will?" she called, and ran over to him.

He blinked up at her, blood smearing his face and hands, and collapsed against her.

Chapter Twenty-One

It took a few minutes to wake him up, but while he was out, Thom and Remy moved him to the sofa in the living room. Venn trembled too much to help, her blood-smeared hands staining the curtains when she went to close them. She peered out to make sure no one lurked in the yard and saw nothing but Frey's shape in the corner of the front garden, stretched out in the sun along some dead hedges.

She kicked herself for sending Will out alone. *I should have known he'd push too hard. Always feels the need to prove himself.*

Taking a breath to steady her nerves, she returned to Will's side, wanting to call him out for getting himself hurt. Thom had already stripped his shirt, revealing pale, clammy skin and the gaping wound in his abdomen.

"It's not as bad as it looks," Thom said. "Lucky for him. Any deeper and he wouldn't have made it here. But he's lost a lot of blood." He handed Will's shirt to Venn. "Keep pressure on the wound. I'll be right back."

He left, and Venn passed the shirt to Remy. "You handle this. I'm going to check outside for Hollis, and make sure no one followed him here."

"Venn, I'm sure he'd rather—"

"I'm sure he'd rather live. I'll be back in a minute."

Remy huffed, but didn't waste time trying to change her mind, dropping down on her knees to press the shirt against Will's gut. He hissed in a breath, releasing it with a groan, and as she reached the door, Venn heard her say, "Hush, love, you're all right now. You're in good hands."

Letting the door close harder than it needed to, Venn stepped into the sunlight, shielding her eyes to look for the charcoal stallion. Anger simmered beneath her skin, bubbling her blood, making her wish she had someone to take it out on. Her fingers twitched towards her knives, although she didn't know who she was angriest at: Will for being careless, or herself for sending him into danger.

Taking it out on yourself won't help anything, she scolded. *Blame the rat testicle that stabbed him.*

Grumbling aloud, she kicked a dirt clod out of her path, blinking to clear the sting from her eyes as the dust blew up in her face.

She wandered down the lane, seeing nothing in the emptiness around her except a hint of the next estate, the beautiful white house beside Pastor's Field. When she reached the side of the house, she saw Hollis grazing near Shalla and Corsa beside the stable.

"I'm glad you made it back," she said, coming up behind him slowly, running her hand over his side and up his neck.

His eyes rolled with fear, and she whispered soothing nothings to him until he stopped trembling under her palm, her own shakes easing.

"What went on out there today, boy?" she asked. "This was supposed to be the safe task."

The stallion snorted, whinnied, and nudged her shoulder, leaning into her. She rested her forehead against him and stroked his coat. "No matter what happened, thank you for getting him here. Now let's get you comfortable."

She left him saddled, but led him into the stall between Corsa and Thom's piebald, leaving a good amount of feed and water for him, as well. His tail swished against the back of the stall, and Venn returned to the house, relieved that the horse, at least, would be all right. She could only hope the same for his rider.

When she returned to the living room, Will was awake, a layer of sweat glistening on his forehead and dripping down his chest. Thom kneeled beside him, a bloodstained cloth and the bottle of nift in his hands.

"One more should clean out the rest of it. You ready?"

Will's jaw flexed as he ground his teeth, hands clenched at his sides, and he nodded, squirming and holding back a scream as Thom poured the alcohol into the wound, pressing the cloth against it after the dirt washed away.

"There we go. You'll be fine, friend. Just stay there a while and we'll get what we need to stitch you up. No lives lost today."

Venn released the breath she didn't realise she'd been

holding.

Remy pointed Thom to Will's satchel that he'd dropped by the door, and the soldier went to claim it, coming back with a long needle and a skein of thread he unwound between his fingers. Venn winced and looked away as he crouched down and started to work.

"It won't look the prettiest, but it'll do the job. Soldier's handiwork."

"I appreciate the help," Will wheezed.

Remy kept hold of Will's hand as Thom stitched, and Venn dragged forward a large blue leather chair, sinking into it and trying not to watch the needle move in and out of Will's stomach, the skin pulled taut with the thread. When Thom finished, Will released a breath and panted through the pain. As it eased, he relaxed into the sofa.

Thom poured another glass of nift and handed it to Remy. "Give him that to sip on. Should help him forget the pain if it doesn't take it away."

The scout smiled and tilted Will's head up, giving him a drink. His face turned red and he sputtered on the first swallow, wincing as his stomach tensed, but he took the glass on his own and took another sip, then a third, and Venn was relieved to see him look less like walking death.

"Think anything in this house won't be covered in blood by the time we resolve this mess?" Venn wondered aloud, trying to distract him.

He breathed a chuckle and glanced up at her though lowered lashes. "Glad to know I'll have left my mark, no matter what else happens."

His voice sounded rough and ragged, and she reached out for him, only to pull back. It wouldn't do any good giving him mixed signals now.

"You able to tell us how you ruined your shirt?"

"Venn, give the man a chance to rest," Remy scolded.

Will patted her hand. "It's all right, Rem. I'm okay now that I know I'll see another day."

The words were said in jest, but Venn felt the pang of their truth and looked away, pressing her finger against her top lip.

He squirmed to pull himself into more of a sitting position, waving Remy away when she tried to help, and then settled back and looked first to Thom.

"I'm Will Stanwell. Thanks for saving my life."

"Thom Foley, but if your friends knew that, you probably did too. You're welcome. Any allies I can keep alive long enough to help me through this crisis, the better. But maybe that would be easier if you told us how you almost became Margolin's latest victim."

Will winced as he made himself comfortable, and he pointed to his satchel. Thom grabbed it and passed it over, careful to set it down on Will's legs and not on his injured stomach.

"I didn't have much luck tracking down Taylor's men, unfortunately. I did my best to find them without bringing too much attention to myself, but many of them are either missing or gone into hiding. Some of their houses are boarded up and no one's seen or heard from them in weeks. Some that remain outright refused to talk to me."

"Not a wonderful start," said Venn.

"Finally I had some luck. Turns out my love of literature has a few unknown benefits. One of Taylor's men is a cartographer, Ben Reeve. He owns a shop selling histories and maps of the country. I started him talking about one map, and slowly worked my way around to Reddington. He looked terrified when I mentioned his name. Couldn't stop looking towards the door. I thought for sure he was going to throw me out."

He pressed his lips together and breathed through another wave of pain. "I was prepared to argue with him, ready to beg for his help if I had to, but he grabbed my arm and pulled me behind a curtain at the back of a shop, into a small closet full of extra books. He told me he'd been waiting to hear from us, that Taylor wrote to him the day we left Addergrove, and he's been watching, taking extra notes now that he knew someone was coming to help. He used to report to both Taylor and Reddington, but since Reddington disappeared he also stopped writing to Taylor in case someone read his letters."

"Did he have anything useful to share?" Thom asked, while Will paused to take another drink.

"He was about to, but then someone came into the shop. His tone changed into something hostile, and he changed the subject, saying he'd put together a package of histories for me. Then he left, greeted the man who'd entered and moved behind his counter, pulling papers and books from underneath. He shoved them into my chest, charged an exorbitant fee, and strongly suggested I leave. I saw the other man watch with approval."

"Friendly," said Remy.

"They'll take the money of foreigners, but have no tolerance for them," Thom said, nodding. "They're being told by the authorities to watch for spies, so they trust no one."

"Sounds like my kind of place," Venn joked, and then frowned. "Except for the poison and centipedes."

Will smiled and reached into the satchel, pulling out two large books and a pile of loose papers. "Most of what he gave me are interesting but useless histories of the area."

"And someone stabbed you for it?" Venn asked.

"I'm not done," he said, looking up at her with a wink. "I needed a drink and wanted to go through the papers, so I stopped by the public house. Figured it wouldn't be a bad idea to assess what the masses were thinking. Blend in — isn't that what you always suggest?"

She smirked, clasping and unclasping her hands to keep them busy. "Something like that. I usually get out in one piece, though."

Will grimaced as he shifted on the sofa, and Thom's gaze shot to his stomach to watch the stitches. "I got out just fine. This hole in my gut has nothing to do with what I learned today. It was just one more thing to learn." He took another drink, leaning his head back on the cushions. "I didn't pick up anything in the pub we didn't already know. Just how businesses owned by non-Margolan people are being shut down without cause. Not blatantly, but with increased taxes and subtle threats."

"That fits with the rumours about Rhoda getting ready for war," said Remy. "Of everything, I think that's the least suspicious thing I've heard since we arrived here."

"Nothing about giant centipedes worming their way through tunnels under the city?" Venn asked.

"Nothing of the sort, I'm afraid. As far as the public knows, their problems are all political and, where the blight is concerned, bad luck. Which is probably for the best. I can't imagine it would go down well if they knew they were living over an unstable insect nest, no matter how many of them we purged yesterday."

Will closed his eyes and fell silent, his chest rising and falling with steady breaths. Venn thought he might have fallen asleep or passed out again, and made to grab his glass before it slipped from his fingers, but after a moment, he opened his eyes and continued, "While I was there, I pulled out the papers to take a read."

Venn rolled her eyes to tease him, unable to supress a smile at the thought of him sitting in a pub, pint in hand, reading. Such a Will thing to do.

"The histories were interesting," he said, "but this one really caught my eye."

He slid out a single sheet of vellum, the top right corner dyed a bright scarlet.

"Is that ink?" Remy asked, her tone hopeful.

"I don't think so," Will replied. "Too bad Ben didn't have a chance to explain what it is, but he gave it to me anyway, so must have thought I'd figure out the message on my own. So far, two names stand out."

Venn took the list from him to scan it. Ambassador Jer Reddington was near the top, but there were so many others. Two long columns, and more on the back. Over a hundred in all. Her gaze caught on one near the bottom, and a stone dropped in her belly, her heart taking an uncomfortable leap in her chest as her mouth went dry. An unpleasant sensation, that "oh shit" feeling.

Frederick Larimer.

"Venn?" Remy asked.

She handed the vellum over to her, and watched her friend pale as she saw the same names as Venn, and flipped to the other side to see the full impressive list.

"You know what it is?" Thom asked.

Venn shook her head. "But I don't think it bodes well for anyone else noted on it."

"So many of them," Remy breathed.

Venn caught Thom's gaze, checking for any sign of guilt or lie. "Based on this, I'm going to guess your captain is dead. Unless you can think of anyone Larimer might have run off to find? We know he was suspicious of the new first counsellor. Is it possible he might have run to find help?"

Thom took the list, green eyes running over it, his skin taking on a grey pallor as he recognised more names on it than Venn had. "Larimer had no one and nothing except his job. I don't think he would have run, even if he didn't trust Danos. So many names on this list are people who have disappeared. I know some of them were arrested, but I don't know on what charge."

He handed the paper back to her, and Venn ran her

thumb over the scarlet mark in the corner.

Remy passed her hands over her face, releasing a huff of frustration. "So we have a missing ambassador, a missing captain of the queensguard, both of whom are on a long list of possible dead people. We have a world-jumping assassin, an army of red soldiers, giant centipedes burrowing under the country, and a brewing war. Can someone please tell me what we have on the other side to counter any of it?"

Venn grinned. "A blind old assassin, a warbear who insists on being my friend, a soldier who only knows a hint of what's going on, a scholar, a scout, and a blade-wielding bloodletter who likes to get her friends into trouble. Sorry, Rem, but if you're looking to get out of this unscathed, I think you're shit out of luck."

Remy groaned and leaned back in her chair. "Someone please pass me that bottle."

Thom handed it to her and she took a swig before passing it to Venn, who followed suit.

The soldier looked between them and took the bottle back, looking ready to down the rest of the contents. "When you came to the palace looking for Larimer, you weren't actually looking to join the ranks, were you? I guessed you were more than you seemed by the way you took down those 'pedes, but all that other stuff you mentioned — world jumping, red soldiers, warbears? There's something bigger going on that even I don't know about."

Venn nodded. "Sounds like it. We're not sure if or how it all ties together, but I think we can agree it's bigger than some poisoned wine and a hundred missing people."

"Shit," said Thom.

"A hundred times over," she agreed and turned back to Will. "So you left the public house unscathed…"

He nodded. "What came next had nothing to do with me. At least, I don't think it did. I was passing by a shop where these two men were arguing over the price of silk. They both had hold of it, and were almost screaming at each other. Not so unusual in itself, but a nearby soldier went into a panic. He pulled his sword, swung at the merchant, and started shouting at the customer to run, that he would protect him. The people in the road went into mass hysteria, sure that the merchant had done something more than yell at the man, so then more weapons came out. The mob had me pressed into the middle, and I was trying to push my way out when someone got me. I managed to reach Hollis and get out of there, but I'm sure there were some lives lost."

Thom's shoulders sank, the soldier a crushed and broken man. "It's getting worse. I knew it would."

Venn filled Will in on what they had learned, while Remy rested her hand on Thom's shoulder.

"We'll figure this out, Thom," she said. "I don't know how yet, but we will."

A shadow passed over the window, and Venn rose to peer behind the drapes. The clouds from the storm last night had started to gather again, hiding the sun that had progressed further across the sky than she'd realised.

Thom noticed the same and jumped to his feet. "I need to get back. Thank you for coming, and for doing what you could. If there's any information I can help you get, I will, but please, let me know if you learn anything else. I need to figure this out as much as you do."

"You know where to find us," said Venn. "If you pick up anything new, leave a message for us here. Top right drawer of Reddington's desk. We'll make sure to come back often and check. If you think you're able to do the same? I know it'll be dangerous if anyone sees you."

Thom nodded. "I'll be careful and make it work."

Venn hesitated, chewing on her thumbnail as a thought toyed in her mind. Finally, she let her hand drop, and sagged into the chair. "At this point, we need something to move us forward or we're stuck. Could you find us a way into the palace?"

Remy's mouth fell open. "The palace?"

Venn kept her attention on Thom, who appeared as flabbergasted as Remy. "I just want to walk around, poke my nose into a few rooms. No one has to know I'm there — and trust me, I can go unnoticed. What do you think? Can you get me in?"

His green eyes switched between each of them before landing back on Venn. "I—" he stammered, licked his lips, and tried again. "I'll think it over. Try to come up with a way."

Venn pulled her lips into a grin. "Excellent."

She extended a hand to conclude the deal and he shook it, then rose to his feet.

"Thank you," he said again. "For trying."

He left the house and a few moments later they heard the horses whinny as he grabbed his piebald and rode down the lane.

Alone in the house, the silence now pressing on them in the absence of the fourth voice, they considered each other.

Venn looked down on Will, scanning the lines of his stomach to rest on the cloth still pressed over the wound. It had started to bleed through, but not enough to worry her. Soldier's handiwork or not, Thom was a good man to have in the field.

"Think you'll make it home?" she asked.

He nodded, brown hair falling across his forehead. She struggled not to brush it away. "Whatever was in that bottle is bracing. It should get back me back to Kell's with no problem."

"Good." Venn stood and peered through the window, staring up at the sky. "I don't know about you guys, but I don't want to be caught in this storm."

Chapter Twenty-Two

The ride home was slow, and Venn noticed the pain on Will's face whenever Hollis took too sharp a step, jarring him in the saddle. They'd helped him put his ruined shirt back on to avoid extra attention on the roads, but it wouldn't have mattered for long. The rain started before they reached the halfway point, and it fell hard enough that she couldn't see more than a few metres ahead, her friends becoming undefined shadows beside her. Lights from the rows of cottages they passed helped keep their route, but it still felt like too long a trip.

Lewyn waited in the doorway when they arrived, ready with stew and a fire, and it popped into Venn's addled thoughts that he must have gained second sight with his white eye to see them coming up the road.

"Took so long I figured something must've happened," he said, helping them get Will into the house.

The younger man looked pale, but was still awake, his eyes clearer than when he'd first woken up.

"I'll see to the horses," Remy said, and melted back into the rain.

Left to wrangle Will someplace where he wasn't likely to fall and tear open his stitches, Venn guided him towards his pallet on the floor. Lewyn waved her away and directed them to his bed.

"I'm not above giving up comfort when other people have more need of it."

Will sank onto the mattress, and Venn kept him propped up while Lewyn pulled off his boots, which dripped water into pools on the floor, and helped strip him down to his smallclothes, his shirt and trousers soaked through.

"Feel like I'll never be dry again," Will mumbled as Lewyn peeled off his socks.

"I won't be happy if you go mouldy in my bed," Lewyn said, "but the fire should help soon."

Will lay down, his face pinched in pain. The effort of getting home and undressed was enough to put him to sleep as soon as his head hit the pillow. Venn covered him with a blanket, and dragged a chair to his side, watching his chest rise and fall.

"Is someone going to tell me a story?" Lewyn asked, pulling the other chair closer.

"Riot in the street. Turns out someone's using the dinner wine to poison the queen and the soldiers. Reddington's serving girl, Rhasha, was friends with one of the guards and told him about the centipedes after she came across them by accident. Now she's dead." Venn frowned, slicking her wet hair out of her face so she wouldn't drip on Will's arm. "It wouldn't surprise me if Foley is the next to vanish. I knew his name from the letter Reddington wrote to Ansella. If anyone else read it, they know Foley's blabbing."

Lewyn snorted. "Not sure who's stupider, the boy for flapping his gums, or the ambassador for writing it down. The coded message Will crafted the other day wasn't a bad cover, but I've always preferred bird messengers as extra security. No one can force a bird to spill its secrets."

"Should we expect a pigeon to bring Ariana's reply?" Venn asked, half-mocking.

"Don't be stupid, girl. Pigeons might have more brains than you, but they're still not good for messages. Watch for the magpies. They steal and follow the shiny goals. Kind of perfect for people like us, wouldn't you say?"

Venn didn't answer, distracted by the way Will twitched in his sleep.

No wonder he's having nightmares.

"You had it out with him?" Lewyn asked.

She didn't bat an eyelash at the sudden change of subject and prodding into her personal life. "Yes."

"Good. Truth is, I think more of the boy than I did when he first got here. He's got a good head on his shoulders, and I think he'll make it far if he sticks with what he's doing. He's stronger than he looks, and he can handle what you throw at him."

Venn looked up so quickly her neck cracked, but she didn't know if she was more surprised by the turn of

Lewyn's opinion, or that he was speaking well of someone.

"But you'll still break him. He's stubborn and determined, and he'll push himself to match you. He'll dig into his darker side to join you in the shadows, but he might not be strong enough to come out the same man he is now. Sure, you could tell him how you feel and try to make a go of it, but do you want him to go as far as you did? Do you want him to have to see what you saw just so he can believe himself your equal in the night?"

Venn swallowed hard, blinking as her vision clouded. Unable to say anything, she reached for Will's hand and shook her head.

"Then you made the right call. He'll have your back out here if he needs to, but are you open to a suggestion?"

"Since when do you ask, old man?" she asked, tone dry and bitter.

"Since you've proved to me you've grown up from the little girl I caught in the woods. You've done well since I left you, that much is clear, but your job isn't finished yet. I think it might be best, when this is all over, if you come back here for a while. I have some work I can get you into, something of the old vein you used to enjoy so much. It'll keep him safe, keep you safe. Give you a bit of cash. What do you say?"

The suggestion came as a surprise. It appealed to the shadows inside her, but offended the new emotions that had been sparked when Will offered the image of a life spent in the light instead of the darkness.

Venn thought of what her life had become, what she had

fought to get over, and the people who wanted to help her make the most of herself. But in staying with them, she would grow soft, and if something happened to strip them away, she would be alone and unable to cope. With Lewyn, she would always be alone, but at least she would be strong in her solitude.

"I'll consider it," she said.

"Do that. In the meantime, don't forget to grab something to eat."

He walked away, and Venn remained still, legs shaking too much to stand.

***

For two days they remained at Lewyn's cottage, giving Will a time to rest, and the others a chance to make their plans. Thom had answered some of their questions, but, from where Venn stood, all roads now led to one path.

"I still don't think weaseling our way into the palace is a good idea," Remy said one evening, having to raise her voice over the sound of thunder.

The rain had held up for days, thunder and lightning competing for their chance to perform. The wind stirred up the mud so the entire back side of the cottage was coated with spray. The horses were safe — Venn made sure of that a few times a day as an excuse to get out of the house — but looked as anxious for the weather to clear as any of their riders.

Once the thunder petered out, Remy continued, "With the soldiers as paranoid as Thom says, it would be us against hundreds if we were caught."

Venn dropped her head against the wall, finding satisfaction in the loud *thump*. "I'm open to suggestion if anyone can come up with something better, but from where I'm sitting, it's the next logical step. Besides, we wouldn't be alone in here. We'd have Foley to get us through the doors."

Lewyn scowled. "Don't be so naïve, girl. You think they trust him? They have to be watching their people closely, and by now they know he hasn't been drinking the poison. He's bound to be on that list and likely you are, too, now that you've met with him. If he's not dead yet, it's because they need him for something."

"And what would that be?" Venn asked. "Aren't you curious to find out?"

"Curiosity is as much a waste of time as hope. Too much of it can get you killed."

Remy smirked. "You say that about everything."

Lewyn bobbed his head. "Because it's true. The only thing you can't have enough of is caution, and I think the cautious thing to do would be to get out of the country, go back to where you started, and find out from a safe place what your next step should be. Think about the old days, Connell. What did we do whenever we finished a contract?"

Venn narrowed her eyes. "We went back to camp."

"Right. To gain perspective. To recharge. Keep going without that and you start making mistakes."

"It might not be a bad idea to head back to Addergrove. We won't be worried about Margolan soldiers breaking down the door." Remy paused, cleared her throat, and focused intently on her bracelet. "What if we took Thom with us?"

Venn eyed her with suspicion, noting a certain tone to her words. A thought dawned on her and she groaned. "No, Rem, don't. Please don't tell me you're attracted to the man."

The scout turned pink up to her roots. "Like Lewyn says, he's a soldier stuck in a dangerous situation. With what he knows, he'll be more use to us alive."

Venn turned to Lewyn, and her mentor held up his hands. "I'm not usually one for teaming up, but if you're looking for information, it might not be the worst way to go."

"Because four people riding across the border, one of them obviously Margolan, won't attract more attention than the three of us?" she asked.

"If you think you're getting over the border the way you came in, you've been hit over the head one too many times this week. You try it, and I wouldn't be surprised if they locked you up and never set you free, no matter who your contacts were. Especially if that contact happens to be me."

He threw the last line in as an afterthought, and Venn caught the way he averted his gaze, his white eye and blue roving back and forth across the flames.

"What's going on, Lewyn?" she asked, concern seeping into her veins. "You were all over us to fill you in about Will, but did we miss something while we were gone? Something we should know about?"

He tilted his face towards her, and she searched his gaze as though the explanation would lurk behind his expression. She found no trace of fear, but worry lines creased around his eyes and mouth. Something had happened, and she refused to let go until he told her what it was.

No stranger to her stubbornness, Lewyn stamped his stick on the floor between his knees. "A few of Larimer's men came to the door while you were out. Told me I was on warning and that if they heard anything about me subverting the queen's law, they'd be over here in a heartbeat to shove me in the depths of the palace never to be seen again, etcetera, etcetera. My association with Larimer is well known, and now it's come to their attention that my house guests are from a country that's growing increasingly hostile…" Snapping his hand together in a gesture of someone spouting nonsense, he then waved his fingers in dismissal. "They left without hassle. In my opinion, they should have waited until they were actually arresting me. At least then they'd have the element of surprise. Now I know they're waiting for a reason, and we know something about Andvell's perceived hostility."

"Which is ridiculous," said Remy. "If anything, it's Margolin getting hostile towards Andvell, not the other way around."

"Why are you preaching at me?" he asked. "I know that."

"More thinking out loud," she said.

"Since they can't use the centipede venom to poison the entire country into paranoia, the story that Andvell is preparing for war must be what they're using to get people worried." Will's forehead gleamed with sweat as he stowed the salve in his satchel and started wrapping the bandage around his waist. "It would be nice to know their endgame. Is it just to start a war? For what gain?"

"And why are they abducting people to make it happen?" Remy asked. "It would make sense if they wanted to provoke Andvell into declaring war, but then why would they keep it a secret?"

Lewyn brought his stick down again to get their attention. "None of which you'll be able to answer if you stay here. If you hope to convince the soldier to leave with you, I would prepare to be out by the end of the week. Even that might be cutting it close."

Venn still heard a deeper fear under her mentor's urgings. In spite of his protestations, he knew something else that he wasn't telling them, and was either trying to get them away to protect them, or for less altruistic reasons. No matter his motivation, she knew she had to increase her guard, even where she had started to feel secure.

As they got ready for dinner, she moved to the window to see if the storm showed any signs of letting up. Large grey-blue pillows padded the sky, releasing the torrents of thick rain and bright lights. The darkness stretched as far as her eye could see, with no daylight to break through the grimness.

Sort of like our situation, she thought, and wondered if somehow the Sisters were trying to send her a message through the weather.

Sudden glittery movement caught her attention from the corner of her eye, and she turned her head towards a run-down shed. A black and white bird perched on the roof, something shiny in its beak. It twitched and hopped along the boards before taking off and disappearing into the storm.

Venn wondered what news the magpie had brought that Lewyn wasn't sharing.

Chapter Twenty-Three

A second magpie, although Venn never mentioned to the others about seeing the first, appeared the next morning with a message full of warnings from Addergrove.

"*Dear Cris,*" Will read. "*Thank you for the updates in your letter. It was so good to hear you arrived safely in Margolin. It was worth the try to see if you could help them, but I worry the weather is not about to improve. I'm afraid I also have to break some bad news. Your father's heart gave out in the field. The healer made it to him in time, but I don't know how much longer he'll be with us. I write to ask that you hurry your return, as I'm sure he's anxious to see you. Loving regards, Mam.*"

Remy and Will exchanged worried looks as Venn took the letter and scanned it over herself. "What a shame about Father. I knew he pushed himself harder than he should. Hopefully now he'll realise he needs to slow down."

She threw the letter on the fire, and they watched the vellum turn black and curl.

"That doesn't sound good," said Remy, interpreting the

message underneath. "As much as I understand the need for code, I wish we had a better idea what they mean."

"I guess that would be the reason behind encouraging us to rush home," said Venn, and she felt torn between necessities. Leaving now would mean leaving Thom and Rhoda in danger, but not leaving might mean abandoning Andvell to whatever new crisis they faced.

She passed a hand over her eyes and stood up to face the others. "Thoughts? What path do we follow?"

Will chewed his cheek in deliberation, then raised a shoulder. "Is there anything more we can do here? I know you want to get into the palace, but I don't see how that's possible without taking some big risks. We got rid of their venom supplics, so without the poison, we can hope Rhoda returns to her own mind and starts solving everything for us. If not, the people behind it might have to tip their hand sooner than planned."

"Still feels like a waste of time," Venn mumbled, grabbing the poker to nudge the burning paper, wishing the sparking flames would do something to ease the frustration growing inside her. "We come out here, nearly die a half dozen times each, and ride back with advice and warnings?"

"Don't sulk," said Lewyn. "Go back to the house. Leave a message for the soldier to follow you when he can, then start packing."

He, Will, and Remy stared at her, waiting for an answer, and Venn wished they wouldn't let everything rest on her shoulders. She had no idea what to do. Returning her attention to the fire, she watched the rest of Ariana's letter burn.

When the last corner crumbled into ash, she knew she had no other option. No matter how detached she'd prefer to be, her family came first.

"Then let's do it," she said, "and hope Thom makes it out on his own."

***

The rain had eased to a light spitting by the time they headed out, so the ride was only almost as miserable as their last one. Will had insisted on joining them, in spite of Lewyn's berating comments and Remy's attempts at persuasion. He never uttered a word of complaint, but Venn noticed the way he held one arm pressed against his waist, keeping pressure on his stomach.

"You all right?" Remy asked with a sharp look at Venn, as if the responsibility to check on his well-being should have been hers.

"Fine," he said. "Just feels tight."

He dropped his arm to avoid further attention and put off their worrying. Despite Remy's continuous looks, which she interpreted as a silent lecture on not convincing him to turn around and go home, Venn ignored his pained expressions and pale skin, willing to leave it in his hands if he rolled off Hollis's back or not.

He's a grown man who claims to know what he wants.

But beneath her stubborn disregard, Venn kept a concerned eye on him the farther they got from the cottage.

When they arrived at the house this time, the door was

closed. With all the rain, Venn knew she'd be able to see muddy tracks or footprints in the layers of dust, but the floor appeared undisturbed.

She headed for the office, checking the drawer where she and Thom had agreed to leave any news, but it was empty. Will sat at the desk to write out their message, and she moved to the window to watch the yard.

"Should we take another look around the place while we're here?" Remy asked, standing on tiptoe to peruse the bookshelves. "I'd hate to leave thinking we missed something."

"Might as well re-check everything," Venn agreed. "The rain is starting up again, so I'm in no rush to leave. If Taylor's man had that list of names, it's likely Reddington also knew how many people were disappearing. Will, did you bring the list with you?"

He reached into his satchel to pull out the red-marked paper.

"Keep an eye out for those names. Any reference to Pastor's Field, or First Counsellor Danos. So far everything points to him, even if we don't know why."

Will nodded. "If Reddington didn't trust him, he must have had a reason. We know he wasn't against writing his thoughts down, so there might be something in these papers. I'll start with the desk."

"I still think it's too bad we can't get into the palace to ask him these questions directly," said Venn. "We'd probably learn everything we wanted to know."

"Before he ran us through with a sword," said Remy.

"Or fed us to the centipedes. What do you think he's after?"

Venn flipped through a book on the table. "Wish I had a clue. It can't be a power thing. He already managed to shoulder his way to first counsellor. Other than being king, there's not much higher he can get. And with the queen out of her mind, he's essentially making all the decisions anyway."

She rolled her shoulders back, her skin prickling with goosebumps as the dampness seeped into her bones.

"You guys keep looking down here, I'll check upstairs. I didn't spend much time in the master bedroom the other day thanks to our Meratis-jumping friend. Could be that's where Reddington's hiding the goods."

"Call if you find anything," said Remy, already lost to the tomes on the shelf.

Venn left them to their books and papers and went upstairs, pausing when she reached the landing to listen to the silence of the house. A floorboard creaked above her head, but then fell quiet. A moment later, she heard a clatter and pulled her blades, heading for the hidden staircase at the end of the corridor. She debated calling down to the others for back-up, but decided to move on her own. No point disrupting their search if nothing was wrong.

Going up the stairs, she wrinkled her nose at the smell of stale blood, wishing someone had come to clean it up. The clatter continued and, as she entered the room, she saw it was the shutters she'd forgotten to close on their first visit slamming against the window frame. Releasing a breath, she went over and closed them, never putting her back to the room. Empty or not, the sound had set her blood racing, and she refused to be taken unprepared by anyone sneaking up after her.

With a quick look out the window to make sure the lane and front yard were empty, she stepped over the blood and returned to the second storey.

To put herself at ease, she checked both the guestrooms first, making sure no one had come in to hide in the wardrobes or under the beds. She checked all the drawers in the night tables and desks, each nook and cranny of the wardrobe. Everything was empty.

The washing room, just as decadent as Remy had described, was equally vacant. She checked the cupboards and found nothing but extra soaps and towels. A good host, but no one to invite over, it seemed. A lonely lifestyle. Too devoted to work and not enough to the people he worked with. Much like what her life would become if she considered taking Lewyn up on his suggestion to return to him. Without the copper washtub.

Smirking at the idea, she left and went into the lavish master bedroom, taking the time to appreciate its unnecessary costliness. For a room that would have been used to sleep and maybe for the odd sexual encounter, if he ever engaged, it looked like he'd put enough money into the decor to set up a child until her final years. A blue and silver silk robe hung over the back of a velvet-upholstered chair at a marble-top table. Fur slippers peeked out from under the side of the bed. Built-in mahogany wardrobes lined the wall to her right, and she remembered from last time that once she opened them, her eyes would be assaulted by brightly coloured outfits, all made of the best materials in the latest fashions.

Her lip twisted in contempt and she shook her head, coming into the room and dropping on her hands and knees to check under the bed. Nothing. Good.

Getting up, she went to the night tables and opened the drawers. She'd checked them last time, but looked again in case she'd missed a diary or journal. Something a man with lots of ideas might have kept by his bedside for late night overthinking. But the drawers were as empty as she remembered.

Having saved it until last, Venn moved to the wardrobe, beginning with the drawer at the bottom of the middle panel. A dozen coloured slippers stared back at her, with darker boots on the lower shelf.

"So ridiculous," she murmured.

As she prepared to close the drawer, she spotted a slip of paper sticking out from one of the slippers. Kneeling down, she unfolded it and squinted at the small words crammed onto the tiny space.

Nightmares getting worse. More people arrested. Sight of red soldiers in the garden. Must meet soon. TF.

Red soldiers, Venn thought. Other than Remy's mention of them the other day, she hadn't given much thought to those red-clad troops on the road. With the centipede nest and missing people, they'd become a low priority. Now Thom had seen them at the palace. But doing what? Attacking someone or as if they belonged there? She wished the soldier had had a slightly larger slip of paper to write his message and provide a few extra details.

She tucked the message in with one of her knives, making a note to ask Thom about it the next time she saw him, and then moved on to the next cupboard. Pushing through the layers of clothing, she saw nothing but silk and corduroy and velvet — the textiles she had neither desire to wear nor ability to afford. Remy might have enjoyed sneaking her nose into the world of the rich, but Venn found nothing that attracted her own interests. No dead bodies and no clues of Reddington's whereabouts.

"Venn? We think we found something." She heard Remy's steps come halfway up the stairs. "It's his schedule from the day he disappeared. Looks like he had a meeting at the palace that morning, but it's crossed out. And then under that is a note saying, 'Meet with TF'."

"From that letter we found, he hadn't met with Foley yet when he disappeared," Venn called back, still rifling through the clothes, hoping to finish up so she could join in with the useful search downstairs. "I can't think of any diplomat that would back out of a meeting with the queen, so either he was scared shitless about something, or they cancelled on him. Either way, he was probably anxious to meet with Foley. Funny he didn't mention the cancelled meeting in his letter to Ansella."

"And have her think the man she trusted to handle her Margolan affairs was skipping out on his duty?" Remy posed. "No, he would have wanted something to present to her before he broke that news. Any luck for you?"

Venn glanced over her shoulder to see Remy pressing her face against the railings, and laughed. "Nothing but more questions. Foley knows about those red soldiers and failed to mention it. Either he doesn't realise they're connected, or there's another reason he doesn't want to share."

Remy shuddered. "So they did come from Margolin. As if we needed another thing to factor in. Great. You almost done?"

Venn took another look around the room. "Almost, thank the gods. I don't think I've ever heard of a man owning so many clothes. Bored blind up here. Want to switch?"

The scout stuck out her tongue. "You wanted to go play loner up here. Finish the job." She winked and started back downstairs. "Try not to hang yourself with any sashes."

"Tempted if I have to wade through many more suits," Venn murmured, opening the last set of doors. "Well, well. Now this is more my style."

On the bottom shelf, under the hanging outfits, rested a collection of three jewelled daggers in a wooden case. Although ceremonial more than useful, the edges glinted. Polished, well oiled, stunning pieces of work. Venn shut the lid on them and slid the case out of the wardrobe, setting it on the floor beside her.

"It's not stealing," she told herself. "It's reusing something that shouldn't be left to rot."

Grinning at her reasoning, she went back into the closet, brushing the robes of state out of the way and revealing a mirror on the back panel.

"Really?" she groaned.

The price of the mirror probably outmatched everything else in the room. She posed in front of it, hands on her hips, twisting her face into grotesque expressions. Then she rolled her eyes and pushed through a few more robes, making sure to check the pockets of each.

A floorboard in hallway creaked. She whipped towards the door and saw nothing.

"Remy?" she called. "Are you messing with me?"

No answer, and the room was silent.

Eyes narrowed, Venn tried to refocus on the task, picking up the pace as she flipped through the last of the clothes.

"At least I found the daggers," she said to avoid feeling too much disappointment at not landing on the answers in the man's underwear drawer.

She straightened up and started to close the doors when she froze, caught by movement not behind her, but ahead. Heart racing, feet glued to the floor, she reached out a hand and pushed the robes aside, revealing the mirror within.

Her own thin, pale face stared back at her. Cornflower blue eyes wide, black hair wild and blending in with the background of a man's chest. Following the seam of his jacket, her gaze travelled upwards to catch the salt and pepper stubble on his chin, and the twisted smile on his lips.

"Hello again," the Meratis jumper said, his cold eyes slanted with his smile.

Before Venn could scream, he grabbed a sash, wrapped it around her neck, and squeezed.

Chapter Twenty-Four

Grabbing onto the silk sash, fingernails scraping into her skin to try to get a good grip, Venn jumped up onto the bottom shelf of the wardrobe, pushing backwards to knock the Meratis jumper off balance. The man staggered, hauling Venn with him, and the silk grew tauter as they slammed onto the edge of the bed.

Venn's lips went numb and her vision hazy as black spots danced in her eyes. To avoid wasting time and energy, she gave up on freeing the sash and snaked a hand under her shirt, grabbed a knife, and plunged it down into the meat of his thigh. He hissed in pain, and released his grip just enough for her to slide two fingers under the silk. With the extra room, she leaned her head forward and slammed it back into his nose.

He growled and let go of the sash to press a blade against the side of Venn's gut, but she knocked it away, slashing the inside of his arm. Rolling across the bed, she landed on the floor and rushed for the door. He blocked her way and shoved her against the window. The glass broke, shards falling down into the yard, smashing on the roof of the porch below. Hand at her throat, he jerked her forward, kicked the window out and tilted her back over the edge.

She grabbed his arm, worked to find her balance to get the upper hand, but he pushed her so far her feet couldn't touch the ground. If he let go, the only thing stopping her from falling was her grip on his arm.

His other hand held the knife to her belly, so her attempts to sit up only pressed the blade deeper into her flesh.

"Before you go, I was asked to pass along a message," he said, his gruff voice vibrating down his arm and into her throat. "It was a nice try, but you never stood a chance. Let your last thought be that you failed."

Venn tightened her grip on his wrist, twisting her mouth into a determined grin. "Whoever asked you to pass along your message shouldn't have had you waste your breath. Too bad you won't be able to tell him."

Bracing her hips against the edge of the window, her stomach muscles screaming with the strain, she brought her knees up and set her feet against the Meratis jumper's waist, thrusting him backwards. As he shifted to catch his balance, he hauled her out of the window into the room. She knocked his knife from her gut with her knee, and heaved her weight towards him. He crashed into the bedpost, the wood splintering under the force of their combined weight.

Jarred by the impact, unable to keep his feet, the jumper slid to the floor. His head bounced against the floorboards, and Venn squeezed her thighs around his waist, her knife pressed into his throat with one hand, the other tight around the bare skin of his wrist.

"We always end up back in his position," she said. "I'm starting to think you like it. Tell me who sent you."

He spat in her face and grabbed her hip, ready to flip her over, but Venn pressed the knife deeper into his flesh, and he paused.

"At least tell me your name. I can't keep calling you Asshole."

The man's mouth stretched into a smile, the same cruel smile that set her teeth on edge and turned her blood cold. He pulled his free hand away, and her gaze flicked down to see him slide it into his pocket. She knew what was coming and shifted her weight to keep his arm still. No way was he going to slip through her fingers again.

"Ah-ah," she said, digging the edge of her knife into his throat until blood beaded up and trickled down his skin. He stretched his neck to relieve some of the pressure, but the smile didn't fade.

"This will go much easier if you—"

He bucked his hip beneath her, his hand reaching his pocket. The world flashed and the room around her disappeared. In her shock, she released the pressure on the knife, tightening her grip on his bare wrist, and stared in amazement at the field where they now lay. A dead, blighted field, covered with machinery and soldiers. Soldiers all clad in blood-red armour. Her mouth fell open as the cold grip of horror clutched her heart. In her distraction, she didn't notice the jumper's fist come up, still clutching the sphere, until it crashed into her cheek.

She tasted blood, and her stomach lurched as the ground disappeared from under her. He flipped her onto her back, forcing the air out of her lungs. She dug her nails into his wrist to make sure her grip never loosened, terrified of being left in this field of faceless soldiers and monstrous weapons.

Having lost his knife, he reached for a rock, but before he had time to bring it down on her face, she swung her free hand up to punch him, his already bloody nose crunching under her knuckles. Through his curses, he slammed his head down against her forehead, wrenching his arm out of her hold.

Her vision burst into diamonds with the hit, disorienting her, and she almost missed him squeezing his hand once more around the sphere. She leaped for him and wrapped her legs around his waist, hands catching his neck, making sure that when the Meratis spell carried him away, she went with him.

When their surroundings came back into focus, they were in a dark room, lit with an eerie red glow around the walls. She could make out nothing else around them, the lights too dim, the shadows too deep.

The jumper didn't give her a chance to adjust before running her into the wall in front of him. She grunted, knife slipping from her grasp, her chest pressed into his face. She slid her fingers up into his short hair and tugged, pulling his head back, dipping her head to sink her teeth into his neck.

He spun her around and slammed her down on an

empty table, the wood cracking under her weight. Reaching beneath her, Venn wrapped her fingers around the edge of a loose board and used the force of breaking it off to smash the wood against his head. Hardly dazed, he brought up the rock he'd stolen from the other world and swung it towards her. She rolled to the side and the rock lodged between the boards beneath her.

Bleeding and out of breath, she caught a glimpse of red as the sphere hit the ground and rolled into the shadowed corner. Both of them lunged after it, scrabbling in the darkness to find the spell. Venn's fingers touched the smooth, cool surface, but an elbow jabbed her lungs, and his hand closed around hers. She spread her other hand over his eyes, digging her nails in. Her fingers turned slick with blood as she broke the skin around his nose and over his eyelids.

He screamed and the spell jarred them again, back into the ambassador's bedroom. Three jumps in hardly as many minutes left her stomach tight with nausea, and in the time it took her head to stop spinning, the jumper shoved her onto her back. Her head struck against the hardwood, and the stars overpowered the adrenaline in her veins.

Loud footsteps bounded up the stairs, and she heard her name being called.

"I'll say goodbye to them for you," the Meratis jumper whispered.

"No," she murmured, refusing to let him get away again. But the fight had left her. Her arms ached, her legs throbbed, and the footsteps echoed in her head so it sounded like thirty people ran down the corridor instead of two.

Venn saw the flash of one of the ambassador's jewelled daggers swing into the air, saw the streak of colour as it plunged towards her chest.

The air crackled with new energy, like a coming storm. Venn's skin tingled, and the jumper was thrown across the room by an unseen force, crashing into the wall next to the window and sagging to the ground. The temperature in the room dropped from warm to cool to freezing, until frost crept across the floorboards and up over her skin. She shivered, body trembling as she fought to stay warm. Behind her, a deep voice rumbled in a language she didn't understand, with words that filled her with terror. She squeezed her eyes shut and brought her hands up to cover her ears.

A hand grabbed her shoulder, and she opened her eyes to see Remy, the scout's face filled with fear. She latched onto Venn's shirt and dragged her across the room, tucking both of them between the wardrobe and the marble-top table. Instead of finding safety beneath the solid furniture, the table rose and, as that voice kept chanting, flew across the room towards the jumper, hitting the wall so hard the marble tore through the plaster, the edge of the stone cracking. The jumper managed to dodge the attack, but couldn't raise himself off the floor.

Venn saw his thigh still bleeding from where she'd stabbed him, and his nose a mashed mess, but in spite of the damage she'd caused, his expression showed none of the fear she expected to see. None of her own dread caused by that ceaseless chanting. He showed interest.

She followed his gaze to see Will in the doorway. She'd known it would be him, that unintelligible voice, so strange and unworldly, all too familiar. But to see him sent another wave of terror through her veins.

Only a shadow remained of the man who claimed to love her, and in his place stood a demon. The veins under Will's pale skin had turned black, creeping up to block out the warm chocolate eyes with its darkness. His lips had faded to a sickly grey, pulled back to reveal sharpened teeth, like rows of fangs. They bit into his tongue, lips, cheeks as he spoke, releasing a black blood that oozed out of his mouth and down his chin.

Remy's fingers tightened around Venn's arm, nails digging through her shirt into the flesh. "What's going on? What is he doing?"

A dark cloud gathered near the ceiling, swirling with shades of black so dark it hurt Venn's mind to watch it. It made her feel empty inside, and the more her emotions and thoughts drained from her, the larger the cloud became.

The temperature in the room continued to drop, and the frost from the floor crept up Venn's boots like ivy, having the same effect on the jumper, except on him the fragile vines morphed into black serpents, climbing up his limbs, binding his arms to his chest. The serpents' heads bared their fangs, slitted silver eyes full of malice.

Venn tensed, torn between running for him and staying out of the way. As much as she wanted him dead, she wanted answers first. They needed something to go on, more information about that army she'd seen.

But no matter how loudly she called out to Will, he didn't hear her. The black veins reached his hair, leaching into the roots and turning the brown locks as black as his eyes.

"He's going to kill him," she murmured.

"Venn, no." Remy tightened the grip on her shoulder, predicting what Venn planned to do.

But she didn't have time to wait. Summoning her courage in the face of that living shadow, she jumped to her feet and ran between the demon and her enemy.

In the corridor behind Will, she saw Thom rush up behind the demon and freeze.

"What the—" he gasped, and she raised a hand for him to stay where he was.

"Wait," she begged the demon, but he only stretched his sick grey lips into a smile.

Spinning around to face the jumper, she saw the serpents wrap tighter around him, their scales slick and glossy, their silver pointed tongues wiggling between their fangs, tasting his blood. He flinched back, still not showing the fear Venn couldn't fight off. One serpent lunged for his neck.

A flash and he was gone, both snakes dropping to the ground, vanishing into dust which rose from the floor in a whirlwind to add to the cloud above.

"No!" She couldn't hold back from stomping her foot in frustration. The jumper was gone, her answers were gone, and this monster still stood in the doorway.

Turning to him, the demon that was Will shifted his attention to her, black tongue snaking out over his lips, those words still repeating, twisting her thoughts into dark shapes.

"Will," she said with as much command as she could summon. "He's gone. Cut it out."

His black eyes locked onto hers, and the coldness cut through her, wrapping around her heart.

"Venn!"

Remy sounded panicked. Venn turned to her to see what was wrong and caught her reflection in the mirror of the open wardrobe. Her own skin had started to bubble with thick black veins, creeping up her neck and over her cheeks. Ice water ran through her blood and twisted her stomach until she thought she would be sick.

Seeing the demon's magic work on her, her determination rose to fight back. She turned to Will and slid two knives from under her sleeves.

"Will, if you can hear me, stop this now. I'm not beyond throwing these into your chest if it means getting out of here alive."

The demon laughed, a raspy sound devoid of kindness or warmth. More ice cut through Venn's veins, and she shivered, gripping the blades tightly so her frozen fingers didn't drop them.

"Venn, you can't!" Remy exclaimed. She remained huddled between the wardrobe and the velvet-upholstered chair, glancing between Will and Venn. Venn wished she'd keep her voice down and stay out of sight. But the demon didn't have eyes for her.

"Join me instead," he spoke, dropping his garbled incantation. "This mortal body I possess would be pleased to have you with him."

Venn glowered, rage sparking. "You don't know the body you possess very well if you think that."

The demon stretched his lips wider, the wicked teeth elongating as his strength grew. His fingers, grey and withered, stretched into long claws that reached for her. Venn stepped back, but he didn't follow.

"I can feel your darkness. You seek strength. We can provide it."

"Not your kind of strength, buddy," she said. "I might not care much for appearances, but fingernails like that wouldn't be very helpful in my line of work."

That raspy laugh again, grating and irritating, ran down Venn's spine.

He stepped towards her and she took another step back, guiding him farther into the room. She hoped Remy would get the idea and sneak out behind him, but the scout stayed put, watching the stand-off.

"Who are you?" asked Venn, aiming to keep his attention on her. She glanced upwards to see the cloud still growing, now covering most of the ceiling. In the centre, the blackness stretched her mind, and she thought she saw faces pushing through, trying to break into the room.

"Irrelevant," he hissed. His shoulders broadened, and his legs stretched, adding another foot to Will's tall frame. "This body knows. This body sought me, hoped to control me. This body will not share its knowledge."

With each change, she worried for the man inside and how much would be left of him if she managed to get him back.

"What do you want?"

"What all creatures want," he said. "Survival."

"Is Will already dead?" The blades in her hands twitched, bracing for the answer.

The demon's smile widened, his face split. "Soon."

Good enough for her. She set her toes against the floor and leaped at him, shouting, "Remy, run!" as they fell together, one knife driving into the demon's side, close to where she knew Will's existing wound to be. The house trembled with their landing, and the vibration split what was left of the bedpost. It crumbled, bringing the silk canopy down with it, crashing to the floor above the demon's head.

Remy broke free from her corner to make a dash towards Thom.

The demon's claws tore at Venn's arms, but she held firm, the other knife ready to plunge into the beating pulse in his throat. She didn't know how human this demon still was, but she hoped his anatomy hadn't changed so much that she couldn't finish him with one good strike.

"I've now killed you," she said, keeping her voice level and soft. "Once I pull this blade out of your side, you'll bleed to death in minutes. If you want survival you've already lost it. So leave. Now."

Those black eyes locked with hers again, but this time

the cold didn't reach her heart. Warm with anger, she pushed back, threatening more pressure on the blade in his side. Above her, she heard moans and screams, and knew that whatever was trying to get through had almost made it.

"If you've killed us, you've also killed him," he rasped, tongue sliding out to catch the blood on her cheek.

"You said he was already dead," she replied. "What's the difference? Can't have an ugly face like yours walking around our world. We've got enough problems."

She hoped he didn't hear the tremor in her voice, or the fear. She had to make him believe her. It was the only chance she saw.

He chuckled, the sound deep and strong enough to strain against the defence of her rage. She felt tendrils of emptiness reach for her and tried to close off from it, focused only on the man behind the demon.

"Prove it," he said. "Pull the blade and kill us."

Venn swallowed hard, breathing slowly, channeling the pain in her body into this one act. No matter what happened next, the demon couldn't live. That was her darkness, her reason. The reason she had to be alone.

Squeezing the blade, she yanked it out, the wound pulsing with thick black blood.

The demon rasped one last laugh. He leaned up, ignoring the knife aimed at his throat. Venn froze, limbs shaking with what she'd done, and she closed her eyes as his grey lips reached her ear.

"The shadows don't fill you as much as you think they do. After this, they will."

His laugh hurt her ears, cut through her anger and left her frozen inside and out. And then he fell back, his shadow dissipating like smoke, the cloud above them closing in on itself, the voices going silent.

Venn stared at the shape on the floor, and saw nothing but her Will lying there, skin ashen and chest still.

Chapter Twenty-Five

"Oh gods. Will? Will, can you hear me?"

Venn felt lost, unable to think straight. She slapped Will's face to get a reaction, but his head wobbled and remained still.

"Fuck, fuck, *fuck*!"

She climbed off him and tore a strip off the sheet hanging down from the side of the bed, running her blade through the smooth cotton.

Mashing the cloth against the gushing wound, she looked to Thom and Remy. The soldier had caught her friend in his arms, and they stood outside the room, statuesque with shock.

"Stop fucking standing there and *help me*!"

She had no room for compassion or sympathy. The four gouges in her arm stung like mad, the flesh around the tears swollen and charred, as if burned by poison. Her skin felt flushed, and now that the demon and jumper were gone, the other injuries she'd received in her earlier fight began to throb. But none of that mattered.

Resting her head against Will's chest, she was relieved to hear the faint, weak heartbeat within. Something to work with. Everything wasn't lost.

Thom recovered first. He hurried over and tried to pull Venn away, but she jerked back, refusing to leave Will. He squatted down, catching her with his green gaze. "You're injured, panicked, and useless. If you want to save him, get out of my way."

His calm confidence seeped through her stubbornness, and she nodded, keeping pressure on Will's side until Thom had taken over. But although Remy tried to convince her to look after her own wounds, she refused to draw her attention away from the unconscious man on the floor.

"You can check my arm here," she said, shaking so much it took effort to get the words out. "I'm not moving until he opens his eyes and gives me some sort of quippy remark."

She noticed the look Remy and the soldier exchanged, their recognition that she might not get what she wanted, but she refused to believe it. They had not come so far only to lose now. She'd not gone head-to-head with a messed up freak of a demon only to lose the man inside.

Remy pushed the sleeve of Venn's black tunic up to her shoulder and gasped. Venn glanced down to see the four gouges had already started to pus, but the black veins creeping out around them were receding.

Too bad, Venn's disoriented and woozy mind spoke up. *Looked neat.*

Her shoulder slumped, and she wavered where she sat,

so she focused her attention on Will as Remy dug through his satchel, pulling out the various salves and vials.

"I have no idea what half of these are," she said, rifling through them with urgency.

"Relax, Rem," Venn murmured. "I'm not about to keel over. They're all useful, so I'm sure no matter which one you use, it'll have some sort of effect."

Remy grimaced. "What about the ones that explode? You in a rush to have the one that peels the skin from your bones?"

"If it gets rid of whatever poison's in my system then sure. Whatever it takes. Just avoid the liquids and stick with the creams. They're probably safe."

The scout groaned with indecision, then grabbed the first salve within reach, spun off the lid, and grabbed Reddington's silk robe to rub it onto Venn's arm.

Venn screamed as her skin set on fire, the pus bubbling under the healing ointment. Remy held her hand against the floor so she couldn't get away, but she squirmed under the pain. She leaned down to rest her forehead against Will's, hiding the tears streaming down her cheeks under her hair as it fell forward.

"Come on, Will," she whispered. Her lips twitched into a smile as she teased for his ears alone, "Wake up so you can be the one to inflict this pain, okay? I deserve it considering what I had to do." He didn't move, his skin clammy as she ran her fingers through his thick brown hair. Remy rubbed on more of the salve, and Venn hissed through her teeth, more tears spilling over. "I'm so sorry, Will. I'm sorry I had to hurt you."

"Once again, it's not as bad as it looks," Thom spoke up. Venn glanced at him through her tear-swollen lashes, and found him staring at her, impressed. "You sure know your anatomy, don't you? Nicked something I'll have to burn quickly to stop the bleeding, but missed all the organs. Not your first stabbing?"

"Something like that." She kept an eye on him as he flipped through the kit he pulled out of his pocket. "So if it's not the stabbing, why won't he wake up?"

"That was some pretty intense magic, Venn," Remy said, and Venn wiped her eyes before sitting up to face her. The scout offered a sympathetic smile and reached out to wipe a missed tear from her cheek. "Probably pretty advanced. We won't know what effects the spell had on him until he snaps out of it."

If... Venn heard the silent alternative hang between them.

"What are you doing messing around with spells like that, Will?" she asked, a new spark of anger warming her insides. "Haven't you learned anything from what's happened in this world?"

Remy rubbed her shoulder when Will didn't answer, and Venn released a breath, hoping she'd get a chance to yell at him later.

"This is going to smell," Thom warned them. "It's a good thing he passed out."

Venn crawled her fingers towards Will's hand and twisted them through his, squeezing tightly as Thom sprinkled a powder into the wound and struck a flint. A flash of bright flame, the smell of burnt blood and flesh, but when it faded away, the bleeding had slowed.

The soldier grabbed the cotton sheet, his hands thick with blood—normal and red, Venn was relieved to see—and pressed it into the wound. "You didn't kill him. No matter what happens now, it's not on you."

Intense relief flooded through her, and she sagged down, not letting go of Will's hand.

Remy and Thom said nothing for a while, one working on cleaning out her arm, the skin numb now after the burning, and the other working on Will. Venn clenched her teeth to hold back her screams, and her sobs, and thought only of Will, imagining him in the murky fields of unconsciousness, trying to guide him back with wishes.

She lost all sense of time, and when Remy poured another salve over her arm, waved in and out of consciousness, unable to tell when she was awake or in dreams as the visions flooded through her mind. The face of the jumper, the sight of that massive red army around the black machinery, the face of the demon, the squeeze around her chest as serpents slithered around her. Will's hand squeezing hers.

The last continued — enough to pull her back into the present. Nothing else had changed, but she felt the unmistakable pressure as Will's fingers twitched against her palm.

She shot up to stare down at him, and Remy gasped at the sudden movement, Thom looking up from his work in surprise.

Venn hardly noticed them, gaze locking on the chocolate brown eyes staring up at her. They crinkled in the corners with a weak smile.

"That's one way to get me on my back," he rasped.

Venn grinned down at him. "The only way I will, Stanwell, and don't ever think otherwise."

Her smile faltered as the demon's face flashed in her mind. The desire to yell at him had faded, but she knew they would have to talk about what he'd done, and what else he was keeping from her. For now, she would just appreciate that his death hadn't been at her hands, and that she wouldn't have to explain anything to Maggie when she got home.

Thom nudged Will's leg. "My back's getting sore. Think you're all right to move?"

Will tried to sit up and winced. "Feels like someone drove a blade through an open wound. But with help, I could manage."

Venn started to move, but Remy held her back. "Not you. I still have more to check with you."

She grabbed Will's shoulders, Thom his feet, and they carried him down the corridor to one of the guestrooms, setting him down on the white coverlet. Venn limped after them, glad the only good mirror in the house was the one in the master bedroom, because she had no desire to see what she looked like now that the demon's influence had left her. She felt broken, her body a wreck, and she wanted to crawl into a hole and sleep until the pain went away.

Will chuckled with a grimace. "Another piece of furniture ruined by yours truly. I hope Queen Rhoda doesn't send a nasty bill our way when it comes time to clear this place out and sell it. I don't think I could afford it."

Venn dropped into the chair at the vanity and slouched against the table, watching Thom clean and re-stitch the wound.

Remy approached her to continue her own ministrations, but Venn held up a hand. "I don't think I can handle any more right now, thanks."

"We should at least reset your nose," she said. "It'll help you breathe."

Venn groaned and squeezed her eyes shut, feeling Remy's gentle fingers settle on either side of her face, thumbs pressed against her nose. A crack, a scream, and Venn was left panting, more tears stinging her eyes as she blinked them away.

"I hate you," she said.

Remy grinned. "I know you do. I love you back. Now let's see the rest of you."

She started from the cut on Venn's head and worked her way down, emitting the odd *tsk* as she went. But she was quick and efficient, and before long, Venn was wrapped and bound and felt more like a preserved corpse than a human being.

"We have a problem," she said after the healing was done and her thoughts could process everything she'd seen in such a short amount of time.

"We have many," said Thom. "That man wrapped in

snakes. That's Brannagh, our new captain of the guard. Where in sunfire did he go?"

"He went to Orland," said Venn, and at their surprised expressions added, "At least I'd guess that's where he went — where we went. That's where they're preparing their war. Why we haven't seen any signs of it here in the capital." She looked to Remy. "Those red soldiers were everywhere. Hundreds of them. But I don't think they're close to done. Foley, I found your note to Reddington. You know something about these soldiers?"

Thom's mouth fell open. "I — yes. Not much. But I saw Brannagh with them." He pointed back to the master bedroom, referring to the jumper. "He was standing in front of them, giving orders. And then —" he passed a hand over his face, leaving blood smears behind, and cupped the back of his neck. "Before today I wouldn't have wanted to mention it. I knew Reddington would call me insane and not believe anything else I said, but now you've seen it for yourselves. Now you have to believe me."

The poor man sounded so desperate that Venn felt compelled to put him at ease. "You saw them disappear."

Thom's expression of relief made her assistance worth the effort.

"Just like that," he said, snapping his fingers. "One second there, the next gone, just like what happened in front of me today. What is going on here?"

Venn pressed her lips together, wincing as her broken nose shifted. "They're transporting these red soldiers to Orland. But it's not just the soldiers. They're creating weapons. I saw trebuchets, battering rams. They're planning for more than a small skirmish."

Worry flitted across Remy's face.

"How did you travel with him this time?" she asked. "That hasn't happened before."

Venn shook her head. "I don't know. It didn't make sense at the time, but thinking about it, I was touching his skin, not just his clothes. It must have been the contact that did it." She rubbed the back of her neck. "I wish it had happened back at that inn. We would have known so much sooner what he was planning."

Will frowned. "If Orland marches, Addergrove will be one of the first places they storm. We need to let them know. Did it look like they would attack soon?"

Venn closed her eyes, trying to conjure the details she'd seen. "They don't have enough men yet to crush Andvell. They must be working fast, but it won't be tomorrow. We might have time to warn Ansella."

Remy released a breath. "There's that at least."

"Then we have more immediate concerns," said Thom. "I wrote a note — anonymously, of course — to the healer, letting him know what was happening to the men."

"Was that smart?" Remy asked. "Won't it come back to you, anyway?"

Thom frowned. "I won't have my men completely blind. If I'm on their list, I had to explain it to someone."

Remy rested her hand on his arm, face creased with worry. "Did something happen, Thom? Do you think they're coming for you?"

"That's why I came here today. Word came out yesterday that they're closing the borders. No one in or out. If you want to get out of here, you should do it now."

Venn looked to Will. "With him in this condition, we can't go anywhere yet."

Will propped himself up on his elbows. "I'll manage. If it's a choice between certain death in bed or a small chance of bleeding out on the road, I'll take the risk. We need to get to Lewyn."

Remy approached Thom. "Come with us."

The soldier's mouth fell open, and he tensed, thrown by the request. "I can't. This is my place."

"This *was* your place," Venn said. "Your brothers are not themselves, and it's only a matter of time before they out you for not being like them. We came here today to ask you to join us. If you really want to help your country and not wind up dead in a week, you'll take us up on the offer."

Thom's eyes tightened with uncertainty, glancing from her to Will to Remy. He locked gazes with Venn and straightened his shoulders. "All right. I don't know if it's the right decision or not, but I'll go."

Venn jerked her head in a nod and stood up, heading to the window. The white house sat tall and coldly majestic against the slate grey background of the clouds, but the rain had let up, and the setting sun cast its shadow over the fields. In the distance, Pastor's Field sprawled out in an endless sea of brown and black. She watched for any long shapes skittering across the earth, but it lay still, and she wondered if Danos and Brannagh — at least now she had a name — had discovered their missing stores.

Wish I could be there to see the reaction, she thought, her face twisting in a bitter smile.

"We'll wait until it gets dark and then we'll ride to the cottage." She wheeled around to face the room. "It doesn't give you much time, Will. I'm sorry about that."

He squared his jaw. "Don't worry about it." Looking to Thom, he asked, "Any more of that nift here?"

"I'll go grab another bottle. Or three."

He and Remy left to check Reddington's stock, and Venn returned to the window, keeping her back to Will, not wanting him to see the emotions she hadn't yet mastered. Too many of them writhed inside her to be able to school all of them at once.

"Thank you."

His low voice barely reached her, but the words worked their way up into her mind, attaching themselves to some of those deeper emotions she thought she'd already restrained.

"I'm sorry for what I almost did," he continued. "For what I almost set loose."

Venn traced her fingers through the dust on the window ledge, watching the dark clouds roll in towards the white house.

"I saw that man about to kill you, and the thought of losing you…" he said. "No matter how you feel about me, I couldn't stand the thought of not having you here. I did what I had to do. I won't apologise for that, but I'm sorry it went so far. That my efforts to save you almost killed you."

Venn swallowed the whirlwind of questions, blinked to clear her vision, and pasted a smile onto her face before turning around. "Don't worry about that yet, all right? You saved my life again. We both tried to kill each other. I think we can call it even. It's fine. Just focus on getting better."

He must have seen something in her eyes that told him she didn't want to talk about it, because he dropped his gaze and fell silent.

Thom and Remy returned with four bottles of amber liquid, and passed them around, one to each of them.

Thom raised his bottle. "To getting through this."

"To getting through this," the others repeated.

Venn opened the bottle and took a swig, grimacing as it burned down her throat.

That's all that's left. Just to get through this.

***

As soon as the sun set, Remy and Thom propped Will up between them to get him down the stairs and out to the horses. Frey sat near the gates waiting for them, watching as Thom mounted Hollis behind Will, leading his own piebald behind them. Will protested, but they all knew there was no way he could make it back on his own.

Venn and Corsa led the way, Frey at her side. His red eyes gleamed in the darkness, and Venn felt a chill run through her at the sight. She kept watch on him as they rode, sensing nothing different about him, but shaken from her association of red with those red-clad soldiers. Adding what Thom had seen to what they had already experienced, she knew that army could grow to be bigger than they could handle. Danos could recruit from anywhere in the world. He wouldn't have to wait for reinforcements to arrive. It would be a never-ending army against their limited forces.

Ansella had to know. If they could set out first thing the next morning — or even that night — they could keep a fast pace to Addergrove and get the family to safety.

If the capital will be safe enough. Where would they go if the gates fell?

Her stomach clenched with the possibilities, none of them good.

As she rode in silence, a plan formed in her mind.

They couldn't afford to wait until the war began, cutting down one soldier at a time. There would be no one left in Andvell to fight. The problem had to be cut off at the source. They had to get to Danos.

She would go with the others to warn Jayden and Ariana, and then she would see about coming back. With a bit of time, with a plan, she could come back.

Unless Rhoda does it for me.

She pushed the hope down. Whether the queen was under the effects of the poison or not, the first counsellor wouldn't give up the power he'd claimed. Venn was sure he'd have prepared an alternative plan.

His downfall would have to come from someone he didn't expect.

A shadow like me.

Leaving the idea to ferment, she urged Corsa into a

canter and they rushed back to Lewyn, who sat with a mug of tea when they barged into the cottage.

"What happened now?"

Venn led the way, with Thom and Remy helping Will in behind her.

"Long story," she said. "Very long story."

Thom took Will's full weight to guide him towards the bed.

"Again?" Lewyn asked, flabbergasted. "How do you get into so many scrapes, kid? Who was it this time?"

"Me," Venn growled.

Lewyn raised a brow, but didn't press for details. Venn and Remy went out to take care of the horses, and by the time they returned, Lewyn had tea steeping on the table. Remy grabbed a mug and went to sit beside Thom.

"The plan's changed," she said, dragging a chair up to the table and straddling it, pulling a mug towards her. "We'll head out within the hour."

He nodded his head towards Will. "He's in no shape to travel."

"He'll have to suck it up. You, Ariana, Larimer, you were all right. There's a war coming, and once it starts, it will raze Andvell to the ground. I might not be able to stop the war, but I can help them prepare for what they're about to face. It won't be pretty."

Lewyn frowned. "You learned something."

Venn crossed her arms over the back of the chair. "We learned a lot. Orland is the stomping ground for the red soldiers. The Meratis jumper's name is Brannagh. He's the new captain of the guard, and he and Danos must be working together. Will knows how to summon dark scary ass demons that make me have to stab him. It's been a busy day. We leave in the hour."

The old man shuffled towards his bed and the grim-looking man who lay on it. Thom didn't look up from his work as he inspected the wound once more.

"Wait until morning," Lewyn suggested. "I understand your rush, and I agree you need to get out quick, but the clouds are rolling back in. A few more hours, you'll have the rain to cover your tracks. Make it easier to get out. Use the time to plan, pack, maybe catch a few winks. You look like you're about to keel over, Connell."

"I'm fine."

"You're mashed to a pulp. A day on the road and you'll be useless. He already is."

He gestured to Will just as the younger man cried out at Thom's prodding. Venn wanted to argue, but knew the old man was right. Nodding her concession, she rested her forehead on her arms and took a deep breath.

Lewyn shuffled behind her, brushing his hand gently across her shoulder as he passed, and dropped onto the chair beside her.

"And here I thought my homeland would be a nice quiet place to retire and eventually die," Lewyn said, stamping his stick against the floor. "Teach me to ever expect peace."

Venn caught his concern beneath his grumbles and a wave of guilt passed through her. She thought of Remy's observation about his motivations, of how he wanted what was best for her. Growing up, she never would have thought it. Even in her years away from him, she'd only ever seen him as the man who pushed her too far, hurt her and warped her. In that moment, she realised how hard he'd worked to instil her survival skills, and even after ten years, still wanted to make sure she made it out of their mess alive.

"Sorry to have brought you deeper into this than I meant to," she said, testing her new awareness as she watched the steam rise from her tea. "At least this way we'll be out of your hair. Maybe the peace you want isn't so far out of reach."

He sniffed, and Venn got the sense there was something he wanted to tell her — the way he scanned her, the white eye seemingly staring deeper into her than the blue one — and then he dropped his gaze and smacked his stick against her calves. "Serves no good being nice to me, girl. The war would have come whether you were here or not. This way I get a head's up. I always prefer to have more information than not enough. And I see you got your soldier boy to agree to come with you."

Thom rose to his feet and extended his hand, dropping it when Lewyn did nothing but stare.

"Hope he's worth the extra baggage."

Venn rolled her eyes at Thom, telling him to ignore it.

Lewyn rose and *shuffle, shuffle, thump*ed to his cupboards. "If we're moving fast, we might as well eat. You're going to need stores for the trip."

With their focus redirected on the practicalities of their journey, the evening passed quickly. Will fell asleep shortly after Thom left him alone, and the others stayed quiet, each set on his own task. When their bags were packed and ready beside the door, the horses brushed and fed, Remy, Thom, and Venn stood in the middle of the room.

"Nothing to do now but wait for the rain to fall," said Remy. The scar along her cheek twitched with the stress of what they faced, her fingers spinning her bracelet in a never-ending circle.

"Nothing but to get some sleep," Lewyn directed from his place at the table. "It'll be a rough start if you don't."

Remy looked to Venn, checking to see if she had any last minute orders, but she nodded her head towards the pallets.

"He's right. Get some rest."

Thom pressed his lips together in an understanding smile, and, before he turned away, said, "Thank you for trusting me. Considering everything else, you didn't have to. I know that."

Venn met his green gaze and bobbed her head. "You've proved you'll be good to have on the trip, but I wouldn't go so far as to say I trust you. Nothing personal. I don't trust anyone."

He stared at her, confused and surprised, and made no reply.

"Get some sleep," she repeated, and sank down at the table across from Lewyn.

Remy and Thom stretched out on the floor, and for a while the room was silent. Soon, Remy's snores vibrated on the air.

"You should join them," said Lewyn. He poured two

glasses of the nift Venn had stolen from the ambassador's house. It seemed a shame to let them go to waste.

"Soon enough," she said, downing the contents of the glass, hoping the buzz would get rid of the throbbing in her head. "Thinking too much to sleep."

"It's not going to get any better. You know that."

She nodded, refilling her glass. "You didn't see what I saw. I have a good idea what we're getting into and trust me when I say no one's ready for it." Meeting his gaze, she said, "Be ready for me to come back."

He frowned. "What do you mean?"

"I mean I'm going to get these guys to the capital, fill Ansella in on what I saw, and then I'll sneak back into Margolin, find a way to get into the palace, and drive my blade through Danos's heart. Brannagh's, too, if I can get my hands on him long enough."

Lewyn eyed her over the edge of his cup. "That your reason talking or the rush of today? Sounds like a stupid plan."

"Danos is behind it all. Between what Foley told me and what we've learned since we arrived, there's no doubt of it. People disappearing, the poison. We know half the story, but it doesn't take Will's brain to know the rest is connected through this first counsellor. If we find a way to take him down, we could end all of this before it starts."

"And how are you going to go about it? Knock on the door and politely ask to come in? You're drinking instead of thinking."

Venn pushed the glass away. "I'm doing nothing but

thinking. He has to go."

"You think you're good enough to do it?"

The question made her pause, and she tilted her head, eyes locked with his. "I better be. I'm the only one who will."

Silence fell between them, and Lewyn shrugged his brows. "Then I wish you the best, girl, but I can't guarantee I'll be here when you get back. Still, you're welcome to use the cottage if you want."

Venn narrowed her eyes. "What do you mean?"

"Things change every day. Your sudden disappearance, the disappearance of another soldier that I'm sure won't go unnoticed — they're coming for me. Tomorrow, the day after that, next month. Doesn't matter. I intend to get away before they can."

"Where will you go?" asked Venn.

Lewyn tapped his thumb on the top of his stick. "Places. Probably for the best you don't know where. Just in case."

"You could travel with us for a while. We could have your back," she said, surprising herself with the suggestion.

She didn't know if she wanted to go back on the road with her mentor. She'd been hesitant with his offer to return to him when it was all done, but the thought of leaving him behind didn't sit right either.

Considering her torn feelings, she didn't know whether to be disappointed or relieved when he shook his head. "No place for me on your team. I have things to wrap up here first. I'll focus on that and you do what you need to do."

Venn grabbed her glass again and took another sip.

"You do what you like for tonight, but I'm going to sleep." He pointed to the glass. "And don't drink too much of that. We won't be able to haul you out of bed in the morning."

Blowing out the candle on the table, Lewyn lapsed them into darkness, only the low fire lighting his way to Will's pallet. She heard him groan, his knees popping as he sank down onto the floor, and for a while she stayed at the table, enjoying the silence.

When her thoughts grew to be too much, she walked over to Will, keeping her tread light so as not to wake him. She stared down at his sleeping form, the way his face looked so calm, his heavy healing sleep unburdened by the nightmare he'd summoned earlier in the day. She thought about the pain he would be in over the next week as they rode, and considered whether it would be better to leave him behind, to follow when Lewyn left. The old man would make sure he was safe.

But she knew he wouldn't agree to it. His wound might tear him apart on the journey, but she knew he would chance it to see his family before disaster rolled in.

"We just need to get through it," she whispered. It wasn't a question of whether they would. She couldn't allow for doubt.

A rumble of thunder brought her away from Will's side towards the window. In the distance, the first signs of the coming storm rolled in, and Venn berated herself for not at least trying to sleep. Soon they would be on the road, and she would have to trust Corsa to lead her safely while she dozed on his back. Not something she looked forward to.

Lightning flashed above the clouds, and in the extra light she saw shadows in the distance. Leaning forward, she squinted to make them out, fingers latched onto the window frame, knuckles aching with the strain.

As they came closer, the shadows bobbed up and down as though in a dance, and she stepped backwards into the room, nearly tripping over Remy's arm. The next flash of lightning brought out human shapes on black horses. The people looked massive, distorted, until she caught the glint of metal in the light.

Red metal.

The storm had arrived, and so had the soldiers.

Chapter Twenty-Six

Shit.

The word drummed through Venn's mind in time with her heart as she moved away from the window.

"Guys," she said, and when no one moved, she repeated it at a shout.

Only Thom reacted, but he jumped to his feet without delay, and Venn was relieved to see at least one of them was already dressed and ready to go. Not that the poor man had much of a choice, having had no chance to grab his personal effects.

"Get Will up and ready," she commanded him. "And make it quick. We've got company." She gave a sharp kick to Remy's side. "Rem. Up."

"Wha—" the scout stopped mid-snore. When she saw Venn standing over her, the confusion and sleepiness vanished and she threw off the blankets, reaching for her sword. "What's going on?"

"Soldiers," Venn said. "Don't bother with the sword —

we couldn't fight them if we tried. Get up, get the stuff ready."

Remy hurried to throw on the few items of clothing she'd stripped off before bed, and rolled up the blankets.

Venn marched over to Lewyn, surprised he hadn't woken at the rush of activity. "Wake up, old man."

He grunted and rolled onto his side, but didn't move.

Not wanting to waste time, she moved back to the window. Four riders had reached the ragged tree stumps in the distance, all in the blood-red armour she had already learned to hate.

Frey rose from his sleep on the shelter of the shed, his black lips pulled over his metal teeth. Venn knew he would stay to fight, but she feared for him standing against them on his own. Last time, he'd taken them down with no trouble, but she didn't want to take the chance.

Blowing a sharp whistle through her fingers to get his attention, she waved him towards her, hoping Frey understood the message before she stepped away from the window out of the soldier's line of sight.

Thom and Remy hauled Will up between them, the injured man pale and sweating with the pain and effort of moving. Blood seeped through his white shirt where the wound bled through his stitches, but they'd have to worry about that later. First they had to survive an escape.

"Will we make it out in time?" he asked, glancing towards the window.

"Do we want to give ourselves the choice?" she asked in return. "Let's hope the shadows still work on my side. You three get the horses. If you can't saddle them, don't worry about it. I'd rather be alive than comfortable."

A loud *thock* hit the roof, and the thatch began to crackle.

"And we just lost a few more seconds. Hurry."

She grabbed two of the packs and shoved them at Thom and Remy before going back to Lewyn, who had finally woken up at the commotion and rising heat in the cottage.

"Trying to rob me of some much needed sleep, girl?" he demanded.

Outside, the hoofbeats galloping over the packed earth competed with the rumble in the sky. The patter of rain followed the riders as the storm swept in, and with each crack of thunder, Venn's heart jumped, her head light as she rushed to get the last of their belongings packed up without losing herself to panic.

A high pitched noise and another *thock* as a second arrow flew through the window and lodged into the table leg, sprouting fire across the far side of the room.

Lewyn's head snapped towards the window.

"What in the gods-be-damned—"

"The red soldiers decided to pay us a visit," Venn explained, strapping her knives around her hips and her waist. She shoved the sheaths usually strapped around her arms into her pack. "I don't know about you, but I don't want to stick around to see what they're trying to sell. We have to go."

A third arrow hit the outside of the cottage, and flames licked up over the window.

"They really want to make sure, don't they?" Venn spat, guessing the arrows were doused in more than just oil for the fire to have moved so quickly over the damp wood. The table had already been consumed, the chairs and far wall the flames' next victims. Venn knew they only had a few moments before the fire reached the door and they'd both be trapped inside.

Snatching a blanket from the floor to protect herself from the worst, she wrapped it around herself, ready to drop it as soon as she got outside. Frey appeared in the doorway, facing the approaching soldiers, rising up onto his hind legs with a growl that would have taken out Venn's knees it if it had been directed at her.

"Let's hurry the fuck up, old man. Addergrove needs us."

She grabbed another blanket for Lewyn, but he grabbed her arm and pulled her close. "Forget Addergrove. Get to Cordelay."

Confusion pushed her thoughts away from her rush to leave.

"What? Why?"

"You really going to choose now to question me, girl?" His fingers dug into her arm in his urgency.

"I'm not going to abandon my family to this war without any kind of warning," she returned. "Not without a damned good reason."

"Gods-be-damned, Connell, you're enough to make my blood boil." He pushed his hand over his hair. "I gave my oath not to say anything, but if you want to take the risk of going after Danos like you say you do — really bring this whole mess to an end — you go to Cordelay and you get there fast."

"What about Jay and Ariana? I just leave them next door to these bastards?"

Lewyn tightened his grip on her arm. "Do you trust me?"

She wanted to throw his lesson back in his face never to trust anyone, but the horses were getting closer. Pressed for time, she nodded.

"Then go to Cordelay." When he saw she still hesitated, he forced a sigh. "The soldier will help, but that's all I can say."

"What—"

He shoved her towards the door before she could ask any more questions, but she didn't step over the threshold, gaze locked on him even as the fire licked towards her boots.

"What about you?" she demanded.

Frey stuck his nose into the cottage, his large paw batting at Venn's leg, as eager to get her gone as Lewyn was, but she ignored them both.

"An old man like me would just slow you down. You already have one invalid to worry about. Now move before we all go up in flames." When she still didn't leave, he rolled his eyes and pushed her outside. "Why am I surrounded by such jackasses? *Go!*"

Remy already had Corsa waiting by the door, but before she mounted up, Venn stopped and looked over her shoulder, frozen for an instant as she saw Lewyn standing amid the flames, his entire home ablaze. In that moment, he wasn't the old man she'd found in Margolin, but the man who had trained her. In the shadows of the fire, he stood tall, the stoop gone, his blue eye sharp against his dark skin.

"Stop dawdling, Connell, and *move*!" she saw him mouth the words, but didn't know if he actually shouted them aloud. A section of flaming roof caved and fell into the cottage, blocking him from her vision.

A hand grabbed her shoulder and she jumped, turning to see Will, mounted on Hollis, his eyes full of panic as he looked across the field. She followed his gaze to find the riders almost on the cottage. It was possible the soldiers hadn't spotted them yet through the rain, but their window was closing fast.

She grabbed onto Corsa's mane and hauled herself up into the saddle. Beside her, Remy and Thom rode bareback, not having had time to finish tacking the horses.

"I set the nags free and they're running," Remy said. "If we move now, maybe we can get past these guys unseen."

"It's a small chance, but I'll take it," Venn said, turning Corsa towards the road. Her shaking fingers wound through the reins, and she felt the stallion tremble between her thighs. It took no urging to get him to a gallop. Frey's hulking shape stayed close by her side until the horses outpaced him, and then he faded into the night.

Venn wished he could stay, but knew he'd find them when it was safe.

She glanced over her shoulder, tightening her grip on

Corsa to keep her balance.

The entire cottage was a blaze of light in the storm. She heard no screams, but saw no sign of Lewyn finding his way out of the wreckage.

Grief filled her heart as she looked away.

Not fair, old man. You were supposed to be my kill.

"So?" Remy asked as they flew down the road, guiding Shalla up beside Corsa. "What do we do now?"

Practicality pulled Venn away from her emotions, and Lewyn's final order filled her mind. She hated the thought of leaving Addergrove to its fate, not knowing who else could warn them, but Lewyn had sounded so desperate. So certain. He asked if she trusted him. Ten years ago she would have spat in his face and said no, but now she knew she did. If she wanted to get the better of Danos, she had to. As if Lewyn were beside her, hitting her with that stupid stick, she felt the weight of his words on her conscience, driving her sense of adventure.

Maybe he's right. Anything is possible.

"We go to Cordelay," she said. Her lips slid upwards into a grin. "And save the gods-be-damned world."

Get your FREE Cadis short story by visiting
http://eepurl.com/bmWp9H

Thank You for Reading

If you enjoyed the read, please help support the author by
leaving a review at the retailer where you purchased the book.

For announcements, promotions, special offers, you can
sign up for The Raven's Quill Newsletter, at
http://eepurl.com/GIJkz

Acknowledgments

With each new book, I grow more amazed by my incredible support system. With unfaltering enthusiasm, my team pushed me through each round of edits, provided invaluable feedback on various drafts, kept me grounded during the emotional ups and downs, and celebrated every achievement — even the minor ones.

A few people deserve honourable mentions. On the book production side of things, a huge thanks to: my editor, Meghan Hyden, for getting *Bloodlore* off on the right foot; Jeff Brown for the beautiful cover art; Kate Sparkes for the feedback, the shoulder, the pep talks; Colin F. Barnes for always being my go-to; and Sadie Scapillato-Hall, Megan Faw, and Chelsea Miller for taking the time to read for me and helping bring Venn to life.

In my life outside of Andvell, my deepest thanks to my family for their love and never-ending support, and to Chris Reddie for the laughs and unlimited hugs during the stressful times. I'd have a lot more grey hair without you guys.

As always, the most heartfelt gratitude to my readers. Without you, Venn would never have existed in *Meratis* or come into her own in *Cadis*. I'm not sure if I should be happy that she has. It's possible I've set loose a whirlwind of trouble, and if she gets out of control, you all have a share in the responsibility.

About the Author

Known for witty, vivid characters, Krista Walsh never has more fun than getting them into trouble and taking her time getting them out.

When not writing, she can be found walking, reading, gaming, or watching a film – anything to get lost in a good story.

She currently lives in Ottawa, Ontario.

You can connect via:

Newsletter
Blog
Facebook
Twitter
Goodreads
Booklikes
At the local Second Cup coffee shop … but only if you come bearing a White Mocha

Other novels by Krista Walsh

The Meratis trilogy
Evensong
Eventide
Evenlight

Made in the USA
Charleston, SC
22 June 2015